CAPTAIN'S KISS

Nora lingered over every detail of Jacob's face, from his intense charcoal eyes to the firm set of his lips. "Why, Captain, are you hinting that you have been courting me? Because if you have, you certainly go about it in the strangest possible manner."

"Miss Seabrook, if I were courting you, you would certainly know it. You wouldn't have to ask."

His touch sent a shiver of anticipation skidding up her spine. "Why, Captain, what would you do to prove it to me?"

With one step, he was in front of her. The hand that had been striking a path of delicious sensation down the column of her throat slipped to the sensitive skin about the bodice of her gown. He laid his other hand flat on the trunk of the palm tree, trapping her with the press of his hips against her knees.

"I would do this," he said, and his forefinger began exploring a lazy, silky trail along the edge of her bodice. "And this." He bent his head until all she could see was the golden sheen of his hair against her skin. His lips moved to where his hand had been, and he kissed her neck, her shoulder, the crest of each breast that suddenly strained against the punishing confinement of satin and lace.

"I see," she breathed. "Yes, all of this would make me think that perhaps you were courting me."

His hands circled her waist again, and he lifted her up and against his chest. With his mouth hovering just inches from hers, he said, "But none of these things would convince you as much as this . . . ."

Books by Cynthia Thomason

RIVER SONG
SILVER DREAMS
HOMESPUN HEARTS
WINDSWEPT

Published by Zebra Books

WINDSWEPT

CYNTHIA THOMASON

Zebra Books
Kensington Publishing Corp.
http://www.zebrabooks.com

ZEBRA BOOKS are published by

Kensington Publishing Corp.
850 Third Avenue
New York, NY 10022

First Printing: December, 1999
10 9 8 7 6 5 4 3 2 1

Printed in the United States of America

This book is dedicated to the memory of my father, Ben M. Brackett, who, while making waves, smoothed the rough seas of my life.

CHAPTER ONE

Nora Seabrook stowed the last of her garments in her steamer trunk just as an insistent rapping sounded on her cabin door. She looked at her second cousin, Fanny, who was lounging on her bunk with a cup of tea in her hand. "I do hope that's Mama," Nora said. "Perhaps she's finally over her seasickness."

"I wouldn't count on it, *cherie*," Fanny advised with a wave of her elegant fingers, "If I know Sid, she wouldn't admit to good health even if her cheeks blushed like roses with proof of it."

Nora shrugged a resigned agreement and took three short steps to the door. "Who's there?"

"It's Captain Murdock, miss. Sorry for the intrusion, but I thought you ladies would like to know that we've sighted land."

Nora felt the surge of excitement she'd been anticipating for seven long days. "Oh, Fanny, we're finally here!"

Fanny Cosette smiled at her young relation. "*Oui, cherie,* so it seems."

Nora flung open the door and resisted an impulsive but

irrational urge to hug the portly Murdock. "How much longer, Captain?"

"We should be at harbor in just over an hour, miss. We have a steady westerly breeze, and the seas are only gentle swells, so I don't anticipate any problems." He peered around Nora to get a clear view of Fanny. "I wouldn't want you ladies to worry," he said. "It's a fine day for sailing, and we won't have any difficulties with the reefs."

Fanny stood up from the bunk and set her cup on the small desk next to it. "I assure you, Captain, I feel quite safe with you at the wheel."

Was it Nora's imagination, or did Captain Murdock suddenly seem to grow two inches in height? She smiled to herself. Fanny had that effect on men, and it was perfectly understandable. Despite her age, which no one really knew for certain, her gorgeous red hair showed no signs of gray, and her seductively plump figure drew appreciative glances wherever she went.

Besides, Fanny *was* French, truly, not just second-generation. She had been raised in Paris and, well, everyone knew about the French, the free-spirited, liberated, joyous French. Fanny Cosette could very well be their ambassador. Poor Nora had never been fifty miles away from Richmond until this trip, and she despaired of ever seeing her mother's homeland.

Captain Murdock's leathery cheeks blazed red above his thick muttonchop sideburns, an obvious reaction to Fanny's compliment. "May I say, ladies, that it has been a particular pleasure having you aboard the *Southern Star* for this voyage. It's a blasted shame that I have to sail again tomorrow; otherwise I would look forward to seeing you in Key West."

Fanny could say more with her eyes than many novelists could in an entire passage, and she did so now by batting her long lashes at the smitten captain. "The pleasure has indeed been ours, hasn't it, Nora?"

"Yes, truly," she answered, suppressing a giggle.

Captain Murdock threaded his hands over his broad chest as if to steady his heartbeat and stepped away from the door. "I'll see you on deck, then. By the way, Miss Seabrook, your father is already there. Shall I inform Mrs. Seabrook that we will be arriving shortly?''

"Thank you, Captain," she said, "but I'll tell Mama myself. You've been most kind."

As Nora shut the cabin door, she caught a glimpse of Fanny's coquettish wave. "Really, Fanny, you are an impossible flirt! That befuddled man won't be able to find his way back to the ship's wheel, and we'll crash upon those dreadful reefs after all!''

Fanny grasped Nora's hands and gave them a gentle squeeze. "Ah, my petite sheltered darling. A little innocent flirting is all part of the *joie de vivre.* Thank heavens I've arrived in time to see to your proper education. Your misguided mama, my own dear cousin, would have you think that all there is to life is a boring succession of musical soirees and quiet meditation. When truly, *cherie,* there is so much more."

As if Nora Seabrook didn't already know that! Even before Fanny arrived in Richmond, Nora had known her life was missing something, and her heart ached to find out just what it was. It was true that Fanny fed the spark of adventure in Nora's soul, but it had been Nora's own longing that had ignited it in the first place.

Refusing to be bound by the limits of her physical environment, Nora had started a journal four years ago when she was seventeen. Because of it, her imagination had taken flight, and with pen and ink she'd eliminated the boundaries of her world.

Now she would soon arrive at a new, mysterious, and challenging destination where nothing would be as it was in Richmond. And as each mind-expanding adventure occurred, Nora would record her impressions and reactions so that she could relive them again and again. Maybe someday she would even write a book and have it published, though that was a secret desire her mother would never understand. Sidonia Seabrook could not condone an activity so crass that it actually merited a paycheck!

Nora put aside her fantasies and regarded her cousin. "Speaking of Mama," she said. "I'll go to her cabin and give her the good news. Surely her humor will improve when she learns we are nearing land.''

"Perhaps so," Fanny acknowledged. "Nevertheless, *cherie, bon chance!*"

Good luck, indeed!

The sun was well above the ocean when Nora joined her father on the deck of the *Southern Star* several minutes after Captain Murdock's visit. When she stood beside him against the rail, Thurston Seabrook put his hand on his daughter's arm and stared into the western horizon. "There it is, Nora. Key West, Florida. I must confess I am most anxious to learn just exactly what makes this interesting little island the subject of so much speculation in Washington."

The southernmost key in the chain extending along the Florida Straits from the state's mainland shimmered on the horizon like a bracelet of pearls on aquamarine satin. "It's as different from Richmond as any place could be," Nora said, noting the low profile of the island. There was an obvious absence of tall buildings and other trappings of a city.

"Truly," Thurston agreed with a decisive nod. "It's a most unassuming spit of land to have earned its unequaled reputation for greed and rivalry."

"It looks beautiful to me, Father," Nora said. "Can't you even for one day forget you're a judge and just enjoy yourself?"

He turned to look at his daughter. "Our government is paying me handsomely to do a job, Nora, and . . ."

"And by golly, I'll see to it they get their money's worth!" she declared in her best impression of her father's voice. She took the sting out of her teasing by smiling up at his stern face.

An answering grin raised one neatly trimmed curve of his handlebar mustache. "I realize you're joking, Nora, though there is truth in what you say. But tell me, what of your mother? Did you inform her we're close to the harbor?"

"Yes. She's coming on deck soon. Fanny stayed behind to help her with the boys."

At that precise moment, a commotion occurred on the companionway behind them that temporarily caused Nora to forget their destination. She whirled away from the rail to see what was happening. A panel of silk burgundy, representing only a fraction of Sidonia Seabrook's voluminous skirt, appeared around the corner of the nearest cabin. Her voice, high-pitched from anxiety, preceded her actual appearance.

"Fanny, are you holding Armand tightly?" she cried. "Oh, this retched boat is pitching and tossing so I can barely keep my footing!"

"Yes, of course, Sid, I have the little beast," came Fanny's response. "He's safe in my arms."

Sidonia approached her husband and daughter near the bow of the ship by grabbing onto any object mounted on the cabin walls that offered assistance. Her progress was slow, and further impeded by a bundle of wiry gray fur protruding from the bend in her elbow. Poor Hubert's eyes nearly bulged from his head, he was held so firmly in Sidonia's grasp.

Nora met her mother halfway and offered to take the dog from her arm.

"No, no, dear, he's already so frightened," Sidonia protested. "If I relinquish him now, he'll positively swoon from fear."

Thurston Seabrook looked over his shoulder and grimaced. "It's a dog, Sidonia. For heaven's sake, dogs don't swoon from anything except perhaps hunger."

After much effort, Sidonia finally reached the railing and stood next to her husband. From her expression, she did not seem in the least amused by Thurston's cavalier attitude. "And that's another thing. The boys have hardly eaten a tidbit since we left Richmond."

"Only mutton and beef and roasted potatoes," Thurston corrected her. Then, to Nora, he added in a whisper, "I'm surprised Mama can still carry the portly pooch at all."

"Now, Father . . ."

Minding his manners, Thurston attempted to interest his wife in the panorama that was their destination. "Look dear, the island is just ahead. Isn't it fascinating?"

In the last minutes, the key had begun to take shape and definition. One- and two-story buildings were now recognizable. Trees unlike those found in Virginia displayed their long, elegant leaves bending in the wind like feathers on a pen.

"It's horrible," Sidonia moaned. "There's not a tall building in sight. Where are the hotels and offices, and where in heaven's name could there even be an opera or theater? It looks as if it's all been cut off at the knees!"

"Mama, you can't compare it to Richmond," Nora said. "It's completely different, and that's what makes it so exciting. If you'd read Father's literature about this place you'd know that."

"I know enough, Eleanor," Sidonia insisted, drawing out Nora's proper name in a way that discouraged further discussion. "It's a land of barbarians."

"Not so, dear," Thurston cut in. "Key West has a doctor, and ministers, and many gentlemen of fine lineage from proper Southern families. There is a hospital . . ."

"Thank goodness for that at least. I would refuse to even leave this ship if we weren't assured proper medical assistance." She looked at her daughter for support. "Eleanor, you're prone to respiratory infections . . ."

Nora sighed with frustration. "Mama, please, I haven't had any problems for at least six years."

". . . and Thurston, there's your stomach. And I . . . well, goodness knows I don't have to tell you . . ."

"And several churches," Thurston concluded, obviously reluctant to listen to the same complaints he was besieged with in Virginia.

Sidonia snorted. "As if heathens need churches."

Turning away from Sidonia's watchful gaze, Fanny clamped her hand over Armand's muzzle to stop the animal from yapping. "Heathens need them most of all, Sid, darling."

Sidonia grasped onto what appeared to be a sympathetic comment from her cousin. "Ah, you see, Fanny agrees with me. We're about to embroil ourselves in a cauldron of ignorance and perhaps even tribalism . . . if we're lucky enough to even encounter human beings!''

"Mama," Nora said, "Father's papers reported that last year, in the census of 1857, there were three thousand residents here."

Sidonia quaked. "And only three of us!" She buried her face in Hubert's fur. "God help us."

Jacob Proctor dipped the nib of his pen into the ink bottle for what seemed like the hundredth time that morning and entered more figures into the giant ledger on his oak desk. This weekly chore was the most ponderous aspect of owning his own business . . . this blasted bookkeeping, which he didn't trust to anyone else. It was especially tiresome on a beautiful February morning when the temperature was a balmy seventy-two degrees and the breeze off the Atlantic was calm and steady, perfect for a leisurely sail.

"Jacob! Come quick. I think the *Southern Star* is approaching."

Even if his first mate's voice hadn't rung with urgency, Jacob would have welcomed the interruption. As it was, the news that came down to him from Willy's position in the cupola was extremely important and eagerly anticipated. It caused Jacob to bound from his chair and climb the stairs two at a time to the catwalk above the two-storied building that housed the Proctor Warehouse and Salvage Company.

He joined Willy in the tower. "Do you think it's her?"

"Aye, Jacob. I'm certain of it now." He handed a brass telescope to his friend. "There's no mistaking the half-moon and star on her flag."

Jacob sighted the approaching clipper ship and nodded. "It's the *Star*, all right. That means our newest judge is about to arrive in town."

Willy Turpin looked down at the floorboards beneath his brogans and shook his head, appearing for all the world as if the weight of the entire wrecking industry was on his thin shoulders. "Let's hope he's a fair man, Captain, or woe be to us all."

Jacob clapped his friend on one of those drooping shoulders. "I've a mind to have a pint, Willy. What do you say to going over to Teague's for a swallow?"

Turpin slowly raised his head and a smile spread under his peppered mustache. "We could sit out on the veranda and perhaps have a look-see at the *Star* as she pulls in."

Jacob urged Willy to the stairs and followed him down. "I never thought of that," he said, though of course he had. "But now that you mention it, it gives us two good reasons for going to Teague's."

The veranda of Jimmy Teague's Tavern looked over the harbor, and it was to this part of the establishment that Jacob and Willy carried their mugs of ale. Settling themselves at a table nearest the water, they had a clear view when the tall masts of the *Southern Star* appeared around the tip of the island.

One by one, each of the sails was goose-winged and then lowered completely as the mammoth passenger clipper inched closer to the longest dock in the harbor. "I'd hate to have to manage her, wouldn't you, Willy?" Jacob said of the cumbersome vessel that measured well over two hundred feet.

"Aye. She'd be as hard to navigate as a three-hundred-pound woman, not that I haven't tried my hand at such a task."

Jacob took a long swallow of dark ale. "But you wouldn't try it again, right, mate?"

Willy chortled with good humor and wiped foam from his mustache. "Never say never, Captain, not on an island where the men outnumber the women three to one."

Jacob laughed. "Good advice there, Will." He angled his mug toward the *Southern Star*. "They're lowering the gangway. Guess we'll have a look at the judge soon enough."

Activity on board the *Star* held both men's attention. They were used to seeing passengers disembark in Key West, but never before had Jacob seen such a profusion of trunks and baskets and valises as accompanied the current arrivals. Though he couldn't yet get a clear glimpse of the passengers, a woman's voice carried to him on the calm breeze. The authority in her tone left no doubt that she was orchestrating the unloading of goods.

"Carry that one straight up," she said. "Don't tip it to the side."

"It will take two men to carry this one," she added. "If one tries alone, he'll surely drop it and ruin all my crystal."

"Do watch that basket," she went on. "The boys' beds are in there."

Willy spoke out of the side of his mouth. "Makes you ever so glad you're not a deckhand, doesn't it, Captain?"

"It does at that."

"We'll proceed first," came the woman's voice again, "and you men follow with our things so I can make sure you tote them properly."

Porting assignments completed, at last the *Star*'s passengers appeared at the entrance to the gangway, three women and one man, each milling about as if deciding who should lead the way. Or perhaps uncertain as to which one would be brave enough to traverse the steeply sloping twenty-foot plank. The matriarchal leader took the situation in hand once again. "Eleanor, dear, you go first. And watch your step."

A slim woman in a dark green traveling suit climbed the stairs to the gangway, took hold of the rope guide, and cautiously took her first steps toward land.

Though the woman made an interesting picture heading toward shore, Jacob's keen gaze darted to movement on one of the mooring lines attached to the stern of the *Star*. A Key West wharf rat, one of many renowned for their acrobatic skills, had jumped onto the rope from the dock and was racing toward the gangway in the center of the ship. The single-minded rodent no doubt intended to make its way to the galley for a snack, and would be no happier to come face-to-face with humans than they would be to meet him.

Jacob anticipated the inevitable encounter. He jumped up

from his chair and leapt over the railing separating Teague's from the harbor. He intended to warn the woman called Eleanor of a possible trauma to her delicate sensibilities should she be the squeamish type, as most women were when it came to nine-inch rats. What he didn't count on was the reaction of two additional members of the animal kingdom, both of whom were every bit as aware of the rat as he was.

It all happened in the blink of an eye. Dogs snapped and yapped in feral excitement. A woman screamed. Eleanor in the green suit stopped halfway down the gangway. A pair of furry cannonballs propelled themselves from the screaming older women's arms. The rat did exactly what it wouldn't have done if it had been thinking clearly, which of course it wasn't in the midst of all that racket. It leapt onto the gangway in front of the woman in the green dress.

Eleanor, to her credit, maintained her dignity and her footing. She appeared to have made the wise choice to let the rat have its run ahead of her to land. The dogs, however, had another plan. They streaked toward the woman, their cockles raised and the fur around their yapping faces laid back as if they were caught in a hurricane.

Running one on each side of her, both dogs disappeared momentarily under the hem of the lady's dress. Their forward speed was great enough that the fabric obstruction barely slowed them down. They emerged on the other side of her skirt still blazing after their prey. And Eleanor went down on her rump.

She grasped one of the rope guidelines with both hands, which caused her to swing to the side. It was this motion, and the moisture on the gangway, that proved her undoing. She slid entirely under the rope, and with feet and arms flailing in the air, she plummeted to the sea. And the older female still on the *Southern Star,* now dogless, screamed even louder.

The billowing skirt of a green dress spread over the water at least two dozen yards off shore. Jacob knew the Gulf was no deeper than the woman's chin at this point; however, she appeared not to be aware of it. She waved her arms frantically and choked and sputtered the distressing fact that she couldn't swim.

"Bloody hell!" Jacob swore as he tore off his boots. Then he jumped off the dock and swam for her.

She wasn't easy to save. When he reached her, the water lapped at his chest, but the victim failed to notice he was standing. She balled the front of his shirt in her fist and tugged with all her might, nearly pulling him under. "Blast woman, hold still!" he shouted.

Her fingers dug into his shoulder blade like sponge hooks, and she squealed in his ear. "But I . . . I can't swim!"

"You can stand, can't you?"

The question calmed her, or more likely shocked her, and she clung to him and stared with large, confused eyes. "What?"

"Madam, it's not deep. Look at me. I'm standing."

Logic registered somewhere in her mind, and in fact even forced something like a giggle up from her throat. Her feet found the bottom of the harbor, and her grip on his tortured body lessened. "Oh. I see," she said.

He pointed toward the shore. "Shall I walk you to Key West, madam?"

She tried to take a step, but was unsuccessful. "I'm afraid I'm mired in something, and my skirts are sodden." She looked at him with eyes the color of the noon sky, and it seemed as if they might fill with tears. "I'm so sorry, but it appears I can't move."

Considering the amount of clothing she was wearing, Jacob wasn't surprised she was stuck in the squishy sand. Water must have added pounds to her natural weight. "In that case, if you'll try to be a bit more gentle, I'll allow you to put your arm around my shoulder a second time."

The eyes grew wide again, so wide a man could get lost in them and forget what he was about. "Pardon me, sir?"

"To keep your balance." He scooped her up in his arms, and she emitted a tiny yelp. Then he carried the entire package— trembling woman, soggy skirts, and at least five pounds of soaked raven hair—to the shore.

"My hat," she said when they were nearly at the dock.

He turned back and saw a little pointed green thing, tipped over like a canoe with an ostrich feather as its rudder. It was floating hopelessly north, well away from the Key West harbor. "I wouldn't worry too much about it, madam. It's not the proper hat for our climate anyway."

He set her on the dock, and was tempted to swim after the hat after all just to escape the crush of agitated humanity that descended upon them. The dogless older woman, who just moments before had been the image of decisive leadership, half swooned in Captain Murdock's arms while muttering a series of unrecognizable squawks about her daughter and her boys. A deckhand worked her fan like a metronome against her flushed face.

A distinguished middle-aged man huffed about in a take-charge manner and inquired after the drenched woman's well-being. That was how Jacob learned that she was called Nora, and how he surmised he was listening to the no-nonsense baritone of Key West's newest Federal judge.

And a female in a striking red dress with hair to match fixed her gaze on Jacob as if he were a worm and she the bird. When he returned her glance, she winked at him, and in a French accent declared that the world could never have enough heroes.

And Nora, still shivering with emotions he could not identify, regarded him with those fathomless blue eyes. Her curling dark hair fell around her shoulders in matted disarray. Her chest heaved against her soaked bodice. Her gown clung to her slim figure, hinting at the shapes underneath. And in a modest voice, she proclaimed, "Thank you for coming to my assistance."

"My pleasure, miss. It's what I do, actually, but I should add that I've never performed a rescue so close to shore."

She looked down at her dripping skirt, raised the hem slightly off the ground, and shook it around her ankles. "Yes, well, I've never fallen off a ship before."

The judge accepted a blanket from the ship's mate and wrapped it around Nora's shoulders. "Yes, thank you, sir," he said. "I'm Thurston Seabrook, and this is my daughter. We are all indebted to you for your quick thinking . . ."

Jacob was only half listening. He was more concerned about a problem Nora seemed to be having with her dress. For several moments the hemline had mimicked a marionette, jerking awkwardly around her ankles. When he had a pretty good idea what was causing the strange occurrence, he bent down and reached under her hem.

"I beg your pardon," the judge blustered. "Remove your hand at once!"

Jacob did, and produced from the folds of Nora's skirt a blue crab who wiggled his appendages in a frantic effort to return to the sea. Jacob grinned as he held the crustacean in the air. "It appears that Nora came ashore with a stowaway in her stitching."

The judge sputtered and coughed. The woman in red hooted with laughter. Nora stared at the creature in awe. And the woman in Captain Murdock's arms shrieked with horror.

Jacob tossed the hapless crab in the water, wiped his hand on his pants, and offered it to the judge. "The name's Proctor, Your Honor."

Regaining his composure, the judge cut short the handshake, narrowed his eyes under bushy brows, and said, "So you're the *infamous* Captain Proctor."

CHAPTER TWO

The man who had come to Nora's rescue dropped his hand from her father's and crossed his arms over his chest. He cocked his head at a slight angle and stared at Thurston Seabrook with cool slate-colored eyes. "I'm Jacob Proctor," he said. "I didn't know I had earned the title 'infamous.'"

"Oh, but Captain, you have," Thurston replied. "Your reputation has spread all the way to our nation's capital."

"And to what do I owe this dubious honor?"

"By virtue of claiming wrecking master rights to more wrecks than any other salvager on the island. By holding more auctions of goods and garnering higher percentages of profit than any other similar business in Key West."

"Since when is it a crime to make money, Your Honor?" Proctor spoke Thurston's title as if the words were dripping in hemlock.

"Making money isn't a crime. The way you go about it may well be."

Proctor altered his stance just a little, and the result was a squaring off, as Nora imagined boxers do in a ring. "I would be careful about insinuations you make, Judge, especially as you're a newcomer to the island . . ."

"Thurston! Thurston, what are you doing over there? Come quickly, please."

Nora had been watching the two men, but her mother's frantic cry drew her attention, and thankfully had the effect of throwing cold water over the tension in the air.

Her father turned away from Jacob Proctor. "What is it, Sidonia? You can see that Nora is quite all right."

"Yes, I know, thank heavens, but the boys, Thurston, the boys have run off. And in this strange place. They could be lost. My darlings could be lost."

Jacob Proctor finally uncrossed his arms, but their impression left his linen shirtfront stuck against his chest. Nora's gaze was drawn to the dark areas under the white fabric. A matting of wet hair lessened in thickness as it trailed to the waistband of his trousers. It was an inappropriate thought, Nora knew, but she marveled that his chest hair could be darker than the hair on his head. That was definitely a question for Fanny.

"Mrs. Seabrook," he said, "your dogs aren't lost." He cocked his thumb toward a tavern on the corner. "See for yourself."

Two men approached. One of them carried Hubert, and the other Armand. The dogs were panting, and their fur was uncharacteristically mussed, but otherwise they appeared unharmed from their ordeal.

Sidonia rushed to them, her arms wide open to receive her boys. "Oh, my babies," she cried.

Jacob introduced the men as they handed over their catch. "Mrs. Seabrook, this is Willy Turpin and Jimmy Teague."

Sidonia barely managed a glance at the two men as she cuddled her boys to her chest. "Thank you," she muttered absently.

Willy Turpin laughed out loud. "Those are some animals, ma'am," he said. "You can't hardly tell the rats from the rat catchers."

Sidonia's head shot up and she leveled a brilliant glare at

the smiling Willy. "How dare you call these dogs 'rat catchers'! I'll have you know these are pedigreed French poodles."

Jimmy Teague rubbed his weeks' growth of stubble and chuckled through missing teeth. After poking Willy in the ribs to get his attention, he said, "Oh, I see. They're really not much good for anything, then."

For once it was fortunate that Sidonia had her hands occupied with the boys. Otherwise, she might have swung her reticule like a medieval mace at both men's heads.

Further incident was avoided when a well-dressed gentleman joined the group and introduced himself to the Seabrooks. He was so remarkably thin that Nora feared a stiff breeze would take him skyward.

"Judge Seabrook, welcome to Key West. I came as soon as I heard the ship had docked. I'm Dillard Hyde, Clerk of the Court. I've arranged to have your things moved to your residence, and ..." He paused long enough to peruse Nora's unkempt appearance. "Perhaps I should take you there right now," he added.

"Yes, I think that's a good idea," Thurston agreed, and briefly introduced his party to the clerk.

"Where is a carriage, Mr. Hyde?" Sidonia asked.

"Oh, there are very few carriages on the island, madam. We've really no need of them. Everything is within walking distance."

"Walking distance? You mean we must walk to our house?"

"It's only a few blocks."

She cast a forlorn look at the pile of trunks and boxes on the dock. "But our things?"

Dillard shielded his eyes and peered up and down the dock. He relaxed when he spotted a Negro boy leading a flop-eared donkey attached to a rickety cart. "Don't worry yourself, Mrs. Seabrook. Felix will bring your belongings."

"Come along, Sid," Thurston said, taking her elbow. He turned back to Proctor before joining Dillard on the street that led through town. "Captain, notwithstanding my gratitude to you for rescuing Nora, I want you to know that in three days

I will officially be holding court. You may spread the word to all your cohorts that at promptly nine a.m. on Thursday, I will expect to see all the wreckers' licenses and credentials. That includes yours, sir."

A smile that was both cocky and foolhardy split the captain's face. "I'll look forward to it, Judge."

Fanny linked her arm in Nora's as they passed Jacob Proctor. "I must give you credit, *cherie,*" she said. "That was an entrance that I, myself, would have been proud of."

"Fanny, stop. It's not as if I meant to fall in the water!"

"More's the pity."

As Nora walked through the center of Key West, she sensed Jacob Proctor's gaze on her back. It created a surge of heat inside her that seemed to hasten the drying of her salt-encrusted garments. She squirmed against the stiff, clammy feel of salty fabric on her skin. Surely the irritation of the chemical explained the strange tingling sensation that rippled through her.

In any other circumstance Nora would have felt self-conscious knowing she was being introduced to a new community looking very much like a drowned rat. This day, however, she scarcely gave a thought to her appearance. She was too engrossed in the sights and sounds and smells of the island, and paid scant attention to gawkers on verandas who were forming their own impressions of Key West's newest arrivals.

It was a five-block walk from Front Street to Southard, where the Seabrooks were to take residence. In that short distance they passed commercial establishments, located nearest the wharf, then simple row cottages, and finally one- and two-story houses that seemed to have come from another country and time entirely. Used to substantial Richmond residences of brick and wrought iron, Nora wondered at the lack of stone and mortar on Key West. Everything but the brick walkways was made of wood.

Some of the homes were easy to see, while others were hidden behind vast tropical foliage, the names of which Nora was determined to discover. Two characteristics were common to all the dwellings. Each house was close to its neighbor and each was close to the street.

"First of all, we have a shortage of usable land, forcing us to build close together," Dillard Hyde explained when Nora asked him about the location of houses. "And secondly, no one *wants* to be far from his neighbor. Originally that was for safety in case of Indian attacks . . ."

Sidonia gripped her husband's arm until he winced. "Indian attacks?" she squealed.

"Not anymore, Mrs. Seabrook, not since the late '40's. Now we continue to build close because it's the most efficient way of dispensing news. On this island, we say the veranda method—that is, calling from one house to the next—works as well as the mainland's telegraph system."

"And why are all the houses of wood?" Nora asked.

"Because wood is what we can get most easily from Central and South America." Dillard stopped in front of a charming two-story residence with palm trees and neatly trimmed plants in front and a veranda that swept around three sides. "Take your house, for example . . ."

Nora drew in a sharp breath and released it slowly. It was the same reaction she had when seeing a beautiful painting for the first time. "This house is ours?"

"Indeed, miss, during the judge's stay, this is where you'll live. The house is made of Honduran mahogany and heart pine. It is similar in design to the homes of British colonials in the Bahamas. Not surprising since it was built by a British sea captain a number of years ago."

Green shutters against milky-white siding made the house look cool and inviting. "It's lovely," Nora said.

"And substantial," Dillard added. "Salt air only makes mahogany stronger, nearly impervious to termites. Why, this house is so sturdy, I doubt fire would even bring it down."

"Why did the sea captain leave such a beautiful home?"

"He still owns it. I imagine he'll sell it one day. His wife grew tired of the island and begged to be taken back to England.

They made enough money here, like so many wreckers have, so that's where they've gone."

Thurston shook his head. "Too much money too fast. It's the root of all evil. These wreckers are like drunken sailors off a boat after a year at sea. Spending wantonly, living wild. It's a sin, I tell you. Making money off the misery of others."

Tired of hearing from both her parents about everything that was wrong with Key West, Nora walked away from them and entered a gate in the picket fence that surrounded the house. She approached the front door, but still heard bits of her father's observations.

". . . false beacons on the shoreline . . ."

". . . needless loss of innocent lives . . ."

Perhaps there was something wicked after all on this tropical isle. Nora was willing to concede it was possible. And she supposed it was also possible that her savior that afternoon was part of this unpleasant picture. But at this moment, walking under the shade of a canopy of palm leaves toward abundant plants covered with the most colorful large blossoms she'd ever seen, she didn't want to acknowledge wickedness. She only wanted to feel the silken softness of the petals and breathe in their sweet scents.

Her father's heavy footsteps sounded on the walkway behind her. "It's a good thing I've come," he said to Dillard. "And not a moment too soon."

The front door was opened by a cocoa-skinned woman in a cotton dress and apron. A colorful cloth was wrapped around her hair and tied at her nape, accentuating large almond eyes and a full mouth. She stood at the entrance without speaking until Dillard noticed her.

"Ah, Portia, your employers have arrived." As each member of Judge Seabrook's household was introduced, the woman responded with a nod of her head.

Soon another, younger, and equally exotic, dark-skinned woman came to stand beside Portia. She was introduced as Lulu. Dillard explained that the two women, as well as a gardener, comprised the household staff, unless Mrs. Seabrook determined that other servants were needed.

"Are they slaves, Mr. Hyde?" Sidonia asked.

"Oh, no, ma'am, indeed not. Portia and Lulu are mother and daughter. They are both members of the Obalu family, free blacks from the Bahamas. They came to this island like so many Bahamians during the raids of the pirates at the end of the last century. The Obalus have lived here for nearly sixty years."

Nora anticipated her mother's reaction. While the Seabrooks were not landed people, they did own three slaves who had stayed behind with Sidonia's brother in Virginia to care for the family's town home and country house while the Seabrooks were in Florida. Her mother was not accustomed to paying wages to Negro servants.

"Does this mean we must pay these people?" she asked.

"Yes, madam. The women each earn five dollars a month, and the gardener, Portia's son Hector, earns four dollars fifty. They are well worth the money. We have very few slaves on this island, and those principally work at the salt ponds."

Salt ponds? Nora had never heard of such a thing. Key West grew more interesting every moment.

"But Florida is a Southern state," Sidonia protested, as if that statement negated everything Dillard had just said.

"Never mind, dear," Thurston interjected wisely. He walked her toward the house. "The wages are quite in line."

Nora was the last to enter. She started to cross the threshold into a wide hallway with rooms on each side, but stopped when she realized she would be treading on a polished wood floor. Looking down at her soiled dress, she said to Lulu, "Perhaps I shouldn't come in. I might mar the floor."

A tentative giggle came from the girl's coral lips. "Young missy fell in the ocean?"

"I'm afraid that's exactly what happened. Now my dress is probably ruined and I'm itchy all over. What should I do, Lulu?"

"No problem. I'll hold the dress while you go upstairs to

the second room on the right. That's your room. Then I'll take the dress away and put you in a barrel.''

Nora wasn't so sure she wanted to be put in a barrel, but anything sounded better than spending another minute in her stiff, uncomfortable clothes. With Lulu following, holding the soggy hem above the flooring, she quickly ascended the staircase in the center of the hallway and found her room. She wished she had time to fully appreciate the charming appointments of her new chamber ... the floral wallpaper and bedcover, the pastel settee, lace curtains billowing at French doors to the second-floor veranda. But Lulu was all determined efficiency.

In minutes Nora was stripped to her camisole and pantalettes. Her hair was free of the last of its pins and hanging loose down her back. The green traveling suit had been bundled up and removed to the hallway. Lulu helped Nora into a thin robe and ordered her to the garden in back of the house.

"But someone will see me," Nora protested. "How can I pass through the house with nothing on but these undergarments and flimsy robe?"

"Pooh, missy," Lulu said. "This is Key West. We don't wear so many clothes here. You go outside and get in the barrel. I'll come soon to wash you free of salt.''

Nora did as she was told, but she fancied herself a streak of lightning as she ran down the back staircase to the rear entrance. Relieved to find that the sizable backyard was enclosed by a tall fence, she found the barrel Lulu had spoken of. It was mounted on an iron stand next to the house and was raised approximately two feet off a wooden platform on the ground. A panel opened when Nora loosened a latch, and she stepped inside.

Almost immediately Lulu appeared and began filling a bucket with water from a cistern near the barrel. "Take your clothes off," she said when the bucket was full. "This is cool rainwater. It makes the hair soft and shiny.''

She then stood on a stool and doused Nora completely with the bucket of water. Handing her a ball of soap, she said, "Now you wash. Then I'll rinse again.''

Sputtering through a mouthful of water and shivering with its chill, Nora scrubbed away the remains of the salt water and endured Lulu's second rinsing. When she dried herself and emerged from the barrel in her robe, she ran her hand down her damp hair. It did indeed feel softer. Turning to Lulu, she said, "Don't people ever take civilized baths around here?"

"Oh, yes, missy, but this is faster, and you smelled like fish. Bah!"

The next day dawned crystalline with a sky so blue it defined the color, and air so fresh it seemed to have been made for that morning alone. Nora chose the early hour while her family slept to explore the garden.

She'd learned the day before that preparations for the Seabrooks to move into the Samuel Rutherford house had begun weeks before. Portia's son Hector had tended the trees. Varieties of fruit, most of which Nora had never seen, hung heavy from pruned limbs. She recognized bananas and grapefruit, but had no idea what to call the oblong green specimens, and decided to find Hector later and ask him.

A vegetable garden flourished with potatoes, tomatoes, and peppers. Herbs grew in boxes along the fence line, and a special place was reserved near the cistern for cultivating the medicinal plant Lulu had shown her called aloe. "You will appreciate its qualities the first time your skin burns, missy," she had said.

It was a practical, bountiful, and peaceful garden, and Nora looked forward to halcyon days and cool sunsets in its comforting surroundings. Solitude was not destined for her this first morning, however. She hadn't been in the garden a quarter hour when she heard a knock on the back-fence gate.

She opened the gate and stared down into three inquisitive brown faces. She recognized one child as the boy, Felix, who'd pulled the donkey cart. A little girl and another boy were with him, and at the end of a short rope they were holding on to was, of all things, a goat.

Nora smiled. "You're Felix, aren't you? You brought our trunks yesterday."

He seemed pleased that she remembered him. "Yes. Did I do a good job?"

"Certainly. A very good job." It occurred to Nora that perhaps he'd asked the question and returned this morning because he hadn't been paid for bringing their belongings. In all the excitement, she hadn't thought of it, and perhaps it had slipped her father's mind as well. "Were you paid for that service?" she asked.

"Yes, miss," he answered. "Mr. Hyde paid me." He worried a small stone in the street with his bare toe and grinned up at her. His eyes were like chestnuts under thick lashes. "But sometimes, if my work is thought to be very good, I get a little something extra."

So that was the reason for this visit. "I see," Nora said. "Your work was very good. If you'll wait here, I will bring you a coin to say thank you."

"Wait, miss, before you go. I want you to meet my sister and brother." Felix took hold of the girl's hand and coaxed her forward. "This is Esmeralda. She is eight years old." He did the same for the boy. "And this is Ty. He is seven. Portia is our grandmother. We are the Obalu family," he said proudly.

Bending at the waist, Nora shook hands with each of the children. She decided that large, expressive eyes and honey-toned skin must be an Obalu family trait. "It is very nice to meet you," she said. "And if you wait, I will get Felix's coin."

"One more thing before you go, miss." Felix took the rope from his brother and held it out to Nora. "You must also pay for your goat."

"*My* goat? I don't have a goat."

"Now you do. This is your goat. Everyone on the island has a goat. This one is named Reckless, and he's yours."

Nora put her hand over her mouth to suppress a bout of giggles. "I'm sure he is a fine goat, but I don't want a goat," she said.

"But you will. Goats eat garbage. It's the way we do things.

Otherwise the island would fill up with garbage. Humans make a lot of garbage, but goats don't mind. They eat it all.''

Nora studied Reckless's face. What Felix said did make sense. She knew very little about goats, but she remembered hearing once that they ate many odd things. And this goat had a sweet, serene look about him with his interesting short horns and a wispy, almost dignified beard. She supposed it might be all right to have Reckless around. "How much must I pay for my goat?" she said, suddenly suspicious of Felix's round, innocent eyes.

"Only one dollar fifty," he said.

That wasn't so bad . . .

". . . a month. You only rent your goat. I will collect on the first day of each month."

Still, if this was how the residents solved the problem of too much garbage, it wasn't much to pay. "All right, then. Wait here," Nora said. When she came back, she handed Felix two dollars and he placed the goat's rope in her hand.

"You are very kind, miss," he said.

The goat, which up to this time had been the picture of docility, began to prance about uncertainly. He strained against the rope, lowered his head, and butted it into the folds of Nora's skirt. He darted back out again, but with a sizable chunk of green and white striped percale in his masticating jaws.

Not another dress ruined, Nora thought. And I haven't even been here twenty-four hours! "No, goat, no," she said, pushing at the part of Reckless's head between his horns.

The children dissolved into fits of laughter until Felix came to the rescue. "Watch, miss," he said, and stuck his finger in the goat's ear. The animal immediately let go of the dress. "That's all you have to do."

Nora answered Felix's self-assured grin with a smirk of disapproval. "You could have told me this goat trick before you handed me the rope," she said.

He shrugged his shoulders. "I thought everyone knew the ear thing."

"What goes on out here?" A sober-faced Portia came

through the gate and approached the children. Her fist shook in the air, threatening to land on someone's head if she were the least provoked. "What are you all doing here bothering Miss Seabrook?"

Nora immediately came to their defense. "They weren't bothering me, really. They're quite charming children."

"Humph! I know how my grandchildren can be." She cast a stern eye on each of them that Nora was certain would have stopped a charging elephant. But her face softened when she saw Reckless. "You've brought our goat, I see."

The children nodded.

"Good." She took the rope and pulled an obedient Reckless behind her into the yard. After tying the rope to a stake, she came back to the gate. "Did you tell Miss Seabrook we must keep the goat tied in the yard, or he will eat all our vegetables?"

Nora looked at all three angelic faces. "I'm sure they were just going to tell me that."

Portia huffed again. "Then go. And stop at the market for fresh conch. Tell your mama to make fritters."

Soon all that was left of the children was the cloud of dust kicked up by their bare feet.

"They're adorable children," Nora said, expecting a glow of pride to brighten their grandmother's face.

Instead she saw a wrinkled brow. "They seem so to you, eh?" Portia waggled her finger at Nora. "Take some advice, Miss Seabrook. Never tell them that when there is still a whole day of mischief to get into."

A whole day of mischief? It was a weekday in the middle of February. Many free blacks up north were in school getting an education. "Why aren't these children in school?" she asked.

"Bah! The only school on this island is for whites. And it costs money. My children learn what they can, and they get by."

Portia went back to the house, but Nora stayed at the gate pondering the dilemma of these Bahamian children. They had so much time on their hands. They should be learning, and yet there was no school available to them. It wasn't right. She experienced a rumbling in her stomach in response to the smell of breakfast foods coming from the kitchen house, and decided to think more about this problem later. Right now she was starved.

She had just started back inside the gate when movement from across the street caught her eye. Someone stood under a gigantic tree with a wide trunk and large roots that climbed clear to the lower limbs. The unusual tree was interesting enough, but the man leaning against it was more fascinating by far. He was dressed in a white shirt and dark pants, and when he realized she'd spotted him, he pushed away from the trunk and took a step closer to her.

He crossed his arms as she'd seen him do the day before, but this time it was a casual gesture, not a defensive one. She knew this for certain because he was smiling. Actually, he was more than smiling. His lips curled upwards in a grin of such absolute delight that she might have felt inclined to answer it with a smile of her own. But she didn't, for she knew instinctively that his amusement was at her expense.

She didn't know how long he had been standing there, but she felt sure he'd seen her entire get-acquainted scene with the goat. One little voice inside her told her to return to her backyard and shut the gate immediately. But another voice, one that was much more persuasive, made her stay. In fact, she even shut the gate behind her and waited near the street as he came across.

CHAPTER THREE

Watching Jacob Proctor approach, Nora took a deep breath to calm an odd quaking in her stomach. He stopped within a few feet of her and let his gaze wander from her hastily combed and restrained hair to the ruffled hem of her striped dress. His grin, which, on closer inspection, hinted more of friendly interest than ridicule, spread across his face and was reflected in his eyes. Despite the amusement in their gray depths, or perhaps because of it, Nora sensed an indefinable power about the man, as if he truly could be the force her father had come to Key West to deal with.

The sun glinted off strands of wheat-colored hair that swept over his ears and brushed his collar. This also said something about Jacob Proctor. Nora rarely saw a man without his hat in Richmond, and even this seemingly small defiance of convention marked Proctor as one who did not follow rules.

He assumed a casual stance, resting his elbow on one of the tall fence posts that enclosed the family's backyard. Still smiling with white, even teeth, he said, "Lovely morning, isn't it, Miss Seabrook?"

She nodded with as much disinterest as she could muster. It

would be well if he knew she was concerned with more important matters than the weather. "Captain, do you enjoy watching me make a fool of myself?"

The smile grew broader. "I hardly know how to answer that. No matter if I say yes or no, it will imply that I agree that you have indeed been making a fool of yourself. That is hardly a gallant way to begin our conversation."

Nora glanced over the fence posts toward the house. This was a conversation she probably shouldn't be having in the first place, and if anyone saw her, she'd pay dearly for this indiscretion later. "Then perhaps I should start it by asking why you were across the street watching me with the children."

"I was merely protecting my business interests."

"Oh, really? What business is that, Captain?"

"The goat you just received. It's mine."

The matter of the goat was becoming more perplexing by the minute. "You mean that you are in the goat-peddling business as well as your other endeavors?"

"Guilty as charged, Miss Seabrook. It's in every wrecker's license that he must have a *legitimate* business, other than merely saving lives and property. Another one of the decrees of our procession of judges," he added. "Goat renting is mine. Reckless, as Felix so aptly named him, is one of fifty goats I imported from Mexico to keep up with the island's growing population. He is an especially fine specimen, too. Always hungry, and not a picky eater. When I heard he was to be yours, I knew he would suit your needs."

A gust of wind pulled a strand of Nora's hair from her chignon and tossed it across her face. She retrieved it and tucked it back inside her snood, all the while aware that the captain's eyes followed her movement. Such attention unsettled her while at the same time causing a flush of guilty pleasure to warm her cheeks. "So my father will be paying our monthly rental for the goat to Proctor's Warehouse and Salvage Company?"

Proctor nodded. " 'Fraid so."

Thurston Seabrook was not likely to enjoy lining Jacob Proctor's pockets with goat money! He'd made it clear that this salvager was to be the focus of his investigation of the wrecking industry.

Proctor angled his head to better see into Nora's downcast face. When she met his gaze, she stared into gray eyes that were alert and subtly probing, almost as if he could see more with them than most mortal humans. "If it bothers you, Nora, to tell your father I own the goat, you can always give the lease money to Felix. After all, he's the one who brought Reckless here this morning. I just followed him to make sure he delivered him to the proper residence."

Most of what Jacob had said faded into insignificance. Nora was more concerned that he'd just called her by her first name. In Richmond, no gentleman with such limited acquaintance with a lady would dare address her so informally. She waited, expecting to see evidence that he realized his social blunder, but what she perceived instead in his clear, cool gaze was bold self-assurance. Captain Proctor no doubt rarely defended or apologized for what he did. "Perhaps it would be best if I say that Felix owns the goat," she said.

"Suit yourself." He pushed away from the fence. "I'll say good day to you, then, until we meet again."

"Yes, well, good day."

He started to cross the street, but stopped halfway and turned back to her. "And Nora, one more thing. I realize you are new to the community, but I caution you to be a bit more prudent where money is concerned."

"What do you mean?"

A corner of his mouth quirked up to laughing eyes. "Goat rental is only seventy-five cents. Felix Obalu is an enterprising young man. It's a trait which I admire, but I don't want to see him take advantage of you."

Before she could argue that she could take care of herself, or some other equally foolish thing, he touched his fingers to his forehead in a parting gesture and disappeared around the corner of Duval Street. It should have been Felix's deceptively innocent grin etched on her mind, but Captain Proctor's easy

smile wouldn't go away. She should have been thinking about
the next time she saw Felix, but instead she recalled Proctor's
words: "... until we meet again."

Nora stared at her reflection in the mirror next to the front
door, angled her hat a bit off center, and tied a wide satin
ribbon just to the left of her chin. She thought it added a bit
more flair to arrange it that way. The brim of the new straw
bonnet nearly spanned the width of her shoulders, and would
certainly keep the sun off her face. When she'd spotted it in
the milliner's shop on Duval Street the day before, she knew
it was what Captain Proctor had meant when he'd said "a
proper hat for our climate." Fanny had bought a similar one,
and now the only problem they would have is being careful
not to walk so closely they would bump brims.

The smile that had been on Nora's face faded when she
caught a glimpse of her mother behind her, one of her "boys"
as usual tucked in her elbow. Apparently Nora wasn't going
to get away this morning without a lecture after all.

"Really, Eleanor, I don't see why you have your mind set
on venturing out among this riffraff for the second day in a
row."

"Please, Mama, we went all through this last night. A girl
can only do needlework so long without going out of her mind.
The unpacking's all done, Father is going to court this morning.
And besides, you have no reason to assume that everyone here
is riffraff."

"I walked through the center of town myself when we arrived
three days ago, remember? I believe nearly everyone in this
town is like that horrible Willy person, and that rude Mr.
Teague. Once you're two blocks from this house, why, there's
nothing but shacks and taverns and chandleries and"—she
wrinkled her delicate nose—"fishy-smelling places."

"And a ready-made dress shop and a chemist. And a market
and a butcher, and ..."

Sidonia waved her free hand to dismiss Nora's words.

"Never mind all that. It's seedy, I tell you, and no respectable girl . . ." She stopped talking when Fanny came into the room.

"What's this about a respectable girl, Sid?" Fanny asked with a wink at Nora.

Taking advantage of Fanny's appearance, Nora planted a kiss on her mother's cheek. "That's exactly why I'm taking Fanny!"

"That's right, Sid," Fanny chimed in. "No one has ever accused me of being respectable, so it's all right, you see. Nora will seem a saint next to her shameful relation. I'll take care of her." She put a hand on each side of Hubert's face and kissed him square on his muzzle. "*Au revoir,* beast!"

They went out the door and down the sidewalk with Sidonia's warning trailing behind them. "That's it, tease all you want, but don't bring home fleas, and keep your hands on your reticules."

"And our bloomers tied tight!" Fanny called over her shoulder.

Nora didn't risk looking at her mother's face. She'd seen that stern expression of disapproval often enough. "You really do goad her unmercifully," she said to her cousin.

Fanny grinned with mischief. "You're welcome, *cherie.* I just wish it would do some good."

Nora administered a playful jab to her cousin's arm. "Let's take Whitehead today," she said when they reached the street. "I haven't been that way."

They had progressed three blocks to an area of cottages and small businesses when they noticed a crowd gathered at the next corner. "I wonder what's going on," Nora said. "It's barely eight o'clock."

"There's one sure way to find out."

They joined the crowd, though their late arrival kept them at the very back. All the onlookers craned their necks to see over a tall fence. From Nora's position, it was impossible to see anything specific on the other side. She estimated the fence to be at least ten feet tall, and only the top of a building was visible. It was constructed of an odd type of stone, light-colored and pitted. Remembering facts she'd gleaned from her reading, she assumed it was limestone, one of the few masonry materials available in Key West.

They'd only been waiting a minute when a chant rose from the throng. It was only a two-syllable sound, yet indecipherable to Nora. As she strained to hear, a hand settled on her elbow.

"Do my eyes deceive me," came a familiar low voice, "or has Miss Nora Seabrook come to bear witness this morning?"

She whirled around to stare into eyes the color of the peppery clouds trailed across the early morning sky. She backed away a step to keep the brim of her hat from hitting Jacob Proctor in his perfectly square chin. He was close enough for her to catch a distinctly male scent, a combination of leather and sawdust. Perhaps it was a warehouse smell, earthy and natural, and most pleasant.

It was a moment before she realized her mouth was open and no words were coming out. The captain continued to hold her arm while the space separating them grew narrower as the crowd pressed against them.

"Why, Captain Proctor, what a delightful surprise," Fanny said, sidling up beside her, and Nora breathed a sigh of relief. She was grateful to her cousin for breaking her own inept silence. Why was it, she wondered, that words flowed effort-lessly from her pen when she wrote in her journal, but stuck like dry pastry in her throat when she tried to speak them?

"I don't think we were properly introduced the other day," Fanny said. "I'm Fanny Cosette. There is, of course, no need to tell me your name since it has been permanently affixed in my mind after your heroic rescue of my dear cousin."

Jacob Proctor nodded. "My pleasure, Miss Cosette . . ."

"Fanny, please, Captain. I don't think formalities are neces-sary in these quaint surroundings, do you?"

Oh, how Nora envied her cousin! Fanny actually encouraged familiarity with the captain, while Nora had only blushed at his boldness in using her first name.

"So tell me," Proctor said, "why have you ladies come this morning? It's not often we see females of such genteel dispositions at these gatherings."

For the first time, Nora studied the faces of the people around her. It was true. There were few females present, and those that were looked to be more at home in a barroom than a sitting room. Meanwhile, their chant had grown to a crescendo.

"Why, my cousin and I wouldn't miss an event of such importance," Fanny said. "Would we, Nora?"

Finding her tongue at last, Nora said, "No, we wouldn't dare miss it."

The captain rubbed his chin thoughtfully. "Imagine Miss Seabrook wanting to see a hanging."

His pronouncement cut straight through her pitiful pretense, and she gulped back a squeal of surprise. "A h-hanging?"

Proctor flashed her a knowing grin. "Well, of course you knew that. Chauncy Stubbs is being hanged this morning. That's him—just climbed the gallows."

So that's what the crowd had been shouting. *Chauncy, Chauncy.* She recognized it now. Giving in to morbid curiosity she'd never realized she possessed, Nora struggled forward against the crowd to get a better view, and felt a pair of strong hands on her waist. She was lifted a few inches off the ground, and was able to see the top of a wooden structure and a man's head and shoulders. When a black hood was placed over his face, and a noose was lowered from scaffolding to his head, she sensed the first bitter taste of that morning's breakfast in her throat.

"Captain, please, I've seen enough."

He set her on the ground, but maintained his hold around her waist. She was thankful for his solid support since the earth beneath her feet seemed to have become quicksand. "Why . . . why are they hanging him?" she asked.

"Oh, he deserves it," Proctor said. "He stabbed a poor man for robbing his crab traps. Cut him up until there was no more left than fish bait."

"How deliciously wicked," Fanny said.

"Claimed he'd do it again, too. A remorseless criminal is Chauncy Stubbs. There was nothing to be done but let him swing."

The gruesome crime recreated itself in Nora's mind. At the same time the morning sun became unbearably warm. Her knees wobbled like a newborn foal's, and before she realized what was happening, her toes left the ground. In the next instant, her back was pressed fully against Jacob Proctor's muscled chest. His hands tightened on her waist, and his words came soft and low in her ear. "What's the matter, Nora?"

"I . . . I think I need some air."

Quickly, Proctor removed her from the scene and escorted her to a bench nearby. After a moment, Nora's senses began to return to normal. Those senses affected by the tale of Chauncy Stubbs, anyway. The ones still swimming from contact with Jacob Proctor, however, made her grateful for the solid structure under her backside. The captain sat next to her. His thigh touched hers.

Fanny fluttered a lacy handkerchief at Nora's face. "*Cherie,* are you all right?"

"Yes, I'm, fine now. Captain, does my father know this is happening?"

"I couldn't say. It was a circuit judge who issued the sentence, so your father probably wouldn't have stopped it. It's island justice, Nora. Everyone here believes in it, just as nearly everyone in the country believes in capital punishment."

That was true, Nora knew, but she'd never been this close to an execution before. "But the fence," she said. "Why is the fence there if everyone believes?"

"It was only built a couple of years ago. Before that, hangings were in full public view. It was the influx of society people, ladies mostly, who insisted the fence be built. But you know the strangest thing?"

She stared at him, admitting her curiosity about what he would say, though she suspected it would be another unsavory detail.

"After the next hanging, the public outcry was so strong that carpenters were ordered to shave off the first twelve inches of the fence they'd just built, so the people who wanted to could still see, some of it anyway."

A loud clap splintered the air, followed by a hoot of triumph from the crowd. Nora grabbed Proctor's hand. He held hers tightly. "It reminds us who we are, Nora," he said, "and what we too easily can become."

She pulled her hand away and reached for her cousin. "Fanny, I want to go home. I don't want to walk today after all."

Lulu finished clearing the soup bowls from the table and left the dining room. Nora decided she'd waited as long as she could before asking the two questions that had been on her mind since coming down for dinner.

Tapping her fork against her mother's Irish linen tablecloth, she said, "So, Father, did you know a man was hanged this morning in the courtyard of the jail?"

Sidonia's horrified gaze darted to her husband. "What? A man was hanged just a few blocks from our house?"

Nora winced at her father's why-did-you-have-to-say-that look, and waited for his response.

"Yes, I knew it. The sentence was handed down by the circuit judge, and I saw no reason to overturn it. The man was a scoundrel of the worst sort, and it was my opinion that the community was better off without him."

Sidonia took a swallow of wine and spread her hand across her chest. "Really, Thurston, this just proves my point. The element we find on this island . . ."

"The 'element' as you call it, Sid, exists everywhere, not just here."

"Perhaps, but so close to our home. Why, that man could have been our neighbor. Our own Eleanor could have seen him, or worse yet, been witness to his hanging . . ."

These last words hung in the tense air surrounding the dining table. Slowly, as suspicion dawned, both parents looked at their daughter. "Eleanor," Sidonia asked hesitantly, "how did you know about this dreadful occurrence?"

Thurston leaned forward and rested his chin on his fist. "Yes,

Nora, I'd be interested in knowing that myself. I understand that public hangings are quite a spectacle in this town. I would hope that you weren't a participant in this morbid ritual."

"Oh, no, Father, I didn't see anything of the hanging." That part was true, at least. "Fanny and I just heard about it in town." Under other circumstances, that part wouldn't have been a lie either, since Nora was certain the hanging was a topic of conversation in all the shops. If she'd gone to town, she *would* have heard about it. "It sounds just awful."

"Oui, cherie," Fanny said. "Imagine if we had seen the actual gallows and the hood being drawn over the poor man's head and the noose being tightened around his neck. Or if we'd heard the trap falling and seen his head jerking at a crazy angle . . ."

Sidonia pursed her lips before spitting out a warning. "Fanny, please. We won't have stomach for the remainder of our meal."

"Yes, of course, Sid. I'm just saying how fortunate we were to have escaped such an indelicate experience." She grinned at her young cousin. *"C'est vrai, n'est pas, cherie?"*

Nora had been sending Fanny a silent warning with her eyes. When she realized her cousin was not going to give them away, she relaxed. "Yes, it's quite true, Fanny."

"No more talk of hangings, I insist," Sidonia said, and for once, Nora agreed with her mother.

The main course was served, and Nora waited for a pause in conversation before asking her second question. "How did everything go in court today, Father?"

"Well. I would say my arrival has created quite a stir, just as I'd hoped it would. I checked the credentials of over a dozen wreckers this morning."

"Did you find them all in order?"

"All but one actually."

A feeling of unease churned in Nora's stomach. "Really? And whose papers were lacking?"

"A man named Milton. Isaac Milton from Connecticut. Seems he has a criminal record he neglected to report to the previous judge. He'll no longer be salvaging in Key West after today."

"And the captain we met that first day, the one who jumped into the ocean to save me . . . his papers were in order?"

Thurston stopped chewing the forkful of chicken he'd just guided to his mouth and stared at his daughter. She smiled sweetly at him. When he finished swallowing, he said, "Yes, his papers were fine. His attitude, however, was not. He's cocky and brash and gives every indication that he would defy the law as easily as draw his next breath."

"Maybe so," Fanny said, "but he is undeniably handsome!"

Thurston grunted with impatience. "I wouldn't know about that. But I do know I don't like him, and I don't trust him. I don't trust how he's made his fortune or how he conducts his salvage operation."

Thurston narrowed his eyes suspiciously. "And I don't want anyone in this family to associate with him. I may not have caught him with faulty papers, but I'll find another way to put him out of business. I feel strongly that he is at the heart of this island's wrecking problems."

Nora didn't want to argue with her father. After all, she had no reason to, but she didn't want to believe him either. For now, the only thing she really believed was what Fanny had just said. Jacob Proctor was indeed handsome.

CHAPTER FOUR

"Milllk! Milk on the hoof!"

Nora ran down the stairs just after sunrise to get another look at the plump holstein that was led down Southard Street every morning. She nearly bumped into Lulu, who had two empty bottles in her hand. "I'll go," Nora said, reaching for the bottles. "Just give them to me."

"You don't have to ask me twice, missy," the maid said.

Nora hurried out the back gate to meet Abraham, the elderly milkman, and Francesca, the cow. This morning they were accompanied by Felix Obalu. Surprised to see her young nemesis involved in yet another enterprise, she leveled her most sober gaze on him and said, "Felix, you can just get all thoughts of my money out of your head. I've bought milk before, and I know very well how much each bottle costs . . ."

He flashed her a devilishly guilty but charming grin. "You got me wrong, Miss Nora. I'm not here to take money for milk. I just want to learn. Abraham's teachin' me to milk. Then maybe if I do a good job, I'll come back by myself someday."

Felix winked, and Nora couldn't resist him. She laughed and

pretended to cuff his ears. "And probably charge double when you do. Just give me two bottles of milk at five cents each."

The Bahamian milkman slipped a three-legged stool off his shoulders and set it beside the animal. Felix sat down, put a wooden bucket under the cow, and positioned his hands on her swollen udders. With impressive skill he squeezed and tugged until thin streams of milk hit the sides of the pail. When Nora's two bottles were full, he said, "I did good, right?"

"Yes. You did a very good job, and I'm proud of you for wanting to learn." Nora wondered at the boy's interest in expanding his knowledge. Despite his devious image, he seemed proud of his accomplishments. It was a shame he was denied schooling.

Denied schooling. The injustice of it all had bothered Nora since she'd first heard about the children's plight days before. As she carried the milk back to the house she decided to do something about it—today.

Nora determined the milliner's shop was perfect, or at least a small part of it would be. The location was ideal, one block from the wharf on Duval Street. She found the proprietor, a stout Scotsman, on a ladder brushing dust off stovepipe hats on the tallest shelf in the store. "Excuse me, Mr. McTaggart?"

The man peered down at her over his beak of a nose. "Ah, Miss Seabrook, isn't it?"

"Yes, sir. I bought a straw bonnet the other day."

As he came down the ladder, dust motes that had accumulated on his otherwise impeccable suit danced in the rays of sunlight streaming in a large window. Another reason Nora had to have this shop. The lighting was exceptional. Even in the storeroom in back.

"I remember that bonnet," he said. "A wise choice, young lady."

"Mr. McTaggart, I hope you don't mind, but I've had a look around your shop this morning, and I notice you have a small room at the back. I ventured into it, and all I found there was a sewing machine and a few boxes of hat trim.''

"Yes, I haven't much use for trims and shouldn't have ordered so many. The few I sell are to ladies who have enough leisure time to affix their own feathers and flowers on their bonnets.'' He unnecessarily smoothed his hair, which had been plastered with bear grease on each side of his straight middle part. "I don't mind, really. Stitching flowers on hats is not such a manly occupation.''

"Then the room I mentioned is not used very much, is that right, sir?''

"Not so much, why?''

"Mr. McTaggart, I'd like to suggest a proposition to you if I may.''

He was interested, at least so far, and he indicated his willingness to listen by escorting Nora to a pair of chairs under the window. "What is it you have in mind, Miss Seabrook?''

As Nora talked, McTaggart's facial expression changed from alert attentiveness to disinterest and finally to disapproval. "I appreciate what you're trying to do, Miss Seabrook, but frankly, I can't perceive a boon to my business by having a ragtag bunch of Key West's Bahamian Negro children occupying my shop.''

"But Mr. McTaggart, it would only be for three hours a day. Surely you find it deplorable that eager, intelligent young children are denied the opportunity to learn?''

From his expression, he did not find it so at all. At least he had the decency not to verbalize his opinion.

"We wouldn't be a distraction,'' she continued. "I would start class at seven-thirty, and you don't even open the shop until nine. We will be gone when you have only been open an hour and a half. The children would be so grateful, and your name would be recognized in the community as a pioneer in education. I'm quite certain that no account of Key West history would be complete without the mention of Angus McTaggart.''

He scratched absently at his sideburns and considered what she'd said. A good sign, she hoped. "Well, I don't know . . .''

"Mr. McTaggart, I've just come from Richmond where free blacks are being educated in enormous numbers. It's only a matter of time until this trend sweeps the country. You could be an innovator, sir, an explorer into this totally unchartered territory."

"An innovator, you say?"

"Definitely. Few men have such a rare opportunity. And Mr. McTaggart, don't the Bahamian women purchase their bonnets here?"

"Why, yes, yes, they do."

"Then my plan *would* be a boon to your business. Their gratitude would be immeasurable. I'm sure they would decide they need an extra hat or two, from the generous Mr. McTaggart."

He considered his options for a torturously long moment. "Still, you've offered no rent."

"That's because I have no money of my own. Besides, what price can be put on education?"

Her would-be benefactor shook his head, and Nora sensed she was losing the battle. How could she deal with the lack of money for rent? If she could come up with a solution, she was certain the thrifty Scotsman would be swayed. The idea came to her as if delivered by Providence.

"Mr. McTaggart, let me propose a compromise. What if we hold class for two hours only. Then the last hour I will see that two of the children each day volunteer their services to help in the shop. They can dust the hats, or sweep the floor, or even stitch trims if you get a call for that."

His eyes lit with telltale enthusiasm. "Miss Seabrook, you present good arguments. I'll agree to your conditions on a trial basis only. We'll see how this experiment of yours works out for two weeks. After that time we will meet and re-evaluate."

Nora bounded out of her chair. "Thank you, sir. You won't regret this. We'll start Monday morning."

She returned to the small cubicle behind the shop and estimated the size of her classroom. Then she made a mental list of supplies she would need. Slates and chalk and a blackboard and benches. And books and quills and inkwells and . . . the list was extensive. Where would she find these things? Who in Key West was likely to have many of these items and be willing to donate them? One establishment came to mind immediately. Proctor's Warehouse and Salvage.

After thanking Mr. McTaggart again, she left his shop and headed across Duval toward Front Street by the docks. A distant clap of thunder and a darkening of the sky did not diminish her euphoria.

Next to the heart-thumping adventure of racing toward a wrecked ship in competition with his neighbors, Jacob liked watching for wrecks the most. And if he couldn't be on the Atlantic Ocean, the domed cupola above his warehouse was his favorite place to be. Here, in a room without walls, the sound of the sea, the rush of wind, and the smell of salt air brought him as close to a life in the water as a man could get while still admitting his inability to survive in a world of fins and gills.

Jacob didn't even mind the loneliness of the watch. As a man with responsibilities to his business and employees, most days he welcomed his solitary time as lookout. The cool, sleek brass telescope in his hand and the calls of the seagulls were companions enough.

And today there was much to watch for. For the past three hours, since dawn, the sky had been clear, the wind calm. In the last minutes, however, conditions to the east had changed. The sky had darkened to a threatening gray, with thunderheads blocking the sun. Harbingers of a storm rumbled above him. The wind had intensified, and now buffeted the little island.

Jacob had seen sudden, fierce storms often enough during his five-year stay in Key West. He'd witnessed their fury and he'd profited by their destructive power. For with a storm came wrecked vessels, and today, as every day, ships were expected in Key West's harbor.

When he heard footsteps on the stairs to the cupola, Jacob

assumed Willy had heard the thunder and felt the unexpected coolness in the air and was coming up to discuss the possibilities. Like himself, Willy was in love with the sea as a life force and as a business. Jacob didn't mind sharing the cupola with his trusted assistant. This morning Willy's footsteps were soft, as if he were showing respect for the steadily rising crescendo of the storm.

Jacob leaned on the railing three stories above the ground and peered through the telescope at the approaching tempest. "Good morning, Willy," he said without turning around. "I see you've heard her coming."

The voice that answered him was definitely not Willy's. "Excuse me, Captain. Your friend downstairs said it would be all right if I came here to find you. I've come to have a word with you if I may."

Jacob turned to face a frothy, ruffled confection of yellow fabric and white lace draped over the shapely form of Nora Seabrook. The wind sweeping through the cupola played havoc with her attire, pressing the folds of her gown to her legs and revealing their slim shapes beneath nearly translucent organdy. Her woven hat, normally so practical for the island, was losing a battle with the wind. The brim blew back from Nora's face and crackled with rent straw.

To save what was left of her bonnet and to keep the wind from blowing it, and her, back to the stairs, Nora untied the ribbon at her throat and removed the hat. As she did, pieces of straw caught in her hair and pulled strands loose from the heavy net at her nape. Raven tresses trailed around her neck and away from her face.

"My goodness," she said. "It looks like we're in for a storm."

Her observation was as much an understatement as Jacob admitting to himself that he was surprised to see her in his private domain. The daughter of the Federal judge who was determined to undermine Proctor Salvage was the last person he'd expected to climb the narrow stairs to his lookout. After a moment, he found his voice and responded. "Yes, it does.

Hardly the proper environment for a lady of Virginia. One used to the sheltered harbor of Chesapeake Bay.''

She dismissed his concern with a wave of her hand. "Storms don't frighten me, Captain. I rather fancy the wind, actually.''

Letting his gaze sweep the length of her once more, he said, "Not as much as the wind fancies you, Miss Seabrook.'' He pushed away from the railing, and in the confined area of the cupola the simple movement brought her swirling skirt against his pants leg. Jacob stepped even closer. "Tell me, Nora, if not the wind, what does frighten you?''

Something—perhaps his nearness, perhaps the realization that she had come unbidden into his private world, or perhaps the storm after all—brought a flush of color to her cheeks. Or perhaps she had become as fully aware of their surroundings, and their place in them as Jacob himself had.

At that moment Jacob Proctor knew full well what frightened *him.* It wasn't the storm or even the possibility of sailing his vessel into a churning sea. It was the knowledge that he was utterly alone with a woman who awakened emotions in him that had nothing to do with the manly pursuits of wrecked ships and dangerous ocean voyages. And yet these emotions were every bit as male and every bit as dangerous.

Her chin jutted out stubbornly. "Nothing frightens me, Captain. Not even you if you're trying to.''

He smiled in spite of the fact that frightening *her* was as absurdly ironic as was the mysterious power she apparently had no notion she possessed. And despite the ominous voice of his conscience, that had already begun to surface in his mind. "Certainly not. The truth is, Nora, you've scared the dickens out of me by coming to the cupola. You're the first woman who's ever been here.''

She smiled more to herself than to him. It was only a slight twitch of her pink lips, but it was enough for him to know that his declaration pleased her. She walked to the railing and looked out at whitecapped waves, and it occurred to Jacob that even though she was the first woman to come to the cupola, she certainly looked as if she belonged there for all time. She drew in a deep breath, filling her lungs with sea air and raising her breasts until they strained the bodice of her gown. Her skirts billowed behind her. More of her hair escaped the meager hold of the snood at her nape. Yes, the wind indeed fancied Nora Seabrook.

She lifted her gaze to him. "I will probably be the first woman to so blatantly ask a favor of you as well, Captain."

He resisted an almost overwhelming urge to grab a fistful of that luxuriant hair and bring it to his nostrils to recall the scent of lilacs he'd identified when she leaned against him at the courthouse. Then, as now, he couldn't imagine a favor he wouldn't grant her. He took a deep breath himself, for reasons that had nothing to do with getting his fill of salt air, and pulled his gaze away from her. It was wise for him to remember that he didn't grant favors easily, and should do so only with caution for this woman. "I'm listening."

"I came through your warehouse a few minutes ago," she began. "I can't imagine what all those barrels and bins contain. There must be hundreds of items stored down there."

She was interested in salvaged cargo? Strange, but at least it was a topic with which he was expertly familiar. "There are. All those barrels will be opened next week for a public auction. You may come if you like and satisfy your curiosity as to the contents."

"I can't wait that long, Captain." There was an urgency in her voice that demanded his full attention. "And I can't buy anything. I don't have any money."

Her honesty surprised and amused him. Leaning his arm on the railing beside her, he met her gaze and smiled. "Then you have a problem. Or perhaps I do. What is it you'd like me to give you for free?"

She told him her plan to open a school for the Bahamian children and teach them to read. If he hadn't heard such firm conviction in her words, he might have thought she was a bored society woman wanting to help the downtrodden until some other amusement caught her attention. Most of the women he'd known had been like that. But Nora Seabrook seemed truly dedicated to her cause. Enough that she had actually convinced the miserly Angus McTaggart to give her space in his shop. That had required gumption and persuasive skill that Jacob admired.

"So you see my problem, Captain. I am in need of everything. Quills and slates and even seats for the children. Do you think you have any schoolroom items in your warehouse?"

Amazingly, a recent wreck had contained two crates of materials bound for a monastery in Central America. When the brothers learned their cargo had been damaged by seawater, they'd ordered all-new materials for their students. The refused items were slightly stained with salt, but were still usable. Jacob had intended to put the boxes up for auction. Now he knew they would never see the auctioneer's gavel.

"I can help you," he said. "I'll give you lumber for benches and what educational materials I have. It should be enough to get started."

Gratitude shone in her eyes and in her quick smile. "Thank you, Captain. Now, I just hope the children will come."

"You'll have no problem with the Obalu children," he said. "Simply tell Portia you want them there. She'll see to the rest."

Slender fingers wrapped gently around his lower arm. Her touch was hardly greater than a feather, yet he felt it as a sudden tightening in his chest.

"You've been so kind, Captain Proctor. Not at all like . . ." Her words caught in her throat and remained unspoken.

"Like your father would have you believe?"

"He doesn't know you."

As her hand stayed on his sleeve, the first unwelcome tension strained the tendons of his arm. He clenched his fist to keep from drawing away from her. There was no crowd at the harbor to protect her now. No throng at the courthouse. Not even the presence of her family in a house on the other side of the fence. It was just the two of them, and she was so incredibly lovely. Her eyes, as blue as the sea, were innocent and trusting of the stranger who had rescued her from the water and teased her.

He looked away, as he knew he had to before those eyes swallowed him. "You don't know me either," he said harshly.

"Wreck ashore! Wreck ashore!"

The warning echoed through the wind and across the streets of Key West. Jacob jerked his arm away from Nora and brought the telescope to his eye. Damn. He'd been so intent on listening to her, watching her, feeling her . . . Everyone on the island knew but him. It would take a miracle to be the first ship to reach the wreck now.

With a snap of his wrist, he accordioned the telescope into the size fit for its storage box. He didn't need it to see the sheet of driving rain heading for the cupola. Wind howled around them and the first streak of lightning ripped the sky in two. Jacob pulled Nora to the stairs and pushed her ahead of him.

"What's happening, Captain? Has a ship wrecked on the reefs?"

"That's exactly what's happened. And the weather is too foul for you to get home. You'd better stay in the warehouse till it clears."

She nodded. "And what about you? Are you going out in this?"

"Yes. Me and a dozen others, I'd warrant. It's what this island is all about."

When they reached the first floor, Jacob took the slicker Willy held out to him and pushed his arms through the sleeves. As he dashed out of the warehouse he called over his shoulder, "When the storm lets up, Nora, go home."

If she responded, he didn't hear her words. The wind drowned out everything but the fury of the storm. "Yes, Nora, go home," he muttered under his breath. "Don't be here when I get back."

Jacob Proctor was a smart man. That was why he knew he was only lying to himself. For the first time in years, he wanted someone waiting and watching for his return.

CHAPTER FIVE

Without fastening his slicker, Jacob dashed from the warehouse and headed for the docks, leaving Nora to wonder what protection the rain gear would possibly provide in the downpour. She watched him go, the tails of his jacket whipping behind him in a flash of gleaming canary.

He and Willy Turpin reached a vessel at the closest pier and jumped on board. Other crew members were already there, and soon rope riggings flapped freely as sails unfurled to catch the wind.

Nora wasn't going to let the weather stop her from seeing the brave sailors and hardy schooners leave the harbor in their frantic race to reach the stranded vessel offshore. She stood under the wooden roof of the warehouse veranda and watched the ships set sail. The awning kept her dryer than she would have been in the open, but even so, she was soon soaked to the skin.

Jacob Proctor's vessel was not the first to leave, nor was it the last. Still, the chances of him reaching the wrecked ship before all the others had to be slim. And arriving second didn't count in this race for riches. Guilt made Nora ball her hands into fists and stomp her foot. If she hadn't been talking to him . . .

Jacob's trim schooner came about and rode with the wind. Its sails filled to capacity. Nora ignored her nagging conscience as she tried to visualize what it would be like to crest the waves under such treacherous conditions. Part of her longed to feel the excitement of each undulation of an angry sea as the ship tested its strength against the power of the storm. Another part of her, however, cringed at the danger the stranded passengers and intrepid sailors faced. One sailor in particular.

Remembering one of the last things Jacob said to her, she whispered to herself, "It is true I may not know you well, Jacob Proctor, but witnessing this, I can begin to understand the force that drives you."

And she was beginning to understand the very heartbeat of the island that she would write about in her journal that night.

Today I witnessed the most thrilling sight of my life, one that quite unexpectedly took my breath away.

More than a dozen sailing vessels left Key West Harbor, pitted against each other and the elements in a race to save lives and win unknown spoils. Each tall-masted schooner was commanded by a brave captain and crew who sail for riches and to feel the blood thunder in their veins.

"Miss Seabrook, what in heaven's name are you doing outside in this weather?"

Words scattered like storm clouds as Nora spun around to face the gaunt features of Dillard Hyde, the Clerk of the Court. She hadn't seen him since the day she'd arrived when he had patiently explained some of the aspects of life on the island. She shook the folds of her soaked organdy dress and frowned. The official must think she spent most of her life in wet garments. Shouting above the roar of the wind, she said, "Mr. Hyde! How nice to see you again!"

Not the least interested in pleasantries, he made her go inside

Jacob Proctor's warehouse. Searching out a barrel of linens, he chose a bolt of cotton fabric and wrapped a few yards of it around her shoulders. "Really, Miss Seabrook, it is quite foolish of you to stand out in such inclement weather."

"But I had to see the ships leave."

He clucked like a mother hen. "There will be plenty of opportunity for that. We have at least half a dozen wrecks a month on this island, and many of them take place in the full, *dry* light of a noon sun. And when that happens you'll see most of the ladies of Key West on the docks waiting anxiously for the treasures to come in." He pulled her further into the warehouse. "Now get away from the windows. You'll catch your death."

She allowed herself to be coddled and fussed over by the fatherly man, though she'd never felt healthier or more alive in her life. "But isn't it all so exciting?" she said. "To think those men risk their lives for treasure . . ."

Dillard settled his lanky frame on a crate and regarded her seriously. "Theirs aren't the only lives at risk today, Miss Seabrook. This is a wreck of serious magnitude."

His tone sobered her instantly, and her heart pounded with trepidation. "What do you mean?"

"The ship that wrecked today is the *Morning Dove*. She was headed for New Orleans from Baltimore with a full register of passengers. I've watched her continued listing through my telescope, and it's bad, Miss Seabrook. Very bad. The ship's floundering dangerously on the reefs."

"You're saying people could die?" Nora's stomach clenched with a sudden, violent upheaval, and she sat heavily on a crate next to Mr. Hyde's.

He nodded. "This business isn't only about treasure and riches, and with a storm this bad, I fear the worst."

"Is there anything I can do?" Nora asked. "Shouldn't we be preparing?"

He patted her hand. "That's why I came directly to the docks. If my worst apprehensions are founded, then we need all the help we can get. We only have a fourteen-bed hospital on the island. It is possible that many more people than that will need medical attention.'' He looked around the warehouse and sighed. ''I had hoped to see some of our citizens braving the weather to gather here, the ladies especially, since so many of the men are on the schooners. Alas, I think the weather has kept them at home. We need volunteers and bandages and someone to keep a soup kettle going . . .''

Nora jumped up and disentangled herself from her wraps. She ran to the exit calling over her shoulder. ''I'll be right back, Mr. Hyde. We'll have three women here at least!''

Having already fastened the hood on her cape, Fanny Cosette waited by the front door, rolls of cotton bandages in her hand. Sidonia Seabrook, however, was taking precious time, still bemoaning her fate. ''You can't be serious, Eleanor! Go out in this dreadful weather?''

''Mother, get your coat. It's not raining nearly as bad as it was. If we walk briskly, you'll hardly get wet at all.''

''But . . . but look at you! You're positively drenched. Sometimes I wonder if you have a sensible thought in your head, Eleanor. Why, with your propensity for colds . . .''

''Mother, I only have a propensity for impatience at the moment . . .''

Fanny threw a cape at Sidonia. It landed approximately around her shoulders. She then grabbed her cousin's arm and began tugging her toward the door. ''Put it on, Sid, or suffer the consequences. Either way, you're going out that door and down to the harbor.''

Giving in with a resigned and mournful groan, Sidonia straightened the cape and tied the cord at her neck. With a last wistful look at Armand and Hubert, who sat watching the scene with alert, bright eyes, she managed a sorrowful good-bye and entered the elements.

A few other ladies had arrived by the time Nora returned with the Seabrook delegation. The rain had stopped and a makeshift infirmary was taking shape in the courtyard of the

Proctor Warehouse and Salvage Company, presided over by a capable Dillard Hyde. Pallets were set up next to a pile of blankets, and the smell of soup wafted from the interior of the building.

Nora was encouraged to see that at least some of her neighbors had responded to the emergency. She introduced herself and her family to the other women, and soon they all were speculating about the degree of injuries they might expect.

Eventually Thurston Seabrook arrived from the courthouse and commended his wife and daughter for acting as volunteers. He explained to Nora that the first responsibility of the wrecking master was to the passengers and crew of the stranded ship. No cargo could be rescued until every human was accounted for. He had come to the harbor himself to see that this most important condition was not violated.

Less than three hours after they departed, the first of the schooners rounded the bend to the harbor, their decks crowded with passengers. One of those ships, Nora saw, was called the *Dover Cloud,* and it was the schooner owned by Jacob Proctor. He was the first to tie up to the docks, and consequently the first to help stranded voyagers off his vessel. Other ship captains followed quickly.

Despite the possibility of injured passengers, most all Key West citizens at the harbor were concerned with one question. Who had been granted wrecking-master rights? Yes, there may be hardship to deal with, but the recovery of cargo was the lifeblood of the island, and it was uppermost in everyone's mind.

Nora soon learned along with the others that a captain named Moony Swain had arrived first at the scene and had been granted rights by the *Morning Dove*'s skipper. Captain Swain would be the one to reap the rewards of his efforts once all the passengers were saved.

Few of the rescued individuals had suffered serious injuries, but nearly all of them were frightened, cold, and drenched with seawater. The ladies went about dispensing soup and blankets, and the doctor was called to treat the more serious cases. Thurston went back to the courthouse, and Nora helped those she could, looking around at intervals for Jacob. When she saw the *Dover Cloud* leave port a second time, she knew he'd gone back to the reef. She hoped she would get a chance to speak with him later.

"Eleanor, come here, dear."

Having scarcely seen her mother since they arrived at the harbor, Nora responded to her voice and found Sidonia inside the warehouse tending to an injured man. On closer inspection she realized that the man wore a professionally applied splint on his left arm, and her mother was merely talking with him.

"Can I help you, Mother?" Nora asked, smiling at the young man, who was dressed in the soggy remnants of a three-piece vested suit.

"I wanted you to meet our new house guest, Eleanor," her mother chirped. "This is Theodore Hadley, an attorney from Falmouth. Mr. Hadley, my daughter, Eleanor."

He extended his good hand and she grasped it in hers. "How do you do, Miss Seabrook?"

"I'm quite well, Mr. Hadley," she replied, "and I'm sorry to see that the same cannot be said of you."

He regarded the splint, breathed a rather dramatic sigh, followed by a weak imitation of a smile, and then returned a limpid hazel gaze to Nora. "It was a perfectly dreadful experience, but I'm feeling much better now that you two angels of mercy have tended to my wounds."

She delicately tried to extricate her hand, but he held fast. "I'm glad you're feeling better," she said, "but my mother and I are hardly angels, and this warehouse is a poor excuse for heaven."

Sidonia laughed too loudly and fluttered her hand in front of her face. "Oh, silly Eleanor. Let the man say what he wants. I rather like his allusion. It's quite charming."

"Yes, well . . ." Nora finally pulled her hand free. "Did Mama say you'll be staying with us for a while?"

"I am most fortunate to answer that in the positiv
Seabrook, and I find it the one bright star on an otherw

horizon. Your gracious mother has offered accommodations during my recovery.'' He attempted to move his arm, and finally let it hang useless against his chest. ''I daresay, I don't know how long this nasty break will take to mend.''

Sidonia spoke up. ''Now don't you worry about that, Mr. Hadley. If I'd suffered as you have today, I know I wouldn't have the courage to undertake a sea voyage for quite some time. My daughter and I will do whatever it takes to assist you in your convalescence. I believe that coming to the aid of our fellow man in dire times is the least anyone can do.''

Nora pasted a smile on her face for a moment before leading her mother a few steps away from her charge. ''Certainly aiding *this* fellow man is the least you've done, Mama,'' she whispered.

''Don't be unkind, dear,'' Sidonia said, immediately disengaging herself from Nora's hold and returning to an expectant Mr. Hadley. ''I'll arrange for a conveyance to take you to our home as soon as possible,'' she told him.

He struggled valiantly to his feet, uttering groans of discomfort. Nora was tempted to remind him that it was his arm that was injured, not his legs. ''I think I can make it on my own, Mrs. Seabrook,'' he said bravely.

''Very well, then. Come along, Eleanor.''

Nora had no intention of going anywhere yet. She hadn't spoken with Jacob Proctor. ''No, you go, Mother. I need to finish up with some things, but I'll be along shortly.''

''All right, but don't be long.'' She took Mr. Hadley's elbow and guided him to the street. ''Lean on me, Mr. Hadley,'' she said. ''Everyone else does.''

When Nora came out of the warehouse, dusk was settling over the island. It was the first she'd noticed that the day was nearing an end. She'd been working with stranded passengers for nearly seven hours. Few people remained at the harbor now . . . just a few volunteers and, of course, Dillard Hyde, who was wrapping up the coordinated efforts of the community.

"Get something to eat, Miss Seabrook," he said to Nora when he saw her standing nearby. "I just encouraged your brave cousin, Miss Cosette, to do the same while we still have food left."

She followed his advice and went to the large kettle steaming over a low fire. A volunteer gave her a mug of pungent chowder thick with potatoes, carrots, and beans, and a slice of crusty bread. To Nora, who had just realized she hadn't eaten since breakfast, it looked and smelled like a gourmet meal.

She sat on a bench inside the warehouse and scooped up vegetables with the bread. The hearty chowder more than satisfied her taste buds, and she closed her eyes to savor it.

"Good, isn't it? These people can cook, or else my poor little tummy was ready to accept anything edible."

Fanny stood next to her looking almost as fatigued as Nora assumed she herself did.

"Hmmm, it's delicious." Nora refrained from saying more since it would have prevented her from eating.

Fanny sat down and leaned against the wall at her back. She regarded her cousin with a playful sideways glance. "I think Sid has found a colorful peacock for you, *cherie.*"

The bread paused midway to Nora's mouth as she turned to stare at her relative. "What does that mean?"

Fanny laughed. "The bedraggled but obviously fastidious counselor, Mr. Theodore Hadley."

"Nonsense," Nora said, focusing again on her meal. "He's merely Mama's latest cause."

"Indeed he is, but not the way you think. Sid has plans for him, all right, but they don't include her, except perhaps in a roundabout way. My cousin is, and always has been, fiercely and mundanely loyal to her dear Thurston." She grinned over at Nora, the mischief evident in her green eyes. "Which leaves you, dear heart, as the target of Mr. Hadley's undying affection."

"That's nonsense, Fanny," Nora protested. "Mr. Hadley is only staying until he is able to travel again, and . . ."

"Bones heal slowly, *cherie.*"

". . . *and* I have no interest in him whatsoever. He's not a man who would appeal to me, nor I to him most likely."

Fanny tapped a long fingernail against her lip. "Still . . . you could do worse, cousin. He's not hard on the eyes. He has a successful career, and while his clothes were ruined, they were of the best quality, rather like those belonging to that Hyde fellow," she said with a baffling grin. "Perhaps Sid has the right idea after all."

"Humph! What utter nonsense." Totally ignoring her manners, Nora scraped the remaining chowder from the sides of the mug with a thin crust of bread. "Go home, Fanny. I'm beginning to think you need rest more than I do." She plopped the soupy mixture into her mouth and grinned like a cat.

Fanny stood and stretched and looked out a window. "Very well. I'll go." The feline smile was suddenly etched on her lips as well. "I won't be leaving you alone, however. I see the *Dover Cloud* just pulled into port." With a flounce of her soiled skirts, Fanny left.

Nora leaned up and looked out the same window Fanny had. It was almost pitch dark, and yet her cousin had recognized the shape of Jacob's schooner when Nora could only see shadows. "She must have special telescopic vision where men are concerned," Nora said to herself, envying yet another of Fanny's talents that had not been passed down to her.

Within minutes the shadows on the dock moved toward the warehouse. Nora crouched down on the bench as the men came inside and headed directly for the soup kettle. All but one, that is. In the lantern light, Jacob Proctor was clearly distinguishable. He bypassed the food and strode to the staircase leading to the second floor.

"Can I bring you a mug, Jacob?" Willy asked. "You've hardly eaten today."

Jacob's heavy boot hit the first step. "Aye, maybe later, Will. Save me some."

He proceeded up the stairs while his men gathered around the kettle. Now was Nora's chance. If she was ever going to speak to Jacob, it had better be now. The men didn't give her notice as she passed them by and climbed the stairs behind him.

Jacob's back was to her when she reached the cupola. This time he apparently hadn't heard her ascent because he didn't speak. He appeared intent on the dark horizon to the east where the floundering ship still listed on the reef. Lights from houses in town were visible over his shoulder. Stars twinkled in an ebony sky. No one would have known that just hours before, a violent storm had buffeted the small island.

All was calm now, except, Nora thought, for the man whose head was bent in contemplation. His arms on the railing, his hands threaded and hanging in the air, and his shoulders tight with tension, he seemed a coil of pent-up emotions. She considered leaving him to his thoughts, but didn't.

"Excuse me, Captain?"

His back straightened, and a shudder seemed to ripple down his spine as he turned toward her. She couldn't see his eyes in the darkness, but his mouth was set in a grim line. "Nora," he said in a low voice. "What are you doing here?"

She took a step closer to him. "I had to talk to you," she began. "I had to apologize."

"Apologize? For what?"

She ran her hands down her dirty dress in an unsuccessful attempt to smooth the skirt. She was a mess, and yet she had ignored her appearance to follow Jacob to the cupola. Her hair had come loose. Errant spirals spun around her head and neck, a wild testament to rain and humidity. Her dress was smeared with grime and even stained with other people's blood. She left her hands at her sides, since they were useless in repairing her state of total dishevelment.

Taking a deep breath, she stated her purpose for being there. "After you were kind enough to offer your help today with the school, I distracted you from the watch. I know it was my fault you missed seeing the wreck first."

A rasping sigh that came from Jacob Proctor's throat was

edged with derision. Perhaps he was angrier than she'd thought.
He had a right to be. "I noticed you earlier today," he said.
"When I came back from the wreck. I watched you for a time."

Strangely, his voice held no emotion at all. It was almost
frightening in its blandness. If anything, the void hinted of
resignation, defeat. He had obviously paid no mind to her
apology when Nora had expected either accusation or exonera-
tion.

"You . . . you watched me?" she said.

"You were doing an admirable job with the passengers. You
have a kind heart, Nora."

Her breath expelled in one long rush of relief. He wasn't
blaming her. "Thank you. I wanted to help."

He came to within a few inches of her, close enough for a
sliver of moon to capture his eyes. They were like molten
silver, soft and somehow troubled. In their gray depths she read
sadness.

"When I left earlier, I told you to go," he said. "Do you
remember that?"

She swallowed. "I stayed to help the passengers. And I
waited to tell you how sorry I was . . ."

"And you have."

"And now you want me to go?"

His fingers clenched at his sides while a vein worked at his
temple. "Now it may be too late. Now I want you to stay."

She didn't answer . . . couldn't find the words to express the
emotions welling inside her. Partly fear, mostly anticipation—
for what, she wasn't certain. But she suspected, and a strange,
mysterious need to know burned inside her.

He raised his arm and settled his hand around her nape. The
tingling from his fingers spread down her back and fluttered
in her abdomen like a frightened moth.

"You are beautiful, Nora."

She looked away from him, down at her skirt, anywhere but
his eyes. "No, I'm not. I'm . . ."

"Astoundingly lovely."

With his free hand he cupped her chin and raised her face.

He was going to kiss her. She felt it everywhere she had nerve endings. It scared and excited her at the same time, the thought of Jacob's sensuous lips on hers. Even as his mouth descended, but before he touched hers, the image of their lips coming together etched itself on her closed eyelids. But the image was nothing like the real thing.

His mouth was soft and damp, warm and pliant. And she let him mold her lips to his. It was wonderful, the stuff of dreams. And then it changed. His hand slipped to her back and he pulled her roughly to his chest. Her breasts flattened against him. His lips, tasting of salt water, crushed over hers, demanding, insistent. The embrace became hard and hungry. And yet it thrilled her as nothing else ever had.

As suddenly as the kiss had changed, it ended. He jerked his head up and thrust her away. His gaze, fastened on her lips, was glittering mercury. "I told you to go home, Nora. You should have."

"But . . . I told you . . ."

"You have nothing to apologize for. Nothing. Now go!"

He turned away from her, presenting her with squared shoulders that shut her away from his thoughts. Why did he kiss her if he wanted her to go? He gripped the railing and stared straight ahead, resolute in his demand for her to leave. But that kiss . . .

After several seconds, he growled into the empty darkness, "Woman, can't you hear?"

A strangled cry came from deep in her throat and she whirled away from him. She ran down the stairs, holding the handrail to keep from stumbling. She barely noticed Willy when she passed him on the first floor. She entered the night and ran toward Southard Street and home without looking back, or up, at the man in the cupola.

Willy climbed to the tower and offered a mug of chowder to Jacob. He waved it away with a flick of his hand. "Not now."

"You've upset that poor girl, Jacob," Willy said. "She was crying when she ran out of here."

Jacob cleared his throat, then bit back the bile that rose to his mouth. "I can't be blamed for every foolish feminine emotion. She shouldn't have come up here. I told her not to."

"She's a fine little gal," Willy said. "A good woman. I know you noticed that yourself. You shouldn't have treated her badly, Jacob. Maybe she would understand."

"Bah!" The absurdity of Willy's statement only inflamed him more. "You don't know what you're talking about. A woman like that only knows one thing and that's marriage. You know I can never marry."

"But this one seems different. You fancied her from the moment you pulled her from the drink. To deny it is to fool yourself. This Miss Seabrook seems like she might be willing . . ."

Jacob stormed past him and headed for the stairs. "I'm going to Teague's," he barked. "Lottie's the only one who can feed this hunger now. Not your soup or your advice. Don't talk to me anymore of that good woman Nora Seabrook."

CHAPTER SIX

Theodore Hadley took a swallow of wine and wiped his mouth with one of Sidonia's linen napkins. Looking at his hostess, he said, "This is wonderful snapper, Mrs. Seabrook."

"You're too kind, Mr. Hadley," she responded. "It's passably tasty, I guess, though the idea of anything but a roast or duckling for Sunday dinner takes some getting used to. I'm told we'll be lucky to procure a decent piece of beef once or twice a month on this island." Sidonia sighed. "Oh, the sacrifices we make."

Nora couldn't resist an appraisal of the dining room's plush appointments. The gleaming mahogany table with its eight Chippendale chairs. Twin china cupboards filled with her mother's finest French china. A sparkling crystal chandelier raining soft candlelight over the entire scene from two dozen tapers. It was difficult not to voice her opinion on her mother's definition of sacrifice, but she remained silent.

Hadley turned his attention to the head of the table where Thurston Seabrook had been toying with his fish for several minutes. Clearing his throat, Theodore said, "Your Honor, if

I may be so bold as to ask, how goes your investigation of the wreck of the *Morning Dove?*''

Thurston seemed grateful for the opportunity to take his mind off his meal. Something was definitely troubling him. He steepled his hands and looked at the young attorney. ''I've learned a good bit in two days, Hadley,'' he said. ''The saddest fact of all is that two people died as a result of that wreck.''

Nora's fork hit the side of her plate with a clatter. ''Two people died, Father? How did it happen?''

''Really, Eleanor,'' Sidonia interrupted, ''this is hardly appropriate dinner conversation.''

Thurston cut short his wife's opposition. ''She has a right to know, Sidonia. We are all part of this island now, and what affects one of us affects us all. Truly I've wanted to bring this to my family's attention since I learned of it yesterday. The knowledge has been a lonely burden to bear.''

So this was what had been bothering Father, Nora thought. And it was not surprising. He had come to Key West to enforce the laws and prevent such unfortunate accidents from happening. And yet, with the very first wreck since his arrival, two people died. ''Tell us, Father. What happened?''

''One poor fellow died in his cabin when the ship struck the reef,'' he began. ''Doctor Winslow surmises that he hit his head and died immediately. The other casualty, a woman in her fifties, is less easy to explain. For some reason she was not able to board a rescue boat. During her attempt to get safely on deck, she slipped from a sailor's grasp and into the sea. The waves pulled her under right away. Her body washed up on shore late yesterday.''

''How horrible,'' Nora said. She recalled the sadness she'd seen in Jacob's eyes two days before. Perhaps he was aware of the deaths at that time. Perhaps he had even seen the woman plunge into the ocean. Maybe that explained why he'd acted as he had when he'd told her to leave the cupola. It was as good an excuse as the dozen others she'd conjured up the last two days. She'd been searching for any reason that would explain Jacob's behavior, anything that would help lessen the hurt she still felt.

"Horrible indeed," her father agreed. "Especially since both deaths could and *should* have been prevented."

"What do you mean? Both cases sound like accidents."

"On the surface, yes, but the captain of the *Morning Dove*, Lars Deiter, told me that he saw a light on shore during the darkest moment of the storm. Being unable to see more than a few yards ahead of him, naturally he directed his vessel to the safety of the light. Only it didn't steer him around the southern tip of the island and thus to the harbor. Instead, it led him straight into the reef."

Nora felt a shiver of dread creep down her spine. "Someone deliberately led the *Morning Dove* to the reef? That's despicable, Father. Do you know who would do such a thing?"

"I have a strong suspicion," he declared. "Though he didn't reach the wreck first, and did not earn wrecker's rights, I still think it was Jacob Proctor who set the false light."

Nora jolted upright in her chair. What her father said was impossible. "No, Father, it wasn't him. I know it!"

Thurston's bushy eyebrows raised in surprise. "What could you possibly know of this, Nora?"

Should she admit the truth and risk her parents' wrath? To save a man's reputation, she had to. "Because ... because I was with him when the storm broke."

Silence, heavy with implication, filled the room for a few dreadful seconds. It was Fanny who broke the awful quiet. *"Vraiment, cherie?* You must tell us more."

Sidonia found her voice next. "Eleanor, what are you saying? Were you unchaperoned?"

Thurston brought his fist down on the table. "I told you to stay away from that man."

"Please, all of you. It's not what you think ... if you're thinking what I suspect you are."

"Well, *I* certainly am," Fanny said.

"We were discussing a business arrangement, that's all."

All eyes were on Nora, making her wish she could crawl under the table.

Sidonia wiped her napkin across her brow, removing a slight sheen of perspiration. "What possible *business* could you have with that man?"

Then as if remembering their guest for the first time in many moments, everyone shifted their gazes to Theodore Hadley. It was not the Seabrook way to air family problems in front of a stranger. Sidonia dabbed at her mouth. "Thurston, if you please . . ."

"Right, madam." He turned to Theodore. "Mr. Hadley, if you would be so kind. I must ask your leave for a few moments while we discuss a matter in private."

Leaving looked like the last thing Theodore wanted, but he was, of course, a gentleman. Pushing his chair back, he stood and, with his good hand, straightened the vest over his new tan worsted trousers. "Certainly, Judge Seabrook. I'll be on the veranda."

"Fanny . . . if you don't mind as well," Thurston said.

"I do mind, Thurston, but I'll go anyway." She flashed a playful wink at Nora as she stood and flounced her skirts. "I'll just help Theodore practice his French on the veranda."

When it was just the three of them, both parents pinned Nora with their most serious glares. "Now then, Nora," her father said, "what business dealings are you having with Captain Proctor?"

As she told her parents about her plan to teach the Bahamian children to read, Nora watched their facial expressions change. Her mother's went from abject mortification at discovering her daughter had been unchaperoned with a man to almost total outrage at her latest revelation. Thurston's expression, however, mellowed to the point that Nora could almost hope he supported her.

"So that's all there is to it, Father," she said, choosing the least intimidating parent to speak to directly. "I needed supplies, and Captain Proctor had them and offered them for free. We discussed his contribution while the storm was brewing outside his warehouse, so that's how I know he couldn't have been responsible for the light.''

Thurston tapped his spoon against his saucer, thinking about what his daughter said. ''I appreciate what you're trying to do, Nora, and I even admire your ingenuity in implementing this plan, but what you've told me doesn't clear Captain Proctor's name with regard to the false light on shore.''

''But, Father, I just told you . . .''

''What you told me, Nora, is that you were with Captain Proctor. That does not preclude the possibility that another member of his crew, acting on Proctor's order, was at the shore, lighting that false beacon while the captain was engaged with you.''

Unfortunately, her father could be right. ''Yes, I suppose that could have happened.'' An illuminating counterpoint suddenly occurred to her. ''But . . . if Ja . . . I mean, Captain Proctor had gone to all that trouble, then he surely would have left before the other ships to reach the wrecking sight. As it was, he didn't even spot the wreck. I would think if he had been anticipating it, he would have been the first to sail his schooner out of the harbor.''

She neglected to tell her father that she had felt partly responsible for Jacob's lateness and had waited at his warehouse to tell him so.

Thurston was not easily dissuaded, and in fact, seemed to read her mind. ''Perhaps, Nora, but you forget, I'm your father. Too many times I've been sidetracked from a project by your untimely, albeit charming, chatter myself.''

Sidonia suddenly threw her napkin on the table and stared at her husband and daughter. Irritation simmered in her eyes. ''What is the matter with both of you . . . going on endlessly about that wreck, and who did what, and who's to blame. Don't you see what's really important here, Thurston? Didn't you hear what your daughter said?''

Thurston returned a blank stare at his wife. ''Of course I heard her, Sidonia. What do you mean?''

She picked up the napkin again and fanned her face vigorously. She was getting a case of the vapors, and that was not a good sign. "Eleanor just confessed that, behind our backs, she has arranged to spend a good part of every day with a motley bunch of Negro children in what will probably turn out to be a fruitless attempt to get them to read!"

The judge narrowed his eyes in an obvious effort to comprehend his wife's point. "Yes, Sidonia, I heard her say all that, all but the fruitless and motley part, anyway."

"Well, don't you see? How will that look? We've only just moved here. I'm finally becoming acquainted with the admittedly small but finer elements of this society. There happen to be some gentlefolk of good lineage here after all . . . the Wardens from Charleston, the MacDougals from Newport News . . . And now I'll have to live down the distressing fact that my own daughter prefers the company of blacks to her own kind!"

Thurston lowered his forehead to his hand. "Oh, Sid . . ."

"And Thurston, those children probably don't even want to read. Why, I've seen them. They're perfectly happy running around the island barefooted and nut-browned. They're *free,* for heaven's sake. What else could they want?"

It was difficult, but Nora suppressed her anger at her mother. After all, Sidonia was steeped in the traditions of Southern living in America. Even though she'd come from France many years before, she had adapted to her husband's way of life easily, and she was exactly like the other ladies of Richmond society. The issues she brought up could have been voiced by any one of her female friends at home.

Nora feared an argument was about to erupt between her parents, and she would have been the cause. She took her mother's hand and stopped her from fanning the napkin. "Mama, I know that what I've decided to do has upset you. And I know that this project might not be appropriate in Richmond, but you have to realize that this is not Virginia. In the short time we've been here, I've learned that some behaviors which would seem out of place at home are perfectly accepted here. Why, look at Fanny."

Sidonia's eyebrows arched with interest. "What about Fanny?"

"Before we left Virginia you were worried that your friends would take exception to some of Fanny's, well ... eccentric habits. Isn't that right?"

"Yes, but ..."

"And here, you've barely given it a thought. In fact, you have to admit that everyone on the island likes Fanny. They are amused and enthralled by her. Why, just today you got an invitation to tea from Mrs. Arthur Whiting, and the invitation includes all the Seabrook ladies, even Fanny. It just proves that things are different here. The extraordinary is accepted and even sought after."

"I suppose so ..."

"And I only want to teach the children to read because I've discovered that there is no opportunity for them to learn otherwise. And if they want to learn, then that isn't right. These children have no masters forbidding their education. Only circumstance prevents it."

Nora poured more wine into her mother's glass and handed it to her. "You may be right about one thing, Mama. Maybe they won't want to come to my school, but at least I want to try. And besides, I have nothing else to occupy my days."

Sidonia took a long swallow of wine and leaned back against her chair. "Sometimes it's hard for me to believe you're my flesh and blood, Eleanor." She looked at her husband. "You did see her when she was born, didn't you, Thurston? You're quite certain this is our child?"

He smiled at her, his patience restored. "As sure as I am of my next heartbeat, lovey. Anyone sitting across the table from the two most elegant women in Key West would see the resemblance and know it's true."

Sidonia blushed, and Nora knew everything was all right again.

"Very well, then, Eleanor," her mother said. "Do your teaching and reading and such. You have my blessing ... reluctantly."

Nora basked in her father's admiring gaze. "Thank you, Mama." She stood up and gifted Sidonia with a kiss on her cheek. "And now I'm off to the milliner's shop to see what I can do about setting up for my first class." *Since I doubt very much that I can count on Captain Proctor's generosity now.* "I'll be back soon."

"See that you are, dear," Sidonia said. "Oh, and when you go out on the veranda, rescue poor Mr. Hadley from Fanny's clutches, won't you?"

The instant Nora stepped onto the veranda, Theodore Hadley bounded up from the wicker settee upon which he and Fanny were sitting. "Ah, Miss Seabrook. I hope that little situation in the dining room has been resolved without too much unpleasantness."

He was obviously dying to know what the altercation was about, and if Nora truly had been involved in a tryst with Captain Proctor, but to Hadley's credit, he didn't ask. "Yes, of course, Mr. Hadley, everything is fine now," she said, heading for the steps leading to the sidewalk. "I'm just off on a little errand."

She was halfway to the fence bordering the front lawn when she heard him behind her on the walk. "Miss Seabrook, I was wondering. It's such a lovely afternoon, with a delightful breeze. I . . . I haven't had much exercise lately. I'd like to walk with you."

She turned slowly to face him. It would be inconceivable to pretend she hadn't heard him. He appeared so earnest in his request, his pale hazel eyes begging her not to turn him down, his free hand ruffling the strands of reddish hair that threatened to fall in his eyes. In fact, he was more puppy-like than Armand or Hubert had ever been, and this made it impossible to deny him. "I would be happy for the company, Mr. Hadley, if you're sure you're up to it."

He hastened to catch up with her, and offered the bended elbow of his good arm for her to slide her hand through. "I'm very much up to it, I assure you, and please call me by my first name," he said.

She let the tips of her fingers rest on his arm. "All right, then, Theodore . . ."

"Theo, please. It's less formal."

Noticing the glimmer of interest in Theo's eyes, Nora decided that "less formal" was precisely what she didn't want in her relationship with the attorney. Keeping her gaze focused on the scenery, she veered off to Duval Street, more or less pulling Theo in her wake.

Using the key she'd remembered to get from Mr. McTaggart the day before when she dropped off reading supplies, Nora opened the lock to the milliner's shop. She'd been able to procure several elementary books from the library, and she'd made some simple drawings herself with her artist's sketch pad, but she couldn't imagine how she'd improvise the other things she needed.

She expected her students, however many of them actually showed up, would have to sit on crates and barrels, and once her sketch pad paper ran out, she'd have to try to beg writing materials from Key West shopkeepers. Her students would have to share the two bottles of ink she'd brought from home and the half-dozen pens she'd found in Samuel Rutherford's desk.

As Nora strode through the hat shop to her little room in back, she couldn't fight off a wave of depression. If only I hadn't angered Jacob Proctor, she thought. I'd at least have benches and slates and proper writing utensils, and . . .

She halted at the entrance to her classroom and stared in disbelief at the very items she had been mentally listing. Drawing in a quick, sharp breath of utter delight, Nora feasted her eyes on six rows of perfectly aligned benches. Every other bench had been outfitted with wooden foot pads to raise it above the one behind, creating elevated writing surfaces. And placed neatly in intervals across each higher bench there were four slates, each with chalk, and four pads of paper with inkwells and quills. Supplies for twelve pupils in all.

In front of all the benches there sat a small, but proper, desk with a leather top and three drawers down each side. An oak chair with wheels had been pushed underneath, and a large wooden easel sat to the side. A small bookcase against the wall held a dozen books, some of them classics that Nora had read when she was a girl. She clasped her hands to her chest. "Oh, thank you, thank you," she breathed. "It's wonderful."

"What's all this?" Theo asked, walking among the benches and inspecting the items. "Has someone called a meeting in the hat shop?"

"So it would appear," came a forceful voice from the doorway. "At least the three of us appear to have met here."

"Captain Proctor!" Nora whirled around to face him. The captain, his hands on the door frame, filled the entrance with his presence. His loose white shirt, open at the neck, gleamed in the late afternoon sunlight. His eyes shone darkly in contrast.

Nora's inspection of her little classroom had produced a multitude of surprising emotions. There was the unanticipated joy of seeing it furnished so practically, and the exquisite torture of finding herself face-to-face with the man who'd been in her thoughts for the last forty-eight hours.

She certainly hadn't expected the former, and she was definitely confused by the latter. She had decided to avoid the captain at all costs, an easy task since she was fairly certain he would do his best to avoid her. He had made his disinterest abundantly clear in the cupola when he told her to leave.

Her boldness in violating his private space had obviously displeased him. Or perhaps it had been the kiss. While he'd seemed eager at the start of it, he must have been put off by her lack of expertise in that area. How many times since then had she longed for Fanny's worldliness and daring. Then she'd have been a match for this captain! She'd decided to come to terms with the events in the cupola by refusing to regret her boldness and pushing the entire kissing incident to the back of her mind where it belonged . . . and stubbornly refused to stay.

Jacob dropped his hands to his sides and entered the classroom. "Hello, Nora."

Uncertain as to how he expected her to act at this meeting,

she backed away as he came closer, finally retreating around the desk. Seeking the first opportunity to remove her gaze from him, she scanned the interior of the room. "You did this, Captain?"

"Some of it. And some was done by Willy and others."

She looked down at the desk. "I'm surprised. I didn't think . . ."

"I gave you my word, Nora. Does the classroom please you?"

He tapped into that vein of delight she'd experienced when she first came in the room, and she couldn't resist looking at him then. "Indeed it does, Captain. Very much. Thank you."

He cleared his throat and slid his gaze to a corner of the room where a rustling noise caught Nora's attention. Hadley stared at first one, then the other while he fidgeted with his sling.

"Oh, Theo, I'm sorry," Nora said. "Let me introduce you."

Her escort struggled to hide his obvious contempt while he remained on the far side of the room. "I know who the captain is," he said coolly.

Jacob crossed his arms over his chest and regarded Hadley thoughtfully. "And you . . . you're the lawyer who broke his arm on the *Morning Dove,* is that correct?"

"It is."

"And you're currently residing with the Seabrooks."

Hadley raised his face, straightened his shoulders, and glared at Jacob over the bridge of his nose. "I am."

Why did he make it sound as if staying with her family were some sort of badge of honor? As if it implied advantages the rest of the population was denied?

Testing his newfound confidence, Theo approached the desk and stood beside Nora. "I really must suggest that we leave, Miss Seabrook . . . Nora. I'm quite certain your father will be wondering where our stroll has taken us after so long a time."

It hadn't even been a half hour, but Nora refrained from embarrassing Hadley with the facts. Instead, she politely

informed him that she wanted to stay and become better
acquainted with the room.

"Very well, then," he said, leaning against one of the
benches as if he were a marble statue meant to rest in that
particular spot for all eternity. "I'll stay with you for as long
as you like."

Nora looked at Jacob and recognized the familiar flicker of
amusement in his eyes. "If you wish, Theo," she said on a
sigh.

Jacob nodded at Theo and allowed a lingering gaze to bathe
Nora in tingling warmth. "Then I'll bid good day to you both,"
he said, and left the room.

Theo stood straight and affected a shiver in his spine. "I
can understand why your father doesn't trust him, Nora. He
has that look about him. It's hard to explain."

Nora stared at the doorway long after Jacob had left. "Yes,
he does, Theo, I know exactly what you mean."

That night Nora wrote in her journal:

> *I am utterly enchanted with my classroom—its rustic,
> sturdy pine benches, fine new slates and chalk, interesting
> books, and, of course, all the glorious sunshine, which
> is so often lacking in Virginia.*
>
> *One man is responsible for donating all of the items
> except the last, and at times I wonder if he even persuaded
> the clouds to part and fill my windows with light. Despite
> his generosity, the man, a sea captain by trade, is as
> enigmatic as are the creatures that dwell at the bottom
> of the ocean. And I know as little about him . . .*

Nora put her pen down on the delicate mahogany desk that
sat near the open French doors of her bedroom and let the night
breeze cool the flush on her face. And oh, how I long to know
more, she thought, accepting the undeniable truth.

CHAPTER SEVEN

Seven children came to the classroom behind the milliner's shop the next morning. Two of them wore shoes. All of them had shiny, scrubbed faces. The three Obalu children were there, just as Portia had promised, or, in that way she had, threatened. There were four others, three boys and a girl, all of whom exhibited such a glow of hero worship in their eyes for Fclix Obalu, it was obvious they would have done anything he asked them—even if it meant giving up two hours of their morning to learn to read.

Nora was not discouraged that only seven children had come. A firm believer in "Rome wasn't built in a day," she applied that same philosophy to the first school for Key West's free black youngsters and greeted her pupils with keen enthusiasm. "What a fine-looking group we have here for our first day of class," she said. "I am very proud of you for being here. You are charter members of the Island School for Reading, and as other students join us, you will always have the distinction of being the first."

When she smiled at the children, she was grateful to see a slight relaxing of the rigid postures they had maintained since coming in the classroom. All of them but Felix seemed intimidated by her presence. Nora had chosen a soft coral dress with white collar and cuffs, hoping the warm color would be soothing. ''And now I want each of you to tell me your name. My name is Miss Nora.''

Once the introductions were over, Nora explained that they would be learning the twenty-six letters of the alphabet. Scanning each attentive face, she said, ''That's all there are, you see. Just twenty-six letters. I don't think it will be so difficult to learn them. And when we do, we can put them together in all sorts of wonderful ways.''

She held her thumb and forefinger an inch apart. ''We can put as few as two or three letters together and make small, simple words.'' She held her arms apart as if she were demonstrating the size of a large fish. ''And later we can put as many as fifteen or more together and make giant, very smart-sounding words.''

So far so good, Nora thought. They were listening. In fact, a few of her students even seemed intrigued at the notion of stringing those letters together to make words. ''But first we must start with just one.''

She held up her sketch pad, which revealed the letters A and B, one on each page. Pointing to the first page, where she'd drawn a bright red apple, she asked the class to identify the picture.

Nothing. Her request was met with seven blank stares.

She looked at her apple. It was perfectly round, brilliantly red, and topped with a small stem and one green oval leaf. It was indeed an apple.

After several moments, Ty Obalu raised his plump little arm and pointed to the other page, the one with the B. ''Well, that one's a banana!'' he exclaimed.

Suddenly she knew what was wrong. These children had never seen an apple. They were only grown in northern states and rarely shipped so far south. To anyone living in the tropics, an apple had to be a rare delicacy, and almost certainly not one the Bahamian children would know. She decided right then to draw an avocado by the next morning. And in the meantime, they would start with the second letter.

"You're absolutely right, Ty," she said.

He grinned and looked around to make sure everyone had heard her.

"So let's talk about the banana. Everyone say the first sound of banana . . . just the very beginning."

Softly exploding *buh, buh, buh*'s mingled with reserved laughter.

"And when bananas grow all together on one limb, what do we call them?"

"A bunch!" a girl named Dorina answered.

"Right! Say the first sound of bunch."

"Buh, buh, buh."

"Now think of other words that start the same way."

"Button!"

"Boat!"

"Bottle!"

"Barnacle!"

Nora pointed to each child as suggestions were fired at her, one after the other. "Right! Good! Now another!"

A rush of adrenaline fueled her own enthusiasm as the words kept coming. Her children had started to learn, and Nora Seabrook was teaching!

The first hour and a half went by quickly, and at nine o'clock Nora instructed the students to practice the capital B on their slates. Except for the muffled scratch of chalk on slate, the classroom was quiet, the breeze from the open windows still cool and refreshing. Soon, however, outside sounds from increasing activity on the harbor filtered into the back of the milliner's shop. They were ordinary sounds, and occasionally her students glanced toward the window.

But when the harsh tones of a heated argument suddenly shattered the calm morning, the drawing of B's was instantly forgotten. Felix jumped up from his bench and ran to the window. "Cap'n J's fightin' with Moony!" he called to the others.

Chalk rolled to the floor, and benches scraped the pine plank-

ing. The other six children ran to the windows. Nora followed
behind them.

"What's goin' on?" the boy called Jericho asked.

"If you shut up, we'll find out," Felix ordered.

Nora's palm flattened against her chest, a vexation habit
she'd picked up from her mother and was determined to stop.
"Maybe we shouldn't listen," she said. "I'm sure this is private
business between the two men."

"They're standin' in the middle of the darn street, Miss
Nora," Felix pointed out. "They can't care too awful much
who hears them."

She conceded with a shrug and leaned further out the window.
Moony Swain was pounding his fist against his opposite hand
in an effort to make a point. "You've got no right to speak
for your men, Proctor. Let me hire a couple of your divers for
a few hours. Give 'em a chance to make some extra money."

With his hands on his hips, Jacob appeared immovable.
"You'll not take one of my men to the wreck of the *Morning
Dove,* Moony. And that's the end of it. I'll fire any of them
that says they're going with you."

"You're a pompous jackass, Proctor! You always have been.
You think you can preach to every one on the island."

"This isn't preaching. It's common sense. Any idiot knows
you can't send men down thirty feet to the bottom when there's
bottles of liniment leaking all over the ocean floor. Wasn't it
enough that one of your men was blinded yesterday, Swain?
You want every diver in Key West coming down with blisters
of the eyes?"

Moony bent at the waist and leaned so close to Jacob their
noses nearly touched. "At least I don't play God, pickin' and
choosin' who gets a job and who doesn't. You spout off your
righteousness till it sticks in my gut like broken glass. We'd
all be better off if you'd take your operation and get off this
island."

Felix Obalu whistled through his teeth. "Ooo-whee, Cap'n
J ain't gonna like them words a bit."

When Jacob's finger began jabbing at Moony's chest, Nora

decided she'd better get the children away from the window. "Maybe we shouldn't watch anymore."

"We can't stop now!" Felix protested. "It's just gettin' good."

"I don't care what you think of me, Moony!" Jacob shouted. "You're nothing but a greedy fool whose only interest is to pluck the last dollar out of the last crate in the ocean, no matter who gets hurt. I'm telling you one last time. Forget about my divers. If you're so anxious to bring up that liniment, you go down and fetch it yourself!"

Having said his piece, Jacob walked away, but Moony followed him. "I'll get you, Proctor. Somehow I will," he shouted at Jacob's back.

Jacob shrugged off the threat, and soon their voices could no longer be heard in the classroom. The children slowly returned to their seats.

"That's horrible," Nora said. "A diver was blinded from substances in the water?"

"It happens, Miss Nora," Jericho said. "My own papa's a diver, and he's had the blisters lots of times. Guess I will, too, since I'll be a diver just like him. I'll prob'ly be lucky, though, like he is. After a few days, he always gets his sight back."

Nora sat on her chair behind the desk and contemplated the harsh life of the island. She jotted down words she would write in her journal later.

So much wealth and beauty, and so much misery in one mile-wide stretch of land. This is Key West.

A dozen illustrations of her point crowded into her head at once. "It's nine-thirty," she said to her students. "Who wants to volunteer to help Mr. McTaggart today?"

Keeping seven energetic children occupied and interested in learning is not an easy task under the best of conditions, but Nora found it especially difficult her first week as a teacher.

The biggest hindrance to education was that she'd opened her school the same week as Jacob Proctor scheduled his auction. Though the auction wouldn't be held until Friday morning, the island began swelling with visitors as early as Tuesday. When all the rooms in the two hotels were taken, individual residents volunteered to house visitors.

Nora could hardly blame her students for wanting to rush to the window whenever a tall ship docked and a new stream of passengers disembarked. What an interesting assortment of individuals they were! Nattily dressed gentlemen in silk top hats and wool frock coats became commonplace, some escorting elegantly dressed ladies in brocades and satins. The arrivals came from varied ports, including the Bahamas, Charleston, New York, New Orleans, and Havana. They were all interested in one thing—Jacob Proctor's auction of salvaged material and the bargains they would take home.

The sale was the talk of the Key West community also. Young and old, everyone planned to attend the event and bid on at least one treasure from the many barrels and crates to be opened and spilled on the dock that day. After all, nearly every home on the island had been furnished from shipwreck spoils. Key West ladies proudly wore gowns of the finest silk, even though the garments often bore salt stains. And in the best homes, women served tea from sterling pots bearing someone else's initials.

By Wednesday evening, Nora was as caught up in "auction fever" as everyone else. She longed to be at the restaurants and taverns that ringed the harbor so she could be part of the excitement that surrounded Proctor's Warehouse and Salvage.

That night she retreated to the backyard after dinner as she often did. Sitting on the service porch steps with a tin pan in her lap, she fed scraps of food to Reckless. Bright melodies from pianos and stringed instruments carried on a breeze from the harbor. Adding to that were the vibrant sounds of harmonicas, banjos, and drums from the Negro community several blocks in the other direction.

Nora sighed and offered the remains of a biscuit to the goat.

"No offense, Reckless," she said, "but everyone in town seems to be having fun but me."

The goat churned his lower jaw and nuzzled closer to Nora's skirt. Familiar now with his habits, she placed her hand on his chest and gently pushed him back.

"You'll not get my dress this time, silly goat," she said. "Don't make me stick a finger in your ear." She then patted Reckless's head between his horns. "You're really the lucky one here, you know. No one pays you any mind at all. Even Armand and Hubert, now that they've gotten their fill of yapping and carrying on, scarcely give you a second look these days. You could march right out that gate, and no one would even notice until the garbage started piling up.

"Now, me, on the other hand . . . everyone in this household seems much too concerned with what Nora is doing every minute. Lulu, though she's sweet about it, is quite sure I'm incapable of doing anything on my own and fusses over me continuously. Mama is constantly putting me in situations where I'm forced to entertain Theo. Fanny seeks me out to bend my ear with the latest town gossip, and Father . . . heaven only knows why he's been watching me like a hawk. It's as if he thinks I'm going to run off with Captain Proctor on a whim."

Nora set the tin pan down and let Reckless lick the sticky remains. Placing her elbows on her knees and resting her chin in her hands, she said wistfully, "And speaking of Captain Proctor, that strangest of all human beings . . . he's the only one of my acquaintances who doesn't appear the least interested in anything about me."

Her gaze wandered over the fence in the direction of the wharf. "I'll bet he's sitting in one of those taverns right now enjoying the music and the company of any number of gentlemen . . . and ladies. He's definitely the most noteworthy person in town these days."

When a plan came unbidden to her mind, Nora didn't even try to push it away. "I'm going there, Reckless," she declared. "There's no reason why I shouldn't enjoy myself, too. I'll tell Mama I'm going to walk down the block, and then I'll sneak to the harbor. And if I see Jacob Proctor, well, so what? It's like seeing a beautiful dress and knowing I can't have it because it's much too daring. At least I got to see it, and there is satisfaction in that.''

She stood up and grinned at the goat, who stubbornly butted his head against the empty tin in her hand. The goat didn't give up easily and neither would she!

Choosing comfort over fashion, and expedience over preparation, Nora left her hoops and crinolines in her wardrobe and hastily threw on a light cotton lawn dress. It was a pale pink muslin with a scooped neckline, pinafore front, and short gathered sleeves. She pinned the sides of her hair at the crown and let the rest fall in waves down her back. The casual appearance suited both the balmy night and her mood.

Grateful that Theo was involved in a legal discussion with her father, Nora exited the house before he could ask to join her and walked briskly to the harbor. She passed Gentleman Bill Barley's Inn and Eatery, by far the nicest restaurant in town. It was full both inside and on the veranda with couples dressed in their finery. The remainder of Duval Street was dotted mostly with taverns. Nora smiled when she remembered a story she'd heard from Dillard Hyde her first day on the island.

"Oh, yes, Miss Seabrook," he'd said when they'd passed a row of taverns, "Key West has more drinking spots than any other city its size in the country." He'd laughed then and related an interesting tale. "Why, when the citizens were trying to get a minister to stay in town two decades ago, the barkeepers banded together and ran the good reverend out of town, claiming he was bad for business!"

Apparently, the two factions had come to terms, since Key West now had three churches, four if you counted the one for the Negro community. Of course, there was still no shortage of taverns. And each of them was enjoying the profits of the suddenly burgeoning population.

Nora headed directly for Jimmy Teague's knowing that Jacob Proctor was friendly with the proprietor. And, too, laughter and music was loudest at that establishment. She'd chosen wisely. Anyone searching for boisterous entertainment and a jolly crowd needed look no further than Jimmy Teague's Tavern this night. The inside was crammed to capacity, with revelers spilling out onto the veranda. And, sure enough, Jacob Proctor was among them.

Nora had planned to stay on the outside, in the shadows, watching from a safe distance. She did not intend to be drawn into the throng, which represented a wide range of cultural diversity. There were sailors and divers and local businessmen. Men in dress suits mingled with fellows clad in coarse linsey-woolsey. And, most noticeably, there were very few women, and these few looked as natural in their environment as if they spent every night at Jimmy Teague's— especially the golden-haired, buxom beauty on Jacob Proctor's knee.

The woman laughed and bent to whisper some secret in Jacob's ear. It must have pleased him because his mouth sought her neck and he planted a kiss under her ear. She stroked his hair, threw back her head, and laughed again. He picked up his mug, raised it to his companions, and gulped down the dark liquid contents.

Unable to draw her gaze from Jacob and his companion, Nora questioned her decision to come to the harbor. What had she expected when she left her home to follow the sounds of the night and her silly fantasies about a man who didn't know she existed? She had turned to go back to Southard Street when a hand reached out and grabbed her elbow.

"Hello, pretty lass," came a gravely voice with a strong Irish brogue. "Lovely evenin' ain't it?"

She looked up into a ruddy face partially hidden by a full beard and mustache. His facial hair was as red as the thick strands jutting out from the band of an old flat-crowned cap. He was a big man, the tallest Nora had seen on the island, but she wasn't afraid. His smile was ready, and his eyes appeared kind.

"Hello," she said. "Yes, it is a nice evening."

"But e'en so, I must ask, why are ye standin' on the outside lookin' in, when the whole world's on a toot at Jimmy Teague's? Come on, lass, let me buy ye a pint."

"You want to buy me a drink?" She foolishly pointed to herself as if she needed to verify the invitation.

"Now, who else would I be askin' since it's only you and me on the street?"

She looked inside the bar at a crowd of nearly a hundred people, as well as she could determine. Certainly there was safety in such large numbers. She glanced to the veranda, where Jacob Proctor had just slipped his arm around the ample waist of the woman on his lap. She responded by sidling even closer to his chest. Nora had seen enough. Why shouldn't she go inside Teague's Tavern? Why shouldn't Nora Seabrook have as much fun as everyone else was having? There wasn't a reason she could think of. "I accept your offer, Mr. . . . ."

"Mullins, miss. Paddy O'Clerk Mullins, at your service." He took her arm and whisked her into the tavern before she even had a chance to tell him her name. And almost as quickly, she had a full mug in her hand. She took a long swallow and nearly choked on the bitter taste of strong ale going down her throat. The second dose went down more smoothly. Nora didn't really care for ale, but she figured for this night only, she could manage it.

Jacob wasn't at all certain he liked being the center of attention. He could accept easily enough his friends' good-natured teasing about the profits to come his way on Friday. But he resented being asked by out-of-town buyers for tips on which barrels held the best bargains. "You'll have to decide that for yourself," he said time and again. "One man's trash is another man's treasure."

"You tell 'em, dearie," Lottie said in his ear after a particularly tiresome merchant had been a recipient of Jacob's retort. She nuzzled her lips against his neck and nipped playfully.

"I'm feelin' awful tired, love," she said, and then settled her hand boldly between his legs. "How about you, Jacob? You feelin' the urge to go upstairs?"

He wanted to decline her offer as gallantly as possible, but he hadn't been able to think of a reason. In fact, he didn't know why the voluptuous Lottie didn't entice him as she usually did. He looked to Willy Turpin, hoping he would come up with an excuse, but his first mate wasn't paying any attention. His eyes were riveted on a scene in the tavern.

"Look there, Captain," Will said. "Are my eyes playin' tricks on me, or is that lady in the pink dress Miss Seabrook?"

Jacob scoffed, certain there was no way the well-bred Nora would be in Jimmy Teague's. But the proof was in the viewing, because there she was, surrounded by more than a dozen men, some of whom he recognized as locals, and most of whom he didn't like. "What the hell . . ." he muttered, half standing up and dislodging Lottie from his lap.

Familiar strains of an old sailor's ditty broke out in the barroom.

> *Loudly the bell in the old lighthouse rings,*
> *Bidding farewell to the danger it brings . . .*
> *Sailor take care*
> *Sailor beware . . .*

One female voice rose above the gruff baritones of her drunken companions. Nora raised her mug in the air and sang in a clear contralto, *"Danger is near thee, beware, beware . . ."*

Squinting into the low-lit room, Jacob demanded, "Is that Bull Mullins standing next to her?"

Willy put a restraining hand on Jacob's arm as if he knew what was to follow. "I think it is, Captain."

"Has she lost her mind? Does she have any idea what that man is like when he's had a few pints too many?"

"I'd venture to say she doesn't know at all, Jacob."

At that moment the song ended in a crescendo of laughter, and Bull Mullins put his arm around Nora. She wriggled out of his grasp, but he wasn't dissuaded. The beefy arm snaked its way again, this time with more forcefulness. Nora put her hand on his broad chest and tried to push him away, but Bull wasn't going anywhere. In fact his face came down toward hers an instant before Jacob Proctor's chair hit the floor with a thud. Leaving a startled Lottie staring after him, Jacob crossed the veranda in three strides and went inside the barroom.

The crowd in the tavern split in half to accommodate Jacob, who strode through the room with fists balled and fire in his eyes. He heard Nora's clear command for Bull to let her go at the same time he pulled the big man away from her. She squealed in surprise as Bull Mullins was thrust into the brass railing of Jimmy's counter.

"Keep your hands off her, Bull," Jacob ground out.

"And just what gives you the right to order me around, Proctor?"

Jacob may have had a bit too much to drink, but he wasn't drunk enough to be stupid. He knew Bull Mullins could pummel him within an inch of his life if he antagonized the big man. He pulled himself up to his full six feet two inches, which still left him lacking in size compared to Mullins, and fixed a stony glare on the man's swarthy face. Then he called on pure dumb luck and Bull's general ignorance to be on his side. "She's my cousin, and that gives me all the right I need." He glanced over his shoulder at Nora, and she blinked her astonishment. "I told you to stay home tonight, cousin," he snapped at her.

Bull's blurry eyes registered a hint of comprehension. "She's your c-cousin?"

"She is." Jacob risked another look at Nora, and was rewarded with a smug grin. "You're not coming out of the house again during this visit," he threatened her before turning his attention back to Bull. "Sorry, mate, but this one's not for you."

Bull didn't look happy about the unexpected turn of events that had interrupted his evening, but he made no aggressive move. Thankfully, the town was so full of strangers, no one had recognized the judge's daughter, including her amorous suitor. Still, Jacob wasted no time. He grabbed Nora's arm and pushed her ahead of him out a side door of the tavern.

Once outside, he backed her against a wall and held his index finger up like a weapon, daring her to move one inch. She didn't. He paced in a little circle, stopping at each revolution to stare at her until he could get his emotions under control. He managed to quell the anger that had been boiling inside him, but it was replaced by another emotion that was almost as dangerous to his sense of well-being. She looked so damned lovely in the moonlight, her face flushed and her eyes bold as blue ice.

Finally, he found the words he was seeking, and once they started, a geyser of emotion spewed from his lips. "Do you have any idea what you were getting yourself into in there? This isn't Virginia, Miss Seabrook. This is Key West, and you'd damn well better remember it! What the hell did you think you were doing, parading around Jimmy's like that?"

"Like what?" she asked innocently.

"Like that. In that dress." With one finger he flipped the edge of a ruffle that rimmed her bodice. He spun his hands around his head. "With your hair all loose and hanging down like that. If I hadn't come in the tavern when I did, you would have found youself in big trouble. I hope you know it!"

"Jacob . . ." she said softly.

"What?"

"Would you like to kiss me?"

CHAPTER EIGHT

Had those words really come out of her mouth? Nora was standing inches away from the man her father claimed might very well be the most dangerous man in Key West, the same man who'd scorned her a few nights before in his cupola, and seconds ago, she'd practically given him an open invitation to do it again.

Despite these rather shocking facts, Nora almost gave in to a ripple of giggles that threatened to burst from her lips. The truth was, she didn't have the slightest inclination to take back what she'd said. Was life worth living if a person didn't take a few risks? No! And this risk was worth taking, if only to see what this man would do.

And what he did was glare at her in awkward silence. Obviously, there were words inside him trying to find their way to his mouth ... words that demanded to be said. But so far, though his jaw had moved, he hadn't made a sound. And Nora gloried in the notion that she had rendered him speechless.

He looked away from her, and a transformation occurred, for when his eyes captured hers again, he was the old Captain Proctor once more ... cocky, confident, and in charge.

A scowl drew his lips downward and narrowed his eyes. "Did you hear a word I said?" he demanded.

"Yes, I heard every one of them."

"Well, you're obviously not taking me seriously."

"That's because I think you're much *too* serious."

"What does that mean?"

Nora relaxed her stance. She stepped away from the wall so that just her shoulder touched the wooden siding. It was a casual pose, as if she were standing under a shade tree conversing with a suitor at a picnic. She hadn't liked the ale, but perhaps it had given her the courage to pretend to have a blasé attitude now. "Captain," she said calmly, "the day of the wreck, you indicated that you have no interest in me whatsoever. As I recall, you kissed me and then demanded that I be on my way as if I had somehow offended you."

"You didn't offend me, Nora. And anyway, it didn't mean you should parade about in the dark of night seeking the company of the first big ape who comes your way."

"I didn't seek Mr. Mullins' company. He sought mine."

"It amounts to the same thing. You encouraged him at the very least."

"I did not. No more than I encouraged you in the cupola. And you did exactly what Mr. Mullins only tried to do."

A sudden light flashed in Jacob's eyes. It was the proverbial glimmer of truth, and Nora realized he'd had to accept her point as valid.

"Perhaps you're right," he said, "but Mullins would have done it if I hadn't stopped him."

"Or if I hadn't," she said matter-of-factly.

"And yet you say you weren't encouraging him?"

"That's right. I wasn't."

A wry grin of victory slanted across his face. "Well, then, Nora, what do you call what you just did with me? That question you just asked me?"

"When I asked if you wanted to kiss me?"

He nodded.

She reached out and touched his arm. "Jacob, I readily admit to encouraging *you.*"

"Ah-hah! I thought so." Though he reveled in her admission, the grin dissolved from his face. "So, you want me to kiss you?"

"Despite the rude conclusion of our only other embrace, I found the kiss quite satisfactory. And, yes, I wouldn't mind if you did it again."

His hand came up to stroke her hair, tentatively at first, until he lifted a thick wave over her shoulder to lie at her breast. His fingers trailed down the curl as he studied her face in the low light from the tavern window. Could he tell she felt his caress all the way through her scalp to that part of her that governed her senses? Did he know his gaze brought a warm flow of blood to her cheeks?

"But only if you want to," she said.

His other hand settled on her waist, drawing her closer as his head lowered partway to hers and stopped. His smile washed over her like the noon sun. "I think I could endure kissing you again, Nora, but it shouldn't happen without a warning. You've been drinking. Do you really know what you're asking?"

Yes, she'd been drinking . . . a little. And something made it feel as though her feet weren't grounded on the sand, but she doubted very much if it was the ale. She looked into gray eyes that had gone smoky with hard-to-fathom male emotions. "I know exactly, Captain."

He laid his palm against her cheek. His thumb caressed her lips in the instant before his mouth covered them. He tasted of spice and grog, and smelled faintly of salt and leather. He took her with a groan of frustration that soon blended with her own sigh of intense and thorough pleasuring as his mouth moved exquisitely on hers.

His hand spanned her back, urging her closer until their hips touched. Her tummy pressed against his abdomen. Tender breasts swelled against fine muslin and the coarser fabric of his shirt. And the kiss, the sweetly torturous, gently punishing kiss continued until all that existed was Jacob's mouth, and the

only sound Nora heard was the beating of her heart. When at
last he pulled away, she knew why she hadn't been able to
banish the memory of Jacob's kiss from her mind. And why
now she never would.

This time he didn't send her away. He held her against his
chest and rested his chin on the top of her head. When she
sighed, he kissed her hair. "Nora, sweet Nora," he whispered.
"Why do you tempt me? It would be wrong for you to become
involved with me."

She leaned back and looked up at him. "It should *feel* wrong,
then. But it doesn't."

He smiled, but not with contentment. With regret, so that
once again he was a mystery. Once again she didn't understand
him. His lips lowered to take hers in another sublime mating.
"It doesn't, but Nora, it is."

The sad finality of his statement cut to her heart. Why was
it wrong? Was it because he was, after all, the man her father
claimed he was? Was Jacob trying to warn her of that very
thing? How could he be when he had just held her so gently
in his arms? She had to know the truth and would have asked
him, but she heard someone call her name and was denied the
opportunity. "Nora! Miss Seabrook, are you here?"

Jacob stepped away from her as if her flesh had turned to
stone. His face became a mask of indifference, and his voice
droned with the passionless inflection of reason. "I believe that
is the call of your beau, Miss Nora."

She recognized the voice as Theo's, and groaned with impatience at having to face him. But there was no escape. His
footsteps rustled in the low palms that lined the street by Jimmy
Teague's.

Jacob put his hand on the small of her back and forced her
to walk toward the front of the tavern. As soon as Theo came
into view, Jacob called out to him. "Counselor Hadley. I am
bringing Miss Seabrook to you now."

There was no doubt of Theo's opinion upon seeing Nora
escorted by Jacob Proctor. His eyes went round with shock,
and his lips pursed with distaste. "Nora, whatever are you

doing in this part of town at this hour?'' *And with this man?* his voice implied.

Jacob smiled jovially, but his fingers, still on her back, curled with the effort of controlling his temper. He prompted her forward until she was more in the company of Theo than of him. ''Tell him, Miss Seabrook. Tell him about the curiosity which brought you here this evening.''

Nora spun around, only to stare at the implacable restraint on Jacob's features. He was a chameleon, capable of changing on the slightest impulse, while she was a cauldron of emotions, not the least of which was confusion. Though her eyes were fixed on Jacob, she spoke to Theo. ''Yes, that's right. I was curious about what was going on at the harbor, and I'm afraid I allowed my stroll to lead me in this direction.''

Theo reached for her elbow. ''Really, Nora, that was a most impetuous action and one which could have resulted in dire consequences. No young woman of breeding should ever venture into this environment unescorted. If your father knew . . .''

Refusing to look away from Jacob, Nora countered, ''Are you going to tattle on me, Theo?''

''Tattle? Why, no, I would never . . .''

''Good. Because there's no need. I already know my actions tonight display the lack of common sense God granted a common housefly!'' Grabbing her skirts, she whirled away from the man whose eyes tormented her with indifference. ''Take me home, Theo,'' she said, not waiting for the attorney to keep pace with her.

Jacob watched her go until the pale pink of her dress blended with the moonlight, and the flaps of the coat draped over Hadley's shoulders became part of the blackness of the night. Then he went back to the veranda of Jimmy Teague's, ordered a pint, and found Willy. Lottie had diverted her attention to another fellow, and for this, Jacob was grateful.

After a long gulp of brew had taken the first step toward calming his raging emotions, Jacob spoke to his mate. ''Willy, I'll be glad when this damned auction is over. I want you to make arrangements to sail. I want full provisions on the *Cloud* by Monday noon.''

"Full provisions, Jacob? I thought our next trip was just to Nassau.''

"Not anymore. We're going to Belle Isle. It's almost time, and I need to get away. Far away.''

Nora settled back against her pillows and allowed Fanny to press a cool cloth to her forehead. When she and Theo returned home, Nora had whisked past the parlor door, giving only a succinct answer to her mother's questions about where she'd been. Then she'd gone upstairs to her room, hoping her cousin would sense her distress and come to see what was wrong. In only seconds, Fanny had knocked.

"Are you feeling better, *cherie?*'' Fanny asked minutes later. "I must say, I don't know what possessed an innocent such as you to drink that manly brew.''

That "manly brew'' had taken its toll, all right. By the time Nora reached her house, she had definitely felt its effects. To combat Nora's queasiness, Fanny had immediately gone to the kitchen for willow-bark tea and dry bread. Insisting that her young cousin consume both, Fanny now fussed over her with affectionate pats and gentle remonstrances.

"You needn't tell me not to do such a stupid thing again, Fanny,'' Nora said. "I learned my lesson with only one overindulgence.''

"I know, *cherie*. And you are certainly entitled to your bold misadventures on the journey to womanhood. Goodness knows I've experienced one or two myself.''

Despite the veins throbbing at her temples, Nora smiled at her cousin's understatement. "That's just it, Fanny. I'm not at all sure this is a journey I even want to take anymore.''

"Ahh . . .'' Fanny intoned with a nod. "So this misadventure has more to do with a man than all the grog in Key West.''

"How did you know?''

"Some gifted souls read minds, *cherie*. I am blessed with

the ability to read hearts. And since I've guessed the reason for your fall from grace tonight, why don't you fill me in with the details.''

"It's him, Fanny!'' Nora groaned into her pillow. "I can't get him out of my mind, and yet I know I'm not even remotely in his.''

"First, I assume the object of your distress is not the attentive and attainable Mr. Hadley, no?''

"No.''

"Therefore, this heartless creature must be the dashing, but bewildering, Captain Proctor.''

Nora nodded miserably.

Fanny looked into her cousin's eyes and smiled. "A man well worth a little heartache, I must admit.''

"Oh, yes, he is!''

"Tell me what happened, *cherie*. And I will try to figure it out for you.''

Nora poured her heart out to her cousin, beginning with her ill-advised trip to the cupola, Jacob's visit to her classroom, and tonight's disastrous encounter. "He's kissed me twice, Fanny. Yet both times he's acted as though it was the last thing he wanted to do! Well, not when he was doing it exactly, but afterwards. But why would he kiss me when the idea is so repulsive to him?''

Fanny chuckled. "I doubt very much that the idea is repulsive at all, Nora. I've seen the way the captain looks at you. Those dark, mysterious eyes of his hold the heated passion of a paramour. Trust me.''

"Then why does he treat me so callously?''

"That is the puzzle we must solve. And we don't have nearly all the pieces yet. I suspect the captain is a very complex man.'' Fanny touched the tip of Nora's nose with her delicate finger. "But if your heart tells you that it must hold Jacob Proctor, then we must try to find the truth of him.''

Nora began to feel a little better. If Fanny thought Jacob had some feelings for her, then it might very well be so. After all,

Fanny knew all about these things. She squeezed Fanny's hand in gratitude. "What would I do without you, cousin?"

"Probably stay out of trouble, *cherie,*" Fanny said with a frown. "I will help you if I can, Nora, but I must warn you that love is not a game in which the winner is always happy. You should remember that for very serious reasons, your papa doesn't approve of this man. You may eventually get to the bottom of your captain's enigmatic behavior. You may even ensnare him with your charms, my dear, but in the end, your papa might not let you go with him. Are you willing to risk that kind of heartache, Nora? It is, indeed, powerful and wicked."

Fanny's warning held a distressing truth. Nora doubted that her father would ever approve of Jacob. And even worse, what if her father was right? What if Jacob was guilty of luring innocent people to the dangerous reefs? What if he was the one so possessed of greed that he would stop at nothing to amass his fortune? His bold accusations directed at Moony Swain might have been purposely misleading . . . false indictments of greed that should have been directed at the man who said them.

At lunch in the Seabrook household on Thursday, the topic of conversation, much as it must have been in many Key West homes, was Jacob Proctor's auction the next day.

Theo paused between bites of his conch salad. "What percentage has the captain been granted as profit, Your Honor?"

"The judge before me granted him twenty percent of all money taken at auction," Thurston said. "Not that I approve of such a generous amount, you understand."

"That is high," Theo agreed. "I thought wreckers were generally commissioned between ten and fifteen percent."

Thurston sat back and leveled a smile at the young attorney. "You've done some research, Hadley, and you're right. Most wreckers only realize that amount. But Proctor somehow convinced Judge Norwald that he was due a higher amount."

"How did he do that?"

"I read the court records. Apparently Proctor argued that because nearly all the cargoes of the wrecks in question were saved, and passengers were rescued expediently, his cut should be higher than customary." Thurston waggled his fork at Theo. "I don't run my court that way, you understand. I fully *expect* lives and cargoes to be saved. It's the wrecker's job to see the salvage is done properly. I'm sorry to say the judges before me have been an unprincipled lot. Some of them, I suspect, even split profits with the disreputable wreckers. And I believe that what's fair for one is fair for all. But I'm not surprised Proctor had Norwald dancing to his tune."

"And all this explains exactly why you're here and Norwald isn't," Theo said, further embedding himself into Thurston's good graces.

"Correct again, young man. I was sent down here to see what was going on in this court and set it to rights. I can't do much about the conditions in place for tomorrow's auction, but I can damn well see that Proctor doesn't take advantage of a Federal court again."

Theo looked at Nora, obviously gauging her reaction to the conversation. She pretended that she'd dropped her napkin and was retrieving it from the floor. Anything but let Theo see that she was intent on every word being said.

Theo had been overly attentive since escorting her home the previous night. He'd risen early to walk her to school, and even met her at the milliner's shop at ten-thirty to accompany her home. And he'd made his opinions about Jacob Proctor crystal clear. He didn't like the man and didn't think Nora should risk her reputation by being seen in his company.

"I'm not one to gossip, Your Honor," Theo continued after Nora's napkin was back in place, "and it's certainly not my intention to spread ill will in this community, but I think there is something you should know about Proctor."

The soup in Nora's spoon dribbled back to the bowl. Feigning indifference was becoming more difficult. What did Theo know about Jacob? Certainly not that he'd kissed her!

"By all means tell me, Theo," Thurston prompted. "If you have information about Proctor, it's your duty."

"I saw him this morning as I was taking my exercise along the island's southern shoreline."

"And?"

"First you should know he didn't see me. I didn't see him right away, either. I spotted a chestnut horse by the water. Proctor, as it turns out, was down among the coral formations that make up the jetty. Are you familiar with the spot, Judge?"

"Yes, I know it. It's quite rugged at that point. Large masses of jagged coral jut into the ocean. Dangerous for a man to walk upon as I understand."

"Extremely, sir. Nevertheless, Proctor was completely hidden in that outcropping. After a few minutes he appeared at the top of the jetty, climbed back down to his horse, and rode off."

Thurston leaned forward, his food momentarily forgotten. "What do you make of it, Theo?"

"I didn't know what to think, so I pursued the only course of action I could. I waited until he was out of sight, and then I, too, went down into the rocks."

Nora's mother gasped with alarm. "Why, Theo, why would you take such a chance with your arm still in the sling?"

"Thank you for your concern, madam, but I felt I was on the verge of unearthing some important information. I couldn't let my own affliction keep me from discovering it."

Nora couldn't help it. She rolled her eyes to the ceiling. Theo had her parents in the palm of his hand.

"And what did you find?" her father asked.

Theo looked first at Nora to insure she was listening. Then he leaned toward the judge and said, "I found a lantern, sir. One of those large ones usually reserved for ships so they can be seen for quite some distance."

Thurston's eyes shone with interest. "A lantern, you say? Do you interpret that the same way I do, Theo?"

Nora knew what Theo was suggesting, and if he was right,

then it was a damning piece of evidence against Jacob. She
held her breath while he explained his theory.

"I imagine so, Judge. You said the *Morning Dove* was led
astray by false lights on shore. A lantern the size of the one I
saw in the jetty would be plenty large enough to attract a ship
from several miles out."

"And it was well hidden in the rocks?"

Theo nodded. "It's my opinion that only someone who knew
it was there would have come upon it. Or, like myself, someone
who was investigating suspicious activity. If I hadn't followed
in Proctor's footsteps, I'd have never found that lantern."

Thurston visibly brightened at hearing news that corroborated
his theory. "Good work, Theo! Tomorrow I'll have someone
watching that spot every day. If Proctor goes back there, we'll
catch him in the act of rigging his phony lights."

Nora shot a quick glance at her cousin. Fanny shook her
head so that no one but Nora saw her, as if to say, *Not now,
cherie. We'll deal with this later.* And of course Fanny was
right. It wouldn't do for Nora to defend the captain in front of
her family when the evidence clearly was not in his favor.

But what did it mean? If what Theo saw and related to her
father was the truth, and Nora had no reason to believe it wasn't,
then why did Jacob have knowledge of a lantern hidden in the
cave-like jetty? A tremor snaked its way down her spine. Was
it possible that she had allowed herself to become infatuated
with a man who was responsible for the deaths on the *Morning
Dove?* How could her instincts have been so wrong?

Suddenly, Nora had to know. It wasn't enough to listen to
Theo's account of Jacob Proctor's treachery. She had to see
for herself that the lantern existed.

She rose from the table. "Mama, I'm going out for a while.
Would you like to join me?"

"In the heat of the day? Of course not, and you shouldn't,
either." Naturally Sidonia declined the invitation, just as Nora
knew she would. "Go upstairs and nap, Eleanor. It's what
civilized people do here in the afternoons."

"I don't feel like napping, Mama. I feel like going out."

"Then take Fanny with you. I don't want you gadding about alone."

Nora looked to her cousin, and received the anticipated nod of assent. "I'll go, Nora," Fanny said. "I'm lightheaded already, so a little sun shouldn't have any effect." She grinned mischievously at Sidonia. "Isn't that what you always say, Sid?"

Nora's mother waved the comment away with a flip of her hand. "Such silly talk, Fanny, really!"

The two women left the house through the service kitchen and went through the back gate to the street. Then they turned toward the southern shoreline. Fanny took Nora's arm and spoke in a whisper as if she were truly a co-conspirator on a mission of espionage. "We're off on a quest, *oui, cherie?*"

"Absolutely, Fanny. A quest to prove a man's innocence before my family and Theo find him guilty."

CHAPTER NINE

Nora stood at the edge of the water and stared at the jetty. How had Theo managed to do it? How had he avoided all that water and climbed over those rocks with his injured arm and a fastidious nature that should have made the task extremely distasteful? And yet, when he'd related his story at lunch, he hadn't mentioned so much as a split seam in his trousers or a damp shoe sole.

A formidable wave crashed several feet from shore and sent Nora scrambling back to keep her shoes dry. She cast a withering look at Fanny. "Well, I suppose if Theo could do this, so can I."

Fanny shook her head, sending red spirals of hair dancing around her face. "Theo didn't do this, at least not under these conditions. There's no possible way." She nibbled the tip of her finger while surveying their surroundings. "I think this has something to do with the tide. At the harbor I hear sailors talk about loosening the mooring lines or tightening them, depending on the time of day. And I heard one of the Obalu children say he left something by the water's edge and when he went back to get it hours later, it was gone."

Of course. That explained the ease with which Theo was able to cross the jetty. "Fanny, you're a genius. Theo was here this morning when the tide was out. He probably just traipsed around the jetty on dry sand until the last possible moment and then climbed the last few feet to the end of the rocks."

Nora estimated that nearly half the jetty was underwater now, making their exploration much more difficult than Theo's had been. She looked at her cream-colored leather shoes, the ones she'd just purchased in Richmond before they'd left home. She considered the damage salt water would do to her gown. The hemline was already stiffening from just the sea spray. "I suppose the sensible thing to do is forget the whole idea," she said.

Fanny shrugged. "*Oui,* I suppose so. But that's not what we're going to do, is it, *cherie?*"

Nora bit her lower lip to trap a giggle. "Are you thinking what I'm thinking, Fanny?"

Green eyes twinkled under carrot-colored hair with their usual mischief. "*Mon Dieu,* Nora. Poor Sid would suffer from the vapors if she even *suspected* that you and I would have the same thought. But, alas, if you're thinking of the best, and only, way to save your garments from the ravages of salt water, then I'm afraid we are."

Nora scanned the shoreline as far as she could see in both directions. "There's no one around, Fanny. And it is such a warm day. . ."

Both women plopped down in the sand and took off their shoes. Then they removed their gowns and stepped around mounds of fine muslin and silk. Wearing just her camisole and bloomers, Nora reveled in the feel of the sun on her skin, the soft crunch of sand and crushed limestone on the soles of her feet. She twirled to the beat of a melody in her head. "Doesn't it feel heavenly?"

Fanny stretched her arms out, turned her face into the breeze, and sighed with the contentment of pure freedom. "It makes you wonder why we put up with all those silly clothes in the first place." Indicating her undergarments with a quick glance down her plump-in-the-right-places body, she said, "The pieces we have on now are all we really need. All the important things are covered."

Nora laughed, took her hand, and they waded into the surf toward the jetty. Nora squealed when the water reached her knees and soaked the ruffles of her pantalettes. "It's much colder than I thought it would be," she said.

"I know, *cherie,* but it is February. Think how the weather is in Richmond this time of year, and it makes the ocean feel much warmer."

With gasps and shivers and protestations masked with laughter, the ladies waded into water that reached their chests and waves that cascaded over their shoulders. With her toe, Nora tested the depth beyond her current position. "It gets deeper here," she said. "We'll have to climb up on the jetty now. I can't swim, remember?"

The rough coral rock punished the soles of their feet, but they managed to reach the top of the jetty. Then, moving like crabs, they approached the very edge where coral jutted out over the sea. The surface of the rocks provided grooves for their fingers, enabling both women to hold on to the jetty while lowering themselves into the water.

Finding a level plateau of more coral, they stood in waist-high water and explored the cave-like underside of the jetty. Waves crashed on the rocks on either side of their position, but inside the cave it was calmer. "It's rather pretty in a primitive way, don't you think?" Nora said, her voice hollow in accompaniment to the amplified dripping of water.

"Definitely, *cherie.* It's Key West's answer to the Blue Grotto."

"I doubt that, Fanny, but it's a nice thought." Nora scanned the interior of their coral cavern, wishing more sunlight penetrated the solid walls. But in moments she spied the glimmer of brass and glass she was searching for, and she grabbed Fanny's arm. A feeling of utter desolation settled on her shoulders and was released in a long sigh. She had truly hoped to prove Theo wrong. Now it didn't appear that was going to happen. "Look, there it is—the lantern Theo spoke of."

Clinging to the interior wall, they edged over the few feet to where the lantern hung from a hook at the highest point in the cave. Theo's description had been accurate. It was a large marine lamp with heavy glass around three sides. When lit, it would be visible from several miles out to sea, and would certainly represent a beacon of safety to a floundering ship.

Fanny examined the lantern as closely as Nora did. She expressed a similar dismay by putting her fingers to her lips and muttering, "Oh, my."

At that moment Nora was sorry she'd embarked on this mission to convince herself of Jacob's innocence. "Fanny, I wanted Theo to be wrong," she said. "But you know what this looks like."

Fanny moved around the lantern, studying it closely, and managed a thin smile. "What it *looks like, cherie,* is a lantern hung from a nail in a cavern. . . nothing more. We mustn't jump to conclusions."

There was a brief rekindling of hope, meager but persistent, as Nora waded after her cousin. "That's right," she said. "We don't know all the facts."

Her own words didn't convince her, however, because the facts, as they were, were disturbingly clear. The lantern had obviously been secreted in this location by someone who did not want it discovered. And while it was hidden from observers on land, it was clearly visible to sea voyagers. And Jacob Proctor had visited this cavern only that morning. Anyone with the ability to reason could only conclude that Theo truly had discovered the false light that had attracted the *Morning Dove,* and the man responsible for the treacherous deed.

With mounting frustration, Nora slapped at the water under the lantern, sending spray onto the walls of the cave. "Oh, Fanny," she moaned. "I don't want to believe it, but I must. It was Jacob. . ."

Her flow of words halted when a pungent odor made her wrinkle her nose in offense. She sniffed her fingers. She had a pretty good idea what substance was mixed in with the water, but she wanted to know if her cousin could identify it as well. Holding her hand out to Fanny, she asked, "What is that smell?"

Fanny sniffed and pulled her face back. "Kerosene."

"Exactly. The lantern must be leaking." She began a thorough search for the source of the leak, and soon found a rend in the brass fuel well. Because of the bent, misshapen metal, it looked as if the damage had been deliberately inflicted by a blade about the size of a hatchet. She felt along the jagged tear, and then rubbed her forefinger against her thumb. They were slick with oil. She shook the lantern and found that it was nearly empty of fuel.

Hope flickered anew and was fanned to life. "Fanny, do you know what this means? Someone has rendered this lantern useless through an obvious act of vandalism."

"Yes, I see, *cherie*. Do you think it was Theo?"

"Really, Fanny, do you? Can you imagine our Mr. Hadley sporting about an ax in the waistband of his trousers and actually delivering the mortal wound to this lantern? With only one good arm?"

Fanny hooted with laughter. "If our Mr. Hadley carried an ax in his trousers, I fear he would inflict damage on a far more serious instrument than a lantern!"

Nora laughed with her until they both fell against the cavern walls for support. Finally, Nora stated the conclusion that restored her previous opinion of her captain. "That's what Jacob was doing here this morning," she said. "He's the one who damaged the lantern so it couldn't be used in the future to attract ships. Thank goodness we came here before the tide went out, Fanny, or the kerosene would have been washed away. We might never have examined the fuel well."

Fanny hugged her cousin. "I think you're right, *cherie*. The hero who pulled you from the water of Key West harbor can remain your hero after all."

The women left the cave and climbed back on top of the

jetty to make their way to shore. It had been a worthwhile endeavor after all.

Jacob Proctor was grateful he possessed one of only fourteen horses on the island of Key West. Eight of them were privately owned animals like Jacob's, and six were kept by the city to pull the occasional carriage or delivery wagon. All the horses shared the same livery, located a few blocks off Duval Street, and that was where Jacob Proctor went for the second time in one day.

After saddling the sleek chestnut Arabian mare once more, Jacob stroked his hand down her gleaming burgundy mane. "So, Rasha, two runs in the same day. It's quite a treat for you, girl." He swung into the saddle and accepted the reins from the stable boy. "I think I need this ride more than you do," he said to the anxious horse. "I've had my fill of crates and barrels and preparations for the auction. I think a good run by the sea will do us both good."

Besides, he thought as he guided the animal out of the livery yard, it would be an added bonus to catch old Swain cursing his bad luck as he came over the jetty with a defective fuel well in his hand.

Rasha was perfectly suited to the climate of Key West, which was why Jacob had chosen her five years ago from among his father's private stock of horses. Hot-blooded Arabians were bred to endure heat, and in fact thrived in it.

He had to pull back on the reins to keep her from breaking into a gallop despite the cloying humidity that was the only threat to the horse's well-being. "Where's all that horse sense you're supposed to have, Rasha?" he said, keeping the mare at a steady trot. "You should have learned to pace yourself in this climate by now."

Once they escaped the confines of buildings and city streets and rode along a line of sweeping palms, both rider and animal exhilarated in the anticipation of open space and salt air. Ducking his head, Jacob broke through the palms, feeling the brush of fronds on his back. Then they were free. Only sand and crushed shells separated them from the water.

They were free, but they were not alone. Jacob pulled hard on the reins and brought the horse to a sudden stop. He squinted through slanting rays of a sun setting at his back to identify two figures clambering across the jetty. His first instinct was to assume they were island children, since their bodies were slim and their clothing scanty. Besides, only Bahamian youngsters with the skills of mountain goats and the hard-soled feet of native islanders would cross the rough surface of the jetty. . . or someone with the devious motives of Moony Swain.

That was why he shook his head and blinked hard to convince himself that the hardy souls on the jetty could not possibly be who they appeared to be. . . no, it was inconceivable. Yet one had hair the color of red hibiscus blossoms and the other's shone with the ebony of a crow's wing. And now that he could see better, their clothing, what little there was of it, reflected the sun as only fine bleached cotton could.

Jacob sat forward on his horse, his elbow on the saddle horn, and watched the scene at the jetty with mounting interest and increasing certainty. It was painfully obvious that the women were not comfortable in their attempt to cross the punishing rocks. At intervals they shook their hands and feet as if those appendages were in contact with hot coals. . . or the jagged edges of hard coral.

"Well, Miss Seabrook and Mademoiselle Cosette," Jacob whispered to no one but the disinterested horse. "What would His Honor say if he saw you now? And what in God's name are you doing climbing the jetty?"

Surely they hadn't discovered Moony's lantern during the course of their little adventure. Surely they hadn't ventured into the cavern. No, of course not. Nora Seabrook couldn't even swim, and she would never risk her life by doing something so foolhardy. And yet if she did make it to the cave, the water wouldn't be over her head even at high tide.

There was only one thing to do. He had to investigate this situation more thoroughly. If the women had discovered

Moony's lantern, then they probably would tell the judge, and all hell would break loose on the island. There would be writs and rules and more bothersome statutes. A damned bit of bad luck considering Jacob had taken care of this particular problem himself only that morning.

He spurred Rasha to the water where the women were now soaking their smarting feet and hands. One question occurred to him as he approached them. If the lantern hadn't been an issue, would he have found a reason to confront the women anyway? Never was a question more difficult to answer. Was there ever a more tempting, if not forbidden, sight as the two sea nymphs who laughed in the waves in full view of his feasting eyes? But the fact remained that Nora Seabrook was beyond his grasp and intentions. She was, after all, a good woman and therefore had no place in his future. And yet, despite his efforts, he couldn't stay away from her.

Fanny was always fun. Even with the soles of their feet and pads of their hands stinging from the coral rock, Nora splashed her cousin and received as good as she gave in the war of the water. Waves rolled in more gently now in a calm afternoon breeze, and neither lady had the slightest inclination to return to the shore and put her clothes back on.

Nora was just about to comment that it was a welcome luxury to be able to bathe in the ocean in such total freedom without worrying about proper decorum and dress. She was just about to suggest to Fanny that they come back often, when a rippling snort from the shore trapped the words in her throat.

She half stood and whirled around in the water, but lost her balance and fell to her backside in the surf. A wave crested against the back of her head and rolled over her shoulders, sending sea spray into her mouth, which was wide-open in shock. Not ten yards away, a huge chestnut horse pawed pieces of shells with its front hoof and shook its large head in the salty wind. And in its saddle sat Jacob Proctor.

Resisting her first instinct to squeal, stand, and run for her clothes, Nora instead crouched lower into the water. She knew, as she was certain Jacob did, that frilly cotton did an extremely inadequate job of hiding those body parts that should only be exposed in one's bath. Crossing her arms over her chest, Nora finally squawked, "Captain, how long have you been here?"

He smiled a slow, lazy grin of bold delight, which had an immediate effect of raising the water temperature everywhere the sea touched Nora's skin.

"Long enough to see your escapade on the jetty," he said, looking from Nora to Fanny, who sat on her knees casually threading water through her fingers. "You are certainly an adventurous pair."

"Adventurous is one way of putting it, Captain," Fanny said with a bright chuckle. "Addle-brained might be another. A woman should know better than to climb those rocks without gloves and brogans."

"True enough. So why did you do it?"

Fanny looked to her cousin. There was an unmistakable glimmer of devilment in her eyes that made Nora hold her breath in anticipation of her answer. "My dear cousin was on a quest, weren't you, *cherie?*" she said.

"A quest? How silly, Fanny," Nora said with forced gaiety. "It was nothing so important as that."

Jacob pulled his knee onto the saddle and grasped the pummel with both hands. His gaze washed over Nora as completely as the waves that cascaded over her shoulders. "So what were you hoping to find, Nora?"

The last thing she wanted Jacob Proctor to know was that she was so interested in his affairs that she would give up an afternoon to pursue them. Not this man whose attentions to her changed from steam to ice in a moment's passing. Theo's story and her search for the lantern would remain her secret, so long as Fanny kept her counsel. Nora glared at her cousin, imparting a definite warning. "Sea life, Captain," she said. "Nothing more. I have a scholarly interest in my new environment that will only be satisfied by first-hand observation."

Again that confident smile that did more to scorch Nora's

cheeks than the blazing sun. "I see. And what sea items did you find on. . . or around the jetty? You must have encountered any number of small crustaceans or water beetles. . . or other, large things."

The realization that she might have been crawling among insects was far from pleasing, but Nora kept up her pretense and took it a step farther. "Oh, I did. It was quite interesting. How is it that you know so much about what can be found around the jetty, Captain? Do you spend a lot of time here?"

A slight knitting of his brows, which would only be noticeable to one who had memorized every feature of his face in fantasies and dreams, hinted of an alert wariness. Most certainly he was connected with the jetty's secrets. But did he suspect that Nora was as well?

"Only when necessary," he said. "Unlike you, I don't come to the jetty for pleasure . . ."

"Fiddlesticks," Fanny interrupted. "This conversation is getting us nowhere. I can't tell which one of you is *le chat* and which is *la souris.*"

Even with her limited knowledge of French, Nora understood Fanny's reference and simmered with mortification. She just hoped Jacob couldn't identify the words *cat* and *mouse.*

It didn't really matter, because their dialogue came to an abrupt end when Fanny stood up in the water and walked toward shore. Her undergarments clung to her body despite her efforts to pull the fabric away from her skin. "Come along, Nora," she said with as much nonchalance as if she were strolling fully clothed along a public thoroughfare. "We found what we came for, and we've been gone so long Sid will have half the employees of the Federal court out looking for us. . . as well as a certain pesky houseguest I needn't mention by name."

To his credit, Jacob averted his gaze from Fanny's immodest journey to shore, and pretended interest in a patch of whispering sea oats near the water's edge. Perhaps he did have manners after all. Since Theo probably would be searching for them and she could hardly ignore Fanny's warning, Nora raised herself until water rippled at her chest. "My cousin is right, Captain," she said. "If you would be so considerate as to ride away now, I could retrieve my clothing without embarrassment."

He turned his full attention on her, and she felt his warm regard from the top of her head to where the water caressed her breasts. All at once the rippling current touching her camisole created a pleasurable and unexpected friction against her nipples. She refrained from retreating further into her watery cloak. She wasn't ready to sacrifice the unfamiliar yet exciting sensation. And she certainly couldn't get out of the water and risk telltale exposure to the captain's gaze. So Nora sat right where she was.

Still, Jacob refused to look away. In fact, his eyes glittered with challenging intensity. "You present me with a difficult decision, Nora. Consideration for your sensibilities versus gratification for my fantasies. An impossible choice for any red-blooded male. But since I wouldn't want to be responsible for your skin wrinkling, and since I suspect you might have a fascinating story to tell at the judge's dinner table tonight, I will leave you and your cousin alone."

She breathed a deep sigh, which she suspected was the reason a grin curled his full lips. "Thank you, Jacob."

He turned his horse and started away from the shore, but Nora called after him. "Captain, you're wrong. I don't have a story to tell the judge tonight. This afternoon's activities were meant only to satisfy my own curiosity."

He stopped and brought his horse around toward her. "Is that so?"

"Yes, and I am quite satisfied with my findings."

Laughing to himself, Jacob rode to the line of palms. When the trees had swallowed up his view of the ladies on shore, he slowed Rasha's gait to a trot. *Chat* and *souris,* indeed! He enjoyed every moment he spent with Nora Seabrook, and she was beginning to warm his blood as surely as the tropical climate of Key West warmed his skin.

"But this cat-and-mouse business is not the game for you, Jacob Proctor," he admonished himself. "Get this bloody auction over with so Monday morning you can put half an ocean between you and this woman who can only suffer ill in your hands."

CHAPTER TEN

On Friday morning, the seven students in the Island School for Reading had just learned the configuration and sound of the letter H. Examples were given listlessly. *Harbor, hoop, hook, house* . . .

Listening to lackluster responses, Nora leaned against her desk and regarded her students with a frustrated stare. "What is wrong with everyone today?" she asked. "When we get to I, it will be a miracle if I get one example from each of you."

As usual, Felix Obalu spoke for his timid classmates. "But Miss Nora, can't you hear it? Why don't you just once look out the window?"

If he only knew how pointless his questions were. She had heard the commotion, all right, and she had stolen peeks at the activity on the harbor across Duval Street. And though she had a strong motive for remaining aloof from the business at Proctor's Warehouse and Salvage, and its enigmatic owner, she was having a difficult time ignoring it all.

Just that morning she had told herself that she would not succumb to the auction frenzy that had taken over the island. She certainly didn't need to embroil herself in the goings-on of a man who treated her with a cocky disdain that often bordered on outright rudeness.

But auction fever was all around her. Even her mother and Fanny had been up with the sun and talking of nothing but the impending sale. By six-thirty Sidonia had had several outfits spread upon her bed, and she'd been in a quandary as to which one to choose. "You must help me decide, Eleanor," she'd moaned. "Everyone will be there this morning. Mrs. Whiting, Mrs. MacDougal, Mrs. Warden . . . I do so want to fit in."

Nora had given the ensembles a cursory glance and had picked a pale green linen skirt and vest. "You can't go wrong with that one, Mama. It's perfect."

Naturally, it was the advice her mother needed to choose the royal blue silk. Anyway, it had left Nora free to think about her lesson plans for that morning. She'd escaped her mother's bedroom with a sigh of relief.

So here she was in the blessed sanctuary that was her class-room, and still she was besieged by auction mania. She answered her most enterprising and intelligent student with impatience. "Yes, Felix, of course I am aware of what is going on outside, but I believe it is more important to stay focused on what is going on in this room. Now please give me another example of the H sound."

"I have one. A perfect example."

All heads turned toward the entrance Mr. McTaggart had just stepped through. It was the first time the milliner had entered their domain, and it was certainly the first time Nora had ever seen a grin alter the normally staid expression on his face.

"Excuse me?" she said.

"H. I have an H word. Hat! And I hope to sell many of them this morning." He crossed to the window and stuck his head out. "What a glorious sun we have this morning. It's positively flooding the harbor with head-pounding heat and eye-squinting glare. Headwear is an absolute necessity."

He rubbed his hands together as if stacks of gold coins had just passed through them. "I love auction days, Miss Seabrook, especially sunny ones when our visitors arrive hatless.'' His countenance brightened with a germinating scheme. "In fact, I have a wonderful idea for the children who will be volunteering this morning. I have dozens of moderately priced straw bonnets, and perhaps, for a small monetary reward, the youngsters could pass among the crowd offering them for sale.''

The children, who just moments before had been disinterested and sluggish, did everything but stand on their heads to get the milliner's attention.

"Me, me . . . choose me!''

"I'll do it. I'll sell hats!''

Mr. McTaggart clapped with glee. "Perfect. You all can!''

Nora could no longer pretend she was immune to the enthusiasm infecting her students. "I give up,'' she said, laughing. "It's eight-thirty. I suppose it would be all right if we stopped early today.''

Felix Obalu beamed. Suggesting he could earn a few pennies by selling hats was like setting a bowl of honey in front of a hungry bear. "Good for you, Miss Nora,'' he said. "You're all right with me.''

She smiled at him. "I'm so happy to hear that, Felix. It has been my goal all along to win your approval.''

With a charming display of white teeth in a cocoa-brown face, Felix bounded up from his seat and followed Mr. McTaggart from the classroom. In the blink of an eye, the other students had followed. Nora collected their supplies and stored them on one of the shelves donated by Jacob Proctor. Then she went to the window and gave in to the temptation to see for herself what all the excitement was about.

It was a glorious sight, and in fact, reminded Nora of the previous summer just after her twenty-first birthday. Her mother and father had allowed her to accompany them to a garden party at the governor's mansion in honor of Mr. Jefferson Davis. That afternoon the guest list had been representative of the finest families in Virginia.

The "guest list'' at Jacob's auction this morning was every bit as impressive, though slightly more varied. The locals, many

of whom Nora recognized, ambled about the harbor in their
best finery, which had probably been purchased at a previous
auction. In Key West, being witnessed by one's neighbors was
as important as witnessing the activities.

There were at least a hundred people Nora did not recognize.
Not surprising since ships had been bringing potential bidders
from all parts of the Eastern and Gulf Coasts for several days.
Men in broadcloth suits and silk top hats strolled arm in arm
with ladies in satin and brocade. Merchants and more serious-
minded procurers had given up their jackets and vests on this
warm day, and pored through bins and barrels with their shirt
sleeves rolled up past their elbows.

Everyone who converged in the courtyard of Proctor's Warehouse and Salvage had one thing in common. They were all
there to see what treasures had been pulled from the sea over
the last few months and what they would have to pay to own
them. And at the end of the auction, Jacob Proctor was entitled
to keep twenty cents of every dollar collected . . . which might
amount to a very handsome sum.

Nora glanced at the clock on her classroom wall. It was
eight-forty. She just had time to investigate a few of the barrels
herself before the auction started, and she had finally admitted
to herself that it was exactly what she wanted to do. Grabbing
her paper and pencil, certain that what was about to occur on
this mile-wide island was manna for a writer's journal, she left
the milliner's shop.

"Eleanor, Eleanor! Come over here!"

Nora had just begun rummaging through the contents of a
barrel of porcelain when she heard her mother's voice. Though
she was much more interested in the Spode china cups and
saucers nestled within dusty straw, she could hardly pretend to
ignore such a strident call.

She looked to her left, where a large banyan tree provided
shade at the edge of the courtyard, and saw her mother sitting
on a wicker lawn chair with Mrs. Whiting and Mrs. Warden.

Wicker being light and easy to carry, the women had obviously decided they could manage the chairs, a small table, and an entire Japanese tea service.

Nora walked over, greeted her mother and the ladies, and refused a cup of tea.

"Oh, dear, Eleanor," Sidonia said. "How shortsighted of me not to bring you something to sit on." She craned her neck to search the shaded area as carefully as she could without standing up, and sighed in disappointment. Apparently, she'd hoped a chair would suddenly appear out of nowhere, and was distressed when it didn't.

"Don't bother yourself, Mama," Nora said. "I'm much too excited to sit anyway. I really just want to see the rest of the items up for sale."

"Good heavens, Eleanor, you're just like Fanny, always traipsing off somewhere. Flitting about from barrel to bin like a bee in a rose garden."

At the mention of Fanny's name, Nora saw an opportunity for escape. "Maybe I should go find her, Mama . . . just to see if she's all right."

"All right? Why wouldn't she be, for heaven's sake? She's Fanny." Sidonia patted the trunk of the tree. "Here, Eleanor, at least come out of the sun. It was dreadful enough to see such pink in your cheeks when you came home yesterday, and you'll only make it worse if you stay out in the heat."

Reluctantly Nora obeyed, though her eyes wandered to take in all the varied and interesting merchandise displayed in and around the warehouse. But was it just the merchandise she was looking for? If so, then why did her gaze wander from the groups of people milling around and finally through the windows and doors to the darker, more private areas of the warehouse? She had a burning desire to know . . . where was the man responsible for this carnival atmosphere?

"Eleanor, stop fidgeting," her mother warned. "You've kicked my chair twice."

"Sorry, Mama. I just think I should try to find Fanny. She hasn't come back in all this time . . ."

"Well, go, then, you silly girl! But stay away from that horrible Captain Proctor person."

Nora's heart leapt at the mention of Jacob's name, and she grabbed her mother's shoulder. "Captain Proctor? Do you see him, Mama?"

Sidonia jumped, both at the fierceness of her daughter's grip and the tone of her voice. "Well, of course I see him, Eleanor. Why do you think I'm warning you? He's over by the docks speaking with none other than Dillard Hyde and my own wayward cousin. Oh, my, if Thurston could see that . . ."

Nora had already left the circle of women, but she called back over her shoulder, "Thank you, Mama. I'll just have a look at the items for bid."

"Oh, and Eleanor, do watch for our dear Mr. Hadley. The last I saw him, he was going to that . . . that little *teaching dalliance* of yours. I wouldn't want you to miss him."

Mama, I don't think it's possible for me to ever miss *Theo Hadley!* Knowing her mother was watching, Nora headed straight for a display of cooking oils and spices. It was conveniently located in the middle of the courtyard with a clear view to the docks. Whatever Fanny was saying made both men laugh. Oh, dear whatever *was* Fanny saying?

Suddenly, Nora's view of the docks was obliterated by a rush of humanity closing in around her. People who had occupied the entire area of the courtyard and the interior of the warehouse came together en masse and focused their attention on the front of the building, where Willy Turpin was checking the stability of an enormous wooden hogshead cask upended on the ground.

A woman beside Nora hushed her children and admonished them to behave. Two men in front of her in workingmen's clothes smoked cigars and spoke rapidly in Spanish. A middle-aged man in elegant attire was jostled into Nora from behind, and begged her pardon in a Southern accent unlike any she'd ever heard before. It was a mixture of Fanny's educated French and the deepest, most honey-toned Dixie. New Orleans, she supposed. He tipped his top hat in apology. This auction had certainly drawn from all elements of society.

A loud groan from the hogshead drew her attention to the front once more. It had come from a heavyset man in a wide planter's hat and bright red vest who had climbed onto the barrel with the assistance of three other men. He held a polished gavel in one hand and a sheaf of papers nailed to a board in the other. When he raised the gavel in the air, a hush settled over the crowd.

"Ladies and gentlemen," he began in a high-pitched voice that carried to the farthest corners of the crowd. "On this twenty-second day of February, the year of Our Lord eighteen hundred and fifty-eight, let the auction of salvaged goods belonging to Jacob Proctor begin."

A roar rose in the crowd reminiscent of Independence Day celebrations in Richmond. A tingle of excitement raced down Nora's spine. If there was such a thing as auction fever, she was catching it.

She released her anticipation in a burst of laughter when she spied Felix Obalu weaving among the throng holding his precious straw bonnets above his head. "A dollar a bonnet," he called out, until he was told to keep quiet by a stern-looking lady who wiggled her fan at him. Felix might have paid her some mind if he hadn't seen a silver coin glinting in the air several feet away. The lady's fan was no competition, and he scampered away, hats waving.

"Now, folks," the man said from the barrel, "we'll have this auction under way in one minute, but first there are certain rules and regulations you must understand if you expect to ever attend one of these affairs again." He stopped, and a Spanish interpreter repeated what he'd said.

"These items will be sold in bulk lots or individually. We'll tell you how before we call for the first bid, so listen up. Ignorance of the proceedings is no excuse for mistakes. And if a mistake is made it'll be yours, because I don't make any."

Nervous laughter buzzed in the air. The interpreter struggled to keep up with the fast-talking auctioneer.

"Everything is sold 'as is, where is,' which means no guarantee of any kind is either implied or expressed. If it looks like a gewgaw and it turns out to be a gimcrack, well, you still bought it." The auctioneer leveled a no-nonsense glare that encompassed everyone within hearing. "Basically, ladies and gentlemen, if you're the high bidder, you pay for it, and then you take it away. I don't much care if you like it or not. This time tomorrow we expect all this merchandise to be gone."

He pounded hard on the board holding his papers. "Any questions? Good. You all got your bidding paddles? Let this auction begin."

Looking down at Willy Turpin, he said, "My good man, would you show the first item up for bid."

Willy raised a saddle in the air.

"A fine English saddle, my friends. Hand-tooled leather from Harcourt and Stone, London Saddlery. Who'll give me a five-dollar bid?"

The auction was under way.

Before an hour had passed, Nora had seen bidders walk away with wine from Spain, mahogany from Brazil, silk and woven material from China and India, porcelain from France, silver and brass from Morocco, spices from Caribbean islands, as well as dozens of bales of Mississippi cotton and bundles of Virginia tobacco.

Comments from the crowd were often more interesting than the items being sold. When several bolts of identical brocade were sold to the dressmaker, one woman commented that every little girl in Key West would be wearing dresses with gold roses, and every one would be water-stained! When an elderly woman from the island bought a huge cast-iron fire bell, her neighbor commented that now she'd have to endure this new method of bringing an errant husband home to supper.

Nearly everyone bought something. Sidonia bought a set of crystal decanters, "with chips so small no one would notice." Mrs. Whiting bought a sterling silver platter, "with four hall-marks," she was only too eager to point out. And Nora purchased a bundle of playbills that had traveled all the way from New York City. The pages were a little wrinkled, but the words were legible, and she hoped her students might soon be able to read about the details of theatrical productions.

And Jacob Proctor was certain to walk away from it all a much wealthier man.

"Having a good time, Nora?"

It was uncanny. His name had just popped into her head, and now his voice vibrated soft and low in her ear. She clutched the stack of playbills to her chest and spun around. "Oh, hello, Captain," she said, grateful her voice didn't betray her emotions. It was the first she'd seen him since he'd been talking with Dillard Hyde and Fanny at the docks. "It's been an educational experience to be sure."

The corner of his mouth quirked up in a cockeyed grin. "Tell me something, Nora. Does everything you do have to come packaged as 'an educational experience'? Don't you ever do anything for the sheer fun of it?"

A fine question coming from the often-brooding captain! "Certainly I do, Jacob," she answered. "I went to a hanging, didn't I?"

He laughed, and the sound sent little tingles as far south as her toes. Taking her elbow, he leaned close. A strand of his sun-bleached hair brushed her cheek. "That's right, you did, though I might have offered other examples that, as I recall, were far more enjoyable."

He was the most confounding man. His lips touched her hair. His breath tickled her neck. He was so near and hinting at moments that were among the most memorable of Nora's life. Stolen minutes of passion that she would recall forever, partly because he'd heartlessly tried to snuff them out in an instant with a cross word or cool rebuff. Why did he taunt her with those images now? She stepped back. "I have no idea what you're talking about, Jacob," she said. "Besides, you asked me about the auction."

"I did?"

"Yes. You asked what I thought of it."

"I did?"

Maybe he didn't. She couldn't remember. "Why don't you

tell me what you thought of it," she said. "Was it successful? Would you do it again? Does it make the race to the wrecks and the retrieval of salvage worth all the danger?"

She wasn't sure if the intense look in his eyes was his way of analyzing her questions or her face. His gaze moved from her eyes to her lips and back again.

"Yes. Yes. Yes," he said. "What are you doing, Nora? Writing a book?"

She would never admit that she thought his answers worthy of a journal entry. "Of course not. I'm just curious, that's all."

Then he did the oddest thing. He led her away from the mob toward the warehouse. Once inside, he took her to a quiet, dark alcove under the stairs. The noise of the crowd and the chant of the auctioneer were only a low drone of unintelligible sounds. The large room was almost vacant now. There were no more stacks of crates or barrels . . . nothing to stop a breeze from whispering under the ceiling beams and fanning Nora's face. It sent a strand of black hair against her cheek. Jacob caught it between his thumb and finger and tucked it behind her ear. He reached for her playbills and set them on the floor.

"What are you doing?" she asked. "Why did you bring me in here?"

"Go out with me tonight, Nora," he said. "Have dinner with me. Go for a walk with me, and we'll watch the moon rise together."

No, Nora, don't be taken in by yet another mysterious side to this man who has more facets than a prism. This is Jacob Proctor, and he is probably inviting you just so he can change his mind a moment from now and withdraw his invitation.

He took her hands and held them to his chest. "I want to be with you tonight. I'm going away on Monday, Nora . . ."

Ignore that little stab to your heart. Of course he's going away. He's a ship captain, after all. He deals in selling and trading. "But you'll be back, won't you?"

"Yes. But I'm not sure when. Say you'll have dinner with me. We'll go to Bill Barley's. That's public enough, isn't it?"

Cynthia Thomason

She pretended a worldliness she didn't feel and shrugged off his concern. "I'm not worried about that . . ."

"Yes, you are, but we'll be in full view of half the population of Key West and nearly all its visitors. You'll be perfectly safe."

Even in the shadows he could see the uncertainty in her eyes. He wasn't surprised by it. How could a man like Jacob Proctor talk of safety to a woman like Nora Seabrook? She would never be safe with him, not as long as his feelings for her were as turbulent as the tides. Even his motives for asking her to be with him churned inside him like a whirlpool with no definitive beginning or end.

Yes, he desired her, but he could never have her. He should never have asked her to go with him tonight. It was a reckless thing to do, thoughtless and unfair. The actions of a man who knew the consequences and still tossed them aside to satisfy a selfish yearning.

What had he been thinking? That if he had her to himself just once he could rid his soul of her for good? Was he hoping to satisfy his longing for something he could not, and should not, want? Is that why he had pulled her away from the crowd outside . . . to beg her if he had to? Jacob Proctor, you are guilty of crimes against this woman you haven't even committed yet and already you are rationalizing them.

And still the words came out of his mouth again. "Let me take you out tonight, Nora." A fool's brain is no match for the thundering of his fool's heart.

She smiled up at him, a strange, almost reluctant lifting of her lips. Her eyes were an aquamarine magnet for his own. "I . . . I can't go to dinner with you, Jacob."

Disappointment numbed him like a shower of ice, and yet, in a strange way, it freed him. He didn't have to face the devil of his conscience and argue it down. He released her hands. "I understand. Your father wouldn't approve."

"No, he wouldn't, but that has practically nothing to do with my answer. My parents are having a dinner party. They've invited Dillard Hyde and a few of the staff from the court. I must be there. You see, don't you?"

"Yes, of course I do. It's quite all right. Perhaps we can try for another time, when I return."

The grin that flashed up at him now was coquettish in its charm, and definitely un-Nora-like. It was all Jacob could do not to smother it with his own lips. "I must say you're taking this far too well for my pride," she said.

He would have answered her, but a call from the entrance stopped him.

"Nora, Nora! Are you in here?"

That infernal Hadley again! Did the man carry one of Nora's handkerchiefs in his pocket so whenever he was on the hunt he could get a fresh dose of her scent? Jacob hardly needed to worry about his own intentions toward her when the woman had her personal attaché close by every moment of the day.

Resigned to the inevitable, Jacob walked out of the shadows of the staircase to hail the dogged Mr. Hadley. "She's over . . ."

With a force he never would have thought possible from the petite Miss Seabrook, he was hauled back into the darkness. "Be quiet!" she hissed at him. "Not a word!"

She pulled him taut against her side, and he stood there like a scolded youngster—though his reaction to her nearness was in every way adult. "Now I see why you're the teacher," he mumbled into her ear.

"Nora? I say, one last time, are you here?"

The bloodhound's footsteps echoed in the empty room, approached the stairs, and then receded.

Nora stood perfectly still for moments after the footsteps disappeared altogether. Jacob, so close to her he could feel the rise of her breast against his ribs, allowed her to hold him a willing captive.

When she estimated it was safe, she took a step back and pivoted him around until he faced her. The light was dim, but even if they had been in a tunnel three hundred feet under the sea, he still would have seen the blue fire in her eyes. Her hands dropped to her sides and balled into fists that flexed with threatening intensity. "How dare you," she spat out at him.

He'd seen the sweet and gentle Nora, the inquisitive, self-assured one, the curious, softhearted benefactor of the island children. But he'd never seen the fighter she had become before his eyes. And she was stunning. He didn't know what he'd done, but seeing the flush on her cheeks and the heaving of her breasts, he wasn't sorry he'd done it. He held his palms up to her in a defensive gesture. "May I ask what this is about?"

"I am sick and tired of you pawning me off, Captain! I will not allow you to hand me to another person as if I were a piece of your precious merchandise and you've just found an appropriate buyer! I will decide when I leave and with whom I go, not you!"

His heart threatened to leap out of his chest. She didn't give two figs for Hadley! But he had to get out of this sticky dilemma, or she might very well raise that white-knuckled fist after all. "Nora, honestly I thought I was helping you cope with a difficult situation. You had just turned down my invitation to dinner, and frankly, I thought old Hadley came along at an opportune moment."

"Well, don't think on my account, Captain. I'm capable of doing it for myself. And as for that dinner invitation, yes, I did decline, but I believe your proposal for this evening was twofold, was it not?"

Twofold? His mind raced back to grasp his exact words. Dinner? Walk with me and watch the moon rise. "Yes, I guess it was."

"May I respond to the second part, then?"

"Please."

"I accept your invitation to walk with you this evening. You may say where."

She wasn't putting him off. "At the end of Southard Street," he heard himself say. "At the narrow lane that leads to a line of palm trees. It's not far from the jetty."

She nodded. "Shall we say ten o'clock?"

"But your dinner party . . ."

She sauntered past him and stepped into the bright light. "I'm sure I will have eaten my fill by then, Captain."

CHAPTER ELEVEN

Dinner was served at the Seabrook house at seven-thirty. Sidonia had tried desperately to find a rib roast large enough to serve ten, and when one was not available anywhere on the island, she'd had to settle for a trio of capons. A poor substitute, she'd moaned, but at least she'd managed to procure mushrooms, paprika, and heavy cream. With these she instructed Portia to concoct a pretty fair chicken Parisienne. For some reason, maybe it was the amount of white wine in the sauce and in everyone's glass, none of the guests seemed to mind that the capons had not one ounce of beefy flesh on their bones.

Least bothered of all was Fanny. She'd accomplished a quick maneuvering of the place cards before dinner, a sleight of hand noticed only by Nora. It had put her next to Dillard Hyde. What an odd combination, Nora thought during dinner as her gaze passed between the reed-thin Mr. Hyde and the voluptuous Fanny. And yet everything Dillard said sent her cousin into fits of laughter.

At one point, when Theo stopped chattering like a magpie in Nora's ear, she caught her cousin's attention and mouthed the words, "What's going on?"

Pretending innocence, which according to family legend was a trait Fanny had lost just out of her cradle with her first scandalous word, she raised her brows slightly and batted her long lashes several times. It was a *whatever-do-you-mean* gesture, and Nora knew she'd have to wait till later to get any answers.

At nine-thirty Nora refused her dessert and announced that she'd obviously eaten too much and felt the need to lie down. Theo jumped up at once and hovered over her chair. "Let me walk you upstairs, Nora," he said. "Perhaps you need a strong arm to lean on. Or perhaps a walk in the garden is all you need to settle your stomach."

"Yes, Eleanor, that will surely help you," Sidonia agreed. "Do take her outside, Theo. I would be so grateful, and you're such a dear to offer."

Nora clutched her abdomen. "Oh, Mama, I'm afraid my condition has gone beyond a walk in the garden."

Sidonia rose from her chair. "You're not ill, my precious? Oh, dear, Thurston, I told you this would happen. I'll come with you, Eleanor."

"No, no, Mama," Nora insisted with a weak smile around the table. "Don't leave your guests. Nor you either, Theo. Stay, please. I overindulged, that's all. I just need rest." She walked to the other side of the table and stopped behind Fanny's chair. "Though perhaps I could trouble you, cousin, to bring a cup of tea to my room?"

"I'll ask Portia to . . ."

A well-placed jab from the toe of Nora's slipper to the back of Fanny's calf cut short her alternate suggestion. "Of course, *cherie*. I'd be happy to bring your tea."

Minutes later the tea was left cooling on Nora's bedside table while she pressured her cousin for answers. "What's going on, Fanny? What are you doing with Mr. Hyde?"

Fanny pouted and sat on Nora's bed. "Don't give me that look, *cherie* . . . the one that clearly identifies me as the spider and poor Mr. Hyde as the fly."

Nora sat at her vanity, removed the net that held her hair,

and began brushing the loose tresses that fell around her shoulders. She smiled into the mirror at her cousin. "Sorry, Fanny. It's just that I wouldn't have assumed he was your type."

"Why not? Because he is slightly built, and I would make two of him?"

"Partly."

Fanny sputtered with mirth. "You've always known I like men I can hold in the palm of my hand."

Nora pinched her cheeks and combed her eyebrows to a fine arch. "Very funny, but tell me truly. Are you interested in Dillard Hyde?"

"I'll tell you, cousin, if you tell me something first."

Nora pressed a crystal perfume dauber under her earlobe and caught her cousin's expectant expression in the glass. "Tell you what?"

"Tell me why a young woman who suffers from acute food indiscretions brushes her hair until it gleams and applies cologne to her sensitive places before going to her sickbed. A single well-bred young woman, anyway."

Deep down Nora had to admit she'd been preening for Fanny's benefit. She wanted to be caught, because she just had to tell *someone*. Pivoting on her vanity stool to face her cousin, Nora exclaimed in a loud whisper, "I'm going to meet him, Fanny. Tonight, down by the jetty."

Fanny grinned like a satisfied cat and pulled a feather from a seam in a pillow. With a puff of her breath, she blew the feather into the air. "Really? I never would have guessed . . ."

"You knew!"

"I suspected. All one has to do is talk to this captain of yours to know there is a kismet between the two of you that cannot be denied. If not tonight, then sometime."

Nora flung herself on the bed, sending Fanny falling into a mound of pillows. "That's right. You talked to him today. What did you say?"

"Nothing. You'll find out, *ma petite,* that you can learn a lot more by holding your tongue with a man and listening to the subtleties of his dialogue. It's not so much what he says as how he says it. I only spoke with Jacob Proctor for fifteen minutes, and during that time, your name was brought up a half-dozen times.''

A revelation! ''And how did he say it?''

''In frustration. In terror.'' She smiled. ''In awe.''

''Oh, Fanny . . .''

''So, that is that.'' Fanny rose from the bed and pulled Nora after her. ''And as for Mr. Hyde, that is a subject for another night. But now you must get ready to meet your hero.''

She fluffed the ends of Nora's hair and pulled at the capped shoulders of her ivory gown.

''How do I look?'' Nora asked.

''Like an angel.''

''This dress has no sleeves,'' she said, reaching for a shawl. ''I suppose I should take this.''

''*Oui*, I suppose.'' Fanny adjusted the already low bodice of Nora's gown to reveal even more of her breasts. ''But don't use it unless it drops to around thirty degrees tonight.''

''Fanny, you're horrible!''

''It's true, I am. But you, my angel, are not. Take this advice from the cousin who loves you. Follow your heart, *cherie*, but don't let it lead to any place you don't want to go. Now I will check the back stairs to see that no one will witness your escape.''

Nora looked through the palm trees to a silver sea glittering under a full moon like diamonds on a black tabletop. And Jacob Proctor, also a contrast in light and dark in his white shirt and black trousers, sensed her presence, turned from the water, and looked toward the trees.

The wind pressed the front of her skirt against her legs and billowed the rest out behind her. It lifted her hair off her shoulders and back and cooled exposed skin that had warmed the moment she saw him. Her heart beat fast, and she pressed her palm against her bodice to hide the telltale rise and fall of her chest.

What would she say when he reached her? She should think of something clever. Perhaps she should remain silent to see what he would say to her. How she hated the first awkward moments between a man and a woman when no one knew who should speak first or what topics would be broached during clandestine meetings such as this one.

Her first and only word slipped out on a soft breath. "Jacob . . ."

He said nothing at all. He threaded his fingers through her tangling hair, laid his thumbs on her cheeks, and took her mouth in a kiss that lasted only seconds. But it was long enough to shatter the awkwardness she'd feared into a thousand pinpoints of light that shimmered in her mind. When he pulled away, he passed his hand through the crook of her elbow, rested his palm on her arm, and took her to the water.

There was a palm tree a few feet from the sea, a sturdy, proud one that had refused to give in to the ravages of winds and storms. It swept gracefully low to the sand and then grew upward to the sky again. Jacob had laid a Shetland wool blanket over the trunk. Circling Nora's waist with his hands, he lifted her onto the tree. Resting an elbow next to her, he said finally, "I owe you an apology."

Still reeling from his kiss, she felt empowered. She laid her shawl on her lap and gave him a sideways teasing glance. "You owe me several, Captain."

He smiled a subtle admiration. "You're probably right, but unless my misdeeds occur within the same day of my apology, I can scarcely remember what they were. Selective forgetfulness, I call it."

"Then I shall have to be satisfied with the one you do remember." Looking at him from under purposely arched brows, she said, "Apologize at will, then, Jacob."

"All right. It was presumptuous of me to call out Hadley as I did today in the warehouse—to attempt to turn you over to him as if it were a foregone conclusion that it was where you wanted to be."

"Yes, it was presumptuous."

"I assumed—wrongly, I suppose—that Hadley is your suitor as well as your houseguest." His tone was more questioning than definite. The captain was on a fishing expedition.

Nora trifled with the trim on her shawl. She enjoyed the direction this conversation had taken. "No, you're right actually. Lately Theo has been attentive enough to be termed a suitor."

He *harumphed.* A quick, decisive little snort of displeasure. "Much to His Honor's delight, I imagine."

Nora shrugged. "Much to Mama's, actually. My father couldn't care less about my feelings for Theo Hadley."

"Yes, I'm sure. He only has explicit opinions about *one* particular contender for the position of suitor ... a certain wrecker for whom the judge has an intense dislike."

Nora lingered over every detail of Jacob's face, from his intense charcoal eyes to the firm set of his lips. "Why, Captain, are you hinting that you have been courting me? Because if you have, you certainly go about it in the strangest possible manner."

Those lips curled slightly at the corners as his hand moved to settle on her shoulder. His fingers caressed the skin over her collarbone and moved up her neck to her earlobe. "Miss Seabrook, if I were courting you, you would certainly know it. You wouldn't have to ask."

His touch sent a shiver of anticipation skidding up her spine. What coyness she'd pretended took flight on the breeze that ruffled the fronds above her head. She let her gaze be swallowed by the smoldering embers of his eyes. "Why, Captain, what would you do to prove it to me?"

With one step, he was in front of her. The hand that had been striking a path of delicious sensation down the column of her throat slipped to the sensitive skin above the bodice of her gown. He laid his other hand flat on the trunk of the palm tree next to her, trapping her with the press of his hips against her knees.

"I would do this," he said, and his forefinger began exploring a lazy, silky trail above the edge of her bodice. He skimmed the swell of each breast and returned.

"And this," he said. He bent his head until all she could see was the golden sheen of his hair against her skin. His lips moved to where his hand had been, and he kissed her neck, her shoulder, the crest of each breast that suddenly strained against the punishing confinement of satin and lace.

"I see," she breathed. "Yes, all of this would make me think that perhaps you were courting me." Her words came out on a trembling sigh and were barely audible above the lapping of water along the shore and the low, husky murmurs that lips make against skin. His lips. Her skin.

With his hip, he parted her legs and stepped between them. His hands circled her waist again, and he lifted her up and against his chest. With his mouth hovering just inches from hers, he said, "But none of these things would convince you as much as this . . ."

She closed her eyes and held her breath, waiting, wanting the crush of his lips on hers. But he teased her. He only brushed his mouth over hers. His lips were slightly parted, slightly damp. He moved across her mouth from one side to the other. The tip of his tongue flicked out, pressed briefly against the line of her lips, and withdrew, only to do the same thing again and again. A journey of but an inch or two, as he seared his way from corner to corner, took a lifetime.

It was wonderful. Sublime. A kiss for the ages, but it was not enough. A moan escaped her lips. Her arms went round his neck. She wouldn't let him go, not until he did to her what she wanted and needed.

"And finally, this," he said against her mouth. With his hands splayed firmly on her spine, he took her lips in a scorching kiss that exploded in her brain like a riotous fountain of stars. She opened her mouth to him and he plunged inside. His tongue rode the ridge of her teeth, slipped along the insides of her cheeks, and finally circled with her own.

He drew his head back, but still held her close. The tips of her breasts remained in exquisite contact with the hard plane of his chest. He moved his thumb across her lips, removing the moisture his mouth had left.

Slowly, she opened her eyes and met his heated gaze. She saw beyond the molten pewter of his eyes, into the farthest corners of his longing. How could she have thought this man cruel? How could she have thought him confounding and misleading? How could her father suspect him of heinous crimes? How could anyone think him anything but gentle and passionate? Definitely passionate.

"So are you, Captain?" she said.

He placed a finger under her chin. "Am I what, Nora?"

Her words, earnestly spoken, almost pleading, crossed the charged space between them and struck a direct route to his conscience. "Please tell me yes, Jacob. Tell me you are courting me."

He walked away from her, toward the water. What did he think he was doing? The look in her eyes could have felled him sooner than the snapping of the tallest mast on the *Dover Cloud* in a hurricane. This was no game to Nora. This little *courting yes, and courting no* nonsense. There was no dissembling with Nora Seabrook. In matters of the heart there was only trust and honesty, and he saw both in the shimmering aqua of her eyes.

What a fool he was! To think he could rid himself of her foothold in his life and his dreams by stealing this night alone with her. What did he think was going to happen on this beach tonight? That he would kiss her and find the act distasteful? He already knew that was not possible. Did he think he would touch her skin and find himself repulsed by the feel of her? One look at the soft ivory of her face and shoulders convinced a man otherwise. Did he think she would screech and scold him like a harridan when he tried to get close to her? Then he was indeed the greatest fool because there was only passion and sweet longing in this woman.

There was no ridding himself of Nora Seabrook. There was

no getting his fill of her either. She was everything he desired and all he couldn't have. Only distance and time could keep him away from her. And even those would not shake her from his heart. What kind of man was he to treat her the way he had tonight, as if she were an experiment for the abating of his hunger, a hunger he now admitted could only be satisfied by claiming her totally?

He knew what kind of man he was. Deep down he knew. Deceitful, selfish, and most of all, weak. Maybe the wicked curse upon his family had already begun its insidious claiming of his soul.

He heard her climb down from the tree trunk. She came beside him and put her hand on his arm. The muscles tensed all the way to his shoulders. How could she touch him without getting scorched?

"Jacob, what's wrong?" she asked.

Her simple question had a thousand answers and yet not one to comfort her. "You know, I can almost see it," he said. "In my mind's eye it's as plain as the day I sailed away over eighteen years ago."

Her fingers tightened on his arm. "What? What can you see?"

"England in 1839. We sailed from Dover, and I can still see the cliffs, the roofs of the few rugged cottages on the hilltops. I've never been back, but I can still see it."

"Jacob, what does all this mean? What are you saying? Who sailed away with you?"

He looked down at her. Her eyes were filled with wondering. She cared what he would tell her. If she only knew there were no explanations. He'd spent half his lifetime looking for them, and still he was no closer to the truth. There was no explaining why some things happened. "It's nothing, Nora. Nothing to concern you." He stepped away from her again, and she dropped her arm. That was how it should be.

"Why do you do this to me, Jacob?" she asked.

"I don't know what you mean."

"Yes, you do. You know. It's as if you live in this great

mansion, and you allow me entry into the foyer, and you say nice things to me. You're glad I've come. And yet you never invite me into the parlor. I can reach the door but go no farther. And tonight I thought . . . I thought you would let me inside."

He stared at the water. The moon had slipped behind a cloud, leaving the ocean as black as the coal in his own heart. "There is nothing to come inside for, Nora," he said. "Inside my house there is only emptiness."

"I don't believe that, Jacob. I've seen a side to you . . ."

He laughed bitterly. "And you're still here? You should be running through those trees back to your father and your good suitor, Nora. Back to Hadley."

He thought he heard her sob, and wanted to put his hands over his ears. He didn't want to hear her cry and know he was the cause. Lights glimmered on the horizon, out to sea. They gave him a place to focus his sight, away from her face. He pointed to the lights. "See that, Nora? It's a ship, probably going around the island to New Orleans or Texas."

"Why are you showing me that ship?" she cried at him. "What do I care for a ship?"

"Only that it's a possibility. There are many possibilities off this island, you know. And one day you will go away and find them. As you should."

From behind him, her voice was a choking whisper. "I want to hate you, Jacob. I want to, but I can't."

He almost turned to her. Almost took her in his arms and comforted her. His body had started the motion that would have taken him to her side. But a noise up the beach stopped him.

"What's that?" She'd noticed it, too.

He heard the muffled crunch of footsteps on shells before he saw shapes appear out of the night shadows. A combination of man and animal moved down the shore toward them. He grabbed Nora's arm and pulled her under the tree with the sweeping trunk. "Stay down," he warned.

Four men leading two mules walked along the water's edge. The mules were at least a hundred feet apart. A rope was strung taut between them, and hanging from the rope were several lanterns, their chambers glowing eerily in the dark. Jacob swore under his breath as the strange company passed a few yards in front of the palm tree. "A mule line!"

He looked out to sea. The lights from the ship veered toward them. It was too late to stop the vessel. It would soon be upon the reef.

As soon as the men and mules passed, Jacob pulled Nora from under the tree. Keeping low to the ground and ignoring her questions, he ran with her back to the tree line. At the entrance to Southard Street, he left her. "Go home, Nora. There's going to be trouble tonight."

Then he ran to the harbor to ready the *Dover Cloud.* It would not be long until he knew he would hear the cry "Wreck ashore!"

Tears stung the backs of her eyes and blurred the few lights still burning in the houses along Southard Street. But Nora was determined not to cry. She'd cried enough over Jacob Proctor. She blinked hard and her vision cleared. "Don't give him the satisfaction of your tears," she said, too angry to give in completely to the hurt he'd caused her again. What did her heart know of mule lines and ships in the night? It only knew that the man who filled her thoughts from morning to night had scorned her once more.

When she reached the fence surrounding the back property of her house, she stopped and drew a deep breath. She felt like stomping her feet, banging doors, and throwing pieces of glassware. But she had to remember that she'd sneaked out of the house to meet Jacob, and she had to be just as quiet going back in.

The gate made barely a sound when Nora opened it. She slipped inside the yard and closed the latch. Reckless stirred on his straw mat and jumped to his feet. Straining against his rope to get to Nora, he emitted a rolling chortle of greeting. *"Baaahh . . ."*

"Hush, silly goat," she said, going over to give him a pat on his head. "You'll wake Armand and Hubert and they'll yap the rest of the household to attention. I'll take you off your lead and play with you tomorrow."

She led him back to his mat and he settled down. Then she crossed stealthily to the back door. She was just reaching for the handle when the door burst open from the inside and her father stomped onto the service porch.

"Confound it to Hell!" he swore. "If it's not one thing it's another on this blasted island."

His ample waistline connected with Nora's shoulder as she stood on the bottom step and almost sent her sprawling to the ground. Clutching the short stair rail for balance, she croaked, "Father!"

"Nora? What are you doing out here?"

Before she could answer, her mother's voice came from the kitchen, accompanied by a chorus of discordant yelps. "Thurston, what are you doing? Why are you up? Where are you going?"

She screamed, and Armand and Hubert shot out the kitchen door. Hubert ran circles around Thurston, jumping and nipping at his trousers. Armand leapt at Nora's waist, and she caught him in her arms. Reckless bounded up from his mat and added his own high-pitched yodeling to the confusion.

Wiggling one leg ineffectually at Hubert, Thurston hollered at his wife. "Sidonia, for the love of God, can't you keep these beasts at bay!"

Sidonia's mass of thick dark hair had shifted to the side under her nightcap, and the whole frilly thing had gone completely askew. Pushing ruffles out of her eyes with one hand and lifting the voluminous skirt of her nightgown with the other, she headed straight for her boy, the furry one. "Don't yell, Thurston," she cried. "Hubert is so sensitive. He won't eat a bite all tomorrow because you've been cross with him."

She picked up the poodle, whose deep sensitivity was masked by a decidedly feral snarl at Thurston. Seeing Armand safely in Nora's arms, Sidonia sighed with relief and said, "Thank you, Eleanor, for catching him.'' Then her eyes widened in alarm and her hand flew to her chest. ''Eleanor? What in heaven's name are you doing out here? I thought you were ill.'' Turning to her husband, she said, ''Thurston, what is Eleanor doing? What are you doing? Will someone please tell me what's going on?''

''Calm down, Sid,'' he said. ''Piney Beade from the jail just knocked at the front door. Seems there's activity on the beach. Those damn blasted wreckers are at it again with something called a mule line.''

Sidonia gasped. ''A mule line? Oh, no!'' She paused. ''What's that?''

''I haven't got time to go into it now, Sid. Suffice it to say it's a way of luring ships to the reef. And I know who's behind it, too. Beade went to Proctor's warehouse and cottage, and even Jimmy Teague's. The scoundrel's nowhere to be seen. Not surprising since, for my money, he's down at the shore pulling a mule! I'll catch him red-handed this time.''

''How ghastly. Oh, do be careful, Thurston.''

He nodded and headed for the gate. Before leaving, however, he turned to look at his daughter. ''By the way, Nora, you never told me . . . what *are* you doing out at this hour? And with evening clothes on.''

She avoided his eyes since she knew she was going to lie, and settled her gaze on the top of Armand's head. ''I never undressed, Father,'' she said. ''Just fell asleep on my bed. And then I heard Piney knock. Curiosity brought me down here, that's all.''

''Well, stay inside. There's trouble brewing tonight, and I don't want you to have any part in it. I've got to go. I'm going to see to it that Proctor has orchestrated the last wreck on the shores of this island.''

''Of course, Father.'' She watched him go in the direction from which she had just come. She could have told him that Jacob had nothing to do with the mule line, that she'd seen it all with her own eyes. She could have told him he was wasting his time going after the wrong man. But the hurt was too fresh, the pain too deep.

Her father was convinced Jacob was at the root of the wrecking problems, and tonight if Jacob suffered the sting of Seabrook justice, that suited her just fine. Let him simmer in hot water for a while. It served him right, and it was nothing compared to what he'd done to her . . . again! Besides, he might very well be guilty of crimes unrelated to the mule line.

Picturing Jacob Proctor as prime beef in the judge's stew was a small victory, however. And the little smile that had crept its way onto Nora's face was erased the instant she heard the first cry from one of the island cupolas.

''Wreck ashore!''

CHAPTER TWELVE

On an island the size of Key West, gossip affected all citizens from the youngest to the oldest. Monday morning, in the Island School for Reading, the children talked of nothing but the wreck of the *Marguerite Gray*. Nora decided the best way to deal with the weekend excitement was to give her students the first ten minutes of class time to say everything that sat on the tips of their tongues.

Of course Nora was tired of hearing about the wreck and thinking about anything that had to do with the night it had happened. For two days her father had vacillated between ranting because ''that despicable Proctor'' had escaped his clutches again, and chortling with glee that the wicked captain's machinations had yielded nothing but a hold full of smelly fish!

Fortunately, no lives were lost, and all eight crewmen on the ill-fated ship had been rescued by Moony Swain and Jacob Proctor, whose ships arrived first at the site. A rumor circulated that a confrontation between Swain and Proctor as to whose vessel arrived first forced the skipper of the *Marguerite Gray* to proclaim them co-wrecking masters in charge of the salvage. It was an honor that proved quite dubious in the end.

The *Marguerite Gray* herself had suffered little damage. A rend in her hull had been patched in two days, and she'd set sail early this morning on a strong westerly wind. Unfortunately, the buyers of her cargo in Gulfport, Mississippi, who anticipated a shipment of New England cod, would be disappointed. The entire load had to be sacrificed to tug the old scow off the reef and haul her into Key West.

The story of the *Marguerite Gray* was made even more humorous to Nora's students when Felix Obalu added the enticing tidbit that the wreck was caused by some pigeon-head who had rigged a mule line to lure the ship. "It took a lot of work to haul those ol' mules up and down the shore," Felix said, "just to make it look like it was another ship sailing well away from the reefs. I guess the sorry plan worked, though." Felix hooted with laughter. "The *Marguerite Gray* crashed on the reef just like the pigeon-head wanted. Too bad her cargo was tossed into the sea."

"All right, children," Nora said. "That's quite enough talk of the *Marguerite Gray*. I'm sure you all know the important thing is that no lives were lost."

"Yeah," Felix said. "The only creatures that drowned were already dead!"

It was an amusing end to the harrowing tale, Nora had to admit, though she truly had had quite enough of remembering that night. She found nothing else about the incident the least bit humorous. She'd hardly eaten a bite and had slept very little because the details of her meeting with Jacob Proctor kept repeating in her mind.

The intuitive Fanny knew something had gone dreadfully wrong, and used every opportunity to get Nora to talk. But Nora hadn't said a word, even to her. Sidonia suspected something was wrong, too, and tried to fix whatever it was by shoving food under Nora's nose.

"You must eat something, Eleanor, or you'll make yourself ill," she'd said countless times. "Please, for Mama?"

Making up excuses and hiding from the females in her family was only part of the reason it had been such a tedious weekend.

Nora's father wouldn't stop talking about "the one that got away." Of course he had no way of knowing that Nora's wounded heart suffered another pang of anguish every time she heard Jacob's name.

The judge had questioned the suspect for two hours on Saturday, and had come home cranky and disgruntled because he still had no solid evidence to put the captain away. One Key West citizen had seen Jacob leaving the beach about the time the mule line was spotted. When Thurston questioned Jacob about this, Proctor had merely thrust his hands out before him as if daring the judge to fix a pair of shackles to his wrists and snapped back, "So arrest me, Your Honor, if suddenly it's a crime to take a walk on this island at night!"

"He's belligerent and uncooperative," Thurston had railed to the women in his family when he related the tale. "And guilty as hell! The man's become a festering thorn in my hide. He's slippery as an eel and crooked as the devil's staff."

Nora recalled her father's assessment of Jacob as she walked among the benches in her classroom and examined her students' work. I don't know about the crooked part, Father, she thought to herself, but he is definitely slippery and thorny. She glanced out the window toward Jacob's warehouse. *So why is it so impossible for either of us to put this man out of our minds for so much as a day?*

Jacob Proctor stood by the front entrance of his warehouse with a clipboard in his hand. As each crate, barrel, or canvas sack was carried outside to his ship, he checked the contents off on a list. Then he waved to Willy Turpin, who stood near the gangway of the *Dover Cloud,* to tell him the item was accounted for.

Once this task was complete, Willy came inside. "Looks like we got it all, Captain," he said.

"It's about bloody time," Jacob snarled. "We could have sailed an hour ago if it weren't for the pace of this crew."

Willy put his hands on his hips and stared at his friend.

"We've got days of sailin' ahead of us, Jacob. I wouldn't think one hour was all that important."

"Well, it is," he said, tapping the side of his head with his finger. "I'm keeping a schedule in here, and it's what's important. The sooner we get out of here, the better."

"What's the matter with you, Jacob?" Willy asked. "You're snappin' our heads off like you were a shark and we were raw meat."

A fresh stab of guilt twisted in Jacob's gut, a sensation he was all too familiar with lately. He reached out and put his hand on Willy's shoulder. "Ah, sorry, Will. I'm just a bit anxious. I always get this way when I'm sailing to Belle Isle, you know that."

"Aye, I do, but usually it doesn't hit you till we spy Angel Kiss Bay."

"True, but this time the feeling's come early for some reason."

Willy scratched his chin and raised one dubious eyebrow. "Could that reason have anything to do with a certain raven-haired young lady?"

The hand that had just rested affectionately on Willy's shoulder dropped to Jacob's side and clenched in frustration. "Nothing at all. And you can just stop your fool speculating. If anything, it has more to do with her bothersome father and the spies he's had following me for days."

Willy took a chance and grinned up at his agitated captain. "I don't think so, Jacob. It's my opinion that if Judge Seabrook had sentenced you to the gallows, it wouldn't stick in your craw as much as that pretty gal has."

Jacob took one threatening step toward Willy and stopped. He'd never come close to physical anger with this man he trusted with his life, and he wouldn't start now. But Will had a helluva nerve talking about things that were none of his business. "Don't you still have work to do?" Jacob barked at him.

"Not a stitch."

"Well, stay out of my way because thanks to the pace of

this loading, I still do! I'm going up to secure my office, pack the strongbox, and prepare to get under way. In the meantime, you mind your own business for once in your life!''

''Will do, Captain. Matter of fact, I was thinkin' of takin' the crew over to Jimmy's for a last pint and cup of fish chowder. It might be the only decent food they get in days.''

''Then go. But only a pint. A soused sailor in the crow's nest is as useful as a dinghy in a hurricane.'' Jacob pulled his watch from his vest pocket. ''But hurry up about it. Bloody hell, it's already nine-thirty! I'll be ready to sail by ten, with you or without you!''

At nine-thirty Nora followed her students out of the milliner's shop and ran into Fanny sporting her wide bonnet and a wicker basket over her elbow.

''Good morning, cousin,'' Fanny said cheerfully. ''Beautiful day, isn't it?''

''Nice enough, I suppose.'' Nora pointed to the basket. ''What's in there?''

''Fresh-baked croissants, strawberry spread, and a quart of hot coffee.''

Nora grimaced. Now Fanny was trying to force food down her throat. ''That was sweet of you, Fanny, though it was probably Mama's idea. But I really couldn't eat anything.''

''Oh, it's not for you, *cherie*,'' she said with a grin. ''I figure you'll eat when you're good and ready, or half dead, whichever comes first. These treats are for Dillard Hyde.''

Dillard Hyde? Nora smiled in spite of her gloomy demeanor. The amazing Mr. Hyde was actually bringing out Fanny's domestic qualities. ''Fanny, how interesting. A picnic in the middle of the morning?''

''Not a picnic, Nora . . . a *rendezvous*. There's a difference.''

''I see. Still, if you hope to appeal to him with pastry, you'd best go to the courthouse. That's where you'll find him at this hour.''

Fanny cocked her head toward Proctor's warehouse. ''No,

no, *cherie.* He's right there with your determined father. He hasn't moved from that spot for nearly an hour, though Thurston only arrived a few minutes ago."

Nora probably wouldn't have noticed the men if Fanny hadn't pointed them out. She purposely averted her gaze from Jacob's warehouse. But they were definitely there. Her father in his black business attire, and Dillard in a dark green suit that made him look like a praying mantis. They were staring at the *Dover Cloud,* though there was no activity at the clipper ship at this moment. Her father was talking with his hands as much as with his mouth. "What are they doing, Fanny?" Nora asked.

"I haven't the faintest idea. Let's go closer to see what they're saying. If we stay behind them, they won't know we're listening."

Nora planted her feet firmly on the sidewalk. "No, thank you, Fanny. I have no desire to step one foot closer to Jacob Proctor's enterprise."

Ignoring her, Fanny tugged on Nora's sleeve until she was forced to follow. "So you profess, liar," Fanny said. Soon they could hear everything Thurston and Dillard were saying.

"Have you watched the entire loading procedure, Dillard?" Thurston asked.

"Yes, sir, though the whole time that Turpin fellow kept giving me the evil eye. Truly, Your Honor, I didn't see anything suspicious."

"You didn't, eh? It's suspicious enough to my mind that Proctor's sailing away within hours of the *Marguerite Gray.* What do you make of that?"

Dillard shrugged. "Nothing much, sir. Proctor sails often to the Bahamas—Nassau usually. He trades regularly with the islands. I think it's just coincidence that the *Marguerite Gray* sailed this morning."

Thurston's voice shot up a notch. "I don't believe in coincidences, Hyde. A load of fish, bah! I'm thinking now that it's very likely the captain of the *Marguerite Gray,* the old reprobate, is in collusion with our own Captain Proctor."

He leaned in close to Dillard, and Nora inched closer to hear what he said.

"Tell you what I think, Dillard. I think there was something of value on that old ship after all. Something worth a lot more than stinking fish. And I'll bet it's tucked into Proctor's warehouse for safekeeping, or ready to float out of Key West Harbor in the hold of the *Dover Cloud*."

Thurston used the forefinger of one hand to enumerate his theory on the fingers of the other. "First, Proctor is seen on the beach the same time a mule line is running. Second, he is one of the first to reach the wreck of the *Marguerite Gray*. Third, the *Gray* sails at first light this morning, and fourth, Proctor follows on her stern not three hours later with hardly a fare-thee-well to anyone in town. It smacks of insurance fraud, Hyde. It does indeed."

Nora shook her head. *You're wrong, Father. Jacob did tell someone he was leaving, and I know for certain he didn't run that mule line.* She was going to have to set the record straight with her father about the mule line. Even Jacob Proctor didn't deserve all this suspicion when he was clearly innocent . . . of this charge, at least.

"I don't know, sir . . ."

Thurston clapped his hands together once, a sign of inspiration. "Dillard, I want a writ of search and seizure. I want to know what Proctor has in that hold."

"Very well, Your Honor, but we'd better go to the courthouse now and get it. Proctor could sail any moment."

The two men hurried off toward the courthouse. Watching them go, Nora muttered to Fanny, "They're not likely to find anything you know."

"I admire your faith in your hero, *cherie*," Fanny mumbled between wet, slurping sounds. She wiped the remains of strawberry jam off the corner of her mouth with her finger, then stuck the gooey tip between her lips and shrugged innocently. "Don't look at me that way, *cherie*. Obviously, Mr. Hyde can't share the croissants with me, and you don't want any. I couldn't pass up a delicious opportunity, now could I?"

"No, I guess not." *Couldn't pass up an opportunity* . . . Of course! "Fanny, you amaze me."

"I do?"

"Yes. Do you know where the *Dover Cloud's* crew is right now?"

"I saw Mr. Turpin and several others go to Jimmy Teague's a few minutes ago."

"And Jacob, was he with them?"

"I didn't see him."

"Did you see him go on the ship?"

"No."

"Then now is my perfect opportunity. Father may not get back in time with his writ. I'm going into that hold myself. I don't think Jacob had anything to do with the wreck of the *Marguerite Gray.* But if he did, and if the evidence is on that ship, I'll find it. And if he is guilty, I'll turn him over to Father myself!"

"*You,* Nora? Where would you even begin to search a ship?"

"I just sailed on one less than a month ago. Remember when Captain Murdock gave us that tour of the *Southern Star's* compartments?" She laughed at her own silly question. "Well, you weren't paying attention, but I was. I know exactly how to get where I want to go and what to expect when I get there."

"I can't let you do this by yourself. I'm going with you."

"No, you're not. With luck I just might be able to get on without being seen, but the two of us . . . it would never work. Besides, look at you. You're wearing a bonnet large enough to sail a small ship, and carrying a wicker basket. I'd hardly call you inconspicuous."

"Maybe not, but what if Captain Proctor *is* guilty? And what if he catches you on his ship? You could find yourself in a lot of trouble."

Nora squeezed Fanny's hand. "I won't stay on board long enough for that to happen. One quick look and I'll get off. Don't worry. I'd much rather you'd go home and tell Mama I stayed to check some papers. The way she's been acting lately,

I don't want her sending Theo after me again. I'll see you for lunch.''

"Oh, Nora, I don't know about this . . ."

Nora turned her cousin around and gave her a gentle shove toward Southard Street. "Fanny, go! There isn't much time. I'll be home soon."

Fanny left, and Nora hurried across the open courtyard toward the *Dover Cloud*. There were a few people milling around the docks, but no one seemed to pay her any mind. Once at the ship's gangway, she gave a cursory look on deck. Not seeing a soul, she crept quickly on board.

The *Dover Cloud* was eerily devoid of human noise. Only ship sounds accompanied Nora's footsteps as she padded across the deck. The boat creaked with the tug of her mooring lines. Water lapped against her hull, and the wind played around furled sails, causing metal riggings to clank and clatter. But the only words Nora heard spoken were incoherent ones drifting over to her from the harbor.

She quickly located the hatch leading to the ship's hold, slid the brass hasp across, and lifted the wooden door. Looking around the harbor one last time, she sighed with relief when she didn't see anyone coming toward the *Dover Cloud*. Gathering her skirts in one hand, thankful she'd worn only crinolines this morning and not hoops, she lowered herself onto the ladder.

She landed with a quiet footfall on the wood-plank floor, and held onto the ladder until she found her balance on the gently rocking surface. The ship's hold was smaller and darker than Nora had anticipated. Almost no air circulated in the low-ceilinged room. Squinting into charcoal shadows of odd forms and sizes, she felt strangely lightheaded. Maybe she should have taken one of Fanny's croissants after all.

Thankfully, after a moment, her eyes adjusted, and enough sunlight came through the window slits for her to see what was in the hold. She began reading labels on crates and barrels stacked along the walls.

It occurred to Nora that she didn't know what she hoped to find. If she found nothing, then Jacob was an innocent man as far as the wreck of the *Marguerite Gray* was concerned. He would sail away to wherever he was going, and it would certainly be in her best interests to forget him. If she found what looked to be contraband or stolen merchandise, then Jacob would be remanded to custody on the island, probably put on trial, and it still would be in her best interests to forget him. Since both scenarios led to the same miserable conclusion, there didn't seem to be any way for Nora to win. Her relationship with Jacob Proctor, however one might characterize it, was doomed. But then she'd known that since her last encounter with him.

At least now she might learn the truth about Jacob one way or the other. "Truth is always better than ignorance, Nora," she said to herself. "Especially truth about a man who couldn't care less about you."

Putting personal prejudice aside, Nora decided that whoever had packed the hold of the *Dover Cloud* had done an excellent job. One entire wall was taken up with food supplies. Enough, Nora thought, to sustain a crew for a longer voyage than one to Nassau. There were at least a dozen barrels of water and above them crates of potatoes, onions, and turnips. On top of those were twenty-pound sacks of cornmeal and flour, and oilcloths wrapped around mystery foodstuffs that smelled like cured meats. Nora's mouth began to water. Yes, she thought she might be able to eat something today.

Along two other walls were baskets of miscellaneous goods . . . bottles of spices and whiskey, medicines, cook pots, lanterns, and household supplies. There was nothing Nora hadn't seen at the auction or in Jacob's warehouse. And nothing so valuable a man would risk his reputation to steal it from the *Marguerite Gray*. The nonperishable goods were probably items Jacob intended to trade in the Bahamas.

She discovered a large wicker trunk filled with bolts of colorful cloth, and decided it was for trade also.While admiring the intricate patterns and fabrics, Nora heard voices coming from the harbor. She stuffed the material back in the trunk and closed the lid. Then she went to the closest window and looked out. Men were gathered at the entrance to Jimmy Teague's shouting farewells to patrons inside. Jacob's crew.

She could still make her escape. The sailors wouldn't notice her until she was on the dock, and then she'd make up some excuse in case one of them asked why she was there. She looked at the open door of the hatch, but when she took her first step toward it, her foot became tangled in a coil of rope.

"What in blazes . . ." she mumbled into the near-darkness. She tried to kick free, but only buried her shoe deeper into the scratchy sisal, until the rope had formed a loop around her ankle. She reached down to loosen the tightening noose, and the ship pitched in a gust of wind, causing her to lose her balance.

She reached out to grab onto something solid for support. What she found was the corner of a sack of flour. Then everything happened at once. Despite her efforts to remain upright, a sudden dizziness in her head and the swaying of the ship sent her sprawling into a corner of the hold. She hit her head and back on the wall. Pain sliced up her spine and into her temples as her breath whooshed from her lungs.

The darkness around her dazzled with stars. She struggled to keep her eyelids from descending over her aching eyes. In one horrifying instant she glimpsed the sack of flour she had been gripping for dear life a moment before. It had become a living, animated thing. It moved on its perch above her head, rolled once, and tumbled. Three X's danced among the glittering stars on a dusty burlap background. It was all Nora remembered before the hold of the *Dover Cloud* went totally black.

CHAPTER THIRTEEN

A cumbersome weight pressed down on Nora from her neck to her knees. She pushed at it with a hand pinned at her side and wiggled her torso, but the effort to free herself was too great. Besides, it wasn't all that uncomfortable. It resembled a heavy blanket, cloaking her in darkness and warmth.

Her head ached, so much that she didn't even attempt to open her eyes. The darkness behind her eyelids was kind and peaceful. It blocked out the pain that light would surely have intensified. Too, she sensed it was nighttime anyway, just as a blind person feels an instinctive connection with the earth's rotation. The world around her had settled in for the night and hummed to a gentle, steady vibration far removed from the day's activities.

She knew that somewhere above her, in the heavens, the moon turned leaves to silver and water to cobalt. A dark wind rattled sashes and ruffled curtains. Nora half smiled. She wouldn't have to battle with the sun till morning.

She would let herself drift back to sleep. *Drift,* what a lovely image, a one-word lullaby, really. She was drifting now, swaying with a soft, caressing motion, like a baby, safe and secure in a cotton-cloud cradle, drifting across the sky. Nora sighed, a mellow, kitten-like sound, and slipped away from a tenuous semi-consciousness.

Judge Seabrook sent his housekeeper, Portia, to summon a doctor to his home Monday evening when he ran out of excuses for why Nora hadn't come home. His wife was near hysteria, and in the few hours since noon she had conjured up every conceivable vile, insidious image of what had happened to her daughter.

While Sidonia cried and moaned and begged God to deliver her daughter unharmed, Thurston organized an all-out effort to comb the island. Theo Hadley divided the island into manageable quadrants, and the Seabrook house became the headquarters for searchers to report their findings hourly. And with each negative result, Sidonia suffered more, cried louder, and condemned her miserable fate more vociferously.

Once the doctor administered a sedative, Thurston gathered the damp cloths Portia had applied to her mistress' brow that evening, took them and an assortment of half-empty teacups to the service kitchen, and persuaded his wife to come to bed. She didn't protest when he removed her clothing, slipped her nightgown over her head, and settled her against a mound of pillows.

She stared at him with glassy eyes when he tucked a sheet under her chin. "I must brush my hair, Thurston," she said. They were the first words she'd spoken during the entire preparation process. "Do bring me my brush and mirror."

"Of course, pet." Grateful for any semblance of normalcy from his wife, he quickly retrieved the requested items from her vanity.

With rote motion she skimmed bristles down her long hair. "Don't leave me, Thurston," she pleaded. "You will stay, won't you?"

"Yes, love, of course. I must speak with Fanny for a moment,

and then I'll be back. She indicated to me just now that she
had something important to tell me.''

"About Eleanor?"

"I don't know, dearest. Perhaps.'' He kissed her forehead,
patted her hand, and went to the door. "Rest now, Sid," he
said as he went out.

Fanny waited for him at the top of the stairs. Thurston noticed
immediately that her features lacked their usual confidence.
She looked almost cowed, like a beaten puppy. The woman
before him bore little resemblance to the saucy Fanny Cosette.
"What is it?" he asked impatiently. "Do you know where
Nora is?"

"Oh, Thurston," she moaned. "I don't know for certain,
but I have an idea."

He took her elbow and led her down the stairs and into his
study. "All right, Fanny, sit down and tell me what you know."

She wrung her hands at her waist. "If it's all the same to
you, Thurston, I think I'll stand. It makes for a faster escape.''
Her attempt at a small grin fell far short of its goal. "This
morning at the harbor . . .''

Thurston couldn't believe what Fanny told him. He didn't
want to believe it. His only child, his precious daughter was
on board the *Dover Cloud* sailing for God knows where with
the most disreputable man on the island. "My worst fears have
been realized," he said. "She's in the clutches of that brute.
He's snatched her away from us in a cruel attempt at revenge."

"It's not like that, Thurston," Fanny responded. "Nora went
on board the *Dover Cloud* on her own. She was under no duress
to do so."

Thurston pounded his fist on his desk. "Are you saying that
Nora went on Proctor's ship of her own volition?"

"Yes, she did, but only to help you. She thought she might
find something to connect the captain with the wreck of the
Marguerite Gray."

"And you let her go?"

"I didn't want to, but she insisted. She said she would only
stay on board a few minutes, that she knew what she was

doing.'' Fanny's words dissolved into quivers. ''Oh, Thurston, Nora said she'd see me for lunch!''

This story was beyond comprehension, beyond what Thurston, as a rational man, could accept. Fanny was talking about his sensible daughter! ''Why would she do such a thing? I've warned her about that man. I made her promise never to go near him.''

''I'm afraid that was a promise she took rather lightly.''

A vision of his daughter on the *Dover Cloud,* a prisoner in the hands of Jacob Proctor and his foul crew, flashed before Thurston's eyes. What little supper he'd eaten threatened to revolt in his churning stomach. He sat at his desk and hung his head. ''No matter how it came to pass, he's got her, Fanny. My poor, foolish child. What will become of her?''

Self-recrimination slammed into Thurston's roiling abdomen. What did I do wrong? he asked himself. I should have watched my daughter's activities more closely since we came to this wicked island. Then, another thought occurred to him, one that eased his own guilt while shifting blame to another. He slowly raised his head and leveled a threatening glare at his wife's cousin. ''Fanny, you've known this since this morning?''

She emitted a tiny squeak and nodded.

He stood and came around his desk to stand before her. ''Why didn't you tell me? I could have set out after her. Maybe caught the bastard before he put so many miles between us.''

Fanny backed away. ''I should have told you, Thurston, I know that now, but I thought Nora would come back. She seemed so sure of herself. I thought perhaps she and Proctor had just sailed out on a brief lovers' cruise . . .''

''*A lovers'* cruise?'' Thurston's blood pressure shot higher until he felt its flush in his cheeks. ''Are you saying those two have . . .''

''No, no, nothing like that, though it wasn't far from Nora's mind, but no, Thurston. Nora is as pure as . . .''

''Then what are you jabbering, woman? Why the hell didn't you come to me with this news?''

Fanny backed into the closed door and flattened against it.

"Nora didn't want me to tell. And I thought you would kill Proctor. I thought you would be angry with Nora. I thought you might very well kill me . . ."

"I'm damned tempted, Fanny! What am I supposed to tell Sidonia? That Nora ran off with this man?"

"No, I don't think Nora would run off with him."

"Then what *do* you think?"

Thurston found himself dealing with the second hysterical woman of the evening. Fanny's tears ran down her cheeks and tested the limits of his patience.

"I don't know," she cried. "She went on his boat and she didn't come home. I don't know why. I don't think he'll hurt her. I think he cares for her, actually. You can tell Sid that, at least."

Thurston took three long, determined strides, which brought him within inches of Fanny's quivering form. She covered her face with her hands.

"Get out of my way, woman. I'm not going to hit you. I'm going upstairs to my wife." He waggled a finger in Fanny's face. "But let me tell you this. You've handled this badly. Very badly." Shaking his head, he left the study.

"Kidnapped! Eleanor has been kidnapped!" Sidonia Seabrook plunged her face into a crocheted pillow and moaned into goose down. "My poor innocent darling. Who knows what horrors that man will inflict upon her? What are we going to do?"

Thurston sat on the bed next to his wife and took her hand. "Now, Sid, don't get carried away until we know all the facts. I never used the word *kidnapped.*"

She raised moist, red eyes to him. "Well, what other explanation could there be?"

Drawing a deep breath, Thurston prepared to say the very thing he knew would only increase his wife's distress. "My dear, Fanny seems to believe that Nora went on board Captain Proctor's ship of her own volition, born of some misguided attempt to ferret out evidence of his misdeeds in the matter of the *Marguerite Gray*.''

"What nonsense, Thurston." Moments passed while Sidonia waited for some sign that her husband agreed with her, and when it was not forthcoming, she tried to pin him into submission with her most condemning look. "You don't believe that, do you?"

"I have to consider it, Sid. Nora told Fanny that's what she intended to do, and Fanny saw her board the *Dover Cloud*.''

The thought that her daughter could do something so brazen was unacceptable to Sidonia. Thurston saw her blatant denial of Fanny's account in the pout that pulled down the corners of her mouth. He knew exactly what she was thinking. She was sifting the details of Fanny's story through her own system of values until she had an interpretation of the event that supported her own beliefs.

"Perhaps what Fanny saw was not really what happened," she offered. "Perhaps that vile man coaxed Eleanor on board, rendered her senseless, and now plans to use her as his concubine. Oh, Thurston, think of it!"

A persistent, nagging logic wouldn't let Thurston condone this version of what happened. Jacob Proctor might be guilty of all manner of activities that lined his pockets, but Thurston truly could not accept that the man was a totally unprincipled lecher. He'd seen no evidence that the captain's lack of ethics extended to such base immorality.

He soothed his wife's fears with a calm voice. "No, Sid. You mustn't think things like that. If Nora is on the *Dover Cloud*, and there is a strong possibility of that, then we must consider that there is a logical explanation for how it happened." When Sid started to protest, Thurston silenced her with a raised hand. "Besides, Fanny says Proctor wouldn't hurt her. She's quite certain of it, in fact."

"Fanny? How would she know that?"

Thurston grinned. "Really, Sid. Proctor is a man, and your cousin is, well ... Fanny. I, for one, wouldn't question her expertise in this subject area."

He was rewarded with a concessionary smile. "Maybe you're

right. But we must do something, Thurston. We can't just let this situation continue . . ."

"At first light tomorrow, love, I'll find out where Proctor has gone. That's only a few hours from now, and if I discover that he'll be gone for some time, I'll send someone after him or follow him myself." He stood up and pressed the covers around his wife's form. "We'll get our Eleanor back, Sid. Safe and sound, I give you my word."

It had seemed like a good plan when he voiced it. The problem was that the next morning no one on the island of Key West knew where Jacob Proctor had gone. Most people were only certain of the places he hadn't gone, like Nassau or the other Caribbean islands with which he generally traded. In addition, Thurston learned one other very distressing fact. Every few months, Jacob Proctor left the island and sailed to an undisclosed destination that kept him away for three or more weeks at a time. He always took the same abbreviated crew of six men with him. Men who had never told another living soul where they sailed with their captain.

"I've no idea, Your Honor," an ancient, gimpy-legged sailor left in charge of Proctor's warehouse told Thurston. "No one knows but them few that sails with him. The captain always says he's goin' on personal business, and he leaves it at that." The old sailor then dismissed a Federal judge with a wave of his arthritic fingers. "You'd best forget askin' around town, Judge. Ain't no one on this Island gonna tell you what they don't know."

It was hopeless. The *Dover Cloud* had a full twenty-four-hour start on any vessel Thurston might consider hiring to chase her. And no ship currently in Key West could even hope to keep up with Proctor's sleek schooner, much less overtake it. And the old-timers who watched the sky swore a storm was brewing in the southeast, and only a fool would venture into the Atlantic when a blow was coming. Thurston was not a sailor, and he was not a fool. He was a practical man who suddenly found himself having to trust in luck.

With a heavy heart, he trudged toward his home knowing

he would have to tell his wife discouraging news. He thought of his precious daughter, somewhere on the seas with a man she barely knew and he didn't trust. He hoped Proctor had the good sense to return his daughter to Key West. If he didn't, Thurston vowed the captain would pay dearly for this error in judgment.

"My dear Nora," he muttered. "If all this is a result of some romantic notion you somehow got in your little head, I pray to God you don't find your illusions dashed on a dark reef or crushed in the cruel hands of a tyrant."

Sunlight as fuzzy and soft as the down on a duck sat on Nora's eyelids. It was just enough to convince her it was daylight, and dim enough to prompt her to open her eyes without threat of her headache returning. Oh, dear . . . that star-spangled, skull-pounding headache came back to her with startling clarity. Something hard had hit the back of her head just before something heavy covered her—and it did still. She was nearly buried in blunt thickness. She remembered thinking it was nighttime. Now she was glad it was not. She had to put the pieces together, to make sense of what happened. If only she could concentrate.

Strange noises interrupted her attempt to remember. They were creaks and groans, and Nora thought at first they were coming from her. She wouldn't have been surprised. Her body ached as if it could groan its protest.

She managed to work her arm from under the weight pressing down on her and felt behind her head. Her palm met timber, thick and wide, and slightly rough. The odd noises seemed to originate from a sort of wooden fortress surrounding her. And from footsteps sounding on a wood floor.

Oh, God, she remembered! She was in the hold of Jacob Proctor's ship. She had fallen while trying to escape. A coil of rope. A sack of flour . . . it was all too ridiculous. How long had she been unconscious? Not long, she decided, determining from shadows that the sun was near its apex. Perhaps she had time to get off the ship without being seen. If she could just remove the stupid sack. And if whoever was in the hold with her would go back on deck again. With a little luck, she could slip up the ladder and cross quickly and quietly to the harbor.

She remained perfectly still while an inner voice urged her to stay calm and wait for her opportunity. Confidence in her plan faltered, however, when she sensed motion all around her. Her body, though rigid in its burlap prison, rocked in a gentle sway. Her head hummed with an effort to maintain a steady equilibrium. With a quick, hot burst of panic she understood. Her fortress was moving! The *Dover Cloud* had sailed.

"Bloody 'ell! What the devil's goin' on 'ere?" a voice squawked in a strong Cockney accent, and Nora's stomach clenched in fear.

Heavy-soled shoes clomped briskly across the floor away from her, and the same voice hollered up to the deck. "Captain Proctor, come quick. There's a body in the 'old. We got us a corpse on board!"

So much for escaping. Nora pondered her immediate future, and realized the next few minutes could be the most embarrassing and unpleasant of her life. There was nothing to be done but await her fate. Pinned against the walls of the *Dover Cloud*'s hull, and trapped under twenty pounds of flour, all she could do was agonize over the prospect of facing the man she'd least choose to be her accuser. She half hoped he'd actually mistake her for dead and throw her overboard in a canvas sack. But the sad fact remained that if she escaped the sack, she still couldn't swim.

In seconds Jacob's footsteps sounded on the ladder and his voice filled the small room. "What is it, Skeet? Where's the body?"

The sailor's answer reflected the quivering in his body. "It's th-there, s-sir. Just the sh-shoes are stickin' out."

Nora wiggled her feet and shoved at the flour sack. It moved an inch or so, and the sailor named Skeet shrieked. For one crazy moment Nora wished she were Jonah and a giant whale would surface from the bottom of the sea and swallow her whole. She'd rather face the gullet of a monster than the wrath of the captain of the *Dover Cloud*.

Long fingers wrapped around the limp corner of the sack that now tickled the skin between Nora's nose and mouth. She recognized the light matting of hair on the knuckles just as surely as she recognized the deep voice that hovered above her head. "One thing's for certain, Skeet," the voice said as the sack was lifted. "The stowaway's not dead."

Like a crushed sunflower, Nora Seabrook lay crumpled on the floor of the *Dover Cloud*. Her yellow dress, dusted with flour, spread around her face and body, encircling a mass of raven hair in its center. Her legs, bare from the knees down, stuck out like two delicate stems. And Jacob couldn't have been more shocked if he'd uncovered a field of brilliant sunflowers growing in the dimly lit hold of his ship.

He flung the sack away and stared at her, trying to gather wits that refused to do anything but scatter to the four corners of the hold. He closed his eyes and pressed his forefinger and thumb against the lids. When he opened them, she was still there. "You!" The word came out almost as a curse and was followed by an actual one. "What the hell are you doing here?"

She struggled up on her elbows and leveled an icy glare at him that for just an instant made him feel as if he were the intruder, she were Cleopatra, and the *Dover Cloud* had suddenly become a Nile River barge. But only for an instant. "I asked you a question, Nora!" he shouted, for lack of any intelligent thought coming to his head.

"It's not as if I chose to be here," she snapped back. "I would hardly choose these accommodations for a Caribbean voyage, Captain."

"Do you want me to believe you were carted on board against your will with the supplies?"

Some of the blue ice melted in her eyes. "I want you to believe it, yes, but I doubt that you will."

"Nora, how did you get on this ship, and what earthly reason did you have for doing so?"

Her gaze darted around the confined space as if she expected to find answers to his questions carved in the black oak walls. When she glanced down her body and noticed for the first time her disheveled and immodest appearance, she let out a gasp. With quick, nervous hands she attempted to cover her legs, and Jacob felt an unwanted stab of pity. Her rumpled, flour-covered skirt wouldn't cooperate, and she only managed to reveal layers of ruffled undergarments.

He cleared his throat. "Are you hurt?"

"Not that you care, but yes, I was. I've been lying down here with a mountain of flour on me for heaven knows how long . . ."

"For over twenty-four hours, apparently."

Her fingers stilled over the pale bare skin of her calves, and her gaze shot to meet his. "Twenty-four hours? We've been sailing for over a day?"

"Nora, we're approaching the eastern tip of Cuba."

The pageant of emotions on her face matched the ones spinning turbulently in his own head. He'd only begun to grasp the consequences of having her on board, and all of them spelled trouble. He couldn't take her to Belle Isle. He was as certain of that as he was of the wrath that must be building inside Key West's Federal judge at this moment . . . if he suspected where his daughter was.

And worse, Jacob had just left Key West the day before, determined to put distance between himself and the innocently, yet dangerously, seductive Nora Seabrook. He had done the noble thing, dammit, for once in his life. And yet here they were, two of eight people occupying 170 scant feet in the middle of a vast ocean. If ever there was a time Jacob needed to think, it was now. "Can you walk?" he asked her.

"Of course I can walk . . . back to Key West if I have to!"

He extended his hand to her. She took it and struggled to her feet. "At this point I'll just ask you to come to my quarters.

I'm going to get some answers, Nora. Skeet, escort Miss Seabrook to my cabin.''

He turned away from her, but a sudden pressure on his hand brought him back. He stared into a face that had gone milky white and eyes that were suddenly veiled with a soft aquamarine haze. She swayed against his chest, and he caught her under her arms. "I thought you said you could walk," he said.

"I can," she insisted. "I just need a minute."

It was then he saw the discoloration on the crown of her head. Her hair was matted with blood. Scooping her into his arms, he muttered under his breath, "I'm starting to believe that I'm not going to get an honest statement out of you at all, Nora."

CHAPTER FOURTEEN

"Will you hold still? I can't do this if you're squirming." Jacob's voice displayed a mounting impatience, but Nora knew he couldn't possibly be as impatient as she was. For ten minutes he'd been swabbing her head with a strange concoction, not letting her move from the bed where he'd placed her when they first came into this cabin.

He had set her down first, and then lowered himself beside her and turned her around so he could examine her wound. His left leg was on the floor while the other was bent at the knee and drawn up on the bed coverlet. Nora's backside was pressed against his calf. His arm was around her and his hand was holding her brow immobile. She'd endured his none-too-gentle ministrations for about as long as she intended to.

"Ouch!" she cried when his warlock brew seeped into the cut again. "What you're doing hurts worse than my injury."

"Well, it wouldn't if you knew how to be a good patient."

"I'd be a good patient if you had any bedside manner as a doctor!"

"I'm not a doctor, in case I need to remind you of that fact.

I'm a ship captain, one who has the unpleasant task of dealing with a stowaway . . . a stowaway who just happens to be you!"

She ducked her head and spun around to glare at him. "Why is it that every time I'm around you, you make it seem as if my presence is the worst thing that could have happened to you?"

He choked out a sarcastic snort. "In this case, it may truly be the worst thing that's happened to me. What does a man have to do to distance himself from you, Nora?"

She stood up and placed her hands on her hips. Her temper had boiled up through her bloodstream until she wouldn't have been surprised if her hair caught on fire. "Here's a suggestion . . . walk the plank!"

His face contorted with the effort to keep from grinning, infuriating her even more. He leaned back on the bed. "I'll consider it. Now, sit back down and let me look at your head one last time."

"It's fine. It doesn't need more looking at. If you had any compassion at all, you'd know there are other areas of my body that are causing me much more discomfort than that little scratch."

If he possessed the slightest common sense he would understand what she was so delicately trying to express, but apparently, he didn't. So he simply sat forward and stared at her with a wary expression that bordered on sympathetic. "Where does it hurt? I can call for Trevor. He's the closest thing we have to a real doctor."

"I don't need a doctor, Jacob. I need privacy. I've been in that hold for over twenty-four hours. There are certain matters that need to be taken care of . . ."

His eyes widened with understanding. "Oh! Of course." He pointed to a set of short stairs that led to a dark-paneled door. "It's over there." He backed away until he reached the exit. "I . . . I'll just leave you to do whatever you need to do. Take as long as you like. We'll talk later."

At least he wasn't totally insensitive, and she had to admit he was even somewhat endearing in his thickheaded manly embarrassment. "Thank you," she said, "and as long as you've displayed this much concern for my well-being, may I also beg a little nourishment? It's been just as long . . ."

He raised his hands in a sign of capitulation. "I know. Twenty-four hours. I'll have something sent up."

She watched him go and waited until he'd closed the door. Then she investigated the little chamber at the top of the stairs.

A small window near the ceiling provided enough illumination to see without lighting the gas lamp on the wall. She latched the door and looked at the smooth oak seat over a porcelain chamber pot. The facilities were quite adequate, actually. Much nicer than the accommodations she'd had on the *Southern Star*.

Nora smiled at her purely feminine reaction to the water closet. Women could be in the most dire of circumstances, and Nora supposed she was, here in the middle of an ocean with a man who treated her abominably, but one nice little turn of events could make even the gloomiest situation a bit more sunny.

"You can stop grinning anytime, Willy," Jacob said.

The first mate pulled his leg up over his knee and sat back on the wooden bench that flanked the other side of the galley table. His green eyes glittered with foolhardy mirth that seemed a perfect match for the cocky angle of his old British naval cap. To his credit, he did try to straighten his lips into a semblance of seriousness.

"That's better. You do realize we're in a hell of a mess here, don't you?" Jacob warned.

"One of us is, maybe, but it ain't me. I'm just a mate. I don't have to make any decisions. I can just sit back and watch the goin's-on." He pushed the cap back an inch. "That's the way I like it."

"I can't have her on this ship."

" 'Pears she already is, Jacob."

"Well she's got to get off, and the only way I can think for her to do that is to take her back to Key West to her papa. If we're lucky we won't encounter a search and rescue fleet from the U.S. Navy on our way there. It'll put us a couple of days late, but it's better to be late than contend with the judge's revenge if he suspects where his daughter is.''

Willy shrugged. ''We're not likely to meet the navy or anyone else for that matter if we head northwest now, Jacob.''

''Why's that?''

Willy cast him a bemused expression. ''I know your mind's been elsewhere lately, but surely you noticed warning flags on the ships we passed the last half day or so.''

A fine captain he was. For the second time in minutes Jacob felt the unfamiliar flush of mortification. The truth was, he hadn't noticed a single flag and Willy knew it. In fact, he couldn't even remember seeing another ship since they left Key West. He'd obviously spent too much time brooding in his quarters and not enough on deck. He leaned forward and stared at his first mate, trying to regain the authority he'd let slip away. ''Don't keep me in suspense, Will. Get to your point.''

''There's a storm to the north. If we turn back now we'll head right into the center of it. We'll very likely end up shipwrecked ourselves on one of the reefs. Goin' back to Key West isn't an option.''

Jacob threw up his hands in frustration. ''Well, taking Miss Nora Seabrook to Belle Isle isn't an option either! You know that.''

''I don't know any such thing, but I believe that you believe it. I told you once before, Jacob, she seems like an understandin' girl. I don't think you give her enough credit. She might be just the one to accept what she'd find there . . .''

Jacob turned away Willy's comments with a burst of pent-up air. ''Bah! She'd be more likely to accept the Borgia family if you ask me. No, she definitely can't go to Belle Isle.''

''Suit yourself, but what else are you goin' to do with her?''

Jacob pondered the nearly impossible situation for several moments, and then smiled when he came up with the perfect solution. "I've got it. We'll keep heading south, but we'll put Nora on the first ship we recognize that's heading north, one that's going around the tip of Key West. We'll ask the skipper to drop her off at the harbor. She'll be home in a few days at most, delivered unharmed into the judge's arms."

He waited for Willy's agreeable reaction, and when it wasn't delivered, Jacob tried to pry it out of him. "What's wrong with you? It's the perfect plan."

"It's a plan, all right. Whether it's perfect or not, only time will tell."

"I should know never to tell you anything. You're a hard man to convince, Will."

It was the ideal solution, and Jacob knew it. He turned away from his mate and shouted to the *Dover Cloud*'s cook. "Quigley, haven't you got that plate ready yet?"

"Aye, Captain." The portly cook brought a platter to the table. It was piled with slices of ham and steaming boiled potatoes.

"Bloody hell, man! You're not feeding a regiment of infantry. She's just one little woman."

"I know that, Captain, but she's such a shadow of a thing. I've got less than a week to put some meat on her. And my good wife on Belle Isle would never forgive me if I brought that skin-and-bones lass to the island looking like she does."

"For the last time . . . that skin-and-bones lass is not going to Belle Isle!" Jacob cringed. Already Nora Seabrook had disrupted the normal flow of activities on the *Dover Cloud*. If she were on the ship for seven days, think what feminine maneuvers would take place. Jacob was glad he'd thought of his foolproof plan to see her onto a ship in the next day or two at most.

"All right, then," he said to the cook. "Take her the plate, but don't stand by and spoon-feed it to her. She's not as weak as she looks."

Despite his size, and though he was balancing the heavy platter in one hand, the cook darted quickly through the low galley entrance. "Aye, Captain."

Jacob stood, went to the single window in the gloomy room, and looked out on the water. Clasping his hands behind his back, he said, "I guess I've got to come up with a place for her to sleep, at least for tonight, if we don't encounter another ship before dark."

"She can have my quarters," Willy offered.

"That's perfect. We've got four extra beds in the crews' cabin so you can bunk there."

"I didn't mean necessarily that I'd move out," Will said with a grin in his voice.

Jacob turned to face him and answered with a smile of his own. As always, their time-ripened friendship had returned to normal. "Now Will, there's no woman on earth as understanding as all that."

Will went on deck, and for the next hour, Jacob sat in the galley and waited for Quigley to return. Eventually, a lively tune warbled in the cook's familiar whistle announced his presence seconds before he entered the room. He squeezed his bulk through the narrow doorway and set the half-empty platter on the table.

"You still here, Captain?" he said, stating the obvious.

"It took all this time for Miss Seabrook to eat?" Jacob responded impatiently.

"It did, sir. She's got a hearty appetite, which pleased and surprised me. And a gift of gab as well."

How well I know. "So glad you enjoyed yourself," Jacob grumbled.

Oblivious to the sarcasm, Quigley shook his head and chuckled. "Indeed I did, Captain."

"Then I think I'll visit the lady myself," Jacob said. "We have a little unfinished business."

"Oh, I wouldn't go just now, Captain."

Jacob stopped at the doorway and spun around to stare at his cook. "You wouldn't? Why not?"

"She's not properly attired, sir. She gave some of her delicates and her dress to Mr. Skeet. He's taken them to the hold for a bit of a wash. They were smudged with flour, you see. I'm surprised you hadn't noticed it.''

It was happening. His crew was turning into a bevy of ladies-in-waiting. ''I noticed it, Quigley. I simply didn't feel like acting as Miss Seabrook's personal laundress.''

Unaffected by Jacob's outburst, the cook busied himself at a scarred wood countertop, and gave a few scraps of ham to the lackadaisical hound that always sailed with him on the *Dover Cloud.* ''Still, Captain, I'd wait a while before disturbing our guest.''

Our guest! Wait before *disturbing our guest* who sat as cozy as a hen in his own quarters! Jacob hardly gave credence to that notion. No matter how it happened, Nora Seabrook was still a stowaway, and she deserved to be disturbed. She owed him answers, and Jacob was determined to get them. The crew of the *Dover Cloud* might be smitten with the idea of having the beautiful Nora aboard for the seven-day sail, but Jacob certainly wasn't.

Even as he said all this to himself, he berated his fickle mind for thinking of her in such positive terms. Remember why you left Key West in the first place, Jacob, he thought. It matters not that she's beautiful. Pursuing her would only result in a match made at the devil's altar and would lead to the ruination of the poor girl's life. Nora Seabrook was like the Sirens were to Ulysses, and if Jacob didn't keep his mind on his original purpose, he'd be as tempted toward his own demon rocks as surely as the Greek was to his mythical ones.

With any luck, he'd only have to face her one more time. He'd tell her of his plan to send her home and take her to her quarters in Willy's cabin. Then he'd let his fawning crew see to her every whim while he set about the very real business of guiding his ship to its destination.

Jacob strode from the galley with renewed purpose in his step that matched the determination of his mission. He climbed the stairs to the main deck, crossed to his cabin, and knocked on the door. ''Nora, I want to talk to you now!''

In seconds the door opened and Nora stood framed in the entrance. At her back, the sun from the one window cast her in a gilded halo. She was all gleaming white and shimmering gold, with a crest of silken ebony spilling over her shoulders. She was an angel to a man who had never believed in them, and Jacob's purpose dimmed in her presence.

"Of course, Jacob, come in," she said softly.

She stepped back and he crossed the threshold, never taking his gaze from her. The last of his bravado was swept away on the same breeze that rippled his white shirt around her body. The tails reached almost to her knees, and the ivory translucence of his garment revealed a hint of the mysteries hidden now under soft cambric.

Her hair, the color and texture of refined coal, tumbled in thick waves to her breasts. The straps of her camisole were visible under the shirt, as was the delicate lace covering her chest. He detected the swell of her bosom above a ribbon tied at the bodice. The ties, narrow shadows under the placket of his shirt, ran down to her waist like rivulets of water.

"I hope you don't mind," she said. "I had nothing to wear, but as soon as my dress is dry . . ."

He cleared his throat and pulled his gaze away. "You do what you have to do. We'll all make allowances for the short time you're here."

"The short time? Then the voyage we're taking is to a close destination?" Her voice sounded small, hopeful.

He went to his desk and searched for something to look at on its uncluttered surface. Unfortunately, it was free of the usual navigational charts and logs. Not surprising since he was well acquainted with this journey and had little use for them. Needing to gaze upon anything but the soft, feminine swells of Nora, he next went to the window and stared at the sun beginning its decent into the west. "The voyage *I'm* taking is at least six days more," he said. "Yours, however, should prove to be much shorter."

Her fingers closed around his elbow. "You're not putting me off in some strange place? You wouldn't do that."

"It's a far more merciful fate than befalls most stowaways."

"Maybe, but what happened to me was an accident. I didn't intend for it to happen."

She let her hand fall and he couldn't resist the temptation to look at her, to see the ever-changing cast of her sapphire eyes. They had darkened in the last moments to a deep indigo, wary and guarded. Surely she didn't truly fear him. "Oh, come now, Nora," he tested, "you're saying it was an *accident* that you ended up on the *Dover Cloud?*"

"No, not ending up here, but remaining here was."

He crossed his arms and widened his stance, determined to ignore the dangerous combination of seduction and vulnerability that emanated from her eyes, her mouth, the tilt of her head . . .

He couldn't allow himself to succumb to her ability to evoke his sympathy and passion. It was crucial to them both that he remember he was captain of the *Dover Cloud* and his domain had been violated by a trespasser. Never mind that the trespasser was this woman.

"It's time, Nora," he said. "Your medical and physical needs have been met. Your culinary and laundry concerns have been attended to by my crew. I think it's safe to assume that there is no outside influence preventing you from answering my questions."

She stepped away from him until the backs of her knees collided with the bed. Laying her hand on the mattress, she slowly lowered herself onto the coverlet. The cool shadows in that darkened corner of the room bathed her in muted shades of ash and charcoal. Even his shirt against her skin was the soft gray of a dove's wing. But her eyes, those great, luminous blue-gray orbs, were as compelling as ever.

She took a deep breath. "Ask whatever questions you like, and I'll answer them."

Gratified when his voice did not betray the sudden lack of

air in his lungs, he said, "There are just a few. And the first one is, why in God's name are you here?"

Nora had already decided there would be no point in lying to him, partly because no lie would be convincing enough to satisfy the skeptical nature of Jacob Proctor anyway. It wasn't as if she hadn't spent the last two hours trying to think of a good one. It was just that a truly clever fabrication didn't exist for this situation.

She had no choice but to admit to her traitorous spying the day before. But confession would not be easy since he stood so rigidly in front of her. With his arms crossed tightly over his chest and his feet spread wide, he reminded her of a powerful genie bent on granting only one wish ... his own. And that wish would be to have her crumble into dust before his eyes and blow out to sea on the next stiff wind.

And to think that four nights before he had held her in his arms and kissed her with greater passion than she had ever known existed. What kind of flesh-and-blood man was he to kiss her like that and then days later complain so vehemently when she appeared in his life again? What kind of man wishes to distance himself from the same woman he caressed with such tender longing?

He was the captain of this ship, that was who he was. Here his word was law. She tried to ignore the ripple of fear that ribboned down her spine. She would face him with courage and accept her fate. In fact, Nora doubted that there was anything more Jacob Proctor could do to hurt or surprise her than he'd already done.

She locked her gaze with his and stuck out her chin. "I came on board the *Dover Cloud* to find incriminating evidence that would tie you to the wreck of the *Marguerite Gray*."

His reaction was only a slight raising of one eyebrow. "I see. And was your father too busy to get a court order to search the hold himself?"

"He was getting one when I took it upon myself to search

Take advantage of this offer to enjoy Zebra's newest line of historical romance novels....Splendor Romances (formerly Lovegrams Historical Romances)- Take our introductory shipment of 4 romance novels -Absolutely Free! (a $19.96 value)

Now you'll be able to savor today's best romance novels without even leaving your home with our convenient and inexpensive home subscription service. Here's what you get for joining:

- 4 BRAND NEW bestselling Splendor Romances delivered to your doorstep every month
- 20% off every title (or almost $4.00 off) with your home subscription
- A FREE monthly newsletter, *Zebra/Pinnacle Romance News* filled with author interviews, member benefits, book previews and more!
- No risks or obligations...you're free to cancel whenever you wish...no questions asked

To get started with your own home subscription, simply complete and return the card provided. You'll receive your FREE introductory shipment of 4 Splendor Romances and then you'll begin to receive monthly shipments of new Zebra Splendor titles. Each shipment will be yours to examine for 10 days and then if you decide to keep the books, you'll pay the preferred home subscriber's price of just $4.00 per title plus $1.50 shipping and handling. That's $16 for all 4 books plus $1.50 for home delivery! And if you want us to stop sending books, just say the word...it's that simple.

Check out our website at www.kensingtonbooks.com.

4 FREE books are waiting for you!
Just mail in the certificate below!

If the certificate is missing below, write to:
Splendor Romances, Zebra Home Subscription Service, Inc.,
P.O. Box 5214, Clifton, New Jersey 07015-5214
or call TOLL-FREE 1-888-345-BOOK

FREE BOOK CERTIFICATE

SN129A

Yes! Please send me 4 Splendor Romances (formerly Zebra Lovegram Historical Romances), ABSOLUTELY FREE! After my introductory shipment, I will be able to preview 4 new Splendor Romances each month FREE for 10 days. Then if I decide to keep them, I will pay the money-saving preferred publisher's price of just $4.00 each... a total of $16.00 plus $1.50 shipping and handling. That's 20% off the regular publisher's price plus $1.50 for shipping and handling. I may return any shipment within 10 days and owe nothing, and I may cancel my subscription at any time. The 4 FREE books will be mine to keep in any case.

Name _____

Address _____ Apt. _____

City _____ State _____ Zip _____

Telephone ( ) _____

Signature _____
(If under 18, parent or guardian must sign.)

Terms and prices subject to change. Orders subject to acceptance by Zebra Home Subscription Service, Inc. .
Zebra Home Subscription Service, Inc. reserves the right to reject or cancel any subscription.
Offer valid in U.S. only.

AFFIX
STAMP
HERE

SPLENDOR ROMANCES

ZEBRA HOME SUBSCRIPTION SERVICE, INC.

120 BRIGHTON ROAD

P.O. BOX 5214

CLIFTON, NEW JERSEY 07015-5214

lll...l..lll.....lll.l.l.l.l..l.l..lll.l.l.l.l

first. I was afraid he wouldn't get back in time and the evidence would sail out to sea."

"And did you find any of this evidence?"

She squared her shoulders to try to cover the warm flush of guilt that had come to her cheeks. "No."

"That's a shame. I might have enjoyed seeing you run to His Honor with your delicate hands waving rotting fish."

"Obviously, my father thought there was something else, something of value hidden on your ship."

"And it turns out he was right, wasn't he? It's a pity the judge didn't get back before the *Dover Cloud* sailed. What he would have found in her hold would have been the most incriminating evidence of all and definitely something of great value, for he would have discovered his own daughter. Which brings me to my next concern . . ."

Jacob paced along a short path and back again. "If your father didn't know you were coming on board the *Dover Cloud,* then he must have absolutely no idea where you are. This not knowing must be causing your family a great deal of distress, but fortunately it leaves me free of the hangman's noose for the time being, at least."

She drew in a fortifying breath, anticipating Jacob's expression when she revealed the next disturbing detail of her story. "Actually, Jacob, my father might know something . . ."

A tensing of his jaw muscles prompted her to continue, while alarming her at the same time.

"I did tell Fanny what I intended to do."

"You did? So at this very moment, your father, the *Federal Court Judge,* may be under the impression that I have absconded with his only daughter and am taking her God knows where for who knows what immoral purposes."

A shudder quaked through her neck and shoulders. It sounded quite horrible when he said it. "I suppose he might be."

He gave her a thin-lipped smile that was in no way a sign of amusement. "At least I'm glad your papa was so fond of me before all this happened."

She accepted his sarcasm as far superior to rage. "Well, now you know everything, and I suppose if we're to discuss walking the plank again, it will be with me as the one taking the unavoidable stroll to eternity.''

"Not just yet," he said. "In a perverse way I'm enjoying this confessional. And I don't know everything yet, so while you're at it, you might tell me why you and Miss Cosette were at the jetty that afternoon a few days ago. Snooping again, Nora?''

"I prefer *investigating*. Theo saw you that morning coming out of the rocks. When you left, he followed your trail and found the lantern. Naturally, he and Father assumed you'd put it there with the intention of attracting a ship.''

"Naturally. And what conclusion did you come to after your 'investigating'?''

"Only that someone had destroyed a perfectly good lantern.''

He smiled, almost genuinely this time, and she continued. "I decided that either you foiled someone else's attempt to lure a ship to the reef or, frantic to complete your mission, you spent the rest of the day scurrying around for a new lantern to hang in the jetty's cave.''

"And which do you think I did?''

"I wouldn't presume to guess, Captain," she lied. "It has been my own personal experience that you do something one minute that is in complete opposition to that which you have just done the minute before. If you treat a woman with such confounding insensitivity, what chance does a lantern have of expecting more rational behavior from you?''

He had stopped pacing, and now fixed her with a gaze that was almost teasing. "Actually, Nora, I think all men would agree that it is far easier to deal with a lantern than a woman, though in the dark a lantern is not nearly as rewarding.''

A light at the back of his eyes flared with the satisfaction of seeing her reaction to his blatantly sexual comment. He pulled a chair from under his desk and sat backwards on it. He rested his elbows on the top rung so his hands hung relaxed down the back.

If she hadn't learned from previous encounters to be wary

of anything the captain did, she might even term the slight lines at the corners of his eyes and the hint of a curve to his generous lips as a gesture of affection. Or his easy grace in the chair a sign of his acceptance of her presence. But no, she wouldn't be taken in by outward appearances. Not again.

She hid the flush on her cheeks by looking away for a moment. "So what is your decision, Jacob?" she asked finally. "Are you going to turn me into fish food?"

"No, I'm not. You will not meet the fate of other, more hapless, stowaways because I am a kindhearted captain. But as soon as I can, I *am* going to give you back to your papa."

"We're going back to Key West?" Nora hated the petulant edge to her voice, but like it or not, she resented the promise of adventure slipping through her fingers. In her moments alone in Jacob's cabin, she had thought of several enticing entries she could add to her journal. Being trapped on a schooner heading for an unknown destination with a handsome, mysterious man would add an element of excitement to the book she hoped to sell one day.

He stood up and came around the chair toward her. "*You're* going back to Key West," he said. "My crew and I are continuing to our scheduled port."

"But how. . .?"

"The *Dover Cloud* isn't the only ship in the Caribbean, Nora. As soon as I spot one going north with a skipper I know, I'll hail him to drop anchor. Once I determine the ship's destination, it will be a simple matter to deliver you into the care of that captain, who will see you safely home."

"I see." No wonder his mood had improved. All during this conversation he'd had a foolproof plan to banish her from his life again.

He bent slightly at the waist to better see into her eyes. His own seemed to mock her with a dare. "That is what you want, isn't it? After all, you just told me you remained on the *Dover Cloud* by accident. An accident by definition is something we don't intend or particularly wish to happen."

"Of course it's what I want," she said, getting up from the

bed and standing as tall as her barefooted posture would allow. "While most of this ship's crew has been accommodating, even kind, I find one of them to be rude and insufferable. I look forward to returning to the enlightened environment of Key West as soon as possible."

He grinned, apparently amused that she had described their island of thirty-two taverns and only three churches as enlightened. "Good. Then we're agreed. Allow me to show you to your quarters for the hours you will remain on board."

She sashayed by him, his shirttails fluttering at her legs and his wide sleeves slapping against her elbows. "That's fine with me. I only hope it's as far away from this cabin as possible."

He followed her out and guided her around a corner to Willy Turpin's cabin. "Unfortunately, only a wall separates us."

She put her hand on the latch, but before opening the door she said, "That's what you think, Captain. Much more than a wall keeps us apart!"

She went in and slammed the portal shut with a resounding crack. Jacob headed in search of Willy, but the last minutes of his conversation with Nora stayed in his mind. "Damnable woman," he muttered. "She's more fun to lock horns with than most lovers are to kiss."

Seeing Willy at the ship's wheel, he crossed the fifty feet of deck in long strides, all the while shaking his head. You did the right thing, Jacob, he told himself. It's for the best that she hates you. It's for her own good. Despite what that stuffing-for-brains Willy says. No girl could understand the sinister climate that shrouds the very air at Proctor House. No decent girl would want to try.

CHAPTER FIFTEEN

Through the rest of that afternoon and evening, the *Dover Cloud* did not encounter a single ship heading north, no doubt, Will Turpin said, because of the storms in the Florida Straits. Feeling less than sociable, Jacob took his dinner in his quarters, and Nora stayed in hers. Several times Jacob heard crew members talking to her, and he caught snatches of their conversations through the wall.

"More wine, miss?" he heard one sailor ask.

"May I take your dishes, Miss Seabrook?" another offered.

"Will you be needing anything else this evening, ma'am?" *Can I turn down your bed, Duchess? Will you accept this bouquet of fresh posies?* It was all too much!

Certain that sleep would elude him anyway, Jacob volunteered to take the first night watch and relieved Will at ten o'clock. Too anxious to sit, he stood at the wheel of the *Dover Cloud*, his hands loosely on the spindles.

It was a calm night with little wind. The schooner barely needed his guidance as she maintained a steady course south toward the Windward Passage. Jacob was acutely aware that every slow mile took them further away from Key West and

the opportunity to return Nora to her family. And one mile
closer to Belle Isle.

He stared at the horizon where the blue-black water of the
Caribbean Sea met an indigo sky. A three-quarter moon dazzled
spears of light upon the gently rippling surface of the water,
giving it a jeweled look that matched the stars twinkling against
a backdrop of clear, dark heaven.

Jacob wondered if Nora was watching the sky and sea out
her window. His gaze kept returning to the amber glow spilling
onto the passageway from the window of her cabin. She was
still awake, and he pondered what matters kept her from turning
out her light. Probably not the same yearnings that kept him
from sleeping!

Finally, around midnight, the lantern in her quarters was
extinguished. At the same time a gray cloud covered the moon,
and only the single sidelight hanging from the mainsail mast
interrupted the endless darkness. It was lonely on the deck of
the *Dover Cloud* in the middle of the night. He'd never noticed
that before. Or, if he had noticed, he'd never minded until now.

He pushed vain longings from his mind. "Tomorrow," he
muttered. "Surely we'll pass a ship tomorrow that will take
her away." He shook off a bout of melancholy and gripped
the wheel fiercely. "I was right," he said to the night shadows.
"Nora has changed everything on the *Dover Cloud.*"

The next morning after breakfast, Skeet manned the ship's
wheel while Will and Jacob stood at the deck rail scanning the
horizon for other vessels. Nora slipped out of her cabin, and
without uttering so much as a good morning, proceeded down
the narrow passageway by her quarters until she came to the
bow of the ship. She stopped at a crate next to her cabin wall.
Spreading the skirt of her yellow dress, which Jacob noticed
was now free of all traces of flour, she sat on the carton and
leaned back. Looking from left to right, she gazed at the panorama of sea and sky, but stopped just short of looking at the
two men at the deck rail.

"Women!" Jacob grumbled. "Especially that one. You know she sees us, but she's determined not to grant us the courtesy of a simple 'good day.' "

Will remained silent a moment and then said, "Everyone has a different telescope on the world, my friend."

Jacob leveled a condemning glare at his mate. "What the bloody hell does that mean?"

"It means that we each see what we want to see, and the missy there is no different."

"So you're saying she doesn't want to see me?"

Will professed impartiality by merely hunching a shoulder. "Couldn't say for sure, but when I delivered her biscuits and coffee this morning, she greeted me cheerfully as could be."

Jacob turned a quarter way around so he could clearly see into his first mate's eyes. "You're enjoying this, aren't you, Willy?"

"A wee bit, Captain."

Jacob snorted. "Enjoy it while you can, because the truth is I'm glad she's staying on her side of the ship. And I'm happy to stay on mine. It's the way I want it. The way it has to be."

"Right, Captain."

He peered beyond Will's purposely blank face just enough to see Nora's profile from the corner of his eye. She had a book open in her lap and she looked calm and serene and shatteringly lovely. Jacob pressed his hand against the deck rail hard enough to stick a splinter into his palm. It was all he could do not to shout with frustration. How dare she appear so at peace with the world when his insides were coiled tighter than a seaman's knot?

"Hurt yourself, Jacob?" Will asked.

He pulled the splinter out of his palm and shook his hand to relieve the smarting. "No. I wonder what she's reading."

"Ivanhoe."

"How do you know that?"

"She saw it in your cabin and fancied it. Quigley retrieved it for her last night."

"I might have known." Temptation got the best of him and

he risked a long, deliberate look down the passageway. *Ivanhoe* was nestled cozily among the pleats of Nora's dress. Her gaze was intent upon its cream-colored pages, and her hands rested almost lovingly on its sides.

Jacob winced. He had to snap out of this mood. He was dangerously close to being jealous of a book!

Will nudged him. "Looks like your problem with Nora could be solved, Jacob."

Following the line of sight indicated by Will's index finger, Jacob spotted a ship in the southeast. It was heading toward them . . . heading north.

"All right. That's more like it," he said.

They both watched as the ship came closer. "It's a steamer," Will pointed out.

"I see that. It's probably a mail packet," Jacob said without enthusiasm.

"That's perfect. It means it's going to several ports, and Key West is surely to be one of them. What luck, eh, Jacob?"

Jacob flashed a look meant to dispel his mate from making any more such ridiculous statements. "We can't put her on a packet, Will. They don't carry passengers. Would you want her sailing with only men? Would you have her stop at every watering hole between here and Key West?"

Will scratched his chin. "I guess I wouldn't."

The packet steamed by. Nora continued reading.

In the next hour another ship appeared on the horizon. When it was still some distance away, Jacob eliminated it as a possibility for Nora's transport. "It's only a two-masted bark," he said. "She'll be a week getting back to her family on that bucket."

Will scratched his chin again. "I guess that's possible."

The slow and steady bark sailed by. Nora continued reading.

The third ship of the morning was cast aside as being too small, though Will estimated its length as no more than ten feet less than the *Dover Cloud*'s.

"Still," Jacob said, "there have been times when I've wished the *Cloud* had been longer. She'd have handled better in a gale.''

"Aye, Captain.''

A Dutch vessel that from all appearances was totally seaworthy was deemed unsuitable because its crew was, of all things, Dutch. "I can't put her on a ship where she doesn't speak the crew's language,'' Jacob declared. "After all, look at all she's demanded from this crew. She'd be lost if she couldn't order everyone about.''

The four-masted Dutch barkentine sailed by with grace and speed. Nora looked up from her book, cast a brief, questioning look at Jacob, and shook her head.

It was nearly noon when a schooner that could almost be called the sister ship of the *Dover Cloud* came into view. She was of identical length and width, similarly fitted, and was a ship that both Jacob and Will know.

"Look there, Jacob,'' Will said jubilantly. "It's the *Sea Hound* from New Orleans.''

Jacob squinted into the sun. "Can you be sure?''

"Of course. Look at her house flag. It's got the black mastiff. It's the *Sea Hound* for certain.''

Jacob couldn't deny it. The ship heading right for them was the very one that sailed monthly from New Orleans to trade for pottery and silver trinkets in Venezuela. She always carried a respectable cargo and several passengers, and she usually came within a mile of Key West when she headed into the Gulf of Mexico for home. Her capable captain, Monty Vasquez, was a U.S.-born Spaniard who spoke perfect English.

Jacob watched the *Sea Hound* draw closer and tried to ignore a sinking feeling that descended to the pit of his stomach. He looked at Nora and realized she was watching him. Her eyebrows raised dubiously, and her lips slanted in a teasing grin before she finally said, "Is this ship suitable, Captain?''

The only thing worse than seeing the woman go was being made to feel like a fool by her. Jacob suffered both the misery and the indignity at that moment. "Yes, Nora. It's quite suitable,'' he snapped at her. "You may grab a seaman's bag from my wardrobe and pack it with as many of my clothes as you think you might need. Include any books from my shelves that might entertain you, and all the slices of ham you can eat, and prepare to go home."

She stood up, slammed the book shut with a crack, and sauntered past him toward his cabin. "That's music to my ears, Captain."

He turned away from her and barked an order to Will. "Hoist the yellow and blue. Let Vasquez know I want to speak to him."

The rasp of heavy rope sliding along wood filtered through the small window in Jacob's cabin. Probably the anchor being lowered, Nora thought, flinging open the door to his wardrobe. Without analyzing her actions, she followed Jacob's instructions and took a canvas bag from a shelf, and then stood in the middle of the room and simply stared at it.

"What in heaven's name did you get this thing for?" she demanded of herself, and flung the bag on the bed. "It's not as if you truly have anything to pack!"

Then she followed the sack onto the bed, throwing herself into the downy softness of the feather mattress. "I don't want to go," she said to the empty room. She fell back against pillows that smelled of pine and sea spray, and Jacob. There was no denying the truth. She wanted to stay on the *Dover Cloud*. But more than that, she wanted Jacob to want her to stay.

I was so sure he was getting used to having me around, she thought. Especially after all that silly ship business. *This one's too short. This one's too slow.* I believed he was going to give up his plan of sending me home and let me stay, even insist upon it. But as usual, it was just Jacob being Jacob . . . impossible to fathom and as unpredictable as Key West weather.

Now she would never know where the *Dover Cloud* was headed. Damnation! What was so special about this place Jacob was going to? Why was it such a big secret? Nora had tempted

Jacob's crew with some of Fanny's best feminine wiles, and not one of the loyal sailors had told her what she wanted to know. Not one had hinted at so much as the country of their destination. Perhaps her execution of Fanny's talents was pitifully inept, or maybe she was simply not enough like the women these sailors knew. It wasn't fair. Not to a girl who had only known two places in her whole life . . . Richmond, Virginia, and Key West, Florida.

No, it definitely wasn't fair. Not to a girl who had never once in her life known a man like Jacob Proctor. There was so much Nora wanted to discover, and now she probably never would.

The *Dover Cloud* had completely halted its graceful slicing through the ocean, and now bobbed gently with the easy swells that cushioned its hull. They were obviously preparing to meet the *Sea Hound*. Nora stood up and placed the seaman's bag back in Jacob's wardrobe. She would go home with only what she'd had when she left.

"Nora, it's time," Jacob called through the door. "Would you come on deck?"

With a heavy sigh, she went to meet him.

Another ship, an equal to the *Dover Cloud* in almost every aspect, rested at anchor some hundred yards away. A black mastiff was clearly visible on its forward jib. "Is this the dog that is to carry me home?" she asked smartly.

Jacob smiled. "Yes, it is, and we're lucky to have found a hound willing to take you."

She answered his smile with a sweet one of her own. "When it comes to you, Captain, my luck seems never to change."

Confusion marred his previously confident features for an instant before he shouted across the water to a man on the deck of the *Sea Hound*. "Ahoy, there! Is Captain Vasquez on board?"

"He is!"

"Good. We're rowing over." He next issued instructions to his crew. "Lower the boat and let go the ladder."

Once these two tasks were complete, Jacob waited for Will

to go down the ladder first. He followed him, but only descended three rungs before he told Nora to begin climbing down.

She stared at the flimsy webbing of rope that swayed precariously against the side of the ship. A person could easily lose footing just climbing over the edge of the deck and trying to fasten their toes on the first rung. Nora wasn't anxious to try.

"Well, come on," Jacob said with impatience. "What are you waiting for?"

She wanted to shout one of the colorful epithets she'd heard at the Key West Harbor, but knew it would do no good. Instead she gritted her teeth in preparation for her task and tried to decide if she should leave her eyes open or closed.

"It's all right, Miss Nora," Quigley said from behind her. "I won't let you fall."

"Thank you, Thomas. That's kind of you." With the cook's hand on her shoulder, she lifted her leg over the side.

"Not like that," Jacob shouted at her. "Do something with your skirt. You'll catch your foot in your dress and fall like a stone that way."

"What a lovely thought," she yelled back at him. "Thank you for the encouragement." But she supposed he was right. She retreated to the deck again, reached under her dress, and grabbed the back of her skirt. Bringing the material between her legs, she yanked the hem up to her middle and stuck it into a sash at her waist. Her legs were bare to her thighs, but this was no time for modesty. Common sense was required.

With Quigley's assistance, she began the process again, and this time succeeded in connecting her toe with the first span of the ladder. The twelve or so inches of rope felt hardly more substantial than drapery cord. Her foot depressed instantly into the middle of the rung. Her hands froze on the deck rail. And she felt Jacob's hand on her ankle.

"Don't dawdle," he said. "Do it quickly. It's easier in the end. Besides, even if you fall, you'll only land on my head."

Feeling a burst of courage, she craned her neck to see his face. It was lit with a broad grin. "That, sir," she said, "is the only aspect of this ridiculous endeavor which I find the least bit tempting.''

"As do I, Nora," he called back.

"Confound you, Jacob . . ."

"Don't look down," he warned, cutting her off. "Just climb. That's the girl."

Somehow she managed to end up in the rowboat between Jacob and Will. She remembered when Jacob's hands had pressed her thighs through the ballooning material at her hips, and finally when their welcome strength had captured her under her arms. And she recalled how those hands had lingered there even after she'd regained her equilibrium.

She sat in the middle of the small boat and the two men rowed to the *Sea Hound*. Not surprisingly, going up the other ship's ladder was every bit as difficult as descending the *Dover Cloud*'s. And when she reached the deck, mussed and dampened with unladylike perspiration, she found herself the object of intense scrutiny by the *Sea Hound*'s crew. They'd probably never seen such an inept sailor in all their days, and it was all they could do not to laugh out loud at her ridiculously uncoordinated efforts. Nora's face heated with embarrassment. *Thank you, Jacob, for making me feel like an idiot again!*

Jacob, too, noticed the beady eyes of the *Sea Hound*'s crew. His flesh heated with building fury while the muscles in his jaw tensed. What was the matter with these scurvy dogs? Hadn't they ever been close to a pretty woman before? From the looks of them, Jacob thought it quite possible they hadn't. Scruffy old clothes, a week's growth of beard, and a strong scent of grog and garlic marked every crewman of the *Sea Hound*. Funny, as many times as Jacob had come in contact with them before, he'd never noticed what a rotting lot they were.

"I want to see Captain Vasquez," he said.

"That'll be a mite difficult, Proctor," one of the men said. "Unless you go to his cabin. He's got the gout. Been in his quarters this whole trip."

"What? I asked about him before we rowed over here."

The ends of the sailor's mustache curled away from a smattering of brown teeth. "You asked if he was here. And he is. He just ain't operatin' in his official capacity."

"Then who is acting captain?"

The sailor snatched a wool stocking cap from his head, causing strands of greasy gray hair to stand on end. "You're lookin' at him. Reggie Smythe." He emitted a belly laugh and punched at Jacob's arm. "What're you so surprised for? This bucket's still afloat, ain't she?"

Jacob turned around, expecting to have to coax a look of pure terror off Nora's countenance. But what he saw was an odd little twist to her pink lips, and a purely astonishing twinkle in her eyes. She wasn't doing it openly, but inside, Nora was smiling.

If she wasn't afraid of or offended by this ramshackle crew, then maybe he was jumping to unwarranted conclusions. Truly, appearances weren't always an important indication of a man's character. And Vasquez was on board, and no doubt still had his finger on the pulse of everything that happened on his ship. Perhaps Nora could sail safely with this crew after all.

"I'm seeking passage for this woman," Jacob said. "She needs to return to Key West as soon as possible, and the *Dover Cloud* is sailing south. Would you have any objection to delivering her to that destination?"

Smythe looked around at his companions, who, during Jacob's request, had drawn into a tight circle around the threesome from the *Dover Cloud*. The grins on their faces left no doubt of their answer, but Smythe confirmed it with a cackle and a decisive nod of his head. "I don't think 'objection' is the word that comes to mind, Captain, and since we'd already planned to stop at Key West, I'd be mighty glad to have the lady on board."

The sailors of the *Sea Hound* expressed their anticipation with overtly bawdy mannerisms that stopped just short of drooling. Jacob looked at Nora again, expecting a squeal of protest from the Richmond-born debutante. "You heard the men, Miss Seabrook. What do you say?"

She thrust her little chin out as though sheer determination was enough to protect her in this den of lechers. ''The arrangements are fine with me, Captain,'' she said, ''as long as they suit you. I know you only have my best interests at heart.''

Jacob longed to see her knees once more, not for the seductive pleasure of ogling her bare calves, but because he was quite sure her joints were knocking together in trepidation under all that fussy yellow material. But damnation, she was playing her bluff like a New Orleans card sharp. It was a long shot, but maybe she would be delivered safely by this crew of reprobates. But Jacob wouldn't bet on it. The only factor that would convince him otherwise was if the *Sea Hound*'s passenger list included women. If Nora would be sailing with ladies like herself, he might consider leaving her. Ultimately, it would be a far better situation for her than going to Belle Isle.

''Tell me, Mr. Smythe,'' he said, ''have you any passengers on board?''

''Yes, Captain. We have seven paying customers, all bound for New Orleans.''

''I'd like to meet them if you don't mind,'' Jacob said.

''Don't mind a'tall.'' Smythe pointed to a group of young men peering at the commotion from several feet away. ''That's them sittin' over there.''

Jacob had noticed the youths when he came on board, but had taken them for cabin boys. Learning they were passengers, he gave them a stern scrutiny now. They were scarcely out of their adolescence. Not one of them could even have attained Nora's age, though now that he regarded their dress, they appeared to be of the same social status as the Seabrooks.

''These boys are your only passengers?'' he asked.

''That they be,'' Smythe assured him. ''All seven of them sent by their rich pappies to some fancy university in New Orleans. A fairly worthless lot of lazy puffs if you ask me, but for what they paid for their passage, I ain't one to criticize.''

Any number of criticisms came to Jacob's mind. Like why did their jaws practically hit their chests when they stared at Nora? And why did they whisper and chuckle behind their lily-white hands? Did they think social position entitled them to liberties not afforded to more common folk? If Jacob had hoped to find comfort in the *Sea Hound*'s passenger list, he was sorely disappointed. And his mind was made up.

"Thank you just the same, Mr. Smythe, but I've changed my mind." He pivoted around to take Nora's elbow, and practically propelled her to the ship's deck rail before issuing a command in her ear. "We're going back to the *Dover Cloud*." Then, in a gruff whisper, he added, "And you can just wait a minute to hike up your skirt!"

She came to an abrupt stop inches from the rail and gently but firmly pried his fingers off her elbow. "That's fine, Jacob, but first I have something to do and you can just wait a minute."

She went back to Smythe, leaving Jacob to follow the yellow flounce of her hips with his eyes. He strained to hear what she had to say. "Mr. Smythe, would you be so kind as to get me a paper and pen?"

Paper and pen? Now what was she doing? When Smythe returned with the requested items, she quickly scrawled a note across the page, folded the sheet, and wrote several lines on the outside. "If you wouldn't mind seeing that this gets to the proper party . . ." She looked over her shoulder at Jacob. "Captain Proctor will see that you are compensated for your efforts."

He stood dumbstruck for seconds. What? She expected him to pay Smythe to do her bidding? A slight tilt of her head and a pointed widening of her eyes warned him that he'd better do just that. He took a few coins from his pocket and delivered them to Smythe's hand. Only then did Nora proceed to the rail to wait for him to start down the ladder.

Not a word was spoken all the way back to the *Dover Cloud*. Nora stared straight out to sea as if the men in front of and behind her didn't exist. And what was there for Jacob to say? It had been his decision to return her to his ship, and he had to live with it.

As the *Sea Hound* hoisted sail and began a northwest heading, Jacob watched his last efforts to keep Nora from Belle Isle sail with her. The die was cast. He couldn't let her go. So he'd just have to do what he could to protect her.

Once back on board the *Cloud*, Nora went immediately to Will's cabin. When Jacob realized she still wasn't going to talk to him, he followed her. She allowed him entrance, most probably because his large frame prevented her from shutting the door. He crossed the threshold and kicked the door closed with the heel of his boot. Then he paced, though in Will's smaller quarters there really wasn't far to go, and the effort did little to relieve his frustration.

Nora waited, watching him.

"Well," he finally said, "aren't you going to say something?"

"Like what?"

"Like admitting what you really felt about staying on that ship?"

"I'll readily admit to knowing how *you* felt about me staying on the ship."

"Is that so? You know how I felt?"

She smiled with the confidence of a sparrow who'd just found the worm in the apple. "Jacob, when we boarded the *Sea Hound* and I looked at the expression on your face, my only real concern was how I'd manage those blasted ladders again!"

CHAPTER SIXTEEN

Jacob had to admire her mettle. It was equal to that of the Key West wreckers who risked life and limb to reach stranded ships. Nora's pluck was more subtle than theirs, but just as effective. And like most sailors, she didn't hold back saying what was on her mind.

Hell, it wasn't just her grit he admired. It was everything about her, and it was getting more difficult with each passing moment to ignore every tense impulse in his body that urged him to act on his baser, manly instincts.

He'd never known a woman like her. She'd rendered him speechless more than once with a well-aimed dart of truth. And she'd snared him on several occasions in the shimmering nets of her eyes. He turned away from her now before she realized the power she wielded over him with a word and a look.

"What was in the note you gave Smythe?" he demanded, his tone as unyielding as his ramrod posture.

"Nothing important," she said. "Just the very words that could keep you from becoming the next exhibit on the Key West gallows."

"Oh, really? Would you care to explain?"

"I wrote to my father telling him I boarded the *Dover Cloud* of my own free will and have chosen to stay because it is the best way to secure my safety. I told him not to worry. That you would deliver me home unharmed."

He allowed her words to sink in, along with the surge of gratitude he suddenly felt for her admission. It couldn't have been easy for her to tell her father that she had ventured on board Jacob Proctor's ship voluntarily.

After a moment, she said, "That is true, isn't it?"

He faced her at last. "That I will deliver you unharmed? Certainly. I'll do my best. That your father will believe it, I doubt very much."

"The proof of the pudding is in the eating, Jacob. Even for my father's stubborn taste buds. There is, however, one thing which would make me feel more confident about the outcome of this voyage."

"If it's within our power, I will see that my crew accommodates you."

"They've already proven that they're unwilling to accommodate me on this matter." She pulled out the chair under Will's simple trestle desk and sat down. When she looked up at him, her eyes shone with cobalt intensity. "I want to know where we're headed. And since I'm here for the long journey, I think I have a right to know."

Of course she did. And he had to tell her enough to satisfy her curiosity . . . for now. He sat on Will's narrow bed. His knees were mere inches from hers. "We're going to an island in the southern Caribbean, Nora. It's located between Barbados and Trinidad, though compared to those islands, this one is barely a speck on the map."

"And what is this island called?"

"Belle Isle."

"A beautiful name," she said. "Is it truly as beautiful as its name implies?"

He nodded. "It's remote, unspoiled. Raw beauty, I would call it. Very private. Chances are the only vessels you will see in the simple harbor are single-masted sailboats, fishing smacks, and dories.''

"Then why. . .?''

Since she left her question unasked, he finished it for her. "Then why is a schooner the size of the *Dover Cloud* venturing into its secluded port? Why are we welcome there?''

"Yes.''

"Because the island is the property of Harrison Proctor, my father.''

"Your family *owns* the island?''

He shrugged an affirmative response. "My father is the second-generation caretaker of the property. It, and the title of Lordship, was originally bestowed upon my grandfather, Charles Proctor, by the Duke of Wellington in 1815.''

"1815?'' she repeated. "The Battle of Waterloo.''

Jacob cast her an admiring look. "Exactly. You know your history. Though you French must not like to be reminded of this episode from your past.''

She smiled. "I was born in America, Jacob. Long after the Napoleonic Wars were ended.''

"So . . . since there are no ill feelings, I can tell you that my grandfather was somewhat of a military genius. The Duke of Wellington convinced King George to reward Charles for his efforts on the Continent by doling out a small estate near Dover which included all Lord of Manorial Rights. With Braxton Manor came a small island in the Caribbean, one which had been claimed for the British flag some hundred years previously.''

"How interesting,'' Nora said. "Tell me, how did the island come to have a French name?''

Jacob chuckled. "That, I was told, is strictly the result of my grandmother Lydia's fanciful sense of humor. The first time she visited the island, she was struck with its majesty, and the fact that it was hers only because the French lost the Battle of Waterloo. She thought it ironically appropriate to attach a French name to her newfound paradise. Lyme Island became Belle Isle. It's a fitting title and it stuck.''

"Do they live on the island, your grandparents?"

How different Jacob's life would have been if they had lived there. Their presence wouldn't have changed his future, but their cheery demeanor would have done much to alter the gloomy aspects of his past.

Nora's question brought back memories of the day just after Jacob's ninth birthday—the day his grandparents were killed in a carriage accident near Dover. He could still remember his grandmother's bright laughter and her hand gently ruffling his hair. And he recalled nights by a warm fire in the library of Braxton Manor when he sat at his grandfather's knee listening to exploits of campaigns and military heroism. "No," he said. "They've been dead over twenty years."

"How sad they didn't have more years to enjoy their island. But your father and mother? They are at Belle Isle?"

He remembered his mother in nightmares when her pale face and cold, dark eyes came back to haunt him. Memories of the night she died still plagued him. He shivered even now when he recalled her that next morning, her body misshapen, the translucent skin battered and scarred by jagged rocks, her many cuts and abrasions bleached white by salt water. "My mother died when I was twelve," he said.

There must have been something in his tone, something Nora misinterpreted, because she reached out a hand to cover the one of his that rested on his knee. "Jacob, I'm so sorry," she whispered.

"Don't be," he said, and meant it. No one should waste one ounce of pity mourning Sophie Proctor's death. But he took the sting out of his words by turning his hand palm up and entwining his fingers with hers.

"Such a sad childhood you had," Nora said. "One loss after another. You spoke of your father. He's alive, then?"

"Very much alive."

She smiled, obviously relieved to have discovered a secure element of Jacob's desolate youth. If she only knew. If only he could keep her from finding out. But each mile brought them closer to the truth, and the reality of Belle Isle was anything but secure.

"I'm glad for that at least. You have your father and the beautiful island."

A beautiful island with a poisonous underbelly. Soon enough, Belle Isle would reveal its hidden depravity to a trusting Nora Seabrook. She would learn that beauty is only the surface of a thing. And yet, when Jacob looked at her, he found it almost possible to believe that true beauty could touch the soul and live in the heart.

If only Belle Isle were like Nora. If only it was the place it was meant to be, the place a joyous Lydia Proctor designated it to be on the day she first sailed into the protected bay and proclaimed it was kissed by an angel. *If only . . .* Jacob's grandmother used to say, "If wishes were horses, beggars would ride." Wishes were only useless fragments of a dreamer's mind.

Going to the island always made him anxious and melancholy, but this time it was worse than ever. This time he longed for the island to be as Lydia saw it. He wished he were taking Nora to the paradise his grandmother had envisioned before it all went so wrong. Before he learned his own fate was sealed with the woman who plunged from the cliffs that wretched night.

He suddenly needed Nora's beauty and goodness close to him, to remind him that it did exist in some realm. He clasped her hands in his and stood, bringing her with him. Then he pulled her into his arms. She hesitated for just a moment, and then stepped willingly into his beckoning circle. He cupped the back of her head, and she laid her cheek against his chest. "Ah, Nora, enough talk about Belle Isle for tonight. Soon I will tell you more, and then before long we will be there."

She stirred in his arms and looked up into his face. "You do love it there, don't you, Jacob?"

He stroked her hair, trailing raven silk through his fingers. "The island begs to be loved," he said, and that part was true.

"And are you so very sorry that I'm here, that I will get to see this place you guard so carefully with your secrets?"

He was sorry she was going to Belle Isle, but God help him, he was not sorry she was here. He smiled down into her shining eyes. "Do I confound you so much, Nora, that you need to ask?"

"Truly, Jacob, you confound me more than that."

"Then perhaps you need some convincing." He lowered his head and took her mouth in a crushing kiss that stirred longings buried deep inside him, longings he had no right to quench. He flicked his tongue across her lips until she opened them to his explorations. She was soft and warm and deliciously moist inside, and in the haven of her mouth he could forget everything but the tender yielding of her body against his.

When he finally pulled his mouth from hers, he could only whisper into her hair, "Nora, I am sorry about many things, but not that you are here right now."

"Then for what?" she questioned in a teasing voice. "I can't find an objection to anything you've done in the last few minutes."

He smiled at her delightful honesty. She made him happier than he deserved to be. "Then for nothing in particular. I'm just trying to get an apology or two ahead."

"I know you, Jacob. That will never be enough."

For Nora, the next few days passed in languid anticipation. She spent warm, sunny days reading on the bow of the ship, and cozy nights in Will's cabin writing her impressions of her voyage and her ideas of what their destination would be like. She tried to help the crew when she could, and to tend to her own concerns without having to ask for assistance.

One of these concerns was her wardrobe, or lack of one. Remembering the basket of colorful material she'd seen in the ship's hold, she decided to ask Jacob about it one morning with the intention of adding to her one garment. He told her the cloth was meant to be a gift for the women on Belle Isle, that he always brought some little thing the women could not ordinarily procure on the island. When she only uttered a disappointed, "I see," he took the cue and offered her a bit of the fabric.

"I'd much rather you'd make use of a few yards of it than walk around in my clothes," he said, and then smiled wickedly. "Though now that I think of you that night in my shirt, I wonder if I haven't gone addled in my brain to say such a thing."

Nora grinned at the memory herself, recalling the pleasure of bantering with this difficult man. Without responding verbally she ran off to fetch the material with Jacob calling after her, "See Quigley for a needle and thread. He's the one who most often bursts his seams and has need of them."

After that evening in Will's cabin when Jacob had told her about Belle Isle and his family, he had not sought occasions to be alone with her. He hadn't exactly avoided her either. They took their meals together in the galley, sharing pleasant conversation with the crew. He had questioned her often about her welfare on the ship, inquiring as to whether she was keeping occupied and not lacking any necessities. Aloof concern was how she described his behavior in her moments alone when she had time to think about it.

Unfortunately, she also thought about the night they were alone in Will's cabin and about the kiss that still burned in her memory. No girl could ever forget the gentle protection of his strong arms around her and the almost desperate tenderness of that kiss. She sighed wistfully when she recalled the assertive press of his mouth on hers, the insistent plundering of his tongue as if he hungered to fulfill some desire in his soul by subjecting her to his will.

She warmed to the roots of her hair even still, knowing that if he'd longed to conquer her that night, she had been more than willing to be his victim. It was a dangerous reaction to a dangerous man if ever there was one! Perhaps aloof concern was what was needed between her and Jacob.

She learned more about the natives of his mysterious island

one calm, clear evening when he asked her to stay with him a moment at the ship's wheel. He stood behind her, placed her hands on the spindles, and instructed her how to keep the ship on an even keel. She followed the direction indicated by the compass, and fastened her gaze on the horizon where somewhere beyond her view lay Belle Isle.

"Who lives on this island, Jacob?" she asked him after they had fallen into a comfortable silence.

He thought a moment before answering. "A few hundred decent people unaffected by greed or ambition."

"It's a lovely thought," she said, "but what I meant was where did they come from originally."

"Ah . . . Belle Islanders, they will tell you, are a unique combination of Bahamian, Latin, and Dutch influences. When you see them, you might agree. They get their grace of movement and lithe bodies from their Bahamian ancestors, their olive-skinned beauty from their Latin forbears, and their patience and tolerance from the Dutch."

"A nice combination," Nora said. "They sound almost perfect."

His hands covered hers on the ship's wheel and he turned it just slightly, making an adjustment in their direction. "Not so perfect, I'm afraid," he said. "They lack cunning and the ability to see and know their enemies. They are sadly defenseless against attack. Luckily, they've never had to test their combative skills or self-preservation instincts. If they had, I'm afraid the island people would have been easy prey."

She thought about what he said, and found his reference to attack and defense to be at odds with his other descriptions of the beautiful island. "Perhaps as isolated as they are, they will never have to know what it is to have their society in jeopardy. I would think that one would be as safe on Belle Isle as anywhere in the world."

His hands clenched unexpectedly over hers. "One should never be so at ease that he drops his guard completely, Nora. I don't believe any place is truly safe from all harm. This is something you will have to learn ... before we reach Belle Isle.''

Again Nora couldn't understand what made Jacob say such things. In all her life, she had known only security and safety. The warmth and protection of a loving family. A welcoming home as her refuge through childhood. And even now, on this ship, with its captain's arms surrounding her in snug security, she felt safe.

Perhaps she had dwelled in a cocoon of blissful naivety all her years, but she could never envision herself embracing Jacob's cynicism. Or maybe she still had a lot to learn about this man and his island.

The afternoon before they were due to arrive at Belle Isle, Jacob granted Nora a special privilege. Since the ship had made good time, and three casks of fresh water still remained in the hold, he gave in to her desires to have a bath, a real one in which she could soak herself from head to toe, not just wash from a basin attached to her cabin wall.

Her ''tub'' was half a hogshead in the belly of the ship. It was not large enough to allow her to stretch out and leisurely soak, but it did accommodate her body if she pulled her knees nearly to her chin. But when it was filled with warm water from Quigley's stove and she lowered herself into it, it was heaven.

She was so grateful that she wanted to thank Jacob again for his thoughtfulness. After supper that night she abandoned her usual habit of staying in her quarters till morning and went on deck to find him. Several crew members had congregated in mid-deck to play cards. ''Have you seen Jacob?'' she asked them.

''Oh, miss, indeed we have,'' Skeet answered. ''He's at the wheel this very moment. And as you can see, the rest of us are as far away from that location as we can be.''

Thinking the old sailor's remarks odd, Nora questioned, ''Why is that, Mr. Skeet?''

"It's the way it always is the night before we reach the island. We leave the captain be, and he likes it that way. It's when he prepares himself."

Prepares himself for what? she wondered. "Do you think he would mind an interruption from me?" she asked.

Skeet looked at his companions and grinned back at her. "You're probably the only one whose head wouldn't be chomped off at the neck for botherin' him."

Shaking off the gruesome image, Nora left the men to their pastime. She found Jacob alone at the stern, his hands on the wheel, a single sidelight illuminating his face. His features were set in grim determination, but when he saw her, the lines around his eyes and mouth softened.

Nodding toward his crew, but watching her, he said, "If a bath can effect such a transformation on a person, Nora, perhaps I should insist the whole bloody lot of them give it a try."

He seemed much too jovial for a headhunter, and her skin warmed at his praise. She'd only had lye soap and a brush she'd found in one of the crates to work with. And since she wasn't much of a seamstress, she'd felt lucky to have created a sort of sarong-type dress out of a silky flowered material in the wicker basket. Before coming on deck, she'd cinched her creation at the waist with the white sash from her yellow gown. All in all, she thought the effect somewhat exotic, like pictures she'd seen of ladies in India.

When she came close to Jacob, he stroked the back of one finger down her cheek. "Or maybe it's the moonlight that does you so proud," he said.

She turned her face into his hand and her lips brushed his knuckle before he grasped the wheel again. "It's the bath," she said, "and I've come to thank you again for your consideration."

"You're welcome. I'm relieved to know you've recognized some long-buried measure of gallantry in my otherwise rude disposition."

She grinned up at him. "Why, you're not rude, Captain . . ."

''Lying again, Miss Seabrook? I believe you've called me so once or twice yourself.''

''Yes, I have, but you didn't let me finish just now. I was about to say you're not boorish . . . *every* minute of *every* day.''

He laughed, a full rich sound so unlike any she'd heard from him that Nora let it wash over her like the first fresh breeze after a rainstorm. It was just that cleansing, and so utterly male in its resonance that tremors of something exciting and provocative coiled in Nora's stomach. She decided she liked Jacob's laugh.

He reached out and slipped his arm around her, then drew her against his chest so she stood between him and the wheel. He leaned back against a post and bent his leg slightly so she could rest against his thigh. They stayed that way for several minutes, both looking out at the ocean, his lips next to her hair, his hand resting on her shoulder, and her body curved into his as if a sculptor had chiseled them to fit so perfectly.

''I'm glad you came on deck tonight,'' he said after a while.

His words mirrored her own thoughts exactly, and she wondered once more why his crew would avoid their captain on the last night before arriving at Belle Isle. Nora found him wondrously pleasant to be with. ''Why is that?'' she crooned back at him.

''Because I need to tell you more about Belle Isle, Nora,'' he said. Quite unexpectedly his voice rumbled with a feral wariness that shattered her previous impression of him and left her dazzled with doubt, not bliss. ''There are things you need to know, and there are rules. You must follow them exactly or I will take measures to see that you do. You must promise me.''

Rules? Follow them exactly? Take measures? And just moments ago she had almost likened him to a lover! She had thought he might actually whisper some word of endearment to her. *Fool, Nora!*

She unfolded herself from his embrace and stepped back to face him. She hoped he noticed that the stars he'd caused to shine in her eyes had been snuffed out, because it was the cold, hard steel of his voice that had done it.

"And exactly what rules are you referring to, Jacob?" she asked, her eyes the cold blue of an ice floe.

For the first time since he'd met her, he could picture her with a schoolmarm's temperament. She wasn't as harsh as the middle-aged Welsh harridan his mother had hired to tutor him at Braxton, but her posture was suddenly just as rigid and her voice nearly as frosty.

He attempted a smile, but let it fade when it wasn't reciprocated. "I can see I haven't fallen into your good graces with the word 'rules.' "

Her eyes narrowed threateningly, and he sucked in a whistle of air. "These rules are for your own protection, Nora."

"Protection from what?" she demanded. "I'm really growing tired of all this secrecy and talk of danger and lack of security. I would appreciate some answers to the hopefully irrational questions that keep building in my mind, Jacob. Otherwise, I'm apt to become as suspicious and secretive as you are."

He called to his crew playing cards. "Will, would you take the wheel?"

Once free of responsibility, Jacob took Nora's arm and led her to a remote area of the ship. They were hidden from the others by Jacob's cabin walls. Under a cloud-covered sky, the night was pitch black. A light from a lantern in Jacob's quarters provided the only meager illumination in the passageway.

Jacob drew a deep breath while deciding how much he should tell her. Enough to make her wary but not enough to frighten her. He'd made his decision to take her to Belle Isle, and she'd seemed in agreement. Neither of them could go back on that decision now, but Jacob couldn't see a reason for making her days on the island fraught with fear and anxiety.

He'd been staring out to sea, aware of her mounting impatience, but now he turned to face her. "Very simply," he began, "my father is not a pleasant man."

"Then you must be the very picture of the man who sired you," she snapped back. "I've had acquaintance with fathers who are not a picture of amicability all the time," she added.

"If you're referring to the judge, let me assure you, he is nothing like Harrison Proctor. Your father may be prejudicial and judgmental, but he is not bitter and mean and bent on the destruction of everyone and everything around him."

"Oh, Jacob . . ." She rolled her eyes, suggesting his description of his father was somehow a gross exaggeration. He couldn't let her believe that.

"You asked for answers, Nora, and I'm giving them to you. All I ask in return is that you accept what I'm telling you as truth."

The skepticism left her eyes, and was replaced by a reluctant capitulation. "All right, Jacob. What has made your father this way?"

Choosing his words carefully, Jacob only half explained. "Eighteen years ago, he was the victim of a vicious attack with a dagger. The blade pierced his chest and back numerous times, severing nerves in his spine and severely damaging his lungs."

Nora's hand flew to her mouth to cover a shriek of horror. "My God," she uttered through her fingers. "Who did this horrible thing?"

The image of his mother's hands dripping with blood, her clothes covered with the life fluid running from his father's wounds, pierced Jacob's mind again with a force almost equal to the dagger's that night. He winced from the very real pain that sliced through his temples. "We never found out," he lied. "It happened on Belle Isle, and since there are no authorities on the island, the attacker, whoever it was, escaped without detection."

The anguish he relived whenever he thought of that night was reflected in Nora's eyes. He hadn't intended to cause her such pain, but she accepted it courageously, and put her hand on his arm.

"I'm so sorry for you, Jacob. How old were you when it happened?"

"I was twelve." It had happened all those years ago, and yet he remembered like it was yesterday. He had heard his father's shouts of fear and then pain and had run to the solarium. But he was too late to prevent the attack. By the time he threw open the doors and stepped into the room, his father was lying in a pool of blood. His mother, unaware of her son's presence or his screams of terror, dropped to her knees beside her husband's body and wailed, long, pitiful screeches that reminded Jacob of tales of the banshees.

"Jacob, you didn't see your father . . ."

"No," he answered sharply. "I was only told about the incident after the island healer had been called."

"Thank God. And your mother? Was she with him? Was she hurt?"

"She wasn't hurt. But she saw him . . . the way he was, before the healer came."

"How awful that must have been for her."

He remembered her uncontrollable trembling, her wretched cries, the oaths against God. She tried to turn the dagger into her own chest, but Jacob, with all the strength of his twelve-year-old body, wrenched it from her and threw it out the window. Her curses turned on him, and she struck out with her fists. He dodged her ineffectual punches, begging her to stop, until finally servants arrived and intervened. "Yes, I suppose it was awful for her," he told Nora. "My mother died soon after it happened."

She gripped his arm fiercely and made him look into her eyes. "How terrifying for you, Jacob, and how utterly sad. You were just a child."

Terrifying, yes. But if you only knew, my childhood was over long before that. One violent shudder racked his body the way it always did when he shook off the dreadful images. It was his body's way of purging itself of the poison, if only temporarily. But he knew the venom would come back to plague him again because the nightmares were not only a reminder of his past, but a look into his future.

"Jacob? Jacob, do you hear me?"

He locked his gaze with hers and let her soft blue eyes bring him the rest of the way back from the cold black eddy of his memories to surface in the warm lamplight of her presence. For one irrational moment he let himself hope that Nora might be the magnet that could always coax him back ... that she would never allow him to be lost in the horror that waited for him. What an absurd notion when it was he who must keep her from being victimized by the poison of the Proctor family.

Nevertheless, being near her, he felt a smile come naturally to his features again, and it calmed him. "Yes, I hear you," he answered. "I'm sorry I troubled you with this."

"Jacob, is this why you think of Belle Isle as a place of danger? Do you think the evil person who did this horrible deed could still be there? Or could he return?"

"No, Nora, no, I don't think that. I believe in my soul that the attacker is dead. I just told you about what happened so you will understand about my father. You will meet him, because you must. But stay away from him as much as you can. He is not a kind man."

"But I understand ..."

"No, you don't! Not all of it." Because he insisted too harshly, he gently touched her hand. "Please do as I say. I have affairs to attend to on the island, but I will do my work quickly and we will be on our way back to Key West before too many days have passed. While I'm occupied, stay in your room or the back garden. You will be safe there. But don't venture out on your own, Nora. Promise me."

Interminable seconds passed before she answered him. "All right, Jacob. You don't need to worry about me."

He wrapped her tightly in his arms, marveling at how she merged with the crooks and planes of his body. She was as soft as the grass that carpeted the hillsides of Belle Isle. Her breath against his chest was as the whisper of leaves in the parrot trees. The comfort he felt with her willowy body melded

with his seemed as enduring as the rugged candlebush that
blazed golden beside the island trails to the sea.

Desire heated in his groin and licked with hot flames to every
tingling nerve. He felt himself grow hard against her belly. His
arms ached with the longing to scoop her into his embrace and
carry her to his cabin. There he would strip her of her flowered
garment and shake the pins from her hair. He would feast upon
the perfection of her nakedness and write a love song to her
body with his hands. Then, when he entered her, and her warmth
surrounded him, he knew he would be reborn, and the devils
of Belle Isle would be no more because he would be new.

With his index finger, he cupped her chin and lifted her face.
"You are very dear, Nora," he said, and pressed his lips on
hers for a chaste kiss that satisfied his conscience, but certainly
not his soul. Nor his heart.

"Now go," he said, and shooed her toward Will's cabin.
"Tomorrow will be a busy day."

CHAPTER SEVENTEEN

Thurston Seabrook longed for breakfasts the way they used to be before his life was turned upside down. Of course he wished more than anything to have his daughter back home. Her welfare was on his mind every waking hour of every day.

Her disappearance had disrupted nearly every aspect of his life from his physical health to his personal relationships, and especially his state of mind. The transformation in his breakfast ritual was just a minor example of the upheaval in his routine the last few days, but to Thurston it was a symbol of all that had gone wrong.

It wasn't Portia's fault. Even in the gloomy atmosphere that pervaded every nook and crevice of the Seabrook house, she still managed to set a fine table. Heaped on Thurston's plate this morning was a mound of scrambled eggs seasoned with those little red things that Portia kept shrouded in mystery but that made an ordinary egg a culinary masterpiece. And there were three buttermilk biscuits slathered with honey, six slices of bacon, procured at no small expense, and chunks of golden mango. All of these varied delectable scents mingled with the steam of strong, black, Bahamian coffee. Tantalizing, to be sure, but Thurston had barely eaten a bite.

"Oh, Thurston, I just don't see how I can go on another day," Sidonia moaned from across the table.

As usual he couldn't see her face since it was buried in her hands. Truly, he'd seen very little of her features since Nora had left. If Sidonia weren't crying into her palms or a handkerchief, she was covered in cool compresses or resting with a pillow over her head. If it weren't for her voice intermittently bellowing in grievous despair, Thurston might never have recognized the trembling bundle of silk and lace as his own wife.

"You have to do something, Thurston!" she cried louder.

Fanny patted her cousin's shoulder. "Now, Sid, do calm yourself," she said before she, too, burst into tears. "This is all my fault. If only I hadn't let her go."

Theo Hadley looked up from his half-eaten meal, swallowed, and said, "You know, Miss Cosette, it really is your fault. Nora's actions were guided by a motivation to trap that scoundrel Proctor. Her goals were commendable though naive. But you should have prevented her from doing something so foolish as to board his ship."

Tears flowed freely down Fanny's checks, but she still managed to bark out, "Shut up, Theo, you twit! You're not allowed to agree with me!"

The few bites of egg and bacon that had found their way to Thurston's stomach began their fiery climb back up his esophagus. He tried to utter words of comfort to ladies he knew were beyond comforting, but they were lost in the rumble of an acid-induced belch. He threw his napkin down on the table and stood up. "Ladies, please! I'm doing everything in my power to find Nora, but I can hardly tolerate these tedious outbursts!"

Sidonia looked up with red, swollen eyes and wailed, "Thurston, don't yell at me. I'm much too delicate to withstand such brutal attacks."

Fanny shook a finger at him. "Really, Thurston, can't you see poor Sid is at her wit's end?"

He growled. Thurston Seabrook actually growled at another human being. "And where exactly do you think I am in regard to my own wit, Fanny? Somewhere in the middle?"

Further confrontation was avoided when Portia came into the dining room from the front of the house. "Excuse me, Your Honor. I hate to interrupt tender family moments but there's someone here to see you."

Thurston frowned at the impertinent maid. She'd become much too comfortable with her employment lately, and he meant to speak to her about it when all this was over. She'd even gone so far as to suggest the day after Nora's disappearance that if Nora were with Jacob Proctor, she didn't know what all the fuss was about.

"Well, who is it, Portia?" he demanded.

"It's Mr. Hyde. He says it's important."

Fanny bounded from her chair before Thurston could instruct the maid to show Dillard in. Apparently, her guilt and despair were momentarily forgotten in favor of more salient emotions. She soon reentered the dining room with her hands draped around Dillard Hyde's arm.

"Good morning, Your Honor, Mrs. Seabrook, Hadley," the clerk said. He took a piece of paper from the pocket of his impeccably groomed suit coat. "A man just delivered this note to the courthouse for you, sir. His name was Smythe, and while his appearance and demeanor were less than admirable, the message itself is most significant." He waited, knowing he had everyone's attention. "It's from Miss Seabrook," he said.

"Eleanor! My baby!" Sidonia squealed.

"Dear Nora," Theo added, finally resting his fork on the rim of his plate.

Thurston rounded the dining room table with his hand outstretched. "Good God, man, give it to me."

The note had obviously been hastily scrawled and bore the scars of indelicate handling, but Nora's words were still legible. Thurston read aloud:

Dearest Father and Mama,

I am sorry for the distress I know my absence has caused. I am on the Dover Cloud *where I found myself as a result of my own devices, though it was not my intent to remain for the entire voyage. Jacob Proctor will return me to Key West safely when his business is concluded. Haven't time to write more.*

Your loving daughter,
Nora

Sidonia, whose weeping had subsided during the reading, grabbed the letter from Thurston's hand and reread it silently. Thurston's tortured digestive system settled into a tentative calm. His precious daughter was alive.

Dillard Hyde was the first to speak. "This is good news, isn't it, Your Honor?"

"Yes, yes," he responded cautiously. "I suppose it's better than bad news, at any rate."

A wide grin split Fanny's face. "See? I told you. Everything will be all right. Nora's fine." With a pointed look at Theo, she added, "Captain Proctor will protect her. Now maybe we can all get back to normal and go on with our lives. Nora will soon be home safely."

Thurston was almost inclined to agree with her, and even cast a longing look at his breakfast plate. However, a steadily increasing keening from Sidonia banished all thoughts of life returning to normal. Her sobs grew in intensity until she was crying louder than ever before.

"You foolish people," she blubbered through her tears. "Can't you see what our poor Eleanor is telling us? She's crying for help. She's begging to be saved from that monster."

Thurston took the note back and tried to blot some of the moisture that had begun to blur the writing. "Why do you say that, Sid? It seems to me that Nora is telling us she's all right."

Sidonia jabbed one plump finger at the paper. "It says right there that Eleanor did not intend to remain on *that man's* ship.

Don't you understand, Thurston? He's holding her captive! He forced her to write this note to throw us off the trail. She so much as admits that by saying she hasn't time to write more. He probably had a knife at her throat as she penned this. Our Eleanor fears for her life!''

Sidonia sank into the nearest chair, slumped over the table, and buried her face in her arms. ''My poor baby is a pr . . . prisoner of that monster! Who knows what horrors . . .''

The gurgling started again in the pit of Thurston's stomach, nearly drowning out his wife's howls. ''Oh, Sid . . .''

''Sir?'' The dyspepsia increased with the sound of Theo's voice.

''What is it, Hadley?''

''I'm afraid I must agree with Mrs. Seabrook.''

Nearly snarling at the young attorney, Thurston said, ''Well, must you do it *now*, Theo?''

''I'm sorry, Your Honor, but I think Mrs. Seabrook has touched on the crux of this thing. Look at this handwriting. I know Nora's penmanship to be flawless. I think she's giving us clues, sir. This is a desperate plea from a terrified woman.'' He bunched a handful of his sling in his good fist and moaned, ''Blast this infernal injury. Would that I were able to sail the seas looking for her. I would, Your Honor. I would if I were able, and I would bring her back.''

Thurston tossed the note on the table and pushed past Theo. ''Get out of my way, Hadley. I'm going to find that man Smythe and see what else he can tell me.''

''You won't find him, sir,'' Dillard said. ''He's already sailed. But I did ask him how Miss Seabrook appeared. If she seemed fit.''

''And?''

Dillard stepped cautiously back out of danger. ''You wouldn't have liked the way he phrased it, Your Honor, but he said Miss Seabrook was, let me recall his wording, 'as fit a pigeon as the last buxom wench he'd coddled on his lap in a Newcastle tavern.' I believe those were his exact words.''

''Oh, my God,'' Sidonia screeched.

"Oh, my God," Fanny cooed.

"This looks bad, sir," Theo observed.

Thurston kept walking out the front door of his house. He wouldn't catch Smythe, and he for damned sure wasn't getting his breakfast, but outside the Seabrook house, there was plenty of fresh air.

Nora had never heard of trade winds until the *Dover Cloud* approached Belle Isle. While she had expected the heat to be oppressive in this region so close to the equator, that was not the case because, she discovered, of those mysterious winds that kept the Caribbean at a near-constant temperature all year.

"The sun's rays hit the earth in a nearly direct path at the earth's center," Jacob told her, "But heat rises, and so do the winds along the equator. They rise and expand, allowing room for polar air to flow underneath. That's why the air is almost always dry and cool. Except for the months of midsummer when the trade winds are replaced by the doldrums, the temperature rarely rises above eighty degrees."

It was a cool, clear morning with a strong wind propelling the *Dover Cloud* when Nora first caught sight of Belle Isle. From some distance away it seemed a shining emerald in a rippling bed of cobalt and teal. They had passed other, larger islands during their voyage, but none as fortunately located as Lydia Proctor's paradise. The closer they came, the more the ocean surrounding Belle Isle appeared streaked with shimmering ribbons of aqua and white, as if they had been painted from an artist's pallet.

As they neared shore, Nora noted varieties of sweeping palms, tall ferns, and flowering shrubs bordering the harbor and its cluster of small buildings. The harbor itself was nestled into an elbow of lush green land that provided a protective barrier for two wooden wharfs. The water had the sparkling clarity and glass-smooth surface of a peaceful lagoon.

"This must be Angel Kiss Bay," Nora said to herself, remembering the picturesque name she'd heard for the harbor.

Jacob appeared beside her. "It is," he concurred with an unmistakable hint of pride. "The first time she came here, my grandmother said the natural inlet looked as though it had been kissed by an angel."

Nora understood what Lydia Proctor had seen that day. It truly seemed as if an angel with gossamer wings had left some of her heavenly dust sprinkling on the water in the golden sun.

The longer of the wharfs jutted into the ocean no more than three hundred feet. It was barely long enough to accommodate the *Dover Cloud*. Other vessels tied to the docks were small fishing crafts and rafts. Most of the boats did not have any sails at all, but relied on oars and poles to navigate the sea. Many of these crafts ventured into the water to meet Jacob's ship as it drifted under minimal sail to shore. Jacob's crew stood by the deck rail and caught fruit thrown up to them by olive-skinned natives who had rowed out to escort the *Dover Cloud*.

"These people are happy to see you," Nora said, and then gave Jacob a teasing grin. "It's nice to know you have a commendable reputation in some parts of the world."

"It's not so much my reputation," he said. "They know I bring goods they can't get on the island."

"So you are a sort of Father Christmas to them."

He smiled as if the image pleased him. "Maybe, but I think this time they are more interested in you than in the items in the hold. See how they are pointing up at you and talking to each other? By tonight you will be the gossip at all Belle Isle dinner tables."

"Just as you are the gossip at Key West tables," she said.

He leaned close and whispered in her ear, "Ah, but aren't you glad the rumors spoken about you are not nearly so slanderous as the ones spoken about me?"

He left her then and went to oversee the docking procedure. Nora watched indistinct shapes of pitched-roofed structures slowly become square clapboard or daub-and-wattle cottages.

When the ship was secure and Nora first stepped onto the wooden dock, she realized that the Belle Isle harbor was different from any other she'd seen. Most noticeably, aside from a small cafe and a larger tavern, there were no business establishments. There was, however, an active marketplace, and Nora was drawn to it immediately. With baskets swinging from their arms, women in colorful dress walked among the vendors. They purchased fish and produce mainly, though bits of cloth, straw goods, and household trinkets were available in limited quantities.

Nora tried to imagine her mother shopping in this market, and the notion brought a smile to her lips. *Mama thinks Key West is barren of goods. She would consider this a wasteland. What it must be like to pick from merchandise that is totally lacking in luxuries.* Yet to Nora, the market had a simple rustic appeal. "Raw beauty," she remembered Jacob calling it.

Just as his name came to mind, the man himself appeared beside her. His hand rested on her elbow. "For a minute I thought I'd lost you," he said. "You shouldn't wander off by yourself, Nora."

She let her gaze roam the length of the market, which couldn't have been more than a city block in size, and then pinned him with a disapproving glare. "That's ridiculous, Jacob. I could hardly get lost here."

His hand tightened on her arm. "Not here, but I told you not to go off by yourself anywhere on the island. It will be very important for you to remember that when we get to the house."

Yes, he had told her, and she had reluctantly agreed. "All right," she sighed. "I promise to be a good girl."

He relaxed his hold and called for a carriage that had appeared amidst the confusion at the end of the market. It was a smart two-seater, as elegant as any Nora had seen in Richmond, and it was drawn by a pair of matching Appaloosas expertly handled by an olive-skinned islander.

When Nora raised her brows, questioning such an unexpected extravagance, Jacob shrugged. "My father refused to live on the island without the barest necessities. Through the years he has imported most of what existed at Braxton Manor."

He supervised the loading of several baskets and crates onto the carriage, and then assisted Nora into one of the seats. After instructing Will to unload the rest of the *Dover Cloud*'s cargo into a thatched-roof warehouse, he climbed in beside Nora. The driver turned the horses around and they headed away from the harbor on a narrow road paved with crushed limestone and coral and bordered by brilliant tropical shrubs.

The trail wound through level countryside to the interior of the island, where the topography suddenly became hilly and thick with lush vegetation. Jacob explained that his grandmother had brought many of the flowering plants to Belle Isle from other, more populated islands in the Caribbean. Through the years the gardeners had kept them pruned and fertile.

Soon the primitive road merged with an even narrower one-lane path that twisted up a steep hillside through gum and chestnut trees. When they were nearly at the top, the lane widened to offer a view of a sprawling, one-story wood and brick residence. Sun filtering through leafy tree branches gleamed starkly off white walls. Six columns supported a massive front porch that stretched almost the entire length of the house. Each room opened onto the shaded veranda with French doors stained a light apple green.

The driver stopped in front of the main portal, carved of deep walnut with an elephant's head for a door knocker. Jacob stepped down from the buggy and offered his hand to Nora. "Welcome to Proctor House."

Scents of jasmine and gardenia filled the air until Nora was almost dizzy from the fragrance. Brilliant orange-flame vines climbed the columns to meet blossoms of poincianas draping the rooftop of the low house. "It's absolutely magnificent," she said.

A large-framed woman in a white dress and flowered bandanna came out the front door. She cast a familiar glance at Jacob before her gaze raked Nora from top to bottom. "Welcome home, Captain Proctor," she said.

"It's good to see you, Juditha," he responded formally. There appeared to be no affection between these two. "Does he know I'm here?"

"He knows. I had him outside in the garden when the ship came into the harbor. He saw everything from the hilltop."

"And how goes he today? Fair or ill?"

She descended the one step to be nearer to Jacob. She tried to keep her voice at a low level, but obviously a demure manner of speaking did not come naturally to this commanding woman. "Not well, Captain, I'm afraid."

"And Dylan?"

Dylan? Having never heard this name before, Nora wondered about the identity of this person.

"He's quiet. He doesn't understand that you've arrived today. Probably won't until you visit him." She passed a clandestine glance at Nora and added, "You've never brought anyone here before, Captain. I really must question the wisdom of doing so now."

Jacob's jaw clenched, though he said not unkindly, "It's not up to you to question anything I do, now is it, Juditha?"

"As Dylan's primary caretaker, I . . ." She stopped and clamped her lips shut at Jacob's scowl. "No, sir, it isn't up to me."

He brought Nora to the entrance. "Juditha, this is Miss Seabrook. Please make her feel welcome and prepare the south bedroom for her stay."

The servant nodded once at Nora. "Of course, Captain."

"Oh, and Juditha, there's a basket of fabric in the carriage. Miss Seabrook has very little in the way of clothing. Would you see to it that Polly stitches up a few simple dresses and accessories as soon as possible?"

"Yes, sir." With a small bow she went back into the house.

Jacob turned his attention to Nora. "Are you ready to go in?"

"I'm not sure. I doubt that you are making me a welcome guest since you've doled out orders concerning my stay. The servants will find me a nuisance."

He smiled at her. "You'll find out soon enough that doling out orders is what I do best on Belle Isle, but in exchange I receive just as many."

As if on cue, a voice bellowed from inside the house. "Jacob, is that you? Get in here this instant!"

He took Nora's arm. "I suggest you leave any warmhearted sympathy for the people at Proctor House at the door and cloak yourself in emotional armor, Nora. You are about to meet Papa."

The room was shrouded in shadow though it was the middle of the day. All but one of the heavy draperies had been closed to the sun. Still, there was enough light for Nora to see that the man in the wheelchair, despite his years and physical disability, was every bit as formidable as his son. Broad-shouldered and thick-chested, with a full crop of coarse gray hair streaming back from his forehead, he did not seem in the least dwarfed by the conveyance in which he was forced to live his life. In fact, it seemed as though this barrel of a man should be able to leap from the chair and push it away without so much as a tremble in his limbs.

Leaving Nora at the threshold, Jacob strode across the room. "Father, how are you?"

Ignoring his son's outstretched hand, the elder Proctor spoke gruffly. "What are you doing here? I didn't expect you for at least another month. Has something gone wrong?"

Jacob dropped his hand and stepped back, putting more distance between him and his father. "No, nothing has gone wrong. I decided to come early, that's all there is to it."

The man tilted his head and squinted at his son. "I hope you're telling the truth. You've brought currency, haven't you?"

"Of course. Plenty to see you through."

"The wrecking business is good?"

"As ever."

Jacob's father snorted, a most unpleasant sound, though it signified his relief. "You must indulge me my suspicions, Jacob. I have nothing to do all day but sit in this damned chair and watch them grow."

"Father, I've brought . . ."

At that moment Harrison Proctor's milky gaze fell on Nora. He wrapped a fist around one wheel of his chair and pushed himself closer to the door, forcing his son to step out of the way. "Who is this?" he demanded in a tone that might have been more appropriate if he'd inquired as to whether his son had brought cholera onto the island.

Jacob made no move to bring Nora and his father closer together. "Father, I'd like you to meet Miss Nora Seabrook. Nora, this is my father, Lord Harrison Proctor."

Nora tried to smile, but it came across as a timid gesture. "A pleasure to meet you, Your Lordship. I appreciate your hospitality . . ."

He pointed a thick, quivering finger at her and she stopped speaking, realizing the man did not intend to return her cordiality with his own.

"What have you done, Jacob?" he demanded of his son, though he continued to stare at Nora. "Why have you brought this woman here?"

"She is my guest, Father. I brought her because I chose to. That's the last I'll hear on it."

"No, you'll hear this. You're a damn fool, Jacob Proctor. And you, Miss Nora Seabrook, are as big a one for coming here." He whirled his chair around until his back was to both of them. "Go on and get out of here, both of you. And Jacob, keep a tight rein on her if you know what's good for you." He waved his hand in dismissal. "Now *that's* the last you'll hear on it from me. You've boiled the water, Jacob. Now it's your own goose that'll be cooked."

CHAPTER EIGHTEEN

Working with Polly, the Proctors' elderly maid, Nora had two additional dresses to add to her wardrobe in less than two days. They weren't works of art. Nora's talents did not lie with needle and thread, and Polly's eyesight was not what it used to be. Therefore the garments were lightly basted, simple dresses with straight lines and imperfect hems. But after a few nips and tucks in the right places, Nora was pleased with the outcome of their hours of work.

And she was pleased, too, with the friendship established between her and the talkative Polly. A servant of the Proctors since before Jacob was born, Polly had delightful stories to tell of Jacob's boyhood in England. Unfortunately, she had little to say when asked about Jacob's life since his mother's death. In fact, she became almost morose in her silences. It seemed the demise of Sophie Proctor was a subject no one in the Proctor household wanted to talk about. Still, despite the difference in their ages, Polly and Nora giggled and chattered about matters great and small while they stitched and pressed.

During this period, Jacob left Nora to herself while he supervised the transfer of goods from the harbor to Proctor House, traded merchandise in the market, and dispersed the trinkets that validated his Father Christmas reputation. Nora was grateful she had Polly's cheerful company and the dressmaking to keep her busy.

When she did see Jacob, he seemed tense and guarded. His discomfort eased somewhat when she assured him she was staying in her room, the kitchen, or the garden. "Though my curiosity about this island has not been satisfied in the least," she told him one night at dinner. "I want to see all of it, not just the part I can see from your father's terrace."

"And you shall," he promised. "Before we leave, I will take you on a tour around Belle Isle's perimeter. You will have an opportunity to write all sorts of impressions on that writing pad you always seem to have by your side."

Lord Harrison Proctor was present for dinner in the evenings, and these strained, silent periods were the only contact Nora had with him. Considering his gruff, ill-mannered behavior the day they met, Nora wasn't sorry her time with Lord Proctor was limited.

During their meals, he responded to his son's questions and comments with an occasional grunt or wave of his hand. He never spoke to Nora at all, and she soon gave up any attempts to engage him in discourse. When he finished eating, he rang for Juditha, who pushed him to some remote region of the house where he apparently remained for the rest of the evening.

Jacob was pleasant and companionable, but he seemed determined to continue with the aloofness he'd established on the *Dover Cloud*. After inquiring about Nora's day and what she planned to do for the rest of the evening, he retired to the library, where he insisted he had correspondence to answer and ledgers to update. Consequently, it was the spindle-thin, white-haired Polly who provided Nora with most of her human contact during her first days on Belle Isle.

Truly, Nora had no intention of breaking her promises to Jacob, but the afternoon of her fourth day on the island an opportunity to explore a small part of Jacob's secret world presented itself and she couldn't resist. She'd run out of things to do. She'd visited with Polly, read three chapters of a book, and written a lengthy journal entry. A full afternoon and evening stretched ahead of her. Seeking any occupation that might draw her interest, she wandered off the terrace and proceeded to the furthest point of the sculpted garden.

A manicured area gave way to fruit trees, palms, and tropical ferns. This untamed section of Proctor land was shady and inviting. Nora walked along a gravel path that led to an iron fence and gated trellis. When she could go no farther, she peered through the gate and spied a small white cottage in the middle of thick island greenery.

The structure was like something out of a fairy tale with its pointed rooftop and pastel shuttered windows. Adding to this charming picture, tinkling strains of a music box drifted from the cottage to where Nora stood entranced, her hands on the iron rods of the gate.

Who lived there? she wondered. It had to be someone who liked music. She recognized the light airy notes of a Viennese waltz. Tapping her toe in time to the music, she visualized elegant ladies and gentlemen twirling around the dance floor at one of the Richmond balls she'd attended before leaving for Key West.

The tune ended, but another just as beautiful began right after it. Nora leaned her cheek against the gate, closed her eyes, and floated with the music. Suddenly, the pressure of her body caused the gate to swing open wide. Whoever had last passed through had neglected to secure the padlock, and it dangled uselessly from the hasp.

What good luck, she decided. She would follow the music and find someone else to talk to, possibly a friendly soul. It was hardly violating her promise to Jacob to venture just a few yards from the Proctor garden. She slipped through the gate, closed it behind her, and walked to the cottage.

The door was open, and Nora stopped on the flagstone entry. A young man was inside. Though he faced away from her, she could determine several things about his appearance. He was tall and thin, and dressed all in white so that he resembled a snowy willow branch, with the same grace of movement. He swayed to the music as if it were part of him. Strands of fine golden hair brushed his shoulders as he dipped and stretched to the strains of the waltz.

At precise intervals he raised his arms above his head as though he were reaching for endless sun and sky instead of ceiling. His long fingers moved to and fro, stretching and curling with the rotation of his wrists.

When the music stopped, so did the man. Nora thought another tune might start up again, and when it didn't, the man remained where he was, neck arched, arms outstretched. He stood for a full minute like a swan frozen on a winter pond.

"Excuse me," Nora said softly.

He emitted a startled cry, shook off his statue-like pose with a violent quaking of his body, and whirled to face her. His eyes widened in shock. He clawed at his open mouth with trembling fingers.

Nora stayed on the flagstone, but reached out her hand. "I'm sorry," she said. "I didn't mean to frighten you."

He dropped his hands from his mouth. "You did frighten me," he accused her. "That wasn't nice."

"I know. I was watching you dance. It was lovely. You move beautifully."

He rolled his shoulders and tilted his head. The fear and suspicion that had glazed his eyes were replaced by a sort of innocent curiosity. The corners of his mouth pulled up in a puzzling grin. "Did you hear that, Marianne? She was watching us dance."

Nora looked around for the person he might be speaking to. Seeing no one, she still returned his smile. "My name is Nora. What's yours?"

"Dylan."

So this is Dylan. "Do you live in this cottage?"

He nodded. "Here, and in the trees and in the water. I live everywhere. And I dance. I love to dance. I dance with beautiful ladies like Marianne."

He made an open circle of his arms in front of his body as

if he were holding a dancing partner. He took a first step, stopped, and cocked his head . . . waiting, listening. Finally, he glared angrily at Nora. "Go away. Marianne says you must go. You made the music stop."

Nora laughed, a nervous sound that seemed forced. "Marianne?" she questioned. "There's no one here but you and . . ."

"Marianne is here," he insisted. "She's always here and she doesn't like you because you stopped the music. Go away."

Suddenly, Nora understood that the man in the cottage was not playing a game. Dylan truly believed he was dancing with a partner, and just as fervently, he was certain that Nora had intruded and interrupted their afternoon. She'd never met anyone like Dylan, but she'd heard her parents talk about people who weren't like the rest of society. People who were ill, who imagined things. And she had an idea what happened to them.

They were most always put away, like Juliet and Francis Butler's daughter. The poor girl had been no older than Nora was now when she'd begun acting strangely, and her parents had sent her away. Nora never saw Charlotte Butler again. And it occurred to her now that no one had ever mentioned her name again.

"You're not nice," Dylan said. The downward tug of his lips and knitting of his brows indicated his escalating anger. "You took the music."

"No, no I didn't, Dylan, but I will go if that's what you want." She began easing away from the open door. Instinct told her that slow, careful movements would be less likely to inflame the man's antagonism.

He watched her go until uncertainty veiled his eyes. "No, wait!" he called, running to the door. "Marianne is wrong. She can be bad sometimes. Marianne stopped the music, not you." He kept his hands on the door frame and leaned out toward Nora. "Who are you?"

"I'm Nora, remember? I told you. I'm a friend of Jacob's."

Dylan's face lit from within at the mention of Jacob's name. He clapped his hands like an excited child. "Jacob's here. Jacob's here," he said.

"That's right, he is."

"Does Jacob like you?"

Dylan's pale face became a picture of innocent trust and childlike hope. Nora wouldn't have told him no even if she had believed that to be the honest answer. "Yes, Jacob likes me," she said.

"Good. Then I will like you." He went to a table in the center of the room and picked up a painted metal teapot. It was just like one Nora had owned as a child and kept in her playroom for imaginary tea parties. Dylan came back to the door and proudly displayed the pot. He reached out with his other hand and grabbed her arm. "You can come in, and we'll have tea."

"I don't know," she said. "Perhaps I should get back."

He stomped his foot. "No. We're having tea!"

Nora thought it best not to argue with him, and was just about to go inside when a look of such intense sadness crossed his face that she remained rooted to the threshold. "Dylan, what's wrong?"

He didn't answer, but suddenly dissolved into tears. The teapot clattered to the stone floor, and he covered his face with his hands. "Now we can't have any fun because she won't let us," he cried.

The meaning of his strange exclamation became clear when a shrill voice split the air behind her. "Miss Seabrook, what in heaven's name are you doing here?"

Nora spun around to see an extremely angry Juditha bearing down upon her. Like a poor girl with her hand caught in the Sunday morning collection plate, Nora could only mumble feeble excuses. "I'm sorry, Juditha. The gate was open. I was only looking for someone . . . I didn't go far from the garden . . ."

Juditha positioned herself in the doorway, blocking Nora's view into the cottage. "Now you've done it, miss. You'll have the both of them coming down on us like God Himself threw a thunderbolt. Now go on, get out of here!"

"I'm sorry. I didn't mean . . ." The rest of her words caught in a choked sob. Nora stumbled away from the cottage and ran as fast as she could to the gate. Through her heart hammering in her ears, she heard Dylan's pitiful wails.

"She scared me, Juditha. She made me fix tea, and I burned myself."

"Where is Vincent?" the housekeeper demanded.

"I think she killed him," Dylan blubbered. "That horrible girl killed Vincent. And she killed Marianne, too."

The rest of their words were lost in the notes of the music box again and the rush of leaves in tall trees at the edge of Harrison Proctor's garden. Nora pushed through the gate and slammed it behind her. Without looking back she ran to the house.

With rote motion that required little thought, Nora dressed for dinner that evening. Certain she wouldn't be able to eat a bite of food, she thought it likely the Proctors wouldn't offer her any anyway. By this time Juditha would have told both Jacob and his father of her transgression that afternoon. There was no denying that she had broken Jacob's primary rule. She'd ventured beyond the confines he'd set for her, and she surely was going to have to pay.

She brushed her hair fiercely before coiling it into a semblance of a topknot. Using the few pins that had survived her ordeal in the hold of Jacob's ship, she stuck first one and then another into her haphazard creation. "Ouch," she cried when one pin found more scalp than hair.

She pulled strands of hair from the unruly mass and tried to bully them into spirals at her neck. Then she spoke to the distraught reflection in her mirror. "For heaven's sake, Nora, you have nothing to feel guilty about. You haven't done anything wrong. *He's* the one who should apologize . . . expecting you to stay a prisoner in his house. All you did was walk less than a quarter of a mile away from his precious boundaries."

And yet, while she outwardly rationalized about Jacob's unfair treatment, a niggling apology kept creeping into her thoughts. She had violated the rules and in doing so, she was sure she had stumbled upon the very thing, no, the *person,* that was the center of the mystery of Belle Isle. She had discovered Jacob's secret, and he was going to be angry.

She tugged at the waistband of the gold and white striped dress Polly had just finished that morning. The bit of fancy frill the maid had added to the scooped neckline and that Nora had thought delightful suddenly seemed too frivolous for the unpleasant evening ahead.

"So what if I did meet Dylan?" she said to her reflection. "The poor confused man shouldn't be kept a secret in the first place. He's probably just starved for companionship. If he's constantly spied upon by that grim-faced Juditha, I can understand why!"

She recalled the range of emotions she'd experienced in Dylan's presence. "I really wasn't so very frightened of him," she said to the face in the mirror. "I could have stayed and had some imaginary tea and gone back to the house later. What would have been the harm?"

"Nora! Are you coming to dinner?"

Jacob's voice boomed from the hallway, and Nora knew that any harm that would come from her encounter with Dylan was about to be realized in the next few minutes. She stuck her head out the door and saw him standing several feet away. He looked achingly handsome in casual attire, his sun-streaked hair brushing the collar of a loose-fitting shirt the color of a ripe coconut.

Nora wanted to believe he would offer his arm and they would stroll together to a candlelit dining room where they would eventually become heady on fine wine and meaningful gazes. But the solemn set of his features and the wide, powerful spread of those gabardine-clad legs told her otherwise.

"Yes, I'm coming," she said, "if I'm not going to be the main course."

Nora sat opposite Jacob at the wide dining table. Neither of them spoke, even when the cook came into the room and asked if they would like wine with dinner. A subtle nod of Jacob's head answered the question, and the servant poured a deep-burgundy Chianti into both glasses. Nora tasted hers, and while it was tart and fruity on her tongue, it burned going down her throat. She regretted having inherited her father's temperamental digestion, and reached for a glass of water. I would be better off starving, she thought, especially if Jacob doesn't quit staring at me like that.

As if reading her mind, he looked away. He rolled the stem of his glass between his thumb and forefinger and watched the contents pool along the sides of the crystal.

When a bowl of steaming clam chowder was set before her, Nora decided that perhaps she could eat a little something. It smelled too heavenly not to, and Jacob was acting his usual remote self. Maybe he wouldn't say anything about the incident at the cottage after all, and it made no sense to waste good food.

She had taken several spoonfuls when he said coolly, "I understand you had quite an afternoon, Nora."

Oh, fine. Her luck just ran out. Jacob used the same tone her father had when she was a naughty child, and rather than intimidating her, the authoritative attitude only infuriated her. She did exactly what a ten-year-old Nora would have done to test her father's patience to its limit. She filled her spoon with creamy liquid and slurped loudly. Satisfied with an expression on Jacob's face that was a combination of amusement and shock, she smiled and said, "Yes, I did, thank you."

He took a swallow of wine that emptied half the contents of his glass. "You realize that your actions today put this house in an uproar."

"I'm sorry that my taking a walk of no more than a few hundred feet beyond my limits had that effect. Perhaps your staff needs more to occupy their time than to vex themselves over my transgressions."

His eyes glittered over the candelabra in the center of the table. "You shouldn't have done it. I warned you and you gave me your word."

She had to concede that point. "I apologize for breaking my word, though I feel it was only to a minor degree, but Jacob, I must tell you how I feel about what I discovered . . ."

She intended to tell him that if Dylan was the reason he shrouded this beautiful island in mystery . . . if that poor befuddled young man was the cause of all the secrecy, then everyone, including Jacob himself, should realize that to hide the man from society seemed to her an inexcusable wrong.

While she had experienced a moment of trepidation in Dylan's presence, she truly doubted that he was dangerous. Confused? Yes. Prone to imaginings? Obviously. But to practically deny his existence to the world was no better than what Juliet and Francis had done to Charlotte.

She would have told Jacob this, except she never got the chance. The metallic hiss of iron on wood announced the approach of Lord Proctor's wheelchair. Pushed into the room by a haughty Juditha, Jacob's father clenched his hands repeatedly on the arms of the chair. His facial expression reminded Nora of a wild animal sensing the close proximity of its prey. Once again she had the impression of her head resting on the silver platter in the center of the Proctor dining table.

Juditha positioned Harrison at the end of the table and stood dutifully behind him. Jacob drained the rest of his wine and said simply, "Father."

Nora wiped her lips with her napkin. "Good evening, Lord Proctor."

He fixed her with a steely glare and raised a finger to thrust it at her. "You're a damned, stupid woman, you know that, Miss Seabrook?"

Jacob rose from his chair. "That's enough, Father. I won't have you speak to Nora that way."

"Well, someone has to. It's obvious your warnings passed through the feathers of her brain like water through a sieve. Your head was so turned by the looks of her that you gave no thought to what is good for this family."

Nora had never known such pure, definitive fury as what

she felt toward Harrison Proctor at that moment. It pounded at her temples and hummed in her ears.

"Stop it," she shouted across several feet of polished mahogany. "You've no right to blame your son. I understood perfectly what he told me, but I chose to wander beyond the boundary of the garden on my own."

"So, you had an original thought, did you?" he sneered. "But you're such a foolish chit that you had absolutely no idea what havoc this one impulsive act might bring down upon this household."

Jacob snapped his gaze to her face. Anger as intense as her own ignited the charcoal of his eyes. "Nora, leave the room."

"No, he must be made to understand . . ."

"Nora! I don't need you to defend me in front of my father. Go out to the garden and stay there. I'll come for you later."

She rose, but didn't move for several seconds. Her breaths came fast and hard so that she felt her breasts strain against the ruffles Polly had sewn on her new dress. "What is the matter with you two?" she cried. "That poor man out there has done nothing wrong. It's no sin to be ill!" She turned the full force of her indignation on Harrison Proctor. "Surely you must understand that more than anyone could!"

He quaked violently in his chair. The pegs and dowels holding it together rattled in the suddenly oppressive silence of the cavernous room. Had he been able to, Nora had no doubt he would have leapt across the table and lunged for her throat. But instead he turned his vengeance on his son. "You see what you've done? You've brought another female onto this island, and she will ruin everything just as surely . . ."

Jacob's voice rattled the crystals of the delicate candelabra. "Nora, go to the garden!"

There was so much she wanted to say, but no words would come. Only a low moan of frustration came from her throat. Both of these men were cruel and heartless, and it was pointless to try to reason with them. All at once she was terribly afraid of these people and this island. And she wished to God she was home in Key West.

She ran from the room and through the kitchen to the back entrance. She stopped in the garden and looked around, frantically searching for an escape that didn't exist. On Jacob's island in the middle of the Caribbean Sea, she had nowhere to go. Among Harrison Proctor's fragrant, colorful blossoms, she imagined only horrors.

The threat of what was in the woods beyond the garden and even in the little cottage beyond the gate suddenly loomed as menacingly as what existed in the house. She sank onto a garden bench. "You were wrong, Lydia Proctor," she said, through tears. "Belle Isle is not beautiful at all."

CHAPTER NINETEEN

By the time Jacob found her, Nora had calmed down enough to face an undeniable reality. Her only hope of getting off Belle Isle was the *Dover Cloud,* and she had to rely on its captain to take her. It had become almost impossible to trust anyone associated with Proctor House, but she concentrated on the man she had met in Key West. Jacob Proctor was the same man who, though he confounded her at every turn, was at times gentle, compassionate, and even gallant. He had given his word to see her home safely, and despite everything, she believed he would.

She was sitting on a bench in the garden when he came up behind her and set a cloth-wrapped bundle next to her. She looked up at him, and then cast a questioning glance at the bundle.

"It's just some bread and cheese and a bit of tonight's flounder," he said. "You missed your dinner."

She picked up the package, placed it on her lap, and unwrapped the food. Jacob sat down beside her and handed her a glass of amber liquid. "It's brandy," he said. "Drink it.

You'll feel better, and after a few swallows, I might not seem like such a monster."

Without looking at him, she nibbled at the fish and sipped the brandy. "I want to go home," she said after she'd had several bites.

"I know. We'll leave at first light day after tomorrow. Do you think you can stand it till then?"

"If I must."

"The day we arrived, I sent a messenger for Dylan's doctor. He arrives tomorrow from Trinidad. I really must be here to . . ."

She put a hand up to stop his explanation. "It's all right. I understand. Of course the day after will be sufficient."

From the corner of her eye she saw the hint of a smile play around his lips. "I've done it again, Nora. Put myself in the position of owing you another apology in my seemingly endless parade of them. I'm sorry I raised my voice in the dining room."

Fresh tears stung the backs of her eyes. She blinked hard to keep them from spilling over. "Obviously, you felt you had reason."

"I was trying to protect you."

She looked up at him. "From what?"

"From him."

"Your father?"

"At that moment, yes. But also from Dylan and Juditha, who seems harsh and unkind to you only because for some reason she loves them both and is devoted to them. She protects them like a mother lion. But to someone who doesn't understand her, it seems she is hard-hearted."

"I think Dylan is afraid of her," Nora said.

Jacob chuckled. "*I* am more afraid of Juditha than Dylan is. He trusts her. Listens to her." He settled his gaze on some distant spot at the end of the garden. "I was also trying to protect you from me. Perhaps mostly from me."

Anguish softened his voice and hinted of his personal torment. Despite her wounded feelings, his words touched her heart. She put her hand on his arm. "It seems to me, Jacob, that there is entirely too much protecting going on around here, and not nearly enough trusting.''

He shifted his gaze to her hand, and she curled her fingers more tightly. Perhaps she was doing some protecting of her own. ''Tell me what is going on here, Jacob. What has happened on this island? Who is Dylan?''

He pivoted on the bench until he faced her and his knees touched hers. ''Will Turpin always said you would understand, but when I tell you the whole story, I don't see how that's possible.''

''I will try, Jacob. You can believe that.''

Her promise was enough. He nodded and covered her hand with his. ''Dylan is my brother, two years younger than I.''

A vision of the pale young dancer came to her mind. *That troubled man, so thin and wan, his complexion the color of gardenia blooms, is the brother of ruddy, handsome Jacob?* It was difficult to imagine the two men coming from the same parents. ''I see,'' she said. ''What is wrong with him?''

Lines of tension radiated from the corners of Jacob's eyes. He bit his lips together, and Nora felt the muscles in his lower arm contract. She sensed that what he was about to tell her could only be related at great personal cost.

''The doctors call it 'Malum Hereditarium,' '' he said. ''What it means is that my brother suffers from a hereditary dementive mania. According to the doctors, and there have been many over the years, some family trees sprout madness like others produce blue eyes or fair hair. The Proctors are so afflicted.

''Dylan sees things other people don't. He hears voices. He believes that nearly everyone he encounters is a threat to his well-being. He lives with fear and anxiety, and he reacts without reason.'' Jacob lifted Nora's hand and held it between his. ''He can be violent, Nora, without provocation or deliberate intent. He simply doesn't know any better.''

Her mind spun back to the details of her meeting with Dylan earlier that day. He had accused her of stopping the music to which he and his imaginary friend had been dancing. He had told her to go away, and then just as suddenly insisted that she stay. He had shouted at her one minute, and then dissolved into tears the next. But hurt someone? Could this confused, disturbed man actually inflict pain on another human being? "But when I mentioned your name, he seemed to light from within," she said. "He was like a child . . ."

"I know. He trusts me. There are only three people who can communicate with any degree of success with Dylan. Myself, Juditha, and a man named Vincent, a male nurse who is Dylan's companion. And music helps to calm him. When you saw Dylan today, Vincent had left for just a few minutes, but he'd turned on the music box. He thought the tune would play until he returned."

"What about the doctor? Can't he relate to Dylan?"

A scornful rush of air from Jacob's lips hinted at his answer. "My brother mistrusts doctors more than any people on earth. He has learned that their poking and prodding only result in further limitations of his mobility. If you only knew what has been tried with him, where he has been confined, what horrors . . ."

He trembled and shut his eyes as if blocking out the memories. "In England, South America, even a sanatorium in Mexico City. Each time we've had hope, but after a few weeks, when I see the effects of the treatments on Dylan, I bring him back here. It's where he's happiest, most content. And I arrange for the doctor to come only when I visit. It helps Dylan get through it."

"Jacob, if you had told me . . . if I had been prepared. Don't you know I would have understood?"

"About Dylan, yes, maybe you would have. But I have become very protective of my brother's privacy. I guess I thought you might try to seek him out, curious about the oddity of Belle Isle . . ."

"Jacob, I wouldn't have . . ."

"Or tried to fix him, as others have. I don't know. I've come to believe that the fewer people who know about Dylan the better. He can't be fixed, Nora. He is permanently broken. And there is more I haven't told you, and I doubt very much you would like to know.''

He dropped her hand and looked away from her again to speak to the shadows. ''I don't think there is that much compassion in any one woman's heart to understand and accept all of it.''

Nora did not shift her gaze from his granite profile, hoping the power of her eyes would draw him back. She sensed there was more to this story before he admitted it, and she suspected what it was. She also believed that Jacob wanted and needed to tell it. Touching his shoulder, she asked, ''Jacob, has Dylan ever hurt anyone? Is that why you were so afraid for me? Is Dylan the one who stabbed your father?''

His head snapped around, revealing wide, dark eyes. ''No. That's not how it was. Remember what I told you about my family and the madness?''

She nodded.

''It was our mother. The genetic properties came from her. She attacked our father and then tried to turn the dagger on herself.''

If Nora could have taken some of the pain reflected in his eyes she would have. ''My God . . . your mother.'' No wonder his childhood was lost. No wonder no one spoke of Jacob's mother. Nora hated to ask the next question, fearing the answer, but he had told her this much, and she imagined the rest . . .

''Jacob, what stopped her from killing herself?''

''I did. I wrested the knife from her hand.''

Nora's heart clenched painfully. He had only been twelve years old.

''But I only forestalled the inevitable. In a very bizarre way, she committed suicide a few days later.''

''Bizarre?''

''It was the beginning of Dylan's symptoms. He was close to our mother, had always been her favorite, really. I never minded. Dylan seemed to need much more than I did.'' He looked toward the cliffs that bordered the sea where Proctor land ended. ''A week after my father's . . . accident, my mother managed to escape the watchful eyes of our servants. She took Dylan to the top of that cliff you can see beyond the grove of trees to the west.''

Jacob paused, and Nora moved her hand to the taut back muscles below his shoulder. A sudden spasm rippled against her palm. ''Juditha followed them and observed what happened, though she was too late to prevent it.''

Nora's words struggled past constricted vocal cords. ''What did happen, Jacob?''

''Sophie, our mother, convinced Dylan that she should be punished for hurting his father, and she told him he must do it.''

''How could a ten-year-old child punish her?''

''She had a way with Dylan. He would have gone to the ends of the earth for Sophie. He loved her without condition. He loved her so much that he couldn't refuse her anything, even when she demanded more than any person should give.''

Jacob pulled his gaze from the cliff and stared at the garden stones beneath his feet. ''She demanded that he push her over the edge.''

Revulsion gripped Nora's stomach, and she fought the urge to be sick. She closed her eyes against the horrible vision that had taken shape on the shadowed mountaintop. She closed her mind to block the cries of Sophie Proctor plunging to her death. ''How could she . . . ?''

''Because she was ill? Because she didn't know what she was doing? That's what they told me through the years. I suppose she was ill. I have to believe it, otherwise I think I would go . . .''

He stopped and took a deep, ragged breath. ''All I know for sure is that my mother's last act of treachery against this family was to take my brother's soul over that cliff with her.''

But hopefully not yours, Jacob. Not yours. ''When I look at you tonight, Jacob,'' Nora said softly, ''I think that perhaps her last act of treachery is still going on and has been all these years. You can see what Sophie has done to everyone else. But I wonder if you fully understand what she did to you.''

He turned a troubled gaze to her face and took her shoulders in his hands. "Willy was right about you, Nora," he said. "You are truly a good woman . . . too good to be here on Belle Isle, too good for . . . I shouldn't have brought you."

How could she tell him that since he had taken her into his confidence there was no place on earth she would rather be? How could she convince him that she understood? How could she make him know that *his* life, not hers, was the true measure of goodness because his virtues had been tested.

And how could she tell him that she had started falling in love with him the day he pulled her from the water at Key West harbor, and she'd been tumbling ever since? And this night she literally spiraled to the depths of her emotions here in his garden. *I love you, Jacob. I love the adolescent boy who lost his innocence and the strong man he has become. I love you.*

The words would not come to her mouth, and perhaps that was best. She feared he would think they were only shallow sentiments cloaked in pity. She did pity him, of course. Her heart ached for what he'd endured. But she was not such an inexperienced girl that she could not recognize the difference between pity and love. She knew. Oh, God, she knew.

"Jacob, I'm not sorry I came," she said at last. "I know I said I wanted to go home, but it was only fear and confusion that made me say that. I'm glad I'm here with you."

One hand slid from her shoulder to her face. He stroked her cheek with his fingers. "In my heart, which is the most damnably honest part of me, I'm glad you are here, too."

"How have you managed?" she asked. "You were just a boy . . ."

He thought a moment, remembering. "We left England just after my twelfth birthday. The scandals about my mother had grown to the point where my father could no longer make excuses for her behavior. In the beginning we had some money. Enough to maintain this house, my father's indulgences, and seek treatments for Sophie. Later, after she died, the money ran out. We sold Braxton Manor and gave up our title."

"But . . ."

"I know, Father still uses his. A harmless enough fantasy, I suppose. When we needed money again, I began trading until I heard about the possibilities in Key West." His mouth lifted in a crooked smile. "The rest I'm sure your father has told you. The 'infamous Jacob Proctor,' the scourge of the Caribbean whose coffers are full of ill-gotten loot and whose profits were pulled from the hulls of dying ships."

She laughed at his exaggeration, which really wasn't so far from the truth, and was gratified to see the sound reflected in his eyes. "He hasn't used such colorful language as that," she said. "And if he had, I wouldn't have paid him any mind anyway. I just believe you are the best at what you do."

"Good enough, thankfully. My father is able to pursue his love of horses and fine brandy. Dylan is cared for and Proctor House is still standing. And here on Belle Isle life goes on. The outside world knows little of this island, and the natives don't speak, to me at least, of the misfortunes of Proctor House." His voice brimmed with refreshing teasing when he added, "And visitors, you noticed, are indeed a rarity, and not at all well received."

She leaned in close and grinned up at him. "Pooh. My only concern is that I am well received by one member of this family particularly."

One eyebrow climbed his forehead in surprise, and a teasing glint sparked silver underneath it. "Miss Seabrook, you shouldn't worry about that. You are indeed well received by one member of this family."

Her heart raced faster than it had through all the trials she'd faced on Belle Isle. "Thank you, Captain, but I'm afraid I'm not quite convinced."

She lifted her face, bringing her mouth to his. She'd never kissed him first, though she'd always kissed him back. But this time she let instinct banish convention to the wind. Her lips touched his like a feather. She pressed gently and retreated, moving around his mouth with airy, noiseless kisses that left traces of dampness on his lips. When she wrapped her hands around his nape and tangled her fingers in his hair, she let her mouth wander to his cheeks, his jaw, and back to his wonderful waiting mouth again.

The initial rigidity she'd felt in his body melted with her insistent caresses. The muscles in his neck eased like warm molasses spreading to her fingertips. She slid along the garden bench until her thigh pressed against his, then moved her lips to his ear and whispered, "Jacob, you are a good man. Much better than you even know. I see the goodness in you."

He groaned and splayed his hands against her back. "Nora, I don't want to hurt you."

She nibbled playfully on his earlobe. "Does this hurt me, Jacob?" She moved back to the corner of his mouth. "Does this?" She lowered her hand to his chest and slipped inside his open shirt. With her fingers, she circled the mat of cocoa-brown hair that surrounded his nipples. She felt his heart beat against her palm. Her mouth hovered over his like a humming-bird, and she said, "This doesn't hurt me, Jacob. This only pleasures me."

She pulled her hand free of his shirt, and his arms tightened around her back. Her breasts flattened against his chest, and his mouth came down to devour hers. His breathing was short and labored, but his kiss was exquisitely long, tormentingly passionate.

He forced her lips open and tasted her, roaming the inside of her mouth and circling with her tongue until she felt a similar coiling deep inside her. Her breasts strained against the weak seams of her poorly sewn dress. The nipples responded with a tightness that was intensified by the hard plane of his chest.

His hand captured one budding tip over the fabric of her dress. He fisted the scooped bodice until his fingers grazed a bare breast. Then he stroked the tip with his knuckles until she wanted to cry out with the sweet friction of his fingers on her skin. When he finally reached inside her camisole to fill his palm with her swelling flesh, his touch weakened her knees, tugged at her abdomen, and shot a honeyed warmth to the dark area between her legs.

She rode on a sea of his embraces, ebbing and flowing on one dizzying wave after another. His hand sought her other breast. His tongue laved her skin above each trembling mound. Deep inside, she sensed the waves would crest with a feeling that would bring all the other sensations together in a mind-numbing finale. And she knew she would never be satisfied until she experienced it with this man. Take me there, Jacob, she cried out in her mind. Take me to the top of the wave and bring me back down with your kiss and your touch.

He crushed his mouth on hers again and gently lowered her onto the bench. His hand felt for her skirt and pulled it up to her waist. "Nora, I want you," he said. "God knows I've no right, but I want you."

"You have the right, Jacob. I freely give it to you. Let me make you happy. I want to please you. This can't be wrong."

His hand stopped moving up the inside of her thigh. With a groan he tore his mouth from hers and sat up.

Confusion and disappointment made her head swim. She looked up at him through eyes blurred with passion. "Jacob, what is it?"

"You don't understand, Nora. Even after all I've told you, you don't see. What we're doing is wrong. Terribly wrong."

"No, I don't believe that."

He didn't look at her. He'd shut her away from his face, his eyes, and nothing could have wounded her more. "I told you about the madness," he said. "I told you how it happens, that it is carried in my mother's bloodline."

"But Dylan . . . not you. You're fine."

"Now, yes, but what does that mean? When I look into the blankness or the violence in my brother's eyes, I know I could be looking in a mirror. It could happen to me. It happens to male children more than to female, and it can happen to more that one offspring in the same family. In a year, maybe two, maybe ten . . . I don't know. I could be as mad as Dylan."

Tears sprang to her eyes and burned in her throat. "No, not to you," she said. "Never to you."

"Yes, to me, dearest Nora. And if you were to get with child . . ."

She reached for him, but he flinched as if her touch were poison. "I don't care," she cried. "It's only a small chance. But my feelings for you are real. Being with you, only you, is my future. Jacob, I love you."

He grabbed her wrist and pulled her up from the bench. His eyes fixed on hers and blazed with raw emotion that could have been either anger or pain. Nora only knew for certain that it scorched her heart. "Don't say that, Nora."

"Why not? It's true."

"Because it would be too easy for me to say it back to you, and I won't. Not as long as my mother's curse hangs over this family. I can't. Go. Go into the house." He turned away from her. "We'll leave day after tomorrow as planned. I'm taking you home."

She waited, hoping, praying he would relent and take her in his arms and swear his love. But she only stared at the rigid muscles of his back. He was lost to her and would not come back. She spun on her heels and ran into the house.

CHAPTER TWENTY

Thurston Seabrook had never been so miserable in his life. No matter how hard he tried, he couldn't make anyone happy, including himself. Sidonia was in a constant state of upheaval, swearing on her mother's grave that she would never again draw an easy breath until her daughter was returned safely. Even Armand and Hubert had turned nastier than usual, nipping at Thurston's ankles until he had tiny teeth marks to prove it.

And Theo Hadley, the never-ending houseguest, added his own complaining to the mix, claiming that when Nora was taken from him, he'd lost the sunshine of his life, and he lived for the day she would return and once more fill his dreary days with light.

Poetic, but Thurston wasn't one to be taken in by fancy rhetoric, especially when Theo's appetite hadn't suffered one whit. In fact, after living with the Seabrooks, the attorney was fairly bursting the seams of his trousers.

But most distressing was the fact that Thurston couldn't help himself any more than he could help anyone else in his household. The simple truth was, he missed his daughter. He'd never before realized what a clever, intelligent, and interesting woman she'd become. Why, he even missed her feminine prattle with Sid and Fanny around the dinner table, and he most definitely longed to see her smile again.

Damn that Proctor! Thurston had cursed the nefarious captain more often than he cared to remember. Even if Nora had stowed away on his ship, he should have turned right around and brought her back instead of taking her God knows where. Once Nora was home, Thurston was determined never to let her within a city block of Proctor again.

An opportunity to insure that reality presented itself one night almost two weeks after Nora's disappearance. The usual pall had settled over the Seabrook dining room, with the exception of Dillard Hyde's attempts to engage the family in conversation. Lately, the man had been present every night for dinner, and he tried so damnably hard to cheer everyone up that Thurston was nearly tempted to dump a bottle of claret over his white linen suit.

During a lull in Dillard's incessant babble, Theo announced that he had a matter of extreme importance to discuss with the judge.

Sidonia perked up immediately, dabbed at her moist eyes, and actually displayed a flash of white teeth that Thurston hadn't seen in ages. *She knows about this, whatever it is,* he deduced, and with trepidation said, "Go ahead, Hadley, speak your mind."

"Well, sir, it's no secret how I feel about Nora, and I truly believe that she feels the same about me . . ."

Fanny suddenly required a smart slap on her back from Dillard to dislodge a bite of food that had become stuck in her throat. "Oh, sorry, Theo," she said when she'd recovered. "Do go on . . . you usually do."

Ignoring her implied sarcasm or oblivious to it, Theo continued. "I know Miss Seabrook and I haven't known each other long, but the time we've spent together, all of it strictly virtuous, Your Honor, has been, well, rewarding, and ever so dear to me. Miss Seabrook is an exceptional woman, beautiful, and . . ."

Thurston squinted his eyes against an impending belch and

said, "I know my daughter's attributes, Hadley. What's your point?"

Sidonia immediately came to the attorney's aid. "Go on, Theodore. Say it. Thurston is listening, and he appreciates forthrightness, don't you, dear?"

Theo smiled tentatively at Sidonia. "Of course, madam." Turning back to his tougher audience, he said, "What I'm trying to propose, sir, is . . . well, propose isn't exactly the right word. I mean it would be if I were talking to Nora . . ."

The evening's melon and cream stuck like plaster in Thurston's gullet. "Out with it, man!"

"Thurston!" Sidonia squealed.

"All right," Theo said. "Sir, I would like your blessing to ask for Nora's hand in marriage if—I mean *when* she returns." Then, in a lower voice, he added, "Assuming she is unblemished, of course."

Thurston's internal mercury, which already measured burning in his throat, leaped to the roots of his hair. "Unblemished, Theo? Did you say 'unblemished'?"

Sidonia's hand fluttered nervously in the air. "Now, Thurston, all Theo meant was . . ."

"I know damn well what he meant, Sid. He's talking about my daughter!"

A line of crimson flashed along Theo's cheekbones. "Your Honor, you've misunderstood. I regard Miss Seabrook as a model of womanly virtue. Why, she is the absolute epitome of fine upbringing and sound parental guidance. I know that anything . . . *untoward* that may have occurred during her absence would certainly not be Nora's fault. I only meant to suggest that . . ."

Thurston leveled a hard stare at his wife. "Sidonia, did you have prior knowledge of this proclamation tonight?"

She smiled almost flirtatiously. "I must admit I did, dear. Theo feels that sometimes you can be a bit hard to talk to, and he tested the waters with me first. And I am heartily in favor of it." She beamed across the table at her expectant future son-in-law. "Theo is a perfect match for our Eleanor," she sighed.

Placing his hands on his roiling stomach, Thurston knew he'd had the last bite he would consume this night. Theo Hadley for a son-in-law? He was far indeed from any matrimonial candidate Thurston himself had envisioned for Nora. But then, Thurston had never really thought any man would be good enough for his daughter. Yet, if she truly cared for him, who was he to stand in her way?

Still . . . Theo Hadley and his Nora? Thurston searched his mind for some snippet of sound reasoning that would explain this anomaly. *Damn! When had this courtship taken place? And where was I when it was happening? But Sid likes him, and she's more privy to Nora's emotions than I . . . And he's certainly a better match than that Proctor!*

His wife's voice cut through his reverie. "Thurston, for heaven's sake why don't you answer Theo?"

"Blast it, Sid, I'm thinking!" He squelched another burp. "All right, Hadley, if Nora wants you, then you've got my blessing. You're a decent enough sort, I guess."

Theo expelled a long breath.

Sidonia clasped her hands under her chin. "Now we won't have to worry about that dreadful ship captain who seems to be constantly at Eleanor's heels. Thurston, isn't there something you can do to insure that Captain Proctor will leave our daughter alone once they return to Key West? After all we've been through, and now that Eleanor's future is settled, I want that man out of her life for good."

Now this was something Thurston could agree with, and he formulated a plan that was certain to please his wife. The thought of dealing a retaliatory blow to that upstart captain gave new purpose to Thurston's life. "Yes, my dear, there is." Turning to Dillard, he said, "Hyde, I want you to go ahead with that search warrant for Proctor's warehouse."

"But sir . . ."

"Tomorrow, Dillard. I want to go inside that building first thing in the morning. Proctor and Swain were the first two wreckers at the *Marguerite Gray*. We've searched Swain's quarters, and we're long overdue searching Proctor's. My gut

still tells me somebody's hiding something." Pressing his hand
to his stomach, he added, "And damn it all, my gut's always
telling me something."

"Yes, Your Honor. I'll have the warrant in the morning."

Fanny snapped such a scathing look at Thurston, he felt its
heat all the way across the table. "What's the matter with
you?" he barked at her. "This is all your fault, anyway."

She stood up from the table and flounced her full skirts. If
her ruffles had been weapons, Thurston would have ducked.
"Come on, Dill," she said. "I need a walk in the fresh air!"

Dill? When had the proper Dillard become the devil-may-care Dill? Speaking to no one in particular, Thurston muttered,
"What the hell is going on in this house?"

The next afternoon, a representative of the Federal Court of
Key West, Florida, discovered a padlocked barrel in the upstairs
office of Proctor Warehouse and Salvage. He smashed the lock
and removed several items from under a layer of straw. There
were Oriental porcelain bowls, a few brass trinkets, and at the
very bottom, a wooden box, its corners crusty with salt. The
man handed Thurston Seabrook the contents of the box—a
bundle of bank notes from the state bank in New Bedford,
Massachusetts.

Flipping through the notes, Thurston spoke to his clerk.
"Dillard, what was the point of origin of the *Marguerite
Gray?*"

"Massachusetts, sir," Dillard answered soberly. "New Bedford." His astounded gaze remained fixed with Thurston's on
the bank notes the judge fanned in his hand.

By mid-morning, Nora's last day on Belle Isle stretched
endlessly before her. The part of her that was terribly unhappy
wanted it to end. But the hopeful part dreaded the next day
when she would have to leave the island. She didn't want to
go, not feeling like this, anyway. Not with her heart torn in

two by the one man who filled her dreams with a future she'd believed might be hers. But Jacob had made it clear that there was no place for her in his life, and the conditions that made it so were unalterable. She couldn't fight the phantoms of Sophie's past. She couldn't change what the doctors had sworn to be true.

She hadn't seen Jacob all morning. Juditha told her he had gone to the village to await the doctor's arrival. She hadn't seen Harrison Proctor or Polly either. She had stared at her breakfast in total silence, completely alone in the dining room, and it looked as if that was the way she would spend her last hours on Belle Isle.

Nora went out to Harrison's garden, and crossed from one side of the flagstone terrace to the other. She looked over the island from every angle. It was indeed a beautiful place. No one would ever suspect what sadness lay beneath its landscape of brightly colored blossoms and abundant trees. If was as if a giant hand had swept the tormenting secrets of the Proctors' past under a carpet of green grass and flowering hillsides.

The sun warmed Nora's shoulders until a profound weariness weighed her down. An oppressive heat from the garden stones penetrated even the soles of her boots. She considered entering one of the shady groves of trees beyond the garden boundary. What did it matter now if she did? Who would care if she broke her word? The damage had already been done.

She chose a path well away from Dylan Proctor's cottage and wandered into a thicket of leafy trees and green shrubs. Following the sound of water bubbling at the bottom of a gently sloping incline, she came upon a small stone house by a clear, narrow creek.

Analyzing its proximity to the water, Nora determined that the structure was most likely a washhouse, a feature common to rural estates. Exploring the little building gave her something to do, so she proceeded to the open door. Someone was inside, and Nora immediately recognized the slight figure as Polly's. Her singsong voice kept time to the rhythmic sounds of wash-day, the wringing and slapping of laundry against a washboard.

They were work sounds, comforting and normal, and Nora leaned against the cool stones to listen.

Her lackadaisical interest grew wary when she realized the maid was crooning an odd ditty that had neither familiar strains nor melodious chords. Furthermore, the lyrics were as strange as the tune. Nora listened closely to discern the words as Polly kept repeating them.

> Heigh ho, fiddle-dee-dee,
> Sir Harry knows the mother not be.
> Heigh ho, fiddle-dee-dum,
> Father has two sons, mother has one.

Shaking her head in bewilderment, Nora started to walk away from the washhouse, deciding not to interrupt Polly's work. But she continued to mull the hypnotic lyrics over in her mind. She had only taken a few steps when icy fingers of comprehension gripped her lungs and stopped her cold in the footpath.

". . . the mother not be," she said. "Father has two sons, mother has one." Nora whirled around, retraced her steps, and rushed into the small building.

Polly gasped and dropped the article of clothing she was washing into the stream. It ballooned out, belched with the weight of seeping water, and floated out of reach of her hands. "Miss Nora," the old lady cried, "what are you doin' here?"

Nora dropped to her knees beside the maid. "Polly, that song you were singing just now . . . what does it mean?"

Polly turned ghostly pale and mumbled a few incoherent sounds before finally uttering, "N-nothin', miss. It means nothin' a'tall. Just some crazy ol' words been stuck in my mind for years."

"No, Polly, that's not true. The words aren't crazy at all. They tell a story. They mean something, and you must tell me. You must!"

"No, Miss Nora. I swear to you, they mean not a thing."

Nora took the maid's shoulders and shook her, not hard, but enough to let her know that she didn't intend to leave the washhouse without answers. "Polly, you know something. You've heard something. Tell me what it is. 'The mother not be . . . Father has two sons, Mother has one.' What do those words mean?"

The old maid's mouth dropped open, and she shook her head. "No, miss, you heard wrong. I meant nothing." She stared at Nora before uttering a small moan of surrender. Dropping from a crouching position, she sat heavily on the stones bordering the creek. "Miss Nora, I can't tell you anything. You'll get us in more trouble than you ever thought of."

Nora entreated the frightened woman with her eyes. "No, Polly, no. I promise you won't get into any trouble. If you know something about this family, about Jacob, you must tell me. Jacob will protect you. He won't let anything happen to you. Besides, I already suspect what the words mean, and I'm not about to forget them. But it would help me so much if you would tell me the truth."

"But Lord Proctor, he warned me if I ever told, he'd send me to Mexico without a cent, and I'd have to work in some poor village. I'd probably starve to death." Her voice trembled, and she nearly succumbed to a fit of crying.

"I won't let that happen, Polly. I'll take you back with me to America before I'd let that happen. Polly, you have to trust me. There have been too many secrets on this island. Too many people have been hurt, and more will be hurt in the future. But I think you can prevent that. Polly, was Sophie Proctor Jacob's mother?"

The maid's resolve wilted, and she collapsed like a damp rag against Nora's chest. Speaking her words in a choked whisper, she said, "It has gone on too long, Miss Nora. Too, too long. Sophie was only Dylan's mother. Jacob's mama was a lady named Anne Hempstead. She died after giving birth to the boy."

Nora felt as if her insides were made of the same weak stuffing as Polly's. Her head swam with the magnitude of the maid's confession. "Jacob doesn't know . . ." she said simply.

Polly looked up into Nora's face. "No. Lord Proctor never

told him. At first Sophie didn't want him to, but then she took with the sickness, and Lord Proctor feared they'd lose everything. When he found out the second boy, Dylan, could end up crazy as a loon, he knew his firstborn, his healthy son, would have to save us all. He had to let Jacob believe that he could turn out just like Sophie and Dylan.''

Nora turned away from the milky mist covering Polly's penetrating gray eyes. She didn't want the maid to see the revulsion in her own eyes for Harrison's lies and the maid's cowardice. "My God, Polly ... all these years. Jacob has financed this island, his father, cared for Dylan.''

Polly gripped Nora's arm fiercely. "But he had to, Miss Nora. There was no other way. Don't you see? Without Mr. Jacob, we'd have all been lost. That's what Lord Proctor told me over and over. We needed Mr. Jacob's money to survive here. Lord Proctor had to keep Jacob's mama a secret so he'd keep bringing the money.''

If Polly really believed that, Nora couldn't change her mind. But the perfidy of Harrison Proctor's lies burned like fire in Nora's chest. Such anguish he'd put his son through. Such nightmares. And for what? If Harrison Proctor had taken the time to get to know his healthy son, to really *know* him, then he would have seen that Jacob's honor would have prevented him from forsaking the family anyway. But now ... Could honor survive such treachery?

Nora forced a steady gaze on Polly's face. "Polly, do you know if there is any proof of the boys' births? Any records in the house?''

The maid shook her head. "I don't know ...''

"Think, Polly. Please.''

She wrung her hands in her lap and closed her eyes tightly. "There's a desk in Lord Proctor's library ... a big, tall one with glass doors on top.''

"Yes, what about it?''

"I don't know for sure, but he's always told me never to lay my hands on it. Never to dust it or go near it. I've always wondered ...''

Nora pressed her lips against Polly's withered cheek. "Thank you." She stood up and went to the door of the washhouse. "Just to be sure, stay away from the house the rest of today. I'll let you know what happens, when it's safe to come back."

Nora hurried up the footpath with Polly's warning ringing in her ears. "Be careful, miss, if you lay a hand on that desk."

The draperies in Harrison Proctor's library were drawn, leaving the room in cool, gray shade. Still, Nora spotted the secretary cabinet against a wall in the farthest corner. When her eyes adjusted to the semi-darkness, she examined the items inside the convex glass doors at the top of the secretary. There were family mementos, silver cups, shaving mugs, and things that had probably belonged to Proctor ancestors.

Below the curio case was a wooden slant front that could be lowered to form a writing surface, and under it, three large drawers formed a wide kettle base on carved claw feet. Nora lowered the writing area. Numerous pigeonholes produced nothing but expected quills, blotters, and stationery.

"Proof of the births has to be in one of these drawers," Nora said to herself as she opened the first one and withdrew the contents. She was careful to listen for footsteps in the hallway or for the creak of Harrison's wheelchair. Once she'd painstakingly examined the items from the drawer, she removed it entirely from the cabinet, turned it upside down, and checked the bottom for concealed papers. Nothing.

The second drawer produced similar discouraging results. Nora had so far invested a half hour of time in her search. How long would it be before Harrison retired to this very room as he did customarily each morning?

She pulled out the third drawer, set it on the carpet, and removed the few items inside, which turned out to be family financial records. Automatically she overturned the drawer to inspect the bottom, and that was when she heard the faint but distinct sound of paper sliding along a wooden surface.

She turned the drawer over twice without locating the source of the sound. It was empty. There were no more papers. Yet the shuffling continued each time she moved the drawer. She set it right side up on the carpet, and ran her fingernail along the bottom, producing a hollow scraping sound on the thin wood. "That's it," she said, her heart pounding with the thrill of discovery. "A false bottom."

Nora retrieved a letter opener from the desk, and pried the bottom of the drawer loose enough to slide her hand inside. Her fingers closed around a thin sheaf of papers, and she pulled it out. The musty-smelling documents were yellowed with age, but the writing was still legible. Nora bit her lower lip to keep from shouting her joy. There, in dulled but readable script on two separate certificates of birth, was the evidence that Jacob and Dylan Proctor had two different mothers.

"What the devil are you doing in my library?"

Harrison Proctor's voice sliced into Nora's brain, and numbed her to her fingertips. She dropped the papers to her lap and shuddered at her carelessness. She'd been so jubilant over the dates and names on the forms that she'd momentarily forgotten to listen for the wheelchair. "L-Lord Proctor," she stammered. "I was l-looking for a b-book to read."

His eyes bore into her until she was forced to look away. "Do you take me for a fool, you stupid girl? I can see quite clearly what you've done." He pointed at the papers in her lap. "Give me those."

Realizing the futility of her lie and the importance of her quest, Nora gathered her wits about her, snatched the papers from the folds of her dress, and stood. "No, you can't have them."

His lips pulled into a snarl and his finger lifted from the papers to center on her face. "Hand over those papers this minute, or I swear to you, I'll . . ."

"You'll what?" she blasted back. "Send me to a Mexican village where I can starve or work myself into an early grave?"

"You'll never be that lucky, you wicked creature! I'll send you to your grave this very day. You've no right to prowl about this house snooping in other people's business like some black-hearted thief.''

She waved the papers at his face. "How dare you speak of *my* black heart? You've kept Jacob's true parentage from him all these years. What kind of a father are you? How could you . . .''

"Shut your mouth, woman! You have no idea what you're talking about, and you have no idea what you've done. If you know what's good for you, you'll give me those papers and keep your mouth closed for eternity about what you saw written there.''

"I will not. I won't let Jacob go on believing in your evil lies. You sit here in your flower-covered castle while Jacob risks his life in Key West to support you. And every day he is plagued with the fear, the horrible nightmares, that he will end up like his brother.''

"My son hasn't suffered from not knowing the truth. He's a wealthy man and lives a damn good life . . .'' Harrison slammed his fist down on the arm of his wheelchair. "A hell of a lot better life than I'll ever see from this infernal contraption. You're wasting your pity on one who doesn't need or deserve it, you witless girl.''

"How can you possibly know what Jacob's life is like? Yes, he can walk, he can leave the island, but for what? Your lies have kept him a prisoner as surely as if he'd been locked away like your other son!''

Harrison grasped the wheels of his chair in his fists and inched closer to her. "I'm telling you for the last time, woman, give me those papers, or I swear you'll never get off this island alive!''

She stuffed the papers into her pocket. "We'll see about that!'' she shouted back. Giving the wheelchair a wide berth, she headed for the hallway. "And we'll see what Jacob has to say about it.''

"Damn you! Damn you to Hell for the devil you are!'' Harrison Proctor's words followed her down the hall and out the front door.

* * *

"Ju-dith-a!"

Harrison's shout brought the servant running to the library. "What is it, Lord Proctor? What's wrong?"

"Tell Vincent to bring Dylan here to me at once!"

"Dylan, sir? I don't think that's such a good idea. He's quite agitated . . ."

"I didn't ask your opinion, woman. Just have him brought here, and then stay out of our way."

Juditha's mouth opened as if she were about to protest the order, but she closed it without doing so. "As you wish, Lord Proctor. I'll fetch Dylan myself."

CHAPTER
TWENTY-ONE

Harrison Proctor looked toward the entrance to the library when he heard the shuffling of feet in the hallway. "Come in, Dylan," he said when his son appeared in the door. "Don't stand there gawking."

Prodded from behind by Juditha, Dylan took short, tentative steps across the threshold. Once inside the room, he clasped his hands at his abdomen while his alert gaze darted nervously around the room. "What do you want?" he asked.

Harrison attempted a smile, but doubted its effectiveness. He felt little but contempt for this weakling son. "I want to see you, of course. Can't a father want to share a conversation with his son once in a while?"

Juditha took Dylan's arm and guided him to a chair. "Sit down, Dylan," she ordered. "You'll be more comfortable."

He wrenched his arm free. "I don't want to sit! Leave me alone!"

Trying to cover an involuntary flinch at his son's whining, Harrison said, "The boy's right, Juditha. Leave him alone. In fact, leave us both alone."

"But sir . . ."

"Go! I'll ring for you when we've finished." He waited until the servant had stepped into the hall. "Close the door, too. And don't listen at the keyhole."

A haughty *harumph* was her response, but Juditha did as she was told.

Harrison turned his full attention to his son. "Now, then, Dylan, it's nice, isn't it? Just the two of us?"

Dylan's hands twisted into a tight knot. "No, it isn't. I want to go home."

If there was anything Harrison despised as much as weakness, it was stupidity. "You *are* home, Dylan," he said angrily, then spread his arm to encompass the library. "This is your home as much as the cottage is." Growing more impatient when his son failed to relax even one tense muscle in his pinched face, Harrison snapped at him. "Sit down, Dylan. You look like a statue standing there."

Dylan sniffed loudly, and chose a low ottoman to comply with his father's wishes. He sat on the very edge of it and hung his white-knuckled hands between his knees. "I want music."

"I don't have any music here," Harrison said. "But if you listen to what I have to say, I'll see to it that you have all the music you want. I will tell Vincent and Juditha to let you listen to your music all night long."

Dylan didn't respond, but he cocked his head to the side, like a bird who's suddenly spotted the worm dangling from his mother's beak. If Harrison wanted his son's attention, he guessed he had it now, at least as much as Dylan was able to give. "I have to talk to you about our home, Dylan. Yours and mine and Juditha's and Vincent's. We are all happy here, aren't we?"

"Can I have music now?"

"No, confound it, listen to me! Our home is in danger, Dylan. Someone is trying to hurt us. A woman has come, and she wants to hurt all of us."

Dylan nodded vigorously, and Harrison smiled. Apparently, this was something his son's confused mind was able to grasp.

"She took the music," Dylan said. "Nora. Her name is Nora, and she took the music."

Harrison had no idea what his son was talking about, but the irrational raving fit into his plans. "Yes, that's right. She took your music. She's evil, Dylan. Nora is a bad woman."

Dylan wrapped his clasped hands around his knees and rocked on the ottoman. "But . . . but Jacob likes her."

"No, no, Jacob hates her. He wants her gone, but she won't leave. She hurt Jacob, and she hurt you."

Dylan rocked and chewed on his lower lip until Harrison thought he might draw blood. "Then I don't like Nora," Dylan finally said.

"That's right. None of us likes her. Jacob and I, we want you to help us make Nora go away."

"How?"

"First you must find her, and then take her up the cliff where you went with Sophie all those years ago."

Harrison did not expect his son's reaction. Dylan wailed a long, low keening sound and dropped his chin to his chest. "Sophie, Sophie," he repeated over and over, finally ending with, "Mama."

"Sophie was bad, Dylan, you remember, don't you? Very, very bad. You saved us all when you helped her leave this island. And you must do the same with Nora." Growing more irritated with the incessant moans and cries, Harrison grabbed his son's hands to stop his senseless, repetitive behavior. "You can save us again, Dylan. I would do it, but I can't. You can. You can make Nora leave the way Sophie did. You must do this, son, you must."

A small strangled sound came from Dylan's throat. His mouth twisted into a grimace. He rolled his eyes to the ceiling and appeared to stare at the iron chandelier.

Harrison fought his mounting impatience. *The damn fool can't even process a single thought like a normal man.*

Finally, Dylan lowered a bewildered gaze to his father. "Can I have the music if I make Nora leave?"

"Of course. Music and dancing and tea parties. Whatever you want."

Dylan stood abruptly and headed for the door. "I'm going," he said. "I will find Nora. Nora is bad, very, very bad."

Harrison wheeled his chair behind his son. "That's right. I'm proud of you, Dylan. I think Nora will be out front waiting for Jacob. She wants to hurt him the minute he comes back from the village. You must take her to the cliff before she can do that." Then, calling to Dylan's back, Harrison added, "And don't tell Juditha or Vincent. Do this by yourself, and be very clever. Remember, Nora won't want to go to the cliff with you, but you must make her go. Then, when it is done, you can have your music back."

Nora never paced. She'd always felt it was a purely male reaction to worrisome problems. Women dealt with such things by confining themselves to their rooms. Men paced. But today, as she waited by the narrow lane leading from the island road to Proctor House, Nora paced as vigorously as any man could have. She didn't even hear footsteps in the low brush surrounding her until a man's voice said her name.

"Nora."

She spun around, and her heart jumped to her throat. "Dylan? What are you doing here?"

"I . . . I want to show you a place."

Reining in her skittering fear, Nora said calmly, "That's nice. I would like to see it. But I can't now. I'm waiting for Jacob. He should be back soon."

Dylan took a step toward her and stopped. She resisted the urge to back away an equal step. "No," he said. "You must see it now. It's not far."

"Where are Juditha and Vincent?"

He thought a moment. "At the place. They want me to go there, but I . . . I'm afraid to go by myself. I want you to take me. It's not far."

''Perhaps we can go later, Dylan,'' she said. ''If you go back to the cottage and wait for me, I'll come as soon as I can.''

''No!'' He came closer, and his face contorted with panic. ''I have to go now. And you have to go, too. I'm afraid.''

Nora exhaled a long breath. Maybe it would be better to take Dylan where he needed to go. He might have gotten lost from the cottage and if he trusted her enough to help him, she should try to do that. She could walk with him to his destination and then come right back. Chances are Jacob wouldn't arrive until she'd returned. ''You say it's not far?''

''No, not far.'' He grinned and nodded his head. Pointing his finger at no particular spot Nora could determine, he said, ''It's just there. Not far.''

Tucking the papers she'd brought from Harrison's library back into her pocket, Nora took Dylan's arm. ''All right. Let's go. But we must hurry.''

Though Nora tried to question Dylan about their destination, he remained sullen and silent until they had left the grounds around the house and even walked beyond the cottage. When she glimpsed the railed catwalk of the little house through the trees behind them, Nora felt a tingling of fear creep up her spine. Their pace had been brisk, and even now as they entered a dense area of shrubs and tall trees, Dylan did not slow down.

Knowing she shouldn't alarm him, Nora laughed and tugged gently on his arm. ''Dylan, please. I can't walk this fast.''

''Yes, you can. You have to.'' He lowered his arm and caught her wrist in his fist. Instead of slowing, he hurried even faster, determined to pull Nora in his wake if she refused to keep up.

She stumbled along behind him a short way, and then stubbornly planted her feet in the brush and halted, jerking him back. ''Dylan, stop this instant. I'm not going any further until you tell me where we're headed.''

Even though they weren't walking, he still kept his feet moving, jumping from one to the other, starting forward and pulling back. "There. Right there," he said, holding tightly to her wrist and gesturing wildly with his other hand.

Nora stared into the distance, looking for any structure that might be their destination. "There's nothing there," she said. "Just trees and rocks, and . . ."

Then she saw it looming ahead of them. The cliff Jacob had pointed out the night before, the one that sloped gradually upwards and ended in a wall of jagged rock overlooking the sea. Fighting to keep her voice steady, she said, "There's nothing at all, Dylan. We must go back."

He stomped his foot and tightened his hold on her arm. Hauling her forward, he said, "No! We're not going back. You have to leave the island."

She staggered behind him toward the base of the cliff. When he paused for a moment, she took a deep breath, filling her lungs. "Yes, Dylan, that's right. I'm leaving with Jacob tomorrow. We're sailing on the *Dover Cloud*. I'll be gone."

"I won't let you sail with Jacob," he said. "You're leaving from the cliff."

"What? No, Dylan, you can't mean . . ." But the single-minded, cold glint of his eyes told her he did. His mission became horrifyingly clear. He pulled her arm so hard, pain shot to her shoulder. She had no choice but to begin the climb up the rocky slope.

Nora tried everything she could think of to escape. She pretended to fall partway up the mountain, thinking he wouldn't have the strength to pull her. She was wrong. He dragged her across rough terrain as if she weighed no more than Armand or Hubert. When her legs and arms suffered cuts and bruises from the rocks, she stood up and tried to keep pace with him.

Her breath burned in her lungs with the effort of the climb, but still Nora tried to talk Dylan out of his terrifying plan. "Dylan, why are you doing this? You don't want to kill me . . ."

He covered one ear with his hand and hunched his shoulder to cover his other ear. "Don't talk to me!" he ordered, and continued up the mountain as if he were more machine than man.

Near the top, Nora's footsteps faltered and she fell for real. When her hand slipped from Dylan's damp grasp, she saw her chance to escape. She crawled away from him, clawing at the underbrush until she had managed to move several feet down the mountain. But her attempt was futile. He grabbed her under her arms, pitched her forward until all the ground she'd gained was lost, and dragged her the rest of the way to the top.

Their entire climb of perhaps two hundred feet had taken only a half hour as best Nora could judge, but when they reached the summit, all she could do was lie in a heap at Dylan's feet. She swallowed short gasps of air, allowing her lungs to fill slowly. Perspiration dripped down her back and between her breasts. Her legs hurt so badly it was only with trepidation that she raised her skirt to check for injuries. Her shins were crisscrossed with scratches, some of them deep enough to have bled onto her underclothes.

Unshed tears smarted in the backs of her eyes and closed her throat. But she would not cry. Any show of emotion would only confuse and anger Dylan further. Instead, she looked up at him and tried to speak rationally. Her voice came out as a hoarse croaking. "Dylan, it's me, Nora. You wanted to have a tea party with me yesterday, do you remember?"

The man who only twenty-four hours ago had swayed like a graceful willow to the strains of a Viennese waltz now glowered down at her, a snarl marring his thin, pink lips. "You took the music. You made Marianne mad. You are bad."

Despite her efforts, one tear fell down her cheek and mingled with the grime of Sophie's mountain. When it reached her lips, it tasted of salt and grit. "No, I liked the music. I liked watching you dance. I'm your friend, Dylan."

"You're evil. My father says so. You want to hurt everyone."

Nora pounded her fist in the dirt. *Damn you, Harrison Proctor!* How could she reason with Dylan when his own father had planted lies in his head?

I can't die today, Nora shouted in her mind. *Jacob will never know the truth.* She would follow Sophie off the side of this cliff, adding her own pitiful cries to the mournful ones that preceded her, and Jacob would go on forever believing he was the tortured woman's son. Only now he would have the guilt of Nora's death to carry as well.

Dylan reached down and pulled her to her feet. Then, wrapping his arm around her waist, he half carried, half dragged her to the edge of the cliff.

Finding a burst of energy she didn't know she possessed, Nora fought back. She scratched at his arm, and kicked wildly with her feet. "No, Dylan," she cried. "Your father's wrong."

He wrenched her body around until she faced the emptiness of air stretching to a distant blue horizon. She swallowed hard and resisted looking to the bottom, where the sea crashed against rocks that formed the base of the sheer cliff.

"You want to hurt Jacob," Dylan said.

"No! I love Jacob." Her pronouncement rang with truth in her ears, and she fell limp in Dylan's arms. Huge sobs racked her body. "I . . . I love him," she said again.

Dylan's arm under her breast tightened more, and she fought for every breath. The blue Caribbean air swam before her eyes in waves of shimmering heat.

"You want to kill Jacob," he shouted.

"Listen to me, Dylan," she said through strangled breaths. "I love Jacob, and he loves me."

"You are a liar," he said. "I am the only one who loves Jacob. He will thank me. You are evil, Nora." Her feet left the ground, and Dylan inched her closer to the edge.

Nora struggled to get a foothold, kicking clods of dirt with her toe and sending them skittering over the edge. "You will break Jacob's heart if you let me fall."

"She's right, Dylan."

Everything stopped. The world stopped spinning crazily in front of Nora's eyes. Her lungs stopped struggling for air. Her limbs stopped their fruitless pursuit of freedom. She was suddenly a rag doll in Dylan's clutches as he spun around toward the sound of another voice. Nora closed her eyes, hoping against hope. *Please let it be him. Jacob.*

When she opened them, he was there, standing several feet

away. He was panting. His eyes were wide with horror. But his hand stretched out toward his brother was as steady as the cliff they all stood upon. "Nora told you the truth," he said. "You will break my heart if you let her fall."

Dylan's arms remained tight around Nora's chest. "Nora is evil," he said. "She must leave. She wants to hurt you, Jacob."

Jacob advanced slowly. "No, she would never hurt me. She loves me, just as you do. You would never hurt me, and neither would Nora."

Dylan backed up a step, and Jacob drew in a sharp breath. "Dylan, stop!"

Terrible tremors shook Dylan's body. He teetered on the edge, and sobbed in Nora's ear. "But Father said . . ."

She gritted her teeth and clung to him as if her strength could keep them from going over the edge. *Please don't let him fall. Please God.*

"Father was wrong," Jacob said. He continued to speak, but Nora no longer heard his words. She only saw his actions. He leaped for his brother and grabbed his arm. They all three fell away from the edge of the cliff and rolled over twice in a heap of tangled arms and legs.

When they stopped against a boulder, Dylan crawled away from them and sat in a patch of tall grass, hugging his knees and crying like an infant. Jacob cradled Nora in his lap and wrapped his arms around her. Though neither of them spoke, he made soft cooing sounds against her hair. After a time, the wind cooled her face and dried her tears. And the strength of Jacob's arms eventually calmed the shudders that made her body quake as though her limbs were attached to marionette wires.

"Can you make it back down?" he finally asked her.

She nodded, and he lifted her to her feet. Then he helped his brother off the ground. Letting Dylan go ahead, he supported Nora with an arm around her waist, and they began the slow journey down the mountain.

* * *

"You're going to be just fine, Miss Seabrook," the doctor said. Whatever ointments he'd applied to her scrapes stung like hellfire, but she supposed he was right.

"How's Dylan?" she asked.

"Confused. Upset. And I think maybe a little remorseful. It's a trait we don't often see in him, but perhaps I saw it today." He smiled. "If you're all right, I think I'll go back to him now. Besides, there's a gentleman outside your door waiting impatiently to see you."

"Yes, let him come in."

Jacob shook hands with the doctor in the hallway and then came into Nora's room. He hadn't changed clothes yet. Dirt and bits of vegetation belonging to Sophie's mountain clung to his skin and clothing, and his hair fell in unkempt sandy waves on his forehead and collar. He appeared almost as bedraggled as Nora assumed she did, but to her, he'd never looked more wonderful.

He sat on the edge of her bed, and she immediately gave in to the urge to brush a strand of hair off his forehead. He took her hand and kissed the palm.

"Well," she said. "I finally got to see something of the island and put an end to this interminable stretch of boredom you imposed by confining me to the house."

He stared at her for a long moment, and then threw back his head and laughed. "And the worst part is, I owe you another damn apology for the way my brother behaved," he said.

She raised a finger and slipped it under his chin. "No, this time you don't. Your rescue quite makes up for the abominable hospitality."

He wrapped his hands around her shoulders. "Nora Seabrook, you are a treasure. It's no wonder I . . ."

"You what?"

He looked away, but not before she saw a familiar shadow

darken his eyes. "It's no wonder I . . . thank whatever's holy that I was able to bring you down off that mountain."

"It's been quite a day, hasn't it?" she said.

"Indeed." He kissed her forehead. "I'm glad it's over."

She took his hand and gave it a quick squeeze. "But it isn't," she said. "I'm afraid the worst is still to come."

With his puzzled gaze glued to her face, she withdrew the ragged documents from the pocket of her dress.

CHAPTER
TWENTY-TWO

Nora would always remember the sixty seconds it took for Jacob to realize the significance of the documents she handed him. In that short time, she watched him change from the man he'd always thought he was to the man he would become.

At first, wide, alert eyes and a parting of his lips in silent exclamation revealed his disbelief. Then a sudden flush of crimson to his face and neck, accompanied by the thrumming of a vein at his temple, suggested that he must be restraining a consuming anger. And last, a long, low sigh of grief and his directionless gaze away from the papers told Nora how deeply his father's wounds had pierced Jacob's soul.

She waited for what seemed an eternity for Jacob to look at her. She prayed she would see in his eyes one final reaction, the one that would release him forever from the chains of his mother's madness. She prayed for relief to settle on his face like halcyon breezes after a storm. Laying her hand on his arm, she whispered, "Jacob . . ."

He grasped her hand and held it to his chest. His heart beat erratically against her palm, yet when he looked at her, his face was calm. "I'm free," he said. "It's over." He lifted the documents from his lap. They crackled with age in his trembling hand, but he was careful not to tear them. "These papers, Nora. How did you . . . ? Where . . . ?"

She told him everything, and he drank in the details of her story like a man long denied water. Polly at the washhouse, the strange lyrics, the pieces of the puzzle suddenly falling into place, the secretary in Harrison's library. And when she told him about her meeting with his father and his threats, his eyes glittered with dangerous intensity.

"He did it," Jacob said through jaws clenched so tightly Nora wondered how she'd understood his words. "He convinced Dylan to take you to the cliff. My poor brother wouldn't have done such a thing otherwise. Dylan doesn't understand revenge. His anger is sudden and intense, but only flares to satisfy an immediate emotional craving."

Nora knew it was true. Dylan as much as told her that Harrison was to blame. But she was grateful she didn't have to tell Jacob in her own words of his father's betrayal. "I'm sorry, Jacob," she said.

He stood up from her bed. His face was etched with taut creases. His lips were pressed in a tight line. "Are you certain you're all right, Nora?" he asked.

"Yes, I'm fine."

"There is something I have to do. I've ordered you a bath and a meal. I'll find Polly and have her come to stay with you."

"About Polly," she said. "I'm worried about her. She's afraid, Jacob, afraid your father will send her away."

A scornful laugh came from deep in his throat. "She has no reason to fear my father, ever again. I'll tell her so myself. And Dylan is in the cottage with Vincent. He can't hurt you. I doubt he would again anyway."

"I'm not worried."

"I'll take care of . . . what I have to do and then I'll be back. You rest, Nora."

"Yes, I will."

He started for the door, but turned and came back to her.

"There are things I need to tell you . . ." He held the documents between them, shifting his gaze from them to her face. "I have to thank you . . ."

She smiled at him, realizing that while old burdens had been lifted, new ones sat upon his shoulders. "Jacob Proctor thanking *me* for something?" she teased. "My goodness, that is truly worth waiting for. I'll definitely be here when you come back."

A glimmer of uncertainty, as brief as the glow of a lightning bug, flashed in his eyes. It reminded Nora of a child on the first day of school whose uncertainty about the nature of the being called his teacher had made him awkward. In a way, Jacob was a child again, with new hopes and dreams and a new life to live. "Good," he said simply. "Good."

Then he folded the documents into his shirt pocket and left the room, and the uncertainty was gone. A fierce determination marked his stride as his footsteps echoed through the hallway toward Harrison Proctor's library.

When Jacob entered the room, his father faced a window to the garden, leaving his back to the door. A quick, hot flash of anger gripped Jacob's abdomen at the sight of those powerful shoulders and thick neck. He drew a breath of air to quench it. He could easily have stepped up to the old man in the wheelchair, a man he scarcely knew, and wrapped his hands around that neck. With barely a second thought he could have squeezed the breath out of him and ignored his choking pleas for mercy. He could have, but then he would have been no better than the tyrant he despised.

After a long moment, Harrison Proctor sensed the presence of someone else in the room. Gripping the wheels of his chair, he slowly turned around. When he saw his son, his eyes reflected doubt and fear. It was a reaction Jacob had never seen before, but which he now relished. The old man's gaze then darted to the surface of his desk. A pistol rested on the tooled leather writing area within easy reach of Harrison's grasp. Jacob had seen the weapon when he entered the room, and he was certain his father had intended him to see it.

Always a master at ruling his domain, Harrison quickly hid his apprehension with a slight widening of his eyes. He cleared his throat in that authoritarian way he had, as if he were preparing to speak to a session of parliament. "Jacob, thank God you've come. We have a situation here. You've heard about Dylan? You know what he's done?"

"I know what *you* have done, *Father.*"

"I? What sort of accusation is this? I've been worried beyond measure all afternoon about Miss Seabrook. Juditha only just informed me that the poor girl will recover from her ordeal. You have been told the details, haven't you? If not, I will tell you myself . . ."

"Don't waste your breath. I wouldn't give credence to so much as a syllable you uttered."

Harrison lurched forward in his chair as if he would rise, but the result was only a wretched squeak from the overburdened wheels. "I will not tolerate such contempt from you!" he bellowed.

Jacob snorted his disgust. "Nor do I give a pence or a penny what you will or will not tolerate from this day forward."

Harrison lowered his chin to his chest and massaged his brow with thick fingertips, a fine pretense of anguish, but one which did not fool his son. "I have already lost one son," he said. "Must I lose another in a show of such disrespectful insolence?"

Jacob reached his father's chair in three long strides and gripped the wooden arms. Harrison's head snapped up, and he stared across charged inches of space into his son's eyes. "I've heard enough of your cow dung, Father," Jacob snarled into his face. "It will not serve you this day, except perhaps as fodder for your evening meal."

Pain, a truly admirable semblance of the real thing, marked his father's features. Jacob thought him better suited to a Shakespearean stage than a sprawling island estate.

Harrison shook his head slowly. "How can you speak to me

this way? Dylan has quite gone over the edge. Our worst fears have been realized today. He took an innocent woman to the cliff where he pushed his own mother to her grave. Only by the grace of God did you arrive to save her . . ."

Jacob laughed, a low feral sound that came from deep in his throat. "Yes, God sharpened my instincts and led me to Nora today, but He also gave me you for a father, so I don't know whether to thank the Divine Being or curse Him for playing loose with my life."

"Blasphemy now, too, Jacob? To what depths of depravity has this family sunk?"

"Enough so that you must look up to see the rest of us sinners." In one swift motion, Jacob shoved the chair away from him, sending it scudding into a wall of his father's priceless leather-bound books. Harrison winced in what was no doubt real pain this time, but he shook off its effects.

Jacob was through toying with him. He was through dancing around the issues they both knew must be faced. "This isn't a family," he said with measured calm. "It's a monarchy, and its depraved condition begins with the self-proclaimed king."

Harrison's gaze flitted to the pistol, and Jacob positioned himself between the desk and the wheelchair. He crossed his arms over his chest and looked down at the man who had never shown any signs of weakness but whose eyes now reflected the first hint of panic. "What manner of human being are you, *Father*, to believe yourself justified in ruling people's lives? To map out their futures to fit your own desires? To lie and deceive the very ones you profess to care for?"

Jacob's hands clenched over his chest, and it was only with great willpower that he kept his fists buried against his shirt. It frightened him to think where his anger might lead. "You called yourself *Father*. You called yourself *Husband*. You have no idea what it means to be either! What about the sons you have lied to for years? What about Anne Hempstead, *Father?*"

The wheelchair rattled with the force of Harrison's trembling. His face became an image of fear. "Jacob, you must listen to me," he beseeched. "That woman, Nora, she lied to you. She took things that didn't belong to her and tried to turn you against your family.''

An uneasy calm, which was in a way more dangerous than unbridled anger, suddenly settled over Jacob. With almost a smile on his face, he said, "Yes, she took things that didn't belong to her. But they did belong to *me*. They were about *me*, about who I am. And she gave them to their rightful owner, something you would never have done, you self-serving bastard!''

Bright scarlet infused Harrison's cheeks, and he sat forward, no longer cowed by his son's fury. "Everything I did, I did to protect this family. I am not ashamed of what I've done for Dylan, to keep him safe. And you have had a good life. You've amassed wealth and power. And still you have the gall to look upon me as one who connived against you." He pounded his fist on the arm of his chair. "How dare you, Jacob Proctor?''

"A good life?" Jacob was incredulous. The demented man truly believed what he was saying. "I've been a prisoner of nightmarish visions of what I would become. I've been locked in a self-imposed cell of guilt and restraint for fear of the horrors I could unleash upon the world.''

He pressed his father's hands to the arms of the chair and covered them with his own vise-like grip. "But that's not even what is important. I know that. What matters, *Father,* is what's right, what's decent. And you have no idea what you've done to violate all that is moral and decent and good about a man's life. And you nearly had a woman killed today. In short, you have played God, and no man can do that, not even one whose own misfortunes confined him to a wheelchair.''

An oppressive silence filled the room. For moments neither man spoke. Jacob's gaze never left his father's face. Before his eyes, the great Harrison Proctor, master of his island, lover of fine horseflesh and finer brandy, began to shrink in size and stature. He seemed to shrivel, until his chair virtually surrounded him in an overbearing presence of wood and cane. The man who had always dwarfed the sad conveyance he lived in was now made a small man in its shadow.

When he spoke, Harrison Proctor's voice quivered with weakness. "What are you going to do?"

"If it were just you, I would walk away from Belle Isle and never return. I wouldn't care if you choked on the vines and weeds that would one day invade the walls and wrap their tendrils around your throat. But you're lucky, *Lord Proctor*. You have another son, and ironically it is he who will ultimately prove to be your savior."

"Wh . . . what do you mean?"

"I will take care of Dylan as I always have. He cannot be faulted for what he is. And as long as Dylan lives, I suppose you will also. If you have a prayer left in your shrunken heart, I suggest you pray for Dylan to reach a ripe old age.

"But there will be changes. You will no longer live in the luxury to which you have accustomed yourself. What is not necessary to the survival of this estate will be sold to pay Dylan's medical expenses. What is not essential to your own survival will be turned into profits for Proctor House. Do you understand?"

"You wound me deeply, Jacob," his father muttered. "I never thought you would turn on your own flesh and blood." Then, as though an afterthought, he asked, "Are you going to marry *her?*"

Jacob allowed himself a smile of victory. "So now you are interested in my life, are you, *Father?* Well, now you have no right to answers. But know this, you will never bounce any grandchildren upon your knee."

Jacob sat on the edge of the desk and slid the pistol to the far side. "We have no need of weapons, do we? I think we have a clear picture of who the enemy is, and he is only one defenseless old man. But I am going to give you one chance to redeem a small portion of the nobility you've lost."

"What more can you ask of me?"

"Only this. Tell me about my mother. Tell me about Anne Hempstead."

The old man's eyes filled with tears, and he bent his head.

Jacob sensed a memory had truly weighed upon what was left of his heart.

"She was a good woman, Jacob," Harrison said. "And a proud one. Very much like you. If she were still with me . . . if only . . ."

Jacob swallowed a catch in his breath, and listened to the story of his mother.

Later, Jacob washed the grime and dirt of Sophie's mountain from his body, and wished he could erase the refuse of the past years from his life as easily. He ate his evening meal in his room and thought about everything his father had told him and how the extraordinary details of his past would now merge with his future.

His mother had languished for several days after giving birth to him. She'd suffered from the hardship of the delivery and pining for a husband who was as good as lost to her. Harrison Proctor's voice had broken into sobs when he told Jacob of his indiscretions with Sophie Farrington while his wife, Anne, was expecting their first child. His wild infatuation with the exotic Sophie had become public knowledge, consequently breaking his wife's heart and her will to live.

He told Jacob that Sophie had enchanted him. She'd cast a spell from which he couldn't escape. She was vibrant and shimmering, and her laughter was like a thousand tinkling crystals. She was different from other young ladies of means. She tossed convention to the winds and wore the spirit of individuality like a dazzling cloak. Once Harrison had had a taste of her, he only wanted more. Even knowing he was married, Sophie's parents encouraged the romance. It was as if they suspected what their daughter's future held and were unburdening themselves of a scandalous disaster.

And that was what Sophie became. Shortly after Anne died, Harrison took Sophie for his wife. She insisted vehemently that the infant Jacob call her Mama, not so much from affection, Harrison thought now, as from a need to possess everything that had been Anne's. In time she became pregnant and delivered her own child. She lavished excesses upon "her two boys," parading them around London as though they were royal princes. When young Jacob balked at the attention and the fineries, she took Dylan under her flamboyant wing, and molded him in her image.

At first Harrison thought his wife merely craved the attention she got from owning expensive things. But he soon realized that Sophie's problems were much greater. An imbalance in her brain, the doctors called it. A dementia that, considering her family history, might very well pass to her own offspring.

Her public behavior was an embarrassment to Harrison and his parents. She would not listen to reason, and threatened retribution against the entire family if she were not allowed to continue her extravagant manner of living. She was indiscreet in her affairs with other men. She was garish and outspoken at public gatherings.

And then the worst happened. Harrison's parents threatened to take nine-year-old Jacob out of the household and tell him the truth of his birth. When Sophie got wind of the plan, she bellowed with rage, claiming that no one would take what was hers. Then a carriage accident took Charles's and Lydia's lives. Harrison never proved that Sophie somehow caused the demise of his parents, but in the library at Proctor House he told Jacob of his suspicions.

"I felt I had no choice," he told his son. "I brought my family here to the island. I thought Sophie might get better." He laughed bitterly at the thought. "I might have told you the truth someday," he said, "but Dylan began acting strangely, and then Sophie attacked me with the dagger. I was desperate . . . an old, desperate, feeble man whose only pleasures in life were the ones he could buy and indulge in on Belle Isle. I couldn't take the chance that you would forsake us."

Jacob had left the library with the knowledge his father had finally given him, the sad, shocking knowledge of his past and his father's true character. He had hardly said a word as his father railed on about his miserable life. If Harrison expected absolution from the son he'd wronged, he'd found out he was never to get it.

Jacob would honor his commitment and allow his father to live out his days on the island, but forgive him? Never. Understand why he made the decisions he did? No. Harrison Proctor had chosen greed and deceit over honor. And if Nora hadn't uncovered the truth, he would have persisted in his ignoble ways. This was something Jacob could never understand.

Having eaten very little, Jacob chose clean garments from his wardrobe. He put on his shirt by the open window that looked over the garden. Dusk was settling over the island, bathing the candlebush and fire vines in a rosy glow that was suddenly beautiful in Jacob's eyes. He was done with wretchedness and lies and depravity. Thank God he now knew what goodness was, and that a man was blessed to find it. And he knew, too, that he had been less than honorable in his dealings with it.

Jacob walked into the hallway of the quiet house, shutting his door behind him. Then he went toward Nora's room.

CHAPTER
TWENTY-THREE

Jacob knocked on Nora's door with just the knuckle of his forefinger. Her reply was barely above a whisper. "Come in."

She was wearing a simple white cotton nightdress, probably borrowed from a servant, and she was seated at a mirrored vanity. Her hair streamed over her shoulder in a damp mass of vibrant ebony. A towel was on her lap. The scent of lilacs drifted from soapy water in an oak tub.

Lace curtains at the window billowed into the room with a twilight breeze. A pale glow from the sun sinking below distant hills outlined the tallest trees and bathed the room in soft pink hues. A single flickering lantern illuminated Nora's face in the mirror.

Jacob had to tell himself to breathe, something he'd never had to do before. But then, he'd never seen a sight as lovely as Nora at this moment. The sharp, almost painful catch of air filling his lungs matched the one in his step, and for a moment prevented him from going where his heart tried to lead.

She pivoted on the vanity stool and looked at him. "Jacob, are you all right?"

Her words calmed him, brought him back to himself. "I'm

fine.'' He went to her, laid his hand on the crown of her hair, then trailed his palm down the silky wetness. Her hair was cool and slick and patterned with fine ridges like a grosgrain ribbon. He picked up the towel from her lap and pressed raven strands into its folds, drying her hair slowly, a section at a time. He savored the simple task after the complications of the day. ''I did what I had to do,'' he said finally.

She covered his hand with hers, stilling his chore for a moment. ''Do you want to talk about it?'' she asked.

''Yes, that and a lot more. But not now.''

She turned back to the glass and he watched her reflection. Her feelings were mirrored in the gentle cobalt of her eyes gazing back at him. He saw caring and understanding in their depths, and reveled in the notion that they were for him.

She raised her hand to her chest where ivory skin showed above the worn cotton. Perhaps someday she would allow him to gift her with gowns of the finest silk and satin. She would indeed be lovely in them, but he would always remember her as she looked now, with her hair unadorned and her beauty all the more seductive because of its simplicity.

Standing behind her, he shifted the weight of her hair until it trailed down her back. Then, with his fingertips, he gently pushed the straps of the nightdress down her arms. When her shoulders were bare, he curved his hands over them and moved from their rounded contours to the column of her neck and back again, the smooth texture of her skin a balm for his work-roughened palms. She tilted her head back, and his fingers met at the hollow of her throat and slowly moved down.

When his hands splayed on her chest, it rose with her quick intake of breath. He would have stopped then before it was too late if she'd asked him to, but she didn't resist his explorations. Instead, she closed her eyes and leaned back so her head rested against his abdomen. Her hair swept against his lower body and blanketed his thighs, causing a swift, sweet ache of tension between his legs.

Watching her in the mirror, he moved his hands down her chest, savoring each satiny inch until his fingers slipped under the thin fabric of her bodice and captured her breasts. She sighed and leaned more fully against him. Her nipples strained against his palms, inviting him to cup the fullness of each glorious mound. He moved his hands in small circles, feeling the crest of each breast pucker against his callused skin. The tension in his loins coiled until the tip of his manhood thrust upon an uncomfortable layer of black gabardine.

His hands slipped further down to her ribs, over the flat plane of her stomach, and back to hold each perfectly rounded breast from below. He teased the nipples with the pads of his thumbs, relishing the quick, ardent response. His own breathing sounded like sandpaper to his ears as a moan came from Nora's lips. Her eyelids fluttered open.

Still massaging her, he smiled down at her face. "You are my savior, Nora. You have brought me back from the brink."

Her lips curved upwards in a quiver of delight. "It was you who brought me back, Jacob, in the most literal sense."

Against her murmur of protest, he took his hands from her breasts and stepped to her side. Then he lifted her from the stool. The gown slipped down her arms and chest to her waist. When he pulled her against his body, she molded to him as if made of clay. Her rigid nipples tantalized him through his shirt. "Perhaps it can be said we saved each other today, Nora," he breathed into her lilac-scented hair.

She pulled back enough to see into his eyes and cupped his face with her hands. It was the dearest face in all the world, and if she had had some part in erasing the lines of anguish that had been there, she was thankful. What she saw in his features now was contentment, edged with something sharper, finer, perhaps even a little dangerous, and it thrilled her.

Seeing her own face, eager and expectant, reflected in the smoldering ash of his eyes, she would have passed through them to his soul if she had been able, for she knew that finally peace existed there. "I'm happy for you, Jacob. You have your life back."

His arms tightened around her. "I hope and pray that I have much more than that, dearest Nora."

Her heart understood the implied declaration of his words and rejoiced. "You needn't pray too fervently," she said, and the embers of his eyes flared as if fanned by a bellows. "I suspect that all you desire can be yours if only you would ask."

"Then I'm asking, Nora. I am most assuredly asking." His body shuddered with reckless hunger. He pulled her hard against him and lowered his mouth to take hers in a shattering kiss that ignited the fire of a passion only she could have started.

It was a mad, wild kiss, given and taken, driven by urgency and long-denied need. For one brief moment of sanity he feared the power of his emotions would frighten her. He couldn't get enough of her lips, her tongue, the sweet, welcoming darkness of her mouth. His hands roamed over her back and slipped between their bodies to cover her breasts. He kneaded each quivering tip until Nora moaned against his mouth. She wasn't frightened. She was alive in his arms and matching his hunger with her own.

Nora swept her fingers through his hair to the nape of his neck, massaging, caressing, drawing his mouth even more forcefully over her own. His kiss scorched her lips and poured warm honey through her limbs. Still, it was not enough. She knew instinctively that it wasn't. Her hands came around to his chest and she worked feverishly loosening the buttons on his shirt. Her breath came in short, heated gasps as she pulled the tails free of his trousers.

She thrust the sleeves over his arms and let the shirt fall from his body. Free at last to explore every inch of his broad chest, her fingers played in the short springy curls, danced over his muscular shoulders to descend the rounded biceps and corded tendons of his arms.

When her hands wrapped around his neck again, he cupped the back of her head and turned her face against his neck. His breath was hot and moist on her ear and sent shivers of anticipation skidding down her spine.

"Nora, I want you," he said huskily. "I have wanted to make love to you for as long as I can remember, probably from the first moment I saw you. If you don't want it to happen here, tonight, then we must stop now." His hands moved slowly up and down her back, leaving a trail of tingling heat wherever his fingers touched her skin.

She looked into smoky pewter eyes that melted her heart and filled her with longing so intense she couldn't have let him walk away. "Make love to me, Jacob," she said hoarsely. "It's what I've dreamed of. It's what I want."

In one swift motion he picked her up in his arms. The flimsy gown draped over her hips fluttered to the floor, and he carried her naked to the bed. He sat beside her and placed his hands on the coverlet on each side of her face. "You are as perfect as ivory, Nora, as splendid a creation as nature can achieve. You are beautiful."

She pulled him down until his chest pressed against her breasts, satisfying, for the moment, the aching need for his touch. She pressed her lips on his, giving back for each glorious kiss he had given her. She trailed kisses over the line of his jaw, his cheekbones, his eyes, while he caressed her body with eager hands.

He stretched out beside her to explore every satiny inch of her skin, and she turned into his embraces. He swept over her breasts, lingering again over each thrusting tip. He moved over her stomach to her hips, cresting each mound and exploring each valley of her body with fervent caresses.

When his hand slipped to her inner thigh, a sudden, intense spurt of warmth flared deep in her abdomen, and she opened her legs to him. He lowered his mouth to her breast and teased the taut bud with his tongue, drawing the warmth between her thighs upward. When his lips closed over her and he sucked hungrily on her nipple, she felt the pull deep inside. It seemed a magnet for the searching hand that with aching deliberateness climbed her flesh. He cupped her sensitive mound, and she drew a shuddering breath.

When Jacob's finger entered the place that was all silk and honeyed heat, the world behind Nora's closed eyelids lit with a thousand shooting stars. He entered and withdrew, spreading rich cream around the part of her that became the center of the universe. He massaged her gently *there,* while his lips moved to take hers again. She spiraled upwards, arching away from the bed, until her mind exploded in riotous waves of ecstasy.

"That's it, sweetheart," he said against her mouth. "Let it go." And Nora could only moan a response as she did just what he told her.

He stood up from the bed to remove the rest of his clothes, leaving her senses to flutter like hummingbirds at the precipice he'd taken her to. Then he covered her body with his. In the shadows of descending night, his magnificent torso glistened like copper and sent her heart skittering toward a path of discovery. Her nearly sated body quivered in anticipation of what was to come. In some secret, mysterious, womanly way, she knew he had satisfied her body's yearning for a man's touch, but not yet the longing of her heart. She wanted to be one with him, to find completion with this man as only two hearts could.

"Don't be afraid, Nora," he whispered in her ear.

"I could never be afraid with you," she answered back on a sigh.

"Touch me, Nora," he said, and guided her hand to his erection.

It was firm and strong and leapt against her palm. She brought him to the part of her that still tingled from his lovemaking. Her breath hitched and held when his smooth flesh slipped inside, and he began to move with a slow, natural rhythm. Suddenly, all of Nora's power and energy centered on her core where he'd entered her body. It felt so right having him locked with her in the most intimate way, and soon she matched his movements with the rise and fall of her hips.

"I'm sorry, sweetheart," he mumbled against her ear. "If this hurts you, it will pass. It only hurts for an instant."

"How can this hurt?" she responded in a voice that seemed to drift above them. "It's heaven. Only heaven." But then a swift, sharp stab of pain streaked through her, and she strangled her cry against his neck.

He moved more slowly until a dewy warmth comforted

her. "It's all right, Nora, darling," he said. "Move with me, sweetheart, you'll see."

She did, and soon all traces of pain vanished in the sweet, hot motion of their bodies. She climbed again to the brink of exploding passion. She followed him upwards to the blissful apex where everything rational dissolved into pure pleasure.

His movements quickened, and she met each thrust with her arching body. Together they crested and rode the spasms of passion until it was impossible to tell her heartbeat from his, and their muffled cries mingled with the breeze of the dark Caribbean night.

Without withdrawing from her, he pulled her on top of him. Her legs entwined with his, her head nestled against his neck. "My God, you are wonderful," he said. "Desirable beyond all measure, generous, incredibly passionate. Quite definitely all a man could possibly wish for."

She laughed softly. "You would think me a wanton if you knew what *I* was wishing for right now."

He tilted his head to better see her eyes. "I'm sure I would not," he said. "You have to tell me now, for my curiosity is almost as great as my love for you."

She opened her mouth on a gasp, and her eyes grew wide. "Your *what*, Captain?"

He smiled. "Did I neglect to say it? How ungentlemanly of me, especially when I have so often appeared rude and uncouth in your estimation." He cupped her chin in his hand and looked deeply into her eyes. "I love you, Nora Seabrook, with all my heart and for all my days. And it would be my greatest honor to have you accept my proposal of marriage."

She suppressed a most unladylike squeal. "Do you mean it? Truly mean it? You're not going to change your mind and run off as though being chased by the devil?"

He laughed. "My devils are all gone, my sweet, and it was you who did the chasing. Now it is my fondest wish only to be caught."

She could have sworn her heart leapt from her chest and soared around the room. Her happiness was that complete, her dreams that fulfilled. "Then yes, Jacob, I will proudly marry you."

"Good," he said, and kissed her soundly. When he attempted to draw back, it seemed his lips would not cooperate, for they stayed on hers, tasting and teasing until her giggles turned to sighs and her arms went round his neck. Before they were utterly lost again, he said, "Now tell me, wicked enchantress, what was it you were wishing for that makes you a wanton?"

She felt him grow hard inside her again, and nipped playfully at his earlobe. "I don't need to say it, my love," she snickered. "For it is right now coming true."

CHAPTER
TWENTY-FOUR

On the fourth day of their voyage back to Key West, Nora heeded Jacob's warning to face the serious matter of her family. It was hard to accept that reality would soon descend upon them with the force of a Federal judge's vengeance, yet accept it, she must.

But Nora had never been so blissfully happy in her life. She and Jacob had resolved the issues of his family, and while she had avoided any contact with Harrison, she had bid an almost "sisterly" farewell to Dylan. He seemed to have forgotten the incident on the cliff, and had regarded her with a detached but curious attention. Now, with Belle Isle four days behind them, all Nora wanted to do was float on the waves of enchantment that carried the *Dover Cloud* through calm seas and deliciously warm nights.

"We've caught a good head wind," Jacob told her the morning they navigated the Mona Passage and sailed northwest toward the Bahama Islands. "I have a hunch we'll reach Key West in two and a half days, cutting several hours from our journey to Belle Isle. That means we could be sailing into Key West harbor the evening of our sixth day out."

"So soon?" Nora said. She snuggled against Jacob's side and laid her head on his shoulder. When his arm came around her, she breathed a sigh of utter contentment. She loved being with him when he took his turn at the wheel, especially since he'd altered his normal routine and chosen to guide the ship during daylight hours. That left the nights free for other, delightfully personal pursuits. "Can't you slow the ship down so we'll have a little longer?"

"And risk getting into a storm?" he said. "Any good sailor knows you have to make time when the seas are peaceful and not tempt the caprices of the weather gods." He leaned down to brush a kiss against her hair. "Besides, the storm we'll face when we reach Key West will be quite enough of a tempest for us to handle."

"If you're referring to my family, you shouldn't suspect the worst," she said with more conviction than she felt. "Fanny already adores you, and Mama will grow to love you in time when she sees how charming you are. Though it might help if she were to learn that your lineage includes a manor house and a title."

"Included," he said, with the emphasis on the last syllable. "Remember, Braxton Manor now belongs to a current member of the nobility, Lord Something-or-Other. But perhaps I can appeal to her with my bank balance. If she learns I can afford to keep her daughter in Key West high style, she might think better of me."

"Oh, pooh," Nora said. "Mama cares nothing about money." After a moment of prickly silence, both she and Jacob laughed at the obvious untruth. "Besides," she added through sputtering giggles, "I can't imagine that you've ever had problems winning any woman's heart."

Giving Nora's waist an affectionate squeeze, Jacob said, "There has only been one woman's heart I've ever cared enough to try to win, and according to her, it was rough going from the start. But now it's her father who looms as my greatest challenge."

Nora's smile faded because she knew it was true. "Let me

talk to him first," she said. "He's always listened to me, and
I can be very persuasive." She looked at Jacob and waited for
his gaze to shift from the ocean to settle on her face. She took
confidence from the love in his soft gray eyes. "And this time
my goal is the most important of my life."

"Then I'll put our happiness in your hands, for the time
being," he said. "But sweetheart, now that I've found you, I
won't bow out gracefully, no matter how much pressure your
father applies."

She stood on her toes and pressed her lips to his. "That's
just what I'd hoped you'd say."

Thurston Seabrook had lookouts in half the cupolas and
widows' walks of Key West, and they'd all been given the
same instructions. "I want to know the minute the flag of the
Dover Cloud appears on the horizon," he'd told them all.

And to Dillard Hyde, he'd added, "I don't want to give
Jacob Proctor any chance to slip from my grasp. We'll see
what he has to say when I catch him with my daughter in his
clutches and the booty from the *Marguerite Gray* waving in
his face."

Actively pursuing his nemesis had made Thurston a happier
man of late. One of the crew remaining at Proctor's Warehouse
and Salvage had told him that Jacob could return at any time.
This news and the probability of an impending marriage
between Nora and Theo Hadley had even transformed Sidonia.
She fairly bubbled with enthusiasm at evening meals. Her previous assumption that she would never see her daughter alive
again had disappeared. She now believed wholeheartedly that
her Eleanor would be returned safely to embark upon a life
with Theo. No other possibility existed for the exuberant mother
of the bride.

Theo and Sid often sat together at dusk mulling over plans
for the future. Though he tried to avoid their conversations,
Thurston was occasionally drawn in with a cheerful word or
enthusiastic wave from his wife. He listened to the pair discuss

Theo's occupational choices. Would he continue to New Orleans with his bride, or might he consider, much to Sid's delight, remaining in Key West?

Too often Thurston had to swallow a nagging resentment that his wife and future son-in-law were discussing his daughter's future while she had no say whatsoever in the plans. He did, however, find satisfaction in Theo's consideration of becoming a maritime attorney in Key West. "To deal with scoundrels such as Proctor," Theo had said, and Sidonia had enthusiastically encouraged him. So why, deep down, did Thurston struggle with a recurring notion that despite having the law on his side, the attorney would be a poor match for the likes of Jacob Proctor?

One of Thurston's spies arrived on the Seabrook doorstep one golden-hued evening the first week of April. "It's the *Cloud,* Your Honor," the island street cleaner shouted through the judge's door. Once admitted to the dining room, the messenger elaborated. "I seen it myself from the roof of the courthouse, sir. She'll be comin' round the tip o' the island soon."

Spoons clattered against dessert dishes. Chairs scraped along wooden floorboards as everyone rose.

"Thank God. My Eleanor's home," Sidonia cried.

"Dear Nora," Theo sighed. "May you still be as sweet and pure . . ." He halted his litany when the judge cast a disapproving glare his way.

"Hobbes," Thurston shouted to the street cleaner, "find Piney and tell him to meet me at the harbor!"

Fanny clasped her hands under her chin. "My *cherie* has returned," she said with a twinkle in her wicked green eyes. "Oooo, what stories she will have to tell."

"Oh, dear," Dillard muttered. "I fear all hell is about to break loose."

The messenger darted away toward the jail, his shoes kicking up bits of shell from the road. The five members of the Seabrook household headed down Duval Street toward the harbor, determination and anticipation etched on their faces.

"It seems we have a welcoming committee," Jacob said between issuing docking orders to his men.

Nora tried to remain calm. "Just as I suspected," she remarked calmly. "Nothing to worry about . . . yet."

He grinned at her as he adjusted the wheel to bring the ship closer to the wharf. "They've missed you, that's all," he said with false cheer. "It's only natural they'd turn out to greet you."

"That's right. Only natural." Nora went to the bow of the ship and waved to her family. They responded with varying degrees of enthusiasm. Her mother and Fanny appeared delighted to see her. Her father's hand lifted in a semblance of greeting that was overshadowed by a frown that tugged his mustache below his jawline. Dillard seemed troubled, and Theo . . . Theo?

Nora groaned her dismay upon seeing the attorney was still a resident of Key West and obviously her household—especially since his arm was now free of the sling and he was able to shield his eyes from the setting sun with a perfectly capable hand. Still, Nora allowed her confidence to grow . . . until she saw Piney Beade approach from Whitehead Street. Why in the world was the jailer coming to the harbor to meet the *Dover Cloud?*

The ship's crew tied the *Cloud* to dock pilings and lowered the gangway. Nora was the first to disembark, and she was immediately enfolded in the arms of her mother and Fanny. It was impossible to answer the flood of questions all at once. Yes, she was fine. Of course Captain Proctor had treated her well. No, she hadn't suffered colds or sniffles. "Really, Mama," she said impatiently, "how many times do I have to tell you . . ."

She accepted her father's awkward embrace, and knew from his scowl that she would have to come up with sound, logical answers to the questions and charges that perched on the tip of his tongue. He stood back to look at her and cleared his throat. "Well, daughter," he said, "it appears you have been returned to us in fairly admirable condition."

She smiled uncertainly. "Of course, Father. I've been practically coddled by Jac . . . Captain Proctor's crew. I sent you a note informing you that . . ."

Her explanation was cut short by Theo, who thrust out his arm to grasp hers and pull her away from her father. Surprisingly, her father let him do it. "My dear Nora," Theo said, wrapping his arms around her and trying to draw her close. "My prayers have been answered now that you are arrived safely home."

She pushed him back, confused and uncomfortable at the unexpected show of affection. "Thank you, Theo, for praying for me, but it really wasn't necessary. Actually, I've enjoyed a splendid sea voyage."

Not dissuaded by her cool reaction, Theo took her hands and brought them to his chest. "My dear, brave Nora, how like you to spare us the sordid details of your captivity."

"What sordid details, Theo?" she asked, attempting to disengage herself from the increasing pressure of his grasp.

He inclined his head toward the *Dover Cloud* and sighed sympathetically. "You can be forthcoming with me, Nora. That man can't hurt you or bully you anymore now that you are back among your own kind."

She snatched her hands free and balled them into fists at her sides. "What are you talking about? No one has bullied me in the least. What's come over you, Theo?"

Sidonia inserted herself between them. "I'll tell you what has come over Theodore, my darling." She chirped like a newborn chick, and her hands fluttered like little wings. "Oh, there are so many plans to make now that you have been delivered safely to us." She linked her arms with Nora's and Theo's, and tried to lead them away from the harbor. "Let's go home now, my dears."

"Mama, let go of me!"

Sidonia dropped her daughter's arm and blinked in astonishment. "Eleanor, what's the matter?"

Nora turned back to the ship as Jacob stepped off the gangway. The instant his feet touched the dock, Piney Beade strode up to him. A pair of iron wrist manacles dangled from his hand. His voice cut through the mellow evening air. "I'm sorry, Jacob," he said, "but I'm placing you under arrest."

Nora's first reaction was that she hadn't heard Piney correctly. Her heart thundered in her ears. She looked from Piney to Jacob, hoping to see a show of good-natured raillery that would take the sting from the jailer's incomprehensible words. This must be a joke between the two men that she wasn't privy to.

Instead, an odd quirk of Jacob's lips registered his own surprise. "What's the meaning of this, Piney?" he asked. "What are the charges?"

"I'll answer that," Thurston said, joining the pair on the dock. "There are several, Captain Proctor. Kidnapping, theft on the high seas, and violation of the terms of your salvage license for starters. Any one of these is sufficient to keep you behind bars for a good long time. Together . . . well, you'd best make peace with a Judge higher than I."

Jacob widened his stance and stood with his fists on his hips. "This is ridiculous! I've done none of these things. Piney, you know me. I've never violated my license, never stolen . . ."

Murmurs of assent came from Jacob's crew, who had come down the gangway to stand behind their captain. He stilled their voices by raising his hand, but their demeanor turned threatening. They remained on the dock, flanking their captain, their legs and arms poised for attack or retreat depending on Jacob's instructions. Nora had seen their loyalty to their captain, and knew they would stay beside him.

"Stand away, boys," Jacob said. "I don't want trouble. I'll take care of these false charges soon enough."

The jailer held up the manacles. "It won't be that easy, Jacob. The judge has proof." Thurston held out the notes from the Bank of New Bedford. "These were taken from the *Margue-*

rite Gray, as I suspect you know well enough,'' Piney said. "We found them in a hogshead in your warehouse."

"I've never seen them before," Jacob protested.

"The game's up, Jacob," Piney said. "You can give me your hands peaceably, or I can take them by force. Either way, the chains are going on."

The harbor seemed to quake under Nora's feet. She put a hand to her brow to quell a dizzying rush of panic. The foundation of her life threatened to crumble beneath her if she didn't do something to stop this farce. She confronted the jailer.

"You're wrong," she cried. "Jacob couldn't have done this. He certainly didn't kidnap anyone. I boarded his ship on my own. You can't do this!"

"That's for the judge to work through," Piney said. The cold metallic jangle of the manacles rang in Nora's ears.

Jacob's steely eyes met hers for an instant, and then fixed on Piney's resolute face. He held his wrists together in front of him and allowed the jailer to chain him. "Go away, Nora," he said. "It will be all right. Go with your family now."

She gripped his arm with both hands. "I won't leave you. I'm going with you."

"No!" he said sternly, jerking free of her grasp. "Go home, Nora." Without looking back, he was led to the shore by Piney Beade. His head high, Jacob walked with Key West's jailer toward Whitehead Street.

Nora rushed to her father. "How can you do this?" she shouted at him. "Jacob hasn't done anything. I told you that in the note. Didn't you get the note?" Her words choked her. Her voice showed the first signs of hysteria.

"Nora, you're upset," he said. "After all you've been through, I can understand that. But the truth is, Captain Proctor stole from the *Marguerite Gray.* He was seen on the beach the night false lights grounded the ship on the reef. Her cargo was found in his warehouse. Just as I suspected, there was more than rotting fish in the hold of that ship." He waved the bank notes at her. His eyes were bright with victory. "He stole thousands of dollars, Nora. No matter what you want to believe, Jacob Proctor is a thief.''

''He isn't,'' she cried. ''You're wrong, Father.'' Her protestations dissolved into sobs, and she struggled to take a breath. She clutched her father's wrist, demanding with actions rather than words that he pay her heed. He only stared at the horizon, remaining cool and distant from her entreaties.

''Sidonia, come see to your daughter,'' he instructed.

Nora's mother responded at once. She came to Nora's side and brushed the tears from her cheeks. ''You're distraught, Eleanor. My poor baby. Come home now.'' She motioned for Theo to join them, and he stood on Nora's other side. They each took her elbow and turned her toward Duval Street.

Numbly, Nora let herself be taken away, for there was nothing left at the harbor for her now. Her happiness, her future, her *life* was probably already locked behind bars on Whitehead Street. She looked over her shoulder at her cousin, who followed close behind the trio. ''Fanny . . .''

Her cousin gave her a smile of encouragement. ''It will come out right, *cherie,*'' she said.

Seeing concern etched in fine lines on Dillard Hyde's face, Nora doubted that it would.

The sun had barely risen above the eastern horizon when Nora tied her bonnet under her chin, picked up the straw basket she'd set by the door, and slipped out the back of her house. Reckless strained at his rope, delighted to see her and probably putting all his little goat dreams into finding out what was in the basket.

''Hello, old boy,'' Nora said, patting his plump tummy. ''I see they've been feeding you well while I've been gone.''

Reckless looked at her with round coffee eyes, bleated a response, and pawed at the basket over her arm. She raised it high and shook a finger at him. ''You'll have none of this, silly goat,'' she said. ''But I promise you a treat and a romp later.'' She told herself she really must keep her word. Reckless couldn't understand how her world had fallen apart in the last twenty-four hours. He couldn't know how utterly bereft she was. All he knew was that life was boring when you lived it at the end of a rope.

Nora had spent half the night trying to decide how she could put hers and Jacob's miserable situation to rights, and this morning she felt she had more in common with the goat than anyone in her family. Now she truly could imagine how it was to be tethered by a rope with many more limitations than possibilities.

When no clear solutions had come to her, she'd finally risen at dawn to accomplish the one thing that was foremost on her mind. She would see Jacob. She had to stare into the cool, clear reason of his eyes to know that everything would be all right. And she had to tell him that she didn't believe a word of the horrible accusations leveled against him.

All the previous evening she'd tried to get her father alone. But between her mother's incessant attention to her needs, and Theo's sudden oppressive nearness, she scarcely had a moment to breathe. Finally, once she'd stolen time with her father, she'd tried to tell him that Jacob was not capable of the crimes of which he'd been charged. He certainly hadn't kidnapped her.

Her father had only mumbled something about how Jacob should have returned her to her home immediately, and the failure to do so was almost as serious a crime as if he'd taken her on board against her will in the first place. The result was the same to Thurston Seabrook. Nora was held captive to the captain's whims, and a good many people had suffered for his lack of judgment.

He refused to even talk about the so-called evidence uncovered in Jacob's warehouse. When Nora pressed him to listen to her arguments, he'd lost his patience and told her to go to bed. He'd said that after her ordeal, she was no doubt exhausted to the point of delirium, and when she was more rational, he'd consider listening to what she had to say.

Nora had never seen her father so close-minded. It was as

if he'd already made up his mind about Jacob without even
hearing his side of the story.

She said good-bye to Reckless, crept out the gate, and headed
toward Whitehead Street. Piney Beade wouldn't be at the jail
at this ungodly time. That was why Nora had chosen the early
hour for her mission. She feared her father had left instructions
with Piney prohibiting her from seeing Jacob. She would have
better luck with the night guard.

The streets were quiet. It if weren't for the peddlers and
milkmen beginning their rounds, the only sounds Nora would
have heard were the barks and crows and clucks from Key
West animals. And of course there was the leaves. The ever-
present breeze on the island caused banyan leaves to rattle
against casements and palm fronds to click like nervous katy-
dids.

When she reached the steps to the jail, Nora drew a deep
breath to steady her own frazzled nerves. She simply wouldn't
be denied the chance to see Jacob. She went inside, disturbing
the lone guard, who reclined in a chair with his boots on the
top of a large oak desk. He pushed back his cap and peered
sleepily at her as if trying to place her face.

He doesn't know me, she realized, and muttered a quick
prayer of thanks.

The guard stood and wiped his palms on his baggy trousers
before giving her a quick once-over that started with her modest
bonnet and ended at her practical leather shoes. "Now just
what would you be doin' here, miss?" he asked in a thick Irish
brogue.

"I've come to see one of the . . ." She'd been about to say
"prisoners," but couldn't make the distasteful word come out
of her mouth. "To see one of the men incarcerated here."

The guard rubbed his chin with a ragged thumbnail. "We've
got nearly a dozen right now," he told her. "Which one of the
sorry lot is lucky enough to have the likes of you for a visitor?"

"Captain Proctor," she said.

He eyed her basket. "Is that for the prisoner?"

She gripped it protectively with both hands. "Yes."

"I'm afraid I must have me a look-see," he said. "It's rules, you know. Gotta make sure you ain't bringin' the inmate a file or a knife."

Nora clung stubbornly to the wicker handle until she realized she would not win this battle. "I'm doing no such thing," she said, drawing the checkered cloth over the basket handle. "See for yourself."

The guard stepped up to her and looked into the basket. He moved biscuits and bananas to see underneath them, and lifted a chicken leg out of a cloth napkin. Nora cringed inwardly when she noticed the grime imbedded in the creases of the guard's fingers.

He turned the chicken leg in front of his eyes as if he were admiring a work of art and licked his lips. "Now, just who are you to be bringin' Captain Proctor such a tasty assortment as this?"

Nora truly hadn't anticipated any trouble, and she hadn't prepared excuses for appearing at the jail. Her mind raced for an answer, and she suddenly remembered the night Jacob rescued her in Jimmy Teague's Tavern. "I'm Captain Proctor's cousin," she said. "I'm staying at his cottage. He's been on the sea so long, and now this misfortune, I've been worried he hasn't eaten well. Surely you can't deny the man one good meal."

The guard's lips spread in a wide grin. "His cousin, are you now? Not his kissin' cousin, I hope."

Nora glared at him. "Certainly not."

"Well, then, I guess I can let you in to see your relation."

Relieved, Nora extended the basket, expecting the guard to return the chicken leg. He merely laughed and took a big bite out of the fleshiest part. "Your cousin won't be needin' this bit. We don't want our boys to get used to fowl. They ain't likely to be gettin' much of it in this place."

Nora snapped the cloth over the rest of the food. Her stomach had turned a somersault. She certainly wasn't going to argue with the ill-mannered man, and she didn't want to offer the chicken leg to Jacob now anyway. "Fine. You're welcome to it," she said over the smacking of his lips. "Which way do I go to see Captain Proctor?"

He pointed with a greasy finger. "Through that door. And only for five minutes. This ain't a social hall."

Nora raised the latch on a heavy pine door and it creaked open. When she stepped inside a long hallway, the first thing she noticed were deep, gray shadows cloaking the details of her surroundings. The sun had been up for nearly an hour, but here in Key West's jail, it was still almost as dark as midnight. The reason became clear when her eyes adjusted and she could see into the first cell. It was empty except for a pair of cots and a bucket. A narrow beam of light came through the single small barred window near the ceiling. These men could suffocate from a lack of fresh air and sunlight, she thought, and decided to speak to her father about the conditions.

An unpleasant odor drifted down the aisle, a mixture of sweat and urine, and Nora instinctively covered her nose. She passed the first two cells without disturbing the four snoring occupants inside. At the next cell she wasn't so fortunate. One man sat hunched on the edge of his cot, rubbing his eyelids. Another stood at the bucket relieving himself. When they heard her pass, both men stared at her with suddenly alert eyes.

"Come back here, little pigeon," one of them said as Nora hurried down the hallway.

"I'd like to get me a piece of that," the other hooted.

Nora rushed past two more cells before their occupants could fully awaken and add their own catcalls to those of the other men. And then she saw Jacob. He was alone in his cell. For that, at least, she was thankful. He sat on the floor, his face buried in his hands. His cot had not been disturbed. When she said his name, he slowly stood up, squinted his eyes, and rushed to the bars. His voice hitched and trembled, but his eyes flashed dangerous sparks. "Good God, Nora, have you lost your mind? What are you doing here?"

CHAPTER
TWENTY-FIVE

Jacob gripped the iron bars. His eyes blazed with fury. Nora put the basket at her feet and placed her hands over his. His fingers convulsed. She thought he might draw back, so she gripped his hands more tightly and met his steely gray eyes straight on.

"Have I lost my mind?" she repeated in a harsh whisper. "Yes, I've lost my mind, and my heart, and every other part of my body that thinks and feels. It happened the night you said you loved me, and now all that I am, body and soul, belongs to you. So, Jacob, why should you be surprised that I would be here, that my place is with you, wherever that might be?"

"But not this place, Nora," he gritted back at her. "You shouldn't be here. You don't belong."

"And you do? If our situations were reversed, and I were the one behind bars, wouldn't you come to me?"

He shook his head. "Don't try to reason with what is unreasonable," he said harshly. "I don't expect your loyalty to extend to daily visits to the Key West jail. I don't want you here."

Even after all she'd discovered about him on Belle Isle, after all the terrible secrets had been revealed, the wall around Jacob Proctor still existed. It was an emotional barricade, built of the brick and steel of Jacob's torment, meant to protect him, but now keeping her out. She couldn't let that wall grow any thicker or taller, not since they'd been through so much to tear it down.

"We have pledged ourselves to each other, Jacob," she said. "That is something I don't take lightly. I won't allow you to push me away just because right now our path isn't smooth."

Crude insinuations echoed down the passageway from the other cells. Jacob extricated his hands and raked his fingers through his tousled hair. His panic-stricken gaze darted to the four corners of the tiny cell. "Is that what you want to hear, Nora? Men who aren't worthy of scraping the mud from your shoes calling you foul names?"

"I don't care about them . . ."

"I do. I don't want you in this place. I don't want you to see me here. I don't want *them* to see you." He wrapped his hands around the bars again and clenched until his knuckles turned white. This time Nora did not reach for him. "I can handle this," he said. "The charges are preposterous, and I will take care of it. Until then, you must stay away."

"But it's my father who has put you here. I can help . . ."

"You can help by staying away." He implored her with those same dangerous metallic eyes. "I won't be able to stand it if I have to worry about you sneaking through the streets before dawn, parading in front of jailed men no better than Chauncy Stubbs."

The mention of Mr. Stubbs and the hanging she'd attended her first week in Key West made Nora's stomach lurch. The image of a black hood, the sound of the gallows trap swinging open, the awed roar of the crowd, made her skin tingle with a sudden chill and her head swim just as it had that day. "Don't speak of him," she said.

Jacob sighed and rested his brow against the bars. His eyes dissolved to soft charcoal. After a moment, he reached through the bars toward her. She stepped close to him and he put his hand on her shoulder. "I'll see Willy today," he said reassuringly. "My men will get to work on this. I wouldn't be surprised if the matter were cleared up in a day or so." His voice was so confident, he seemed more like the man he'd been on the ship the last seven days. "Just please promise me you won't come back here again. I'll see you when this is over."

Tears welled in Nora's eyes, and she wrapped her arms around her chest to keep from shivering. "But I can't bear to think of you in this place. It's so dark and cold . . ."

He smiled at her and moved his hand from her shoulder to her face. He gently stroked her cheek. "My sweet Nora. I've been in the pitch darkness of the hold of a floundering ship in the middle of a hurricane. I've been tossed by fifteen-foot waves while clinging to the mast of the *Dover Cloud* during the bleakest of nights." He gestured around the four walls of his cell with his free hand. "This room seems like a palace compared to that."

She managed a weak smile in return, but the effort only caused the tears to overflow down her cheeks. He wiped them away with his thumb. In a trembling voice, she said, "It's just that I love you so . . ."

"Oh, I love ya, ya slimy sod," came a whining falsetto from another cell. Two beefy arms stuck out of the bars and embraced the air. "Give us a kiss now to see us through our darkest days . . ." The air filled with a series of sloppy puckers followed by raucous laughter.

Jacob's face turned to granite. "Leave us be, you sorry bastards!" he called out of his cell. Then he pushed the brim of Nora's bonnet away from her face. His hands met at her nape and he pulled her close. Their lips touched for a brief kiss through the bars before he pulled away. "Now go," he said, "and do what I say. Don't come back. Promise me."

She would have promised him anything, but could not speak this vow. She sniffled back sobs, picked up the basket, and said, "I've brought you something to eat." At least it was something she could do for him.

He took the basket from her, tipped it sideways, and crushed the handle so it would fit through the bars. When he raised the cloth and looked inside, he grinned at her. "A feast fit for a king," he said. "It's no wonder I love you, Nora."

The heavy pine door at the end of the hall creaked on its hinges and a loud voice called, "Let's go, kissin' cousin." The guard's head appeared around the door frame. "Visitin' time's over."

Panic wrapped icy fingers around Nora's heart and she held the bars. "I don't want to leave you. What if . . ."

Jacob blinked hard once. "It'll be all right, love. Go on. Go!"

She whirled away from him and ran past the other cells, blocking the insults and lewd snickers that followed her out. When she'd left, Jacob sat on the edge of his cot and put his head in his hands. He kicked the basket to the other side of his cell, where a skinny rat popped out of a crumbling hole in the wall to see what temptations lay under the brightly checkered cloth.

Blood pounded in Nora's ears as she ran up Whitehead Street toward Southard. She could hear her own heartbeat thundering each time her shoes hit the brick sidewalk. She had to help Jacob, she just had to. Picturing him in that awful cell was too much to bear. She'd talk to her father. She'd find out how those horrible bank notes got into a barrel in Jacob's warehouse. She'd track down the real owner of the lantern in the cave. She'd discover who ran the mule line the night the *Marguerite Gray* was wrecked on the reefs. She'd . . .

"Miss Nora! Miss Nora, you're back!"

She stopped short at the sound of the familiar voice. Spinning around, she stared down into the smiling face of Felix Obalu. "Oh, Felix, it's you," she said, trying to regain enough composure not to look crazed out of her mind.

"Sure, it's me," he said, grinning from ear to ear. "I heard you got back last night." He stepped even with her and coaxed them both into walking a steadier pace toward Southard Street.

"I heard you were with Captain J on the *Dover Cloud*. Fact is, the whole town knew about it. The judge went runnin' around every day askin' folks where the captain had gone and when he'd be back. He was actin' nervous as a bare-skinned boy in a beehive."

Felix knitted his brows and nodded wisely. "I told him to stop his frettin' . . . that the captain'd see you got back just fine and with an explanation that would satisfy God Himself."

Nora smiled at him. "Good for you, Felix. You were exactly right, too."

Shrugging off the compliment, Felix said, "I was just comin' to your place to see you. I brought the cow by this morning, but it was just ol' Lulu who came out of the house."

Nora struggled to keep her mind on Felix's chatter. "I'm sorry I missed you. I enjoy seeing how you're progressing with the milking."

He squared his shoulders. "I'm as good as ol' Abraham, now. Can pump a pint in twenty seconds flat."

She looked down at him. "Very impressive."

"Can't spell 'milk,' though," he said. "It's kind of hard to admit this, but I sort of missed that schoolin' while you were gone. I tried to keep it goin' for a few days, but you know how kids are . . ."

An honest smile came to Nora's lips. "Yes, I was beginning to understand them a little."

"Anyway, I was thinkin'. If you want to start up again, I guess it would be okay. Not more than the two hours a day, though. Gotta tend to business, you know."

She nodded. "I understand completely. You have a lot going on in this town."

"Sure do. Now with Captain J in the jail, I gotta take over the goat-rentin' business." His face expressed the seriousness of a fully grown man, and he looked up at Nora with eyes dark as chestnuts. "I 'spose the captain will get out of this mess okay, don't you think so, Miss Nora? No disrespect to your father, but no one'd ever convince me Captain J did something unlawful."

They'd reached the sidewalk to her house. Nora stopped before going in and laid a hand on Felix's shoulder. "No one would convince me either, Felix, and yes, I think he'll get out of this just fine."

"Good. So when will we see you over at ol' McTaggart's place?"

Surprisingly, the boy had made Nora feel better. Jacob *would* get out of this mess. Felix believed in him, and so did she, and so did a lot of other people. Nora would have faith in him and do what she could to speed his release from jail. It would all work out. She smiled down at Felix's expectant face. "Tomorrow morning, bright and early," she said. "And be ready to work hard. We've got a lot of time to make up."

"Yes, ma'am," he said, and ran off toward town.

Determination making her heart lighter, Nora opened the gate to her walkway and stepped inside. She was halfway to the porch when the front door of the house flew open and Theo stormed out. Her heart took an involuntary plunge toward her stomach.

Theo raced down the steps and took her arm. "Thank heavens, Nora. You're all right."

She was too tired to fight his attention, so she didn't resist his hold. "Of course, Theo. I've been for a walk, that's all."

He shook his index finger at her. "You'll pardon me for saying this, Nora, but you take walks at the oddest hours. I really must advise you to resist this tendency to wander about before the sun has even risen in the sky."

Now Theo was trying to tell her how to run her life! "It's not as if I prowl around in the middle of the night like an alley cat, Theo. You're making too much of it."

His cheeks colored. "I didn't mean . . ." He stopped on the porch before going in, and prevented Nora from entering as well. Turning her toward him, he enclosed her in a sort of embrace, his hands resting tentatively on her back. "I am only concerned for your welfare, Nora. And only because I care for you."

She attempted a smile. "Well, thank you, Theo. That's kind, but you don't need to worry about me."

"You don't understand," he said. "I mean *really care* for you."

Her mouth dropped open. She closed it quickly to prevent the escape of a nervous giggle that had begun to build inside. "Theo, you're not suggesting . . ."

His answer was a lowering of his head. Nora was too startled to react before his lips just brushed hers. "Theo, stop!" she said, backing away from him.

His hands fell away from her, and he knitted them together in front of his body. "Forgive me, Nora. The time was not appropriate for a display of my affections."

"No, Theo, it wasn't."

"But we must talk soon. I cannot hold back the flood of emotion I'm feeling now that you're home. I'm working with the judge this morning on the Proctor case. Perhaps tonight after dinner you will sit on the veranda with me."

Had the world gone completely mad? Even knowing Theo was ignorant of her true feelings for Jacob, Nora couldn't abide the appalling notion that the Benedict Arnold who was working to prove Jacob guilty was actually trying to express his affection for her. She certainly didn't need this complication in her life. What was even more ludicrous was that her father was spending the majority of his time avoiding her, and now she would be doing the same to Theo. There were going to be a lot of closed doors in the Seabrook house.

She sighed and headed for the entrance. "Yes, Theo, we'll talk soon." *And when we do, you won't like what I have to say.*

Will Turpin leaned a shoulder against the bars of Jacob's cell and tried to appear relaxed. His posture didn't fool his longtime friend, however. Jacob knew that inside, Willy's nerves were stretched as tight as the fibers of a mooring line. And for good reason. No one would want to answer the questions Jacob was about to pose.

"So, Will," he said, "how's the news on the outside? Tell me of the gossip and predictions for my future."

Will tried a grunt of nonchalance. "It's only been a few days since they brought you in, Jacob. No one knows what to make of the judge's charges yet."

Jacob approached the bars and stared at his friend. "Nice try, Will, but I know that's not so. Tell me the truth. What do you hear about my chances?"

A shadow crossed Will's face, and he looked away just long enough for Jacob to be certain the news was not good. "I wish I could tell you, Captain, that every wrecker in Key West was ready to stand firm in your defense . . ."

Jacob scoffed at the notion. "I'd know you were lying to me if you did."

"True enough, but for the life of me, I never suspected the depth of jealousy among our own, Jacob. It seems your plight has brought out the worst of the lyin' blokes, and they've come down on you pretty hard."

"Who do you mean?"

It was obvious that Will would rather bite off his own tongue than give Jacob the sorry news. "Clarence Dearborn is one. And Davy McGinnis. Both those lyin' bastards went to Judge Seabrook and told him they'd had suspicions all along that you'd been riggin' false lights. I called them out on it at Teague's last night and told them they were lower than snakes' bellies."

Despite learning the true nature of some of Key West's wreckers, Jacob managed to smile at his mate. "You're a good friend, Will, but don't get yourself in any brawls over this. I need you to keep looking for answers, not end up in the infirmary with McGinnis' knuckle prints on your cheekbone."

Will bristled and stood straight. "It'd take a lot more than Davy's punch to lay me low. I'll keep lookin', Jacob, you can count on it. I'm not forgettin' the other turncoats in town, but my search centers around that weasel Moony Swain."

Jacob nodded. "The seas have been calm of late with no

wrecks called out. That means no mule lines are running either. Makes me wonder where Moony's hiding out these days."

"He's around, down at Jimmy's and workin' a few hours at the salt ponds. I suspect he's layin' low and lettin' the evidence against you build."

Jacob turned away, not wanting to see Will's eyes when he asked the next question. "And about that evidence . . . it is building isn't it, Will? Even here in the jail, the night guard's been talking of getting the gallows ready."

Will pounded his fist on the bars, rattling the cell door. Startled at his friend's vehemence, Jacob spun back around to face him.

"There'll be no hangin', Jacob," Will said. "You have my word on it. If it comes to that, me and the boys will get you out of here and away from Key West. Far away. I promise you, no matter what it takes, your feet won't swing over this island soil."

The fire of determination burned in Will's eyes, and Jacob knew he meant it. "It won't come to that," Jacob said, choking back a bitter acid that rose to his mouth from an empty stomach. "Keep looking, Will. We'll fight this in court. We can win."

"I'll keep lookin', Captain," he said, "but you remember what I told you."

He started to leave, but Jacob stopped him. "Will, what of Nora? Have you seen her?"

"Every day, Jacob. She comes over after her school is out and talks to me. Begs me to talk some sense into you and let her come back to see you."

"Don't let her do it, Will. I don't want her in here."

"I know, but that poor little gal's heart is breakin'. I see tears in her eyes though she tries to hide them. It's hard on a woman when her man's in trouble. She wants to help."

"There's nothing she can do. She's in the middle of this thing between her father and me, and she'll only get hurt. Nora's strong, Will. Tell her I said to keep being strong and I'll see her one day soon when this mess is over."

"I'll tell her, but it'd mean more comin' from you."

Jacob shook his head. "Not yet."

After Will had gone, Jacob crouched in a corner of the cell and contemplated his conversation with his best friend. He hoped Will wouldn't have to make good on his threats. He couldn't live with himself if even one of his men's blood spilled because of him. But that was exactly where this all would end up if the law of Key West tried to hang Jacob Proctor. Jacob knew Will, understood his unwavering sense of loyalty well enough to be sure of that. "God help us," Jacob said.

Then he thought of Nora, and his heart went heavy in his chest. Sweet, loving Nora. He should have known that even if he weren't Sophie Proctor's son, he had no right to the gentle, pure spirit that was Nora's. He had to face the terrible probability that he would never see her again, never hold her in his arms, never kiss her, caress her. It was easier to accept the black emptiness of a hangman's hood than to consider losing Nora.

Jacob crossed his arms over his knees and lowered his brow to rest on them. Seeing nothing but the cold, moldy bricks of the jail floor, he closed his eyes and pictured Nora's face while the minutes ticked slowly toward the end of another day.

CHAPTER
TWENTY-SIX

Every man in Nora's life was either breaking her heart or in some other way conspiring against her. Theo had been doggedly pursuing her for days, trying to get her alone to hear his declarations of love. Apparently, blatant avoidance wasn't working with the thickheaded attorney, and she would have to explain her position with unquestioning frankness even he would understand.

Her father continued to dodge her questions about Jacob and refused to listen to her pleas on his behalf. Piney Beade had turned down her requests to see Jacob with an uncompromising attitude that convinced her that her father was behind his decision. The night guard who'd let her see Jacob before now told her that the prisoner himself had left a strict order that no females were to be allowed to his cell. "I guess that includes you, little kissin' cousin," the guard had sneered, and then followed his cold-hearted teasing with an offer to amuse her himself once his shift was up.

And Jacob was the most aggravating male of all. She'd made several attempts to visit him despite his objections, but he had spun a web of privacy around himself that was tearing her apart. Didn't he see that this isolation he'd forced on them was worse than any taunting she might have to suffer from his cellmates?

At least Will Turpin seemed to understand her plight. Until today. Now he was avoiding her as well. Once she'd dismissed her students, she'd marched across the courtyard of Proctor Warehouse and Salvage as she'd done every day, to see Jacob's first mate. She'd caught a glimpse of his naval cap through a window, but when she'd entered the warehouse, the little man was nowhere to be seen.

"Where is Will?" she asked Skeet, who was standing around idly with his mates.

He looked to his companions for support and shrugged. "Don't know, Miss Nora. He was here a minute ago, and now he's gone." The other men gave her the same halfhearted responses, but one made the error of glancing up the stairs at the same time he professed to knowing nothing of Will's whereabouts.

"Aha!" she said, traipsing toward the stairs. She gathered her skirts in her hands and climbed to the second floor. The mumbled curses of Jacob's men convinced her she was on the right trail.

She found Will in the cupola, which was fine with her since there was no way he could run. "What's happened, Will?" she demanded, "It must be bad since you're hiding out like a coward. You'd better tell me since I've had my fill of cowards and traitors and mule-headed men in general!"

He seemed to shrink before her eyes. "Ah, Miss Nora," he moaned, "it's bad enough. I was going to tell you once I'd had a pint to fortify my nerves."

Her own nerves sent a quick patter to her heart, and she leaned against the cupola railing. "What is it? Tell me."

He took a deep breath and wiped the back of his hand across his mouth. "Your father and his men have finished gatherin' evidence, so I hear. Jacob's trial is set for Monday."

"Monday? That's only three days from now."

"Don't I know it. And I haven't yet found a legal way to save the captain from the . . ."

He refused to say the words, but Nora interpreted the rest of his sentence. She fought the hysteria that threatened to banish all logic from her mind. "From what, Will? From the gallows? Is that what you're not telling me?"

"Aye. There's talk that the sentence will be hangin'."

Anger fought with horror inside Nora and won. "That's preposterous," she said. "You can't hang a man for stealing a few bank notes, even if Jacob were guilty, which he's not!"

"You'll have to talk to the judge about that. I just know what I hear. And as long as you've heard this much, you might as well know that there's also a rumor that the punishment will be swift. It's possible the hanging will be carried out the next morning."

The cupola suddenly seemed to be spinning on its own crazy axis, tilting and whirling with the caprices of the wind. Nora gripped the railing with both hands behind her and grounded her rampaging emotions by fixing her gaze on Will's face. "This can't be happening," she said.

Will came beside her. "You'd better sit a minute, Miss Nora, and then we'll go downstairs."

"I don't need to sit," she lied. "I need to stop this."

"I know. I know," Will said. Then in a low voice, though no one could hear but her, he said, "I give you my word, Nora. The captain won't hang for a crime he didn't commit. Will Turpin won't allow it."

She pushed away from the railing and stood straight. "Neither will Nora Seabrook," she announced. "Excuse me, Will. I've got some work to do. And it involves getting through some mighty dense heads!"

She marched down the steps of the cupola without looking back.

Nora was waiting on the front porch for her father when he came in for lunch. He noticed her when he passed through the gate, and stopped and stared as if this stick-postured woman were a stranger. Finally, he cleared his throat and said, "Well, Nora, what a nice surprise to see you home for lunch."

She never altered the sober facial features, which she hoped signaled her intent. "I'm always here, Father. It's you who's chosen to stay down by the harbor every day ... gathering more evidence, I assume."

He stepped up onto the porch. "I've been busy, yes. But now I'm done and happy to have more time to spend with my family."

She affected a thin-lipped smile, and was gratified when it seemed to baffle him. "I wonder if you'll think that after we've had a little talk."

His jowls drooped with weariness. "Oh, Nora, if it's about that Proctor again ... I'll be on a constant diet of oatmeal and mush if you don't let me do the job the judicial system of this country hired me to do."

"And which you are doing very poorly," she said.

"Now, listen here, daughter ..."

She blocked his way to the door in case he tried to escape to the house. Her heartbeat quickened to a rapid staccato as she prepared to meet the enemy head on. "I'm afraid it's you who's going to listen, Father. We can talk out here in privacy or we can go inside where Mama and Theo and Fanny are right now tucking napkins under their chins. It's your choice."

Her father's lips formed a perfect O as he expelled a long, slow breath of capitulation. "I suppose I've avoided this conversation as long as I can," he admitted. "I choose here. If I have to listen to one more of Sid's giggles or Theo's pompous adages, I think I'll go mad." He removed his jacket and tossed it over a chair. Folding his hands over his abdomen, he said, "Let me have it, girl, but not one foolish word about the supposed romantic adventure of a seafaring life which you seem to think you've had."

"This has nothing to do with any romantic notions of sea voyages. It has to do with a man's life. Jacob Proctor has been falsely accused, and if you continue with this ... this witch hunt, you will be condemning an innocent man.''

"Oh, really? You are singing a different tune now, young lady. Aside from a mountain of evidence which I have gathered in the last month or so on Jacob Proctor, need I remind you that you ended up on his ship in the first place because you went there in search of evidence yourself? Where was this loyalty to Captain Proctor then?''

She'd hoped he had forgotten that, but had an answer prepared in case he hadn't. "Yes, I did, but the difference is, I truly didn't think I would find any evidence, and you anticipated finding tons of it before we even landed in Key West. You arrived here with preconceptions about Jacob, Father, and that is most ... unjudgelike!''

His face reddened with restrained anger. "Why do you think I was sent here, Nora? Because Judge Carlton wanted to reward me with a few years in paradise? No. I was sent here because this island reeked with foul play and thievery and an outright lack of respect for the law. There was something rotten festering on this island, from the previous judge right down to the poorest of the wreckers, who by the way is *not* Jacob Proctor!''

"So from the start, in your eyes, Jacob was guilty of the crime of success? Come now, Father, you can't believe that's a reason to hold a man's life to a microscope.''

"No, but it's a reason to suspect him above all others. And since I've been here I've found sound, irrefutable facts to back up my suspicions.''

She risked opening a Pandora's box when she asked, "Like what?''

"Like several thousand dollars in New Bedford, Massachusetts, bank notes. Like eyewitnesses who saw Captain Proctor running from the beach the night *his* mule line drew the *Marguerite Gray* to the reefs, which was, as it turns out, a signal from Proctor to the *Gray*'s skipper to steer toward the lights. It wasn't an accident that the *Gray* ran into the reefs, Nora. It was a carefully executed plan to make it look like she did. Proctor led her there with a rope and a couple of mules.''

Nora braced herself to admit her culpability that night. "It wasn't like that, Father," she said. "I can vouch for Jacob's innocence."

"And how can you do that?"

"Because he was with me at the beach, not running a mule line."

She'd rendered her father speechless for several moments, but he soon recovered to blast her with his conclusions. "Lying now, too, Nora? I saw you that night, remember? I practically ran into you on the back steps of our house when Piney came to tell me of the mule line. You were home, Nora, not with Jacob Proctor."

She remembered Jacob sending her home and how she'd run from him as fast as she could. Everything had happened in a rush that night. Of course her father would think she was lying now. She truly had met him on the back steps at the same time the mule line was spotted.

"And it's not just that," he continued. "Remember when Theo followed Proctor's trail into the shore cave and discovered a secluded place only the perpetrator would be likely to know about? Theo found a lantern big enough to lure ships."

Nora wished now she'd told her father about finding the lantern damaged and her suspicions that Jacob had foiled the plans of the real criminal. If she told him now, he'd probably only accuse her of lying again to protect Jacob.

"And of course there's the matter of the bank notes," he said. "Irrefutable. They were in Proctor's warehouse buried in a hogshead. And they'd come directly off the *Marguerite Gray*. Add to all this the testimony I've been procuring from other island wreckers over the last few days, and the evidence against Jacob Proctor is most compelling."

"But I know him, Father. I know Jacob, and I am absolutely positive he didn't do any of these things."

Her father leveled a thick finger at her face. "You're trying to argue with a Federal judge by using intuition, Nora? I'm surprised at you! Besides, you only think you know this man. But you don't. I didn't want to have to tell you this, it sounds so callous, but don't you see that Proctor only used you to get to me?''

"That's preposterous. What *evidence* do you have of that?"

"The man sailed away with you, Nora."

Her voice trembled with frustration. "I told you . . . that was my fault, not his . . ."

"Let me finish. When he discovered you on the *Dover Cloud,* he should have done what any man with honorable intentions would have done. He should have turned around and brought you back. Short of that, he should have sent you home on the *Sea Hound.* But did he? No. He would much rather envision the hell he put this family through worrying about you while he wiled away his days on some remote island.

"The only thing which kept me from tearing the man limb from limb when the *Dover Cloud* sailed back into Key West was seeing that you were delivered home safely. He didn't harm you. For that I'm grateful. Apparently there is a thread of decency somewhere in the man."

She wanted to shout that there was *only* decency in Jacob Proctor. There was nothing in him that could make him commit the terrible crimes her father had just listed. She wanted to tell him everything, but what she'd learned about Jacob and what had happened to them on the island was his to tell. She couldn't betray his trust in her by revealing a past he might not want anyone to know. At least she wouldn't tell it now. But if it seemed that Jacob might hang, she would do or say whatever it took to stop that.

"Father, I don't believe Jacob did any of the things you've told me. He is not capable of such deception. He is the fairest, most honorable man I've ever known. But even if he had, why in God's name are you recommending that he face the gallows? None of these charges merit such strong punishment."

Her father's face became as hard and cold as stone. "Treason on the high seas is punishable by death, Nora. And so is murder. In the five years that Proctor has been on this island, twenty-three people have died on those reefs. Twenty-three people, including women and children. You will never convince me that luring ships and innocent people to a watery grave isn't tantamount to murder."

"Father, you can't say that. Jacob didn't kill anyone. He has spent the last five years of his life trying to save lives."

"Maybe he didn't kill intentionally. Perhaps his motives were only to plunder as many riches as he could, but people *have died*, Nora. That is an irrefutable fact you can't ignore. This practice of luring ships to the reefs has to stop, and it's going to stop with Jacob Proctor."

Nora felt the tenuous hold she had on rationality begin to slip. Her father was so sure, so unreachable. She couldn't persuade him with her arguments, because she didn't have facts to back them up. She only had feelings, but to her they were the truth of the matter. She knew Jacob hadn't done any of those things. Her fear for his life boiled inside her and threatened to explode in a torrent of words that could create a rift between her and her father that would never mend.

She bit back her anger and forced a contained calm to guide her actions. Grasping her father's hand, she pleaded, "Give me more time, Father. I'll find evidence to prove Jacob's innocence. Please postpone the trial. Please . . ."

"Eleanor!" Her mother's shriek pierced the air. "What in heaven's name has gotten into you?" She wrapped long fingers around Nora's shoulder. "Why are you defending that horrible man?"

Nora whirled on her mother. "Why, Mama? I'll tell you why. Jacob protected me and cared for me. And loved me."

Her mother's eyes became round as teacups. A tiny squeak came from her pursed lips.

"Yes, Mama, loved me as I never dreamed any man would."

"You're irrational, Eleanor. The man's done something to you. Island voodoo, I'd warrant. Come inside and I'll get you a spot of sherry." She took Nora's arm and tried to coax her into the house, but Nora wouldn't budge. "Theo loves you, Eleanor," Sidonia argued. "Truly loves you, and I know before this horrible sea voyage, you had feelings for him. You'll get them back. You'll marry Theo . . ."

Nora jerked free and backed away from her mother. "Feelings for Theo? Mama, open your eyes! What do you see? A woman in love, yes, that's true enough. But I love Jacob Proctor!" Ignoring her mother's gasps, she continued. There was no stopping the flow of words now. "I love him with all my heart. Mama, Father . . ." She looked from one to the other. "Right now I may be carrying Jacob's child. And all you can talk about is killing its father."

"Oh, my God!" Theo appeared on the threshold and slumped against the door frame. "The woman I'm to marry may be carrying another man's child? And that man is Jacob Proctor?" He dropped to a chair and placed a trembling hand on his forehead. "I know this wasn't your doing, Nora, darling. I know you could never . . . But I must tell you, I find this difficult to forgive. I hope you fought him . . ."

Tears of fury nearly blinding her, Nora reached down and grabbed a handful of brilliant marigolds growing at the base of the porch. Raising the whole mess over her head, stems, roots, and clods of moist, dark earth, she hurled her weapon at Theo. "See if you can forgive this, Theo!"

Sidonia teetered and let out a low wail. "And Mama," Nora shouted at her, "if you're going to faint, you'd better get to the kitchen for your own damn compress, because I'm leaving!"

And that was precisely what she did as she went in search of the one male in all of Key West who, she knew, would help her.

She tracked Felix to Jacob's goat yard. He stood in the middle of a half-dozen clambering billies, and tossed a handful of grain at their hooves. When the goats romped off to nibble something more rewarding than Felix's shirttail, he spotted her and ran over to the chicken-wire fencing. "Hey, Miss Nora. What're you doin' here?"

"Felix, we've got to talk."

"Am I in trouble at school?"

"No, in fact I think I can guarantee you some extra grades

for answering a few questions, and the first one is, who in this town would most like to see Jacob swing from a hangman's noose?''

Though the subject was grim, Felix beamed. ''You can mark down those grades, Miss Nora, 'cause I got the answer. Moony Swain. He's hated Cap'n J for years.''

''My opinion exactly,'' she said. ''Do you think it's possible that Mr. Swain put those bank notes in Jacob's warehouse?''

Felix thought, and then nodded once with conviction. ''You saw those two go at it that day in the courtyard, Miss Nora. Moony has enough hatred for the captain to do most anything.''

At last, an ally. ''I want to find the rest of those bank notes, Felix. I believe there must be more, because if Moony were trying to frame Jacob, he wouldn't have put all the notes in that hogshead. He'd have kept most of them for himself.'' She reached for Felix's hand. ''I don't want you to get in any trouble,'' she said. ''But I want to go inside Moony's warehouse tonight, and I need someone to stay on the outside and be a lookout for me. Could you do that, Felix?''

His eyes shimmered with the spirit of adventure. She'd enticed Felix into the world he loved best. ''I can do better than that, Miss Nora,'' he announced. ''I'll go in with you.''

''No, no,'' she said. ''I don't want you to go inside. It will be dark and could be dangerous.''

''Never has been before, not if you know what you're doin','' he answered with swaggering confidence. ''Besides, I can show you where to look.''

''You've been in Mr. Swain's warehouse before?''

He leaned over the fence to be close to her ear. ''Just between you and me, Miss Nora, it's where I did most of my late-night Christmas shoppin' last year, and the selection wasn't too bad, either.''

Laughter threatened to destroy Nora's stern exterior. ''Shame on you, Felix,'' she said with a grin in her voice. ''That's a terribly naughty thing to do, but it does make me reconsider about you going inside with me tonight. Will your mother be angry if you're out after dark?''

"Leave that to me. My mama won't be angry . . ."

If she doesn't know you're gone, Nora interpreted. She repressed a sharp twinge of guilt that she was probably encouraging Felix to sneak out of his house. "Oh, dear, Felix, what am I doing? You must promise me that if we get into trouble you will run as far and as fast as you can."

"Oh, Miss Nora . . ." He tried to wave away her concerns.

"Promise me, Felix, or the deal is off."

"I promise, but nothin's gonna happen."

"All right. Meet me at midnight in back of Jacob's warehouse. You can show me the way to Moony's from there."

Hours later, Nora found her partner in the deep shadows behind Proctor's Warehouse and Salvage. "What do you mean we're not going to Moony's warehouse?" she asked him.

Felix grinned. "You want to find the bank notes, right?" She nodded. "Well, then, believe me. They aren't in the warehouse."

"Then where?"

He folded his little arms across his chest in the same infuriatingly confident way Jacob had. "If Moony's got them, they're on his ship."

"How do you know that?"

His grin broadened. "Because before I came here, I happened to pass by Jimmy Teague's. It seems all of Moony's men are in there right now, and they're corked as swillbellies."

"So? That's the usual place for Moony and his men, isn't it?"

Felix nodded. "Especially when they're sailing out in a couple of hours."

"Sailing out?"

"Yep. I heard Moony himself tellin' one of his boys that they were meetin' up with Toliver somewhere up the coast."

"Who's Toliver?"

Felix gave a look that said for a teacher, she didn't know much. "Don't you listen, Miss Nora? He's the captain of the

Marguerite Gray. The one who lost a hold full of stinkin'
codfish. Only now I don't think he cried much over that cargo,
'cause now I think him and Moony salvaged something a lot
more valuable than anybody thought.''

"The bank notes.''

Felix clapped his hands once. "You got it, Miss Nora. While
Cap'n J was savin' the sorry butts of the *Gray*'s crew, Moony
and Toliver were savin' the bank notes. They prob'ly planned
to divide them up when the judge wasn't breathin' down their
necks.''

"And after some of them had been used to plant evidence
against Jacob,'' Nora added.

"Yep. And I'd bet a week's worth of milkin' money that
those notes are on Moony's ship right now ready to be split
with Toliver.''

"Do you know where Moony's ship is?''

"You bet I do. We'll have to stay close to Cap'n J's warehouse when we go by the harbor. Nobody'd notice me runnin'
out on the dock, but you, Miss Nora . . .'' He gave her a quick
once-over and clucked his tongue disapprovingly. "At least
you wore a *brown* dress.''

They came around the back of Jacob's warehouse to step
into a strong wind sweeping off the gulf. It was powerful
enough to pull strands of hair from Nora's neat chignon and
whip them around her face. Following in Felix's shadow, she
bundled layers of skirt in her fists to keep her white petticoats
from billowing out and catching someone's eye.

They reached the harbor without being detected. Dozens of
crafts with masts soaring to the sky creaked and moaned at
their pilings, looking like ominous sentinels of the sea. Nora
shivered at the bulky shadows of wooden hulls and the eerie
groans emanating from them. The harbor looked and sounded
almost sinister in the dark hours of night.

"C'mon, Miss Nora,'' Felix called to her. "We don't know
how long those boys'll be over at Jimmy's.''

His voice jolted her to awareness and she ran after him. In
the dim light from a quarter moon, they crept aboard a three-

masted schooner with the name *Raven's Wing* burned into its bow. "Where to now?" Nora asked, grabbing hold of the deck rail to steady herself in a sudden gust of wind.

"We should check the hold first," Felix said. "I figure we're lookin' for a strongbox or somethin' that size. As long as Moony's men are at Jimmy's, we don't need to keep a lookout. If we don't find the bank notes there, we'll search the captain's quarters."

Nora was grateful Felix was there. She didn't want this evidence-gathering mission to end up like her last one had. She certainly wouldn't want to sail anywhere with Moony Swain, but she knew from experience that anything could happen. "All right, but listen, Felix. If there's any trouble, you remember your promise. Get off this ship, even if I don't."

He started to protest, and she grabbed his shoulders. "I mean it, Felix. Promise me you'll run and get help. It won't do for both of us to get caught."

He thought a moment, and gave in reluctantly. "Okay, but don't worry. We won't get caught."

The hold of the *Raven's Wing* was nearly empty. Moony's voyage was obviously not intended to be a cargo transport, and Nora put more faith in the theory that Moony was sailing to a nearby key solely to meet with the captain of the *Marguerite Gray* and divide the bank notes.

"There's nothin' here but ballast and supplies," Felix said.

Nora was relieved to follow Felix out of the hold. Even though it was tied to the dock, the ship pitched and rolled at its moorings, making the simple act of standing a difficult chore. She was glad when they climbed the ladder to open air.

The door to Moony's cabin was unlocked and opened with a reluctant squeak. A small oil lamp burned over a simple desk, its flame dim behind a grimy chimney, but its pitiful light would have to suffice. The quarters were sparsely equipped and not as comfortable as Jacob's more lavish cabin on the *Dover Cloud*. Clothes and papers were strewn about everywhere.

"Just dig in, Miss Nora," Felix said.

She lifted the first bundle of clothes from the bed and felt around on the mattress. "Those bank notes could be anywhere in this mess."

A half hour later, Nora centered her search on a seaman's chest in a corner of Moony's cabin. She lifted a removable tray and rummaged through moldy contents underneath. The stench from an old slicker and rubber boots that hadn't been scraped of fish scales in years nearly made her forget her search and slam the lid closed again. But she was glad she didn't when she encountered the hard, sharp texture of metal hinges.

She muffled a squeal of delight and called Felix over. They lifted a wood and iron box from the chest and set it on the floor. Her excitement gave way to despair when they found a sturdy padlock on the front. Felix scoffed as if it were a minor inconvenience. He pulled a ten-inch crowbar from his pants and ran his fingers down its smooth surface as though it were made of gold. "Never go anywhere without this," he said. "It gets me into some of the better places in town."

Nora stared at him. "We're going to have to talk about this," she warned, and then gently nudged him in the ribs. "But for now, go ahead and open this blasted thing!"

He wedged the crowbar into the padlock, and then jumped up and down on the protruding end until the lock gave way. Inside the box were hundreds of bank notes of varying denominations. And each one originated from the Bank of New Bedford, Massachusetts. A childish grin of pure delight sparkled at Nora in the low lamplight. "Looks like we found what we came for," Felix said.

"Looks like it," she agreed.

"I say we take the whole box."

"I don't think that's necessary, Felix." She stuffed a few notes into her pocket. "We'll take these to the authorities and tell them the box is on board. For now let's put it back in the chest." She stood up and looked around the cabin. "At least this room doesn't look any worse than it did when we came in," she said. "So if we put the box away, Moony will never know we've been here."

Once the box was secured, Felix opened the door of Moony's

cabin and peeked out. Suddenly, his hand waved frantically behind his back as a gust of wind caught the door and blew it open. He spun away from the entrance and flattened his thin body against an interior wall. "Get down, Miss Nora!" he hissed in terror.

There was no time. A burst of wind pushed Nora back from the door. Her heart skipped a beat and then slammed into her ribs. In the wash of moonlight peeking through gathering gray clouds, she stared at the menacing grin of Moony Swain.

CHAPTER
TWENTY-SEVEN

Moony stepped across the threshold, forcing Nora further into the room. A brown-stained grin lifted the grizzled ends of an unkempt mustache to mock her. Moony's tongue flicked out to push a toothpick from one side of his mouth to the other. "Well, what have we here?" he snickered. "Looks like Jacob Proctor's hen if my eyes aren't deceivin' me."

Nora barely heard his words. Every artery rushed blood to her temples, which throbbed with a thunderous roar. At the same time her limbs went numb with the chill of shock.

Moony stalked her to the center of the cabin. "And what might you be doin' on the *Raven's Wing,* missy?"

She couldn't have answered past the lump in her throat, but he didn't give her time anyway. He cocked his head to the side and squinted one glittering eye at her. "Methinks you might be lookin' for something," he said. "Is that what you're doin', missy? Treasure-huntin'?"

She forced a response on a trembling breath. "I don't know what you're talking about. I'm not looking for anything. I ... I came to locate you. I thought you might be able to help Jacob ..."

Whiskey-laden breath exploded in her face when Moony laughed. "That's a rich one, it is. Moony Swain helpin' Jacob Proctor! Case you don't know it, girl, I'm as happy as can be the good captain has his arse in the town jail. And seein' him swing from a hangman's noose will make me positively gleeful."

The vulgar evil of the man fired Nora's loyalty and her anger. "That will never happen, Mr. Swain. Jacob is innocent of any crimes . . ."

"Oh, innocent, is he?" Moony sneered. "We'll see if a court of law decides the same way. A court presided over by your own pappy."

His crude chortles raised the hair at Nora's nape and made her palms itch to slap the taunting grin from his face. She darted a glance to the corner of the room, where Felix was still pressed against the wall. The door was open, giving him a chance for escape if she could keep Moony occupied. She stepped back, knowing Moony would follow. "Fine," she said. "Think what you will. But the evidence will prove otherwise, and Jacob will soon be a free man."

Moony's eyes lit with sudden understanding. "Evidence? What evidence is that?" His mouth curved down into a snarl and he grabbed her arm. "Just what exactly have you been doin' in my quarters, missy?"

Knowing she'd said the wrong thing, Nora used Moony's anger to divert his attention from the cabin door. She struggled against his grasp, keeping his focus on her face. Further help arrived from a gust of wind, which swept into the room, rattling the one window and blowing papers around their heads. Moony tumbled backwards, providing the opportunity for Felix to escape. In a shadowy flash of quick movement, he was out the door, and Nora was determined to follow.

Moony fell against a corner of the desk and uttered a scathing curse. Nora ran past him to the door, and almost made it out before his hands wrapped around her waist. He hauled her back inside and pinned her to the wall. But in the silvery moonlight she'd seen what she'd hoped to see—a slight body slithering over the side of the *Raven's Wing* and dropping into the black water. Moony's crew advanced onto the gangway, but Felix had gotten away without being seen.

Moony's arm pressed against Nora's collarbone. His face was just inches from hers. "We'll just see what evidence you have," he bit out.

She turned her face toward the door and started to scream, but her cry was cut off by Moony's palm over her mouth. An acid taste of dirt and grime mixed with her saliva. Nausea churned in her stomach, gagging her. She sputtered for a breath, and he removed his hand long enough to pull a rag from his pocket. Threading the greasy cloth between her teeth, he bound it in back of her head. Then he pushed her to the door and into the arms of one of his crewmen on deck.

"Tie her hands and keep her flat on her belly so no one'll see her," he instructed. "And don't let her out of your sight." Immediately the edge of a hand slammed into the back of her knees and she went face-down onto the deck. Once he'd made certain her hands were bound, Moony headed back to the cabin. "We'll see if the little darkies' schoolmarm has found herself any evidence," he said, pushing the door closed against the steady roar of the wind.

He came out a few minutes later with the damaged padlock in his hand. Dangling it in front of Nora's eyes, he taunted, "Come to see if I'd help Proctor, eh?"

Nora swallowed against the oily rag and closed her eyes to Moony's sneer. His boots sounded twice on the deck before he grabbed her arm and yanked her to her feet. "Some of those bank notes are missin', little teacher. And they aren't the ones I hid in Proctor's barrel."

Moony fastened his fiery gaze on one of his men and jerked his thumb toward the hatch of the ship's hold. "Open it up."

Once the hatch door swung away, he pushed Nora to the opening. Still holding her arm, he forced her down the ladder. Her shoes grabbed just enough of the rungs to keep her from tumbling headlong into the dark hole. Even so, she fell when she reached the bottom.

Moony followed her down and advanced with threatening intent etched in his features. He flung the padlock across the hold. It clanged against the inside of the ship's hull. A strangled cry tried to force its way past the cloth in Nora's mouth as she watched him reach out a hand toward her.

"Not so cocky now, are we, missy?" he said, pulling her to her feet.

She tried to push him away with her shoulder, but he slammed her against the ribs of the ship and held her fast with his forearm pressed on her chest. "Let's see if ol' Moony can find those bank notes you took," he said. She kicked fiercely, but he only laughed and moved his arm up to her throat so any movement would block her air passage. With his free hand he ripped the front of her dress. Onyx buttons clattered across the floor. Moony groped under the lacy fabric of her camisole with greedy fingers.

"No bank notes there," he said with a leering grin. "Though a mighty pleasin' substitute." He spread his legs to balance himself against the tossing of the ship and leaned into her, pressing his hip against her abdomen. With one sweep he raised her skirt to her waist and jerked her undergarments to her knees.

Tears of shame and fear swam in Nora's eyes. Her throat burned with the need for air. Moony's hand raked across her thighs and around to her backside. When he found nothing, he slapped her hard on her bottom, laughed out loud, and stepped away. She drew a welcome draft of air.

"Now where else could you have hid those notes, little teacher?" he demanded. His eyes went glassy with lust. "Could take me a long time to find 'em, but find 'em I will, and I'll enjoy the search."

He walked to the ladder and called up to his crew. "Shove away, boys. Prepare to sail. We've not a minute to lose." Then he turned back to Nora. "I'll be back, little missy. You wait for me now." With a boorish laugh that mingled with the creaking of the hull, he stumbled up the ladder and closed the hatch. The heavy metal bolt clicked home as Nora slid down the curved ribs of the *Raven's Wing*.

"Cap'n J, Cap'n J! You in there, Cap'n?"

Jacob pulled himself up from the cot and shook his head. For days he'd only snatched minutes of sleep at a time, but tonight exhaustion had claimed him and he'd fallen back on the pitiful straw mattress and slept like a dead man. "Who's there?" he called, struggling to regain the sanity of clear thinking and throw off grogginess that made his head feel as if it was filled with sand.

"It's me, Cap'n . . . Felix."

Jacob pulled the cot to the window, stood on it, and looked out. In a ray of moonlight spearing through the palm fronds, Felix Obalu jumped up and down like a jack-in-the-box. "Felix, what are you doing here? It must be the middle of the night."

"It is, Cap'n, and maybe the middle of the *last* night for Miss Nora."

The remaining cobwebs disintegrated from Jacob's brain at the mention of Nora's name. He leaned his face out the window as far as the bars would allow. "What are you saying?"

"Moony's got her, Jacob. She's on the *Raven's Wing,* and he's plannin' to sail."

"What?" The full impact of Felix's words slammed into Jacob's head with the force of a blow. "How'd it happen? What . . ."

"We found the bank notes on Moony's ship. Miss Nora and me, we both thought they'd be there, and sure enough . . ."

Jacob blocked out the rest of Felix's words. "Is she all right? Moony hasn't hurt her?"

"Not so far as I know. I jumped the ship and came right away to tell you."

Jacob pounded a fist against the rough bricks of the prison wall. He was powerless to help, yet he had to do something. "You've got to get the judge, Felix. Hurry!"

Felix's head bobbed in a frantic nod. "What'll I tell him? That Moony's got Miss Nora?"

Logic and panic warred in Jacob's mind for dominance.

What could Thurston Seabrook do? Jacob was the only chance Nora had if Moony had left the harbor. "No," he said. "Tell him I've got to see him. Tell him I'm confessing . . . tell him I'm escaping. Tell him anything. Just get him here as fast as you can. And then wake Will and tell him to ready the *Cloud* just in case that snake Moony has already sailed."

Lightning flashed over the tops of the trees, and rain began to fall in sheets as Felix darted through the shadows. Jacob paced. Surely no sailor with an ounce of sense would venture out on a night like this, but Moony Swain . . . Jacob wasn't at all sure. He ran to the door of his cell, rattled the bars, and hollered for the guard. "Frank! Come quick!" He was answered with the oaths of his cellmates, until the guard appeared and threatened to beat all of them into silence.

"What is it now, Proctor?" he said, sauntering up to Jacob's cell with lazy insolence. "You got a bedbug in your drawers?"

Jacob was beyond reasoning with anyone. "You gotta let me out of here, Frank. Someone's life is at stake."

The guard laughed. "I know. Yours."

"Damn it, Frank, open the cell!"

"Go back to sleep, Proctor. It's the first peace and quiet we've had here since you became a guest."

Jacob lashed out between the bars with his booted foot. "Damn you to hell, Frankie! There'll be a death on your conscience."

The guard danced free of the danger. "Not yours, Jacob, my boy. Not on my conscience. After you hang I might just have me a shot at them wrecks myself." He turned away and walked back down the hall, leaving Jacob to prowl around his cell like a caged animal.

Once the *Raven's Wing* sailed away from Key West harbor, the wind picked up with steadily increasing intensity. Unable to stand in the pitching of the boat, Nora lay on the floor of the hold, braced her feet against a barrel of fish, and struggled to free her hands from the rope at her wrists. Luckily, the drunken man who'd bound her had done a poor job of it, probably the only advantage she could see to being on a ship in a storm with a half-dozen soused sailors.

She loosened the rope, slipped her hands from the loops, and snatched the cloth from between her teeth. Spitting the rancid taste from her mouth, she gulped in the air of the hold, which was foul with fish and mildew.

It wouldn't do any good to yell. Minutes had passed since the ship had left the safety of Key West. Thunder combined with the howl of the wind and filled the hold with ominous sounds of the storm. No one would hear her through the narrow slits in the bow of the hull that served as the only ventilation. Besides, the last thing she wanted was for Moony to hear her and come back down.

It was so dark. Even after many minutes, Nora could only make out large indistinct shapes in her prison. The *Raven's Wing* rose and fell over the waves, churning its way out to sea. The timbers of its masts creaked with the pressure of overfull sails. Boards at Nora's back moaned with the effort of holding together in the increasing swells.

She groped around the floor for something to stabilize her in the wicked tossing of the sea. Finding the rope that had bound her wrists, she stood and coiled it twice around her waist. Then, sliding her hand above her head, she located an iron hook that would secure her to the side of the ship. With her hands shaking and her body pitching forward and back with the motion of the waves, she finally managed to loop the end of the line around the hook. She drew it as tight as she could, knotting it with the rope at her waist and bringing her back against a rib of the hull. She dug the toes of her boots into the pine planking at her feet, thought of Jacob, and prayed that Felix had made it to shore.

"What's the meaning of this, Proctor?" Rainwater streaming from his hair onto his face, Judge Seabrook scowled through the bars of Jacob's cell. "I don't like being dragged out on a night the devil himself wrought . . ."

Jacob slammed the flat of his hand against the bars. "Stop talking for once, Judge, and listen."

Thurston swallowed his next words in a sputter of indignation. "Now see here . . ."

"Your daughter's life is at stake, Judge. Does that make you want to hear what I have to say?"

Thurston's cheeks puffed out with a startled breath. "Nora? She's home in bed."

"The hell she is. She's right now on Moony Swain's ship, and God only knows what he's doing to her this minute."

The judge clamped his mouth shut and stared at the man who'd silenced him.

"She found the bank notes on Moony's ship," Jacob said, "but unfortunately Moony found her. We can only hope the *Raven's Wing* hasn't sailed." Lightning flooded Jacob's cell, illustrating his frustration. "I pray Moony won't be fool enough to test the seas on a night like this."

Thurston looked to the guard for help. "Go down there, Frank. See if my daughter is on that ship and bring her back here."

Jacob scoffed at the ineffectual instructions. "You're sending Frank? He won't be able to get Nora off that ship." He thrust his arm through the bars and grabbed the soaked collar of Thurston's nightshirt. "Let me out of here, Judge. You've got to open this cell."

"I can't let you out, Proctor. How do I know you're telling the truth? How do I know this isn't a plot concocted by that crew of yours to help you escape? How . . ."

A new set of footsteps sounded through the passageway, and halted the flow of Thurston's words. Gasping for air, and dripping a trail of rainwater onto the brick floor, Felix charged up to the men and leveled frightened eyes on Jacob. "It's gone, Cap'n. The *Raven's Wing* has sailed."

Jacob bunched more of Thurston's nightshirt into his trembling fist and twisted, hauling the judge to the bars. A growl that was primal and fierce came from his throat. "Damn it, Judge, what more do you need to hear? For God's sake, I love Nora. I'd risk my life to save her. I'll bring her home and come right back to this stinking cell. You have my word, but you've got to let me go before there's not a ship in Key West that can chase Moony out to sea."

Thurston quivered against the bars. Fear flickered in his eyes. "All right." He motioned to the guard. "Frank, let him out." He stepped away from the door as it swung open. Jacob raced past him as a cry pierced the incessant roar of the wind.

"Wreck ashore!"

CHAPTER
TWENTY-EIGHT

The *Dover Cloud* was ready, rocking at her moorings like a thoroughbred anxious to leave the paddock for a good run. Jacob jumped aboard amid shouts of welcome from his crew. He loosened a rope from a piling and shouted over his shoulder, "The judge may lock me up again when I return, so if this is our last run for a while, let's make it a good one."

"Aye, Captain," Will said, handing him a slicker, "we're ready."

Jacob thrust his arms into the jacket. "If any of you men don't want to go out in this, I'll understand, but get off now."

Each crew member glanced at his companions' faces from under the dripping brims of nor'westers, and Will spoke for all of them. "It's only a good stiff breeze for a brisk sail, Captain. Not a man here would want to miss it."

Jacob slapped Will's back. "You're full of bilgewater, Will. It's a damn tropical storm and you know it. But I'm grateful."

Jacob took the wheel as the *Cloud*'s sails filled with the howling wind and the ship rode the first of the big waves out of Key West harbor. Other wreckers, hoping for a good salvage, had set out ahead of him, but those ships were turning back.

"It's too rough out there, Jacob," one skipper called to him above the sinister sounds of nature. "Ain't no cargo worth paying for with your life."

Jacob only waved away the man's words. The cargo on the stranded ship at Sailboat Reef was indeed worth fighting for, worth dying for. The precious cargo of the *Raven's Wing* was the very substance of Jacob's life.

The *Dover Cloud* rounded the southern tip of Key West and faced the menace of the Florida Straits head on. Waves topping ten feet buffeted the ship and sent walls of water onto her decks. Jacob's crew cursed and vowed revenge against a sea that showed no mercy. Still the schooner forged ahead, riding wave after wave to dizzying heights before crashing to sea level again.

In the distance, through sheets of rain and charcoal-gray clouds that touched the earth, Jacob saw one single light burning on Sailboat Reef, one light from somewhere on board the *Raven's Wing* that would guide him to the stranded ship.

"A pitiful performance, Moony," he said bitterly, as if his foe were standing in front of him. "All your experience didn't keep you off the very reef you've been plundering from for years. Serves you right, you old bastard, and gives me the chance I need to catch you."

And to the ship that remained sturdy under his feet, he said, "You're a good lady, *Cloud*. You make this run and we'll let you rest. You'll have earned it."

Nora had been almost grateful when the strident scrape of wood on rock jolted her to awareness in the dark hold. She'd almost said a prayer of thanksgiving when the *Raven's Wing* tilted precariously, tried to right itself, and unsuccessful, settled with a mournful groan onto the reef. When the ship's careening, headlong course was brought to a sudden, bone-cracking halt, Nora knew the schooner could not escape the ravages of the storm but that maybe, just maybe, rescue was possible for her.

Voices, mostly indecipherable and muffled by the wind, carried into the hold. Nora made out phrases punctuated by panic. One man's cry announced the demise of the mainmast just before the wood rent and split the air with a thunderous clap. When the huge timber hit water, the ship teetered on its bed of coral, and Nora covered her ears against the moans of a threatened vessel battling an unforgiving sea.

"She's breaking up, Moony!" a sailor called, and proof of his warning sounded in creaks and splinters of wounded wood and bent iron. A piece of the hull gave way, and water leaked into a three-foot slit of torn lumber.

Nora watched in horror as seawater seeped into her shoes. At least fortune had been with her when she'd strapped herself to the side of the hold that ultimately protruded out of the water, but it wouldn't be long before the gash in the hull widened. Water that leaked in now would soon tear through the hold with a vengeance.

When she heard Moony give the order to abandon ship, Nora stared at the round hatch still bolted above her. Would Moony come and take her off the ship? Even if it meant she might live, she prayed he wouldn't come. If the foul hold of the *Raven's Wing* was to be her tomb, it was better than being captive to a cruel monster, one who would probably kill her in his own time anyway.

She identified the sound of a rowboat hitting the water, and the frantic calls of men trying to board it. Then all was quiet except for the storm. Rain pelted the side of the ship with unending fury. Thunder clapped overhead, and the wind continued to howl and taunt the *Raven's Wing* with jolts and jostles that made the beaten ship rasp its death rattle.

Occasionally, a flash of lightning illuminated the hold, providing Nora with the ghastly sight of seawater rising relentlessly. Supplies intended to sustain the crew for the short voyage north floated around her knees now. Bottles of whiskey, smoked meat, and soggy loaves of bread bumped into her legs and floated away on a bobbing trail to ultimate destruction. And she waited for help to arrive or for the last full breath she would take before the water took her.

* * *

Jacob aimed a lantern beam on what was left of the *Raven's Wing*. Flotsam of the ship's deck and masts caught the waves and crashed into the sides of the *Dover Cloud*. Only a portion of the hull remained above sea level, and it appeared the ship's crew had abandoned the wreck to trust their fortunes to the angry sea.

Though he knew it was useless, Jacob called her name. "Nora! Nora, are you here?" His voice was lost to his own ears, claimed by a wailing wind. He made the decision to search the ship before attempting to chase Moony and his crew into the Atlantic.

"Get closer," he shouted to Will, though he knew his own ship might become a victim of the reef. But time was his worst enemy now. If Nora was in the hull, it would only be minutes before the sea would pull what was left of the *Raven's Wing* under the roiling surface.

His crew dropped the rowboat into the water and Jacob and Will jumped aboard. Calmer seas existed in the watery valley created between the two ships. The small boat maneuvered the gentler whitecaps to come aside the hull of the *Raven's Wing*. Jacob threw a rope to a section of ragged, torn timber. After checking its stability, he climbed hand over hand onto the hull. Bracing himself against the wind raging over the shell of the ship, he called Nora's name again.

The sea lapped at her shoulders. Salt water filled her mouth and woke her from a dazed stupor. She spat it out and stared around the hold. It seemed foolish to hope now, and Nora wished she could fall back into the blackness of sleep so she wouldn't have to watch the water inch its way above her head. It would be so much more peaceful that way, but was impossible now.

Fully alert, she drew a deep breath and prepared to battle to the end. She tried to extricate herself from the ropes that had saved her during the worst of the storm. Maybe, if she were loose, she could widen the gap in the hull and escape. Failing that, she would at least be free to find the last bit of air left in the hold.

The sodden fibers at her waist were stretched taut. She rubbed her fingertips raw trying to slip the knots free, but they wouldn't budge. Tears of frustration flowed into her eyes. She cursed the blasted ropes that once had saved her, but now prevented her last desperate attempts to survive. And then a voice came to her through the howl of the storm.

"Noraaa!"

Joyous recognition flooded her heart. It was Jacob's voice, the sweetest, most wonderful sound in all the world. Nora closed her eyes against the ravages of the storm and let her spirit rejoice in survival. She was going to win. She would wake the next morning to the beauty of the island and to the love of her life. "Jacob!" she shouted. Adrenaline pumped through her veins, and she renewed her efforts to untie the ropes at her waist. "Jacob, I'm down here!"

"Nora? Call out again. I'll find you."

Water seeped past her lips. By skidding her boot soles along the side of the hull, she was able to raise her mouth a few inches. "Jacob, the hatch is locked. You have to open the hatch cover."

A full minute ticked agonizingly by before she heard his voice again. "Nora, I've found the hatch, but it's submerged. If I open it the hold will be flooded."

"It already is, nearly," she called. "Hurry, Jacob, there isn't much time."

"I'll get you out, honey. Just hang on."

Seconds turned into precious minutes. Nora struggled for each inch of air. Outside, footsteps sounded on the hull. Jacob called for help. There was a loud crash and, once more, footsteps. Then the entire hold reverberated with a resounding crack. The wood above her head split and revealed the tip of an ax blade. Jacob was literally chopping the hold to bits to get to her.

Water covered her mouth and she tilted her head back to breathe through her nose. The ax came down again. The blade sliced through, twisted, and pulled at jagged timber. A large chunk of the *Raven's Wing* gave way and floated past Nora's eyes. *One more time, Jacob. One more swing and you can reach me.*

Thwack! The blade did its job. A gaping hole appeared in the side of the hull, but not without exacting a price. The ship pitched closer to its grave, and water rushed over the exposed lip of the hole and into the hold. Nora filled her lungs with air seconds before water covered her head.

The sea swelled around her, rolling in waves that pushed her into the wood wall and then tried to drag her back. But she could no longer order her hands to work at the ropes. Buffeted by crates and barrels and bits of lumber, she'd lost control of her limbs. Her lungs burned like fire. And then strong hands were around her waist. A narrow, hard object slid between the ropes, sliced them with one smooth movement, and suddenly she was free.

Propelled upwards, Nora willed the air to stay in her lungs. *Air, sweet, wonderful air.* She kicked with her feet, and stretched toward it, toward the light that seemed to float on the surface of the sea. And then her head broke through and she gulped great drafts of life-giving oxygen into her lungs. She clung to the remains of the *Raven's Wing* until Jacob hoisted himself out of the wreck and pulled her up beside him. Her tears mingled with those of the man who held her in his arms and whispered her name over and over like a prayer.

The winds had died down and a drizzling rain had been burned off by a brilliant sunrise when the *Dover Cloud* limped proudly back to Key West harbor. Her crew had saved the precious human cargo of the *Raven's Wing*. Most of the men, humbled by the vengeance of the storm and the magnitude of their efforts, were ready to accept their due from the citizens of Key West.

Realizing his only reward might be another night in the island jail, Jacob Proctor cared only that he had saved the person who meant more to him than life. It was the reason he would be able to face his fate, whatever it might be, with only prayers of thanksgiving that Nora had been spared.

A rosy-streaked dawn illuminated the sky and the hundred or so people gathered at the dock to watch the *Dover Cloud* slide into its berth. Nora settled deeper into the crook of Jacob's arm, where she had remained the whole of the journey back. She sighed contentedly. "I knew you would come. I knew that somehow you would."

He laughed softly in her ear. "Did you now? You knew I would slip the bonds of a Federal judge, break down iron bars, and battle the fiercest of elements to get to you?"

He sensed her smile. "Yes."

He wrapped a blanket more snugly around her. "Well, as usual, you were right. But did it ever occur to you that I risked life and limb primarily to retrieve the evidence Felix said you'd found?"

"No. Because you never mentioned it till now. And you've asked about my welfare at least . . . oh, five hundred times in the last three hours."

Jacob laughed. "Caught again by a woman with both brains and beauty."

She whirled away from him and jumped to her knees. "Oh, Jacob, the bank notes! I'm not a bit sure I have any brains at all." She began searching for the pocket of her dress among the damp folds. "They'll be ruined by now."

He stilled her hand with his own. "It'll keep, my love." He pointed to the people advancing down the dock. They included Nora's mother, attended by the Seabrook servants, Portia and Lulu, and Fanny Cosette and Dillard Hyde. And leading them all was the judge himself, a seldom-seen smile altering the puffy contours of his face. "Right now I'd better cover you back up." Jacob slid his thumb over the swell of her breast only covered by Nora's thin camisole. "I don't want the judge to add another crime to my noteworthy list."

Nora grinned at him as he replaced the blanket. "Sorry. I'm afraid he's already added that one."

Nora refused to leave Jacob's side even as she was fussed over by her family. Her father enclosed her in a hasty but genuine embrace, and followed it with a stern admonishment for what was again a most foolhardy act. But he softened his scolding by mentioning his pride in her for sticking to her beliefs. Then he turned his attention to Jacob.

Drawing himself to the full height allowed by his portly build, the judge cleared his throat and stuck out his hand. "It seems we meet again on this dock after you've rescued my daughter from an unexpected bout with the sea," he said.

Jacob grasped Thurston's hand. "And again it has been my pleasure, Your Honor."

Thurston looked from Jacob to his daughter, studied their faces, and for once drew the appropriate conclusion. "I can see that it has. My wife and I will be eternally grateful to you . . ."

"And. . . ?" Nora nudged him in his ribs.

He flashed her a look of exasperation. "Let me do this my own way, *Eleanor!*"

He'd used her full name, something he only did when his patience was diminishing or his embarrassment was growing. Nora sensed which it was this time and smiled at him.

"*And,*" Thurston continued to Jacob, "I owe you an apology, young man. I don't often misjudge people, but in your case I did." He glanced at Nora and grimaced. "A sin for which I will probably pay the rest of my life! My daughter tried to convince me with that intuition thing women seem to brag so about, but I'm a hard man, Proctor. I needed facts, evidence."

"And you have evidence now?" Jacob asked.

"Why, yes, indeed I do."

Nora was completely baffled. What evidence did her father have? She hadn't shown him the soggy bank notes in her pocket. The rest of the notes had sailed with the *Raven's Wing*, and were now either floating aimlessly in the sea with Moony Swain or had sunk to the bottom of the Atlantic Ocean. "What are you talking about, Father?" she asked.

"The bank notes, of course." He answered as if her question were ludicrous. "Supplied by young Obalu here."

Felix stuck his head out from behind Thurston's girth and grinned sheepishly at Nora.

"Felix, you didn't!"

"I just filched a few," he admitted. "I was going to put them to good use, believe me, Miss Nora, but I figured Cap'n J could use them more, so I gave them up to the judge."

"You know, Felix," she said, "we really are going to have to talk about this."

"Enough talk for now, though," Thurston interrupted. "Proctor, send one of your men to your cottage for a change of clothes. I'd like you to come to the house with us and have a decent meal and a rest."

Nora bit back a squeal of delight at her father's invitation, and risked a look at her mother. Fanny stood behind Sidonia and emphatically poked a finger into the small of her cousin's back. Then she flashed a smile of triumph at Nora.

"Oh, yes, Captain, do come," Sidonia intoned as she massaged the base of her spine.

"Thank you, Mrs. Seabrook. I'd like that," Jacob said.

Nora sidled close to her father and whispered, "Thank *you*, Father, but we still have the problem of Theo . . ."

"Don't give him another thought, Nora," Thurston said with a grin. "When I was told the *Dover Cloud* was coming into the harbor this morning, I woke our houseguest and suggested he take a room at the hotel until a ship sails for New Orleans."

Nora hugged her father. "Did he go willingly?"

Thurston's eyes twinkled with amusement. "Yes, he did, as a matter of fact. One reason might be that marigold petals were still falling from his hair as he stepped off our porch."

Promising to tell Jacob later what had sent her into peals of laughter, Nora settled next to him as they walked with her family up Duval Street toward Southard. Jacob slipped his arm around Nora's shoulders as neighbors came out on their porches to watch the procession. Nora suspected Key West verandas would soon crackle with the news that the judge's daughter and Captain Proctor were spotted in a most compromising clinch.

Lulu walked to her other side, fingered a section of Nora's dress, and wrinkled her nose. "Every time you come back from that water, you smell like a fish, Miss Nora," the girl scolded. "You're goin' in that cedar barrel the minute we get you home."

Nora agreed at once and giggled, not at the thought of being washed down by Lulu again, but because Jacob had just pulled her a little closer and whispered in her ear, "Do you suppose there's room for two in that barrel, my love?"

EPILOGUE

Nora leaned on the railing of the cupola and waited for her husband. She watched the first lights come on in the houses of Key West. A pink-tinged dusk dissolved to a peaceful charcoal over the rooftops of the small city—the city Nora loved because it was here that she'd met the man who filled her heart and completed her life. She breathed a sigh of contentment that came from knowing that for its own extraordinary, mysterious reasons, fate had shined upon her and led her to Jacob.

She'd never dreamed life could be so wonderful. Her family accepted Jacob. Her students in the Island School for Reading were flourishing. In fact, Nora wouldn't be at all surprised if a few years from now, Felix Obalu was mayor of Key West. The thought pleased her greatly. Her star pupil loved the city as much as she did. His reign would certainly be an interesting addition to future books she intended to write about her adventures in America's wealthiest little city.

Not all the Seabrooks had come to love the island, however. Only this morning, before the wedding, Sidonia had complained of the heat. "It's only May, Eleanor," she'd griped while fanning her flushed cheeks at a furious pace, "and already I'm melting. June, which is really the proper time for young ladies to wed, will be ghastly."

Nora had only smiled. She didn't mind the warm, moist climate because there was always a breeze. Sometimes, however, the gentle winds turned furious, blowing as if they had will and determination. But it didn't last long. Besides, wasn't the wind symbolic of life itself? Strong gales to make the heart beat faster, and gentle breezes to feed the soul? Nora looked forward to riding the crests of every one of them with Jacob by her side.

She would be frightened for him each time he rode an angry sea to a stranded vessel, but she understood that shipwrecking was his life. It defined him, satisfied him as no other occupation could. She would wait for him to return, and pull him close at night and thank God he'd come home safely.

Not like the three bodies that had washed up on Matecumbe a week after the storm. One of them might have been Moony Swain, but it was impossible to say for sure. All the bodies bore scars of the ravages of the ocean and the creatures who live there. At any rate, none of the crew of the *Raven's Wing* had returned to Key West. And neither had the strongbox with the bank notes from New Bedford. Another grim reminder of the authority of the sea.

Footsteps on the stairs to the cupola drew Nora's attention from her somber thoughts. Jacob dropped a bundle of cloth onto the floor of the cupola and came to stand beside her. "All's well," he said to his bride. "I locked all the doors to the warehouse, so we are, for the first time today, utterly alone."

His arm slipped around her, and his hand settled on her hip. She rested her head on his shoulder. The breeze lifted her hair from her forehead, exposing her skin to his kiss.

"Someday, my love, we will have a real honeymoon," he promised. "We can go to Charleston or Savannah, or any of the beautiful islands of the Caribbean. Not Belle Isle, of course," he added as an afterthought.

"This is honeymoon enough for me right now," she said. "Anywhere with you is the most romantic place I can think of. Besides, Mama had to plan this wedding so quickly, we didn't have time for many of the details. She's been so concerned about the possibility of a baby.'' Nora covered her tummy with her hand and imitated Sidonia's frantic speech. '' 'We must marry you quickly, Eleanor, just in case. A judicious use of time is most important now.' ''

''Poor Mama,'' Nora said. ''Perhaps she can talk Fanny into accepting Dillard's proposal, and then she can plan a wedding with all the fuss.''

Jacob laughed. ''Hyde is as trapped as any fox with a pack of hounds on its tail. I never knew the old boy could be so besotted.''

Nora thought of her cousin and smiled.

Jacob picked up his bundle and unwrapped it. ''Speaking of babies,'' he said, ''I've come prepared to deal with that situation tonight.'' He spread a down-filled coverlet over the floor of the cupola. ''Since this is the spot where I first lost my heart to you, I think it's only fitting that we discuss the idea of babies right here.''

Nora's heart rejoiced. Jacob wanted children. This man who only weeks before had been certain his offspring would unleash sadness upon the world was now anxious to be a father. He took her hand and gently lowered her to the pallet until they were both on their knees.

Their hands worked on the fastenings of their clothes while their lips blended in a sublime celebration of their union. Since making babies was the most deliciously satisfying activity Nora could think of, she decided to wait until the morning to tell him their mission had already been accomplished.

ABOUT THE AUTHOR

Cynthia Thomason lives in Davie, FL, with her husband, teenaged son, black Persian cat, and Jack Russell terrier. When she's not writing romances, she is an auctioneer and estate furniture buyer for the auction company she and her husband own. Cynthia loves to hear from readers. You may contact her at PO Box 550068, Fort Lauderdale, FL 33355. Or you may E-mail her at Cynthoma@aol.com

BOOK YOUR PLACE ON OUR WEBSITE AND MAKE THE READING CONNECTION!

We've created a customized website just for our very special readers, where you can get the inside scoop on everything that's going on with Zebra, Pinnacle and Kensington books.

When you come online, you'll have the exciting opportunity to:

- View covers of upcoming books
- Read sample chapters
- Learn about our future publishing schedule (listed by publication month *and author*)
- Find out when your favorite authors will be visiting a city near you
- Search for and order backlist books from our online catalog
- Check out author bios and background information
- Send e-mail to your favorite authors
- Meet the Kensington staff online
- Join us in weekly chats with authors, readers and other guests
- Get writing guidelines
- AND MUCH MORE!

**Visit our website at
http://www.zebrabooks.com**

Put a Little Romance in Your Life With
Fern Michaels

_ **Dear Emily**	0-8217-5676-1	$6.99US/$8.50CAN
__**Sara's Song**	0-8217-5856-X	$6.99US/$8.50CAN
__**Wish List**	0-8217-5228-6	$6.99US/$7.99CAN
__**Vegas Rich**	0-8217-5594-3	$6.99US/$8.50CAN
__**Vegas Heat**	0-8217-5758-X	$6.99US/$8.50CAN
__**Vegas Sunrise**	1-55817-5983-3	$6.99US/$8.50CAN
__**Whitefire**	0-8217-5638-9	$6.99US/$8.50CAN

Put a Little Romance in Your Life With
Rosanne Bittner

__Caress	0-8217-3791-0	$5.99US/$6.99CAN
__Full Circle	0-8217-4711-8	$5.99US/$6.99CAN
__Shameless	0-8217-4056-3	$5.99US/$6.99CAN
__Unforgettable	0-8217-5830-6	$5.99US/$7.50CAN
__Texas Embrace	0-8217-5625-7	$5.99US/$7.50CAN
__Texas Passions	0-8217-6166-8	$5.99US/$7.50CAN
__Until Tomorrow	0-8217-5064-X	$5.99US/$6.99CAN
__Love Me Tomorrow	0-8217-5818-7	$5.99US/$7.50CAN

Call toll free **1-888-345-BOOK** to order by phone or use this coupon to order by mail.

Name _____

Address _____

City _____ State _____ Zip _____

Please send me the books I have checked above.

I am enclosing $_____

Plus postage and handling* $_____

Sales tax (in New York and Tennessee) $_____

Total amount enclosed $_____

*Add $2.50 for the first book and $.50 for each additional book.

Send check or money order (no cash or CODs) to:

Kensington Publishing Corp., 850 Third Avenue, New York, NY 10022

Prices and Numbers subject to change without notice.

All orders subject to availability.

Check out our website at **www.kensingtonbooks.com**